IN THE LADIES' ROOM

ROOM

A Novel

Andrew Smith

Prime Prods Press. New York, NY
www. primeprodspress.com
knatural@aol.com
ISBN: 0692390014
ISBN 13: 9780692390016

Dedicated to:
Ellen Fox Emerson
Albert Oehrle
Oliver Clarke
They read the manuscript more than once

"We have met the enemy and
he is us."

—POGO (WALT KELLY)

CHAPTER ONE

S omething was wrong. Very wrong. Something wasn't right at all. Brendan could feel it.

Even the traffic was wrong. There was none. As he drove north on Laurel Canyon over Mulholland Drive and into the Valley, he was making record time getting to a job he needed badly but couldn't help feeling ambivalent about. It was 6:38 AM. He had to constantly remind himself not to be self-destructive again. He was doing his best to keep his head down, writing on a daytime talk show called "The Ladies' Room"; but he still knew there was something wrong. Something very, very wrong. He felt like he couldn't stand it. But, of course, he could. The women were driving him nuts. He was working on a show named for a toilet, for crissakes. It reminded him of his favorite conundrum: what is the smallest bill—the smallest denomination---you would pick out of a urinal at Yankee Stadium? Working on "The Ladies' Room", in the relentless sun of Southern California, far from his home and his people in New York, Brendan knew he was picking loose change out of pinstriped porcelain and grateful for the opportunity.

The studios of the Swann Broadcasting System were in Reseda, deep in the San Fernando Valley. The building itself rose like a monolith out of the blasted wasteland around it like so many other anomalous structures in the Valley where "nondescript" was an architectural flourish. The building looked as if it had landed rather than been built, and there was something decidedly alien about the place as if it had come from a universe other than our own. From the governmental, brooding looks of the place, Brendan could have been a drone pilot going about the grisly business of remotely killing "insurgents" in faraway places instead of just a comedy writer whose job it was to fashion witticisms for females with no sense of humor. On second thought, it was *exactly* like being a drone pilot, going to work each morning delivering jokes that "killed" in faraway places. The show ran all over the world in one form or another. Smart-ass comments launched from his miserable desk in Reseda would land unceremoniously in the huts of tribal leaders in Pakistan. For all he knew, Osama Bin Laden liked his stuff.

Brendan arrived on time for the "CrossTalk" meeting that began each work day at 7:00 and dutifully wrote his forty jokes based on topics selected there for the live show at 9:00. But today it all seemed in a vacuum that he couldn't fully identify. It was all part of the "something" that was wrong.

There was trouble in the air just as the show was about to go *on* the air. Something didn't feel right when Brendan came into the studio just before showtime with two additional cards of jokes for Marge Foley, the so-called comedian on the show. He would give the new lines to her as she sat complaining into the mirror about her hair and checking her iPad for something, anything, but what she was paid to do. But Brendan knew there was still something very wrong.

Bad Bob Vapors, the executive producer, was backstage shooting the pre-show action on his foolish iPhone in the narrow walkway behind the set. It was there that the women were mic'd before slipping into the small co-host "green room" for their final primping and last minute gossip. There was something very wrong about an executive producer seriously interviewing himself on a cellphone when his network television show was about to begin. But shooting clips for "The Ladies' Room" website had become Bad Bob's main preoccupation thanks to a network order from Sandy Abumpkin, the SBS network executive in charge of Daytime. It represented Bad Bob's own brush with fame. The backstage footage had suddenly became every bit as important as the show itself. Or so he had convinced himself after the network had come up with the idea. Bad Bob wanted "air-time" that bad. His "on air" career was a "selfie".

"We're almost on the air," Bad Bob was saying to his outstretched hand that held the iPhone, "But I wanted to give you a first-hand look at what goes into putting on a hit daytime television talk show like 'The Ladies' Room'."

Bad Bob put the phone down momentarily and looked around for someone or something else to shoot. What he saw was the usual pre-show activity of stagehands positioning equipment, co-hosts arriving on the set, and personnel from the production staff and network milling around trying to look like they had something to do.

"We're backstage where it all happens. Just a couple of minutes before we go 'live' to millions of people," Bad Bob continued.

He began to walk toward the area outside the co-host's green room where the women got their mics.

"There's Beverly Frost getting mic'd and also Marge Foley. It's the only time either one of them will ever let a man put his hand down their shirt. Just kidding. Let's go watch," he said with an inviting wave of his free hand.

Brendan stopped to catch his breath next to Bradley the stage manager. He had run up the stairs to the studio from his office below

"You okay? Or are you acting," Bradley said to him as a joke. Brendan leaned against a rolling hamper and closed his eyes to gather his strength.

"I hate actors, and I hate acting."

"Well, you came to the right place," Bradley replied. Then he saw the blue cards in Brendan's hand. "You want me to give those to Marge?

"No, gotta look busy."

"Right. Act like a writer, so they'll know what you do," Bradley said as he moved on. Brendan laughed once and headed over toward the audio section to intercept Marge.

"The stage manager makes sure everybody's ready," Bad Bob reported to the back of his hand as he panned the iPhone around the set. "There's Brendan White. He's Marge's comedy writer. Those blue cards in his hands are jokes for Marge to use in the "CrossTalk" segment. They better be funny, or that *writer* will be a *waiter* come Monday morning. Just kidding again. Sort of."

Then he turned the camera back on himself. "Marge is the only one of the ladies who has a writer. It's because she's a comedian. I write all my own stuff. Who needs writers?"

A scenery flat that was painted a gaudy shade of green was being rolled into place for the "green screen" Buckingham Palace stand-ups that Brendan had written for Marge. As a result, Bad Bob was not able to immediately move over to where the cohosts were, so he continued to interview himself.

"Backstage at "The Ladies' Room", just before air time, can only be described as 'controlled chaos'. But as executive producer, it all makes sense to me. I love live television."

But there was something wrong with Bad Bob and the way he ignored Brendan and avoided eye contact with him when Brendan squeezed past to get to Marge. But that wasn't what was really wrong. It was something else.

Two stage hands carrying a large vat of water came through the narrow passageway between the back of the set and the audio section. Bad Bob was in their way.

"Look out. Wet stuff. Comin' through." One of the men said without slowing their pace. They incorrectly assumed Bad Bob would move out of their way. But Bad Bob was still talking about himself to the camera.

"You know, a show like 'The Ladies' Room' thrives on spontaneity. You never know from one moment to the next what to......"

The stage hands tried to squeeze the ungainly vat past Bad Bob who was too busy with his self-interview to notice. In the process, they slopped a large amount of water on the bottom of his pants.

"What the...?" he exclaimed without turning off the iPhone. "Now look what you've done. We've got a show in two minutes, and I'm completely wet."

"Sorry, Chief," one of the stagehands said while still trying to shuffle past him.

Bad Bob cut him off before his explanation. "Look at me," he said presenting his drenched trousers to the retreating stage hands.

"Maybe hair and make-up can dry it off. I seen them do it for Beverley's dog when he pisses himself."

"What segment is that for? " Bad Bob demanded.

"Five."

The stagehands were now out of the alley and heading off toward their destination.

"Cancel it!" Bad Bob ordered.

"Can't do that, Chief," the stagehand said.

"Who's the segment producer? Where is she?"

"Pixie. In the green room with the talent," the other one said over his shoulder.

The stagehands were now far enough away to be able to wash their hands of the whole situation. They turned their backs and proceeded on their way.

"Damn!" Bad Bob exclaimed to no one. "Great! Just great!"

He now had to go find the hapless segment producer and ream her out for no reason and then try to get his pants dried before the show. He was about to storm off, but then he remembered the iPhone was still running.

"Just part of the craziness before going on air," he said regaining his cheerfulness into the camera. A little water won't stop me. See you out there." He finally stopped shooting and put the phone back in his pocket. Then he turned toward the main green room, the one with the talent, PR people, and segment producers in it.

"Does anyone have a mop?" He shouted to no one in particular. "There is a dangerous wet spot over here."

Brendan still couldn't put his finger on exactly what was wrong, so he proceeded with his pre-show routine anyway. There was still enough time for him to give Marge two additional "blue cards" with four jokes on each one which she could use in the crucial opening moments of "CrossTalk" after the ladies hit the table. In the few minutes remaining before the start of the show, he could also explain any of the jokes from the seven cards of material she had supposedly already read, or else he could "improvise" and verbally riff with her about some last minute bits like a co-host's quirky wardrobe choice or a piece of breaking news. That is, if Marge had even bothered to look at the *first* set of cards that were, presently, back in her dressing room already discarded in her wastepaper basket; or if she weren't so terminally pre-occupied with her own hair and Beverly Frost's social life to actually care about being funny on the show.

Beverly Frost was the moderator of the show and also its co-executive producer mainly because she owned the whole thing lock, stock, and barrel and licensed it back to the SBS network. Her legendary news status and rarified lifestyle preceded her, and she was more interested in sharing every minute of both with her fellow co-hosts than actually preparing for what was about to happen "live" on the air.

By now Marge had been mic'd and was sitting in the co-host green room in front of a mirror. Her faithful but abused hairstylist, Celeste, was standing behind her trying to console her.

"It's not right. It looks like a mop," Marge said directly into the mirror.

"It *is* a mop."

"What?" Marge said panicking

"That's what you wanted. You wanted to look like a moppet. Remember? I think it's cute," Celeste told her.

"I'm too old to be a moppet. *Or* a Muppet. I look like Elmo's grandmother," Marge said.

"I can comb it out and put in a hair band. We haven't got that much time," Celeste said resigned to undoing a morning's worth of styling.

"Beverly changes her hair all the time," Marge whined. She was competitive with Beverly even though Beverly had hired her from the obscurity of lounge-grade comedy clubs in Las Vegas.

"Beverly has two people working on her even while she's asleep," Celeste said as she began to re-comb Marge's hair.

"Are you serious?"

"I'm kidding. But she does have a lot of help. It's in her contract. She doesn't even have to pay for it. And at Christmastime, all she ever gives anybody is socks."

Marge studied herself long and hard and watched Celeste begin to re-form her hair style into something more familiar.

"I need my own show," Marge said to herself into the mirror.

Brendan had been waiting all this time behind Celeste hoping to get Marge's attention in the last minutes before the show so he could brief her.

"Marge?" he said tentatively. He knew how important her hair was, so it was like asking a mother to turn away from her newborn.

Marge continued to intently study her new hairstyle in the mirror as if she were a surgeon evaluating brain scans. Her hair had been dyed extra red the afternoon before because she thought it made her funnier, like Lucille Ball. Of course, no one told her that the red hair wasn't the funny part of Lucy, Lucy was.

"Now I look like Mrs. Bozo."

Brendan persisted. He edged himself past Celeste and closer to Marge's side.

"The first topic is the Queen's Jubilee. Here are some queenie lines. And don't worry, no Elton John," Brendan said quickly. He knew that Marge's audience was mostly gay men, and she was extremely careful about any material that could be construed as anti-gay or a gay put-down in any way, regardless of the humor.

"I won't be able to get a word in edgewise," Marge said, "You know how Beverly is about the Royal Family.

"It's also Flag Day in Great Britain, so I did some flag jokes just in case Beverly brings it up."

"Flag Day?" Marge whined, "Is that a holiday?"

"It is if you're a flag. But now you'll have material," Brendan said putting the cards in her hand. Marge took them and felt the cards between her thumb and forefinger as if they were fabric.

"Are they funny? They don't *feel* funny."

"Ah, but they smell funny. And that's better," Brendan said cheerfully even though, now, she was being a complete cunt about the work he'd done that morning.

"Anyway, it doesn't matter," Marge said scowling at herself in the mirror, "I'm going to just listen."

"Good. So now you can listen with jokes." Brendan said. He liked what he'd come up with for Flag Day.

Marge took the cards and put them face down on the make-up counter. Brendan knew she wouldn't look at them, if ever, until she actually got out to the table on the air and only then to check on what she was *not* going to say. Such was the M.O. of a comedian in decline who had only recently discovered that people's memory of her was much funnier than anything *new* she might say or do. And the harsh reality of that was proven every time she opened her mouth. Consequently, these days, she preferred to do nothing.

Marge got up from her chair when Beverly came into the little room. By doing so, she accepted the ultimate fate of her hairstyle. She then abruptly dismissed Celeste as if the woman had been an intrusion. There were two minutes before air time as confirmed by Bradley, the stage manager. But still the ladies could not be bothered to look at the cards in their hands which contained a bullet point version of the script that waited for them, in full, on the teleprompters astride each of the cameras.

"Darlings, I've decided to do a "shout out" to me this morning," Beverly announced to anyone within earshot, "If that's all right with you." She paused for a reaction, but there was none. "I want to say something about my special last night."

"You mean, you want to plug it *after* the fact?" Marge said as if setting up a joke.

"Well, not in so many words, darling. Let's just say it's an acknowledgement that we *did* win the night. And, also, for all those tedious TiVo people who haven't watched it yet."

"Beverly, the fox that bit you died," Marge told her with a smile. Beverly took it as a compliment, which it was in a way; but not in the circles she travelled in. "But go, do. Plug away," Marge continued. "I wouldn't call your special a 'dead horse', but whatever it is, you're not above giving it a good beatin'."

At that point Bradley stuck his head into the room like a vaudevillian. "One minute to air!"

So far, neither Beverly nor Marge had looked at their show cards where the rundown of the show was and also the questions they would ask. They were too busy.

"Darling I'm going to be out at the Colony this weekend with Zubin Mehta and Vladimir Putin. Will you be at your rental in Venice?" Beverly asked Marge.

Beverly stood stiffly with her hands at her side and her torso slightly arched backward as a bulwark against any osteoporosis trying to assert itself in her heavily fortified eighty-three year old body. But the forced good posture made her look, instead, like someone else had gotten her dressed that morning (which was true); and she was waiting to present herself before a panel of nuns rather than about to appear on her own television show.

"Yeah, sure," Marge replied. "You gonna have a party? I love the Colony," She was referring to the Malibu Colony, a stretch of beachfront homes reserved for reclusive Hollywood types and moguls. Streisand has a place there.

"God no," Beverly said. "But if I need something I can call you."

"Of course," Marge said with a shrug. "Just ring a bell."

At that moment, Moonie Brown arrived in the room completely out of breath on account of her "forced march" from the elevators to the studio, a distance of less than sixty feet, downhill. Moonie, as her name implied, was as round as a planet and just as full. She probably even had her own gravitational field. But she was far from pale. Her race existed somewhere between Native American and African Anything, depending on which constituency she was trying to con.

"Am I too late to get mic'd," Moonie said between inhales.

"Hell, no," Marge said being unable to resist a straight line and especially one from Moonie. "But somebody warn Mike."

A sound man took a deep breath and rapidly attached a mic to the heaving Moonie.

"Marge, Jesus will forgive you. But I will make you pay first," Moonie wheezed.

"I was joking," Marge replied trying to assess exactly how much she had really offended her.

"Ohhhhhhhhh. It's so hard to tell," Moonie said smiling. "I get it. You were trying to be *funny*." Now Moonie had gotten in her own licks, and it felt good.

Bradley entered the little green room at that point to make sure there was a smooth transition onto the set. "In ten," he began; counting down like it was a NASA launch. "Nine, eight, seven...."

At that moment, Bambi Crutchfield, the young one, burst into the room. She was out of breath, too, but her hyper-ventilation was because she had run, full tilt, from her dressing room on the floor below, up the stairs, and into the studio. She recovered immediately.

Bambi was perfectly formed and perfectly blonde. The fact that she could walk and put on earrings at the same time was one of her greatest achievements. This day she had outfitted herself with *five* inch heels which made the muscles in her perfectly turned calves stand out even more invitingly.

"Sorry, everybody, I was cleansing." She announced benignly.

"That's the filthiest thing I ever hoid," Marge said á la Groucho. She was doing more comedy, now, backstage than she would ever do on the air.

"Four, three, two…. And we are on the air," Bradley intoned with a sweep of his hand to indicate that the ladies should line up at the entrance to the set while the theme, title animation, and voice-over billboard for the show played on the monitors in the studio and on the smaller flat screen monitor in the corner of the co-hosts' green room.

It always seemed to require two sound men to attach a lavaliere mic to Bambi, but this time she took it as an emergency measure. In truth, it was merely because neither sound man would release that distinct pleasure to the other. It was the only time the job was truly worth it. But this time, they actually were racing against time, so Bambi decided to facilitate the process by popping her blouse open and exposing her perfectly formed breasts cupped in a Victoria Secret Wonderbra. She was proud to be felt up that day.

The pre-packaged billboard of what was coming up on the show began to play as Ed Kendall, the announcer, sonorously read the copy that Leo, the other writer on "The Ladies' Room", had written for him the day before.

"It's August 15th, and the ladies are bustin' out all over for summer fun," he began as if he were announcing the Second Coming.

Still, the co-hosts had refused to look at their cards or even to begin to focus on the task ahead. Marge and Beverly continued to talk about Malibu and a bitchy anecdote and put-down of Calvin Klein that Beverly was proffering. Calvin was a guest on the show that day, but Beverly never missed an opportunity to diminish anyone who had the temerity to step into her penumbra. Moonie tried to catch her breath with her hand over her mic so the wheezing wouldn't go out over the airwaves, and Bambi bent over the make-up table in her heels in order to check herself in the mirror and apply an extra layer of lip gloss to her lower lip in case anyone asked her anything serious.

"Who's on the show today?" Marge asked the group as they stood waiting to go on.

"Oh, darlings. Let's just have fun out there and wing it," Beverly said.

"I thought that was our job description," Marge quipped.

"Great, because I haven't had time to look at anything." Bambi said. Beverly shot her a look indicating that "the young one" was not supposed to indulge in that whim.

The "walk on" music was cued when the billboard ended. Then Bradley took a cue from Hal, the director, through his headset, and hustled the women out onto the stage for their entrance to thunderous applause.

"…And you're on." Bradley said with another sweep of his hand like the ringmaster at a circus. "Have a nice show, ladies."

At that precise moment, Leo, the continuity writer and the one most intimately involved with the script of the show, appeared at the door of the green room. His face was ashen and full of doom. Brendan looked at him and decided that, maybe, there really *was* something wrong.

"What's the matter, pal?" Brendan asked.

"Stop!" Leo said with his hands outstretched toward the stage entrance as Bambi, the last of the co-hosts, disappeared onstage. "No!" he said as if he could stop time and turn back a live show.

"What's wrong, Leo?" Brendan asked again.

"Everything," Leo said, "The cards. The cards are wrong. We're fucked. Totally fucked." He sat down on the whorehouse-grade couch and held his head in his hands. On the monitor, the ladies were acknowledging the applause and crossing to the table.

Bad Bob had followed Leo into the room and was still talking, at arm's length, into his silly iPhone like an intrepid reporter on the trail of a big story.

"Well, the show has just started, and I have to get out there to guide the ladies through the subjects they've chosen for today's 'CrossTalk' segment," he said as if he'd been asked. "Normally, union rules would prevent me from bringing a camera onto the set, but I'm going to do it anyway," he continued with a union-busting wink to his outstretched hand. He began to walk past Leo and Brendan on his way to the set. The applause persisted past its normal duration, but Bad Bob took it as affirmation of his own impending appearance.

On the monitor, Brendan could see the women at their chairs, still standing around the table. Beverly and Moonie sat down and smilingly acknowledged the long applause as if they actually deserved it and as if the audience had finally realized the enormity of their true worth.

Leo was in a state of shock.

"That new piece of fucking shit-fuck-piss script software we just got printed out the cards for last year's 'Vagina Special' instead of the ones I wrote" Leo said. He waved a set of correct cards at Bad Bob and the women in the monitor.

"Great! Do it for the camera." Bad Bob said not getting it. He turned the iPhone on Leo and then back to himself. "This is Leo, the writer, who says there seems to be a problem." Then he turned the phone back to Leo, but Leo's head was in his hands.

"No good, no good. It's all wrong," Leo was saying to the floor.

The women in the monitor were silent and motionless as they noticed the teleprompter for the first time. They fumbled through their cards trying to make sense of them. Then Beverly made a rolling motion with her hand to have the teleprompter scroll down to something intelligible.

"What're you talking about?" Brendan said.

"They have the wrong script. The script software printed out the "Vagina Special" instead of today's show. It's all wrong on their cards and in the teleprompter. We're fucked. It's the Vagina Show out there right now, not the Queen's Jubilee."

Bad Bob had swung the camera over to Brendan who under-stood immediately what was happening. Brendan could only stare at the monitor with his mouth open but with a certain amount of evil glee at the predicament unfolding, "live", on stage.

"Get to the control room and change the prompter." Bad Bob said turning his phone off and slipping it into his pocket. Then he pressed the little intercom button on his headset and bent his head to his chest. "We have a problem," he said with NASA-grade gravitas.

The ladies on air were completely flummoxed and tried to make the best of the situation.

"Well, ladies, today's show is all about Vaginas," Beverly began.

Then, to make matters worse, a huge picture of the Queen Elizabeth in her jubilee crown came up on the massive monitor behind Beverly. "I don't quite understand," she murmured half to herself. But then, 55 years of slavish fealty to teleprompters and the possibility of a breaking news story kicked in; and she plowed on regardless. The prompter always knows best.

"That's right. Vaginas. Every woman has one. They come in all shapes and sizes, but nobody talks about them," she continued reading cheerfully.

At that point, the screen split, and a drawing of an 8 foot high vagina appeared on one side of the monitor and the Queen of England on the other. The audience was confused.

"Well, that's the biggest pussy I've ever seen," Marge exclaimed, doing her Groucho again. Of course, the word "pussy" was imme-diately bleeped by the Jeanie the Censor, so what went out over the air was "That's the biggest 'bleep' I've ever seen," which was, really, just as bad.

"Darling, please. Try to restrain yourself. It's just a picture." Beverly said looking over her shoulder at the Queen she so loved who was now paired with a giant sexual organ.

"I was talking about the other one." Marge said because even though she had stopped doing comedy, she did know her jokes.

Bad Bob knew he was in trouble now. The audience tittered nervously at the co-hosts' obvious dilemma

"Go! Go! Go!" Bad Bob shouted at Brendan. "Change the prompter." Then into his intercom mic he asked, "How much time before commercial?"

Back on stage the situation was rapidly spinning out of control. The graphic of the Queen was replaced by portraits of famous royals from Camilla Parker Bowles to Kate Middleton to Queen Victoria all with the accompanying giant vagina graphic.

"Beverly, have you gone crazy today?" Moonie asked.

Beverly tried to maintain a news anchor's control in the face of disaster. "Darling, it's a new day," she said. And then she continued down the teleprompter road.

"Welcome to "The Ladies' Room", everyone," she began again. "Today we're going to talk about vaginas."

"My cards look like a mash note from my gynecologist," Moonie added.

The images on the jumbo monitor began to race through pictures of famous women from Hillary Clinton to Madeleine Albright to Martha Stewart. The audience was stunned. But Beverly could not be stopped.

"Well, apparently, today is vagina day, so let's just make the best of it," she trailed off realizing that the situation was hopeless and irretrievable.

Brendan ran out of the studio and headed for the stairs that would take him up to the control room. There was no time to wait for the elevator.

The control room for "The Ladies' Room" was on the floor above the studio just as the dressing rooms were on the floor below. But owing to the height of the studio to allow for the lights and sets, the stairs up to the control room floor were twice as long. By the time Brendan arrived, he was as winded as Moonie would've been getting up from a couch.

For Brendan, entering a television control room was always like going into a secure bunker, except there was really no reason why it should be so. Nothing inside the room ever went out over the air even though, often, there was much shouting. Yet television control rooms were always secured by thick, heavy doors; and their entrances constructed like airlocks.

Brendan pulled the first door open with a "wump" owing to its seal and quickly move past the audio room and announce booth where Ed, oblivious to the crisis, was practicing the "bumper announce" for the first break.

"Still to come on "The Ladies' Room", more "CrossTalk" with the ladies," he said with announcer delight. Then he tried a different read on the same material. "Still to come on "The Ladies' Room", *more* "CrossTalk" with the ladies." He nodded professionally to Brendan racing past without asking what his hurry was for.

By the time Brendan stepped into the darkened control room itself, all hell had broken loose.

The control room was a two-tiered affair. On the upper level there was a bank of chairs in front of a long counter with phones and gooseneck intercom mics. It was there that the senior producer, the line producer, Jeanie Murphy the Censor, and the PA's sat. In back of them, on the same level, sat the network liaison (known as "Madam Defarge" for her diabolical death grip on the purse strings of the show), the senior production manager, and several unassigned chairs along the back wall for visiting clients and guests.

The actual directing of the show was performed by Hal Jennings several steps down from the "producers level" in a pit before a wall of monitors and esoteric electronic displays. Hal chose to direct standing at a lectern as opposed to seated in a chair because he liked the idea of being above everyone else. It made him feel more like a "director". He was a workman-like technician who ran his shop with an iron fist and never missed a shot... as long as it was scripted. Anything that *hadn't* been written into the script, or actually happened spontaneously in the studio, stayed in the studio. He missed more shots than a blind man at a shooting range. To either side of him, in front of a solid wall of monitors and oscilloscopes were the technical director, the lighting director, the assistant director, the DGA PA and other technical people who did the actual switching of the various camera shots and previewed the waiting ones.

When Brendan stepped down to Hal's level in the control room, he could see, on the various monitors, that the women were still trying to cope with the bogus "CrossTalk" script despite the fact that they were now completely on their own.

"What the fuck is going on?" Hal shouted. "Vaginas?" Then, feverishly leafing through his show script, "Where the fuck did all this vagina shit come from? Why is everybody talking about pussy all of a sudden? And kill the graphics on the Queen."

"Too many 'vaginas', Jeanie said loudly, meaning some words were acceptable for network consumption but not a barrage of them. You could say, "penis" once but not ten times, even if you were a urologist. She had reached her "vagina" limit. "I'm bleeping all the rest."

The split of the Royals and the giant vagina on the set monitor suddenly went black. But, after a beat, it was replaced by Lindsay Lohan getting out of a car with no panties on and a black strip obscuring her genitals.

"How you gonna bleep that, Jeannie?" Hal asked.

"I'm calling someone. This has gotten out of hand," Jeannie said reaching for the phone.

The women were still trying to get it straight.

"I thought we were going to talk about the Queen and her pet Corgi," Bambi said on the air.

"You mean, the royal pooch?" Moonie said.

"There you go again," Marge shot back.

Nobody seemed to have a clue about exactly what was going on and, certainly, even less about what to do about it.

"They have the wrong script and the wrong prompter. They're going to have to adlib," Brendan announced to everyone.

"Fat Chance," Hal said. "They couldn't adlib a fart."

"Mugsy" Muggeridge, the senior producer and former lover of Bad Bob's, felt she should make some sort of executive decision even though she had studiously avoided any such utterance in the fifteen years she had been with the show.

"Can't we go to commercial?" she said to the back of Hal's head.

"Too soon. I need three minutes," the technical director said who was timing the show. He knew that the affiliates down the line were unprepared to roll on anything local that early in the show.

"What about the disaster button? We could go to bars," Mugsy said referring to the test pattern of colored bars that usually meant something cataclysmic had occurred.

"How about *a* bar... and fast," Hal replied. "Jesus Christ! They've got brains and mouths, don't they? What's wrong with them?" Hal shouted to no one.

"If we can just get them through the next couple of minutes, it'll be okay." Brendan said as he vaulted down to the far right of the consoles to where the teleprompter operator sat.

"Fix it, Baby," Mugsy said to Brendan in her best kittenish voice which meant that she really wanted him to do something. "You're the writer."

The women had begun describing what they were wearing. They continued to vamp but made no sense at all; and they kept returning to the prompter hoping it would bail them out, but the prompter, in its current state, only sent them deeper into the "Vagina Special".

"Well, ladies and gentlemen. It's fairly obvious we have the wrong script for our show today," Beverly announced to the audience when, along with the graphics, the vagina script had made the show sound as if the women had a terminal case of Tourettte's. "Of course, we don't really need a script," she couldn't help adding, "Our show is completely spontaneous."

"That's live television, folks. But at least we have pictures of women," Bambi said and turned to look at the monitor. "At least we used to."

At that moment, a shot of Prince Charles popped onto the screen.

"Ah, Bonnie Prince Charles," Marge said. "The man who would be a tampon. Wait a second. This is all starting to make sense."

Brendan stood behind Millie, the teleprompter operator, and put his hand gently on her shoulder.

"The script in the prompter is all wrong. But it's not your fault. It's the new software we started using," Brendan said. "So now we have to wipe the whole thing out and start over. Can you do that?" he asked.

"Sure," Millie said.

Millie pressed a 'delete' button, and the prompter screen in front of her went completely blank. She then scrolled to the top of it.

"You know, I should be in the Writers Guild," Millie chose to say at that moment.

"You're already in a union," Brendan replied.

"But I do all the writing," she persisted even though a disaster was unfolding right before her eyes.

"Okay, go," Brendan said, calling her bluff.

Millie wrote "Go" in the teleprompter and then stopped and looked up at him.

"See?" Brendan smiled thinly. "Okay, just type, 'Please ad-lib to commercial'," he said.

Millie dutifully typed in what she was told.

Immediately, Moonie looked into Camera Three and said, "Go. Please ad-lib to commercial." Then she covered her mouth when she realized the foolishness of what she had just said.

"Still, I think I should get WGA benefits," Millie said.

"This is going to be harder than I thought," Brendan said, mostly to himself. "Type in, 'Discuss Flag Day'".

19

Millie typed it in. This time Beverly actually started talking about Flag Day. The only problem was she had no idea what the hell she was talking about.

"Well, as you know, today is Flag Day," Beverly began not knowing where she was going. "It's a most wonderful day because of… because of …well…because of all the glorious flags we love and enjoy so much. What're you girls doing for Flag Day?"

At that point, Marge actually looked down at her cards for the first time and picked up a line that Brendan had written.

"Oh, yeah, Flag Day," she said, "In my old neighborhood we used to love Flag Day. We'd have Flag Sucking Parties. We'd sit around blindfolded, suck on a flag, and try to guess what country it was from."

It was a joke Marge would never have done had she not been desperate. The audience was nonplussed at first because it came out of nowhere; but then, because it *sounded* like a joke, in that it had the rhythm of something funny, the audience laughed lightly. Basically, they liked the sound of Marge saying the word "suck". So the line actually scored, but for all the wrong reasons. But Marge, herself, had no idea exactly what it meant because its construction was somewhat hip.

"Nice line," Hal turned and said to Brendan.

"Pat McCormick, 1981," Brendan replied.

"Geez, you even steal from dead people, you old geezer."

"But from the best," Brendan said proudly when, in fact, he felt guilty that Marge had actually used the line which he had put in just to entertain her and himself. But then, as a result of the mild laugh, he watched Marge literally sit back in her chair and decide to remain silent for the remainder of the segment and help no one.

"Write, 'In England, this is a Flag Day to honor the birthday of Princess Anne. In America, Flag Day commemorates our flag's adoption by the Continental Congress in 1777,'" Brendan said.

Millie wrote this into the prompter and rolled it. Immediately Beverly was correcting everyone as if she were the only one with a brain out there.

The script in front of Mugsy was the "Vagina Special"; unlike Hal, who had had the correct "Queen's Jubilee" one. Consequently, what Mugsy had in her hands bore no relation to the script that was supposed to be in the prompter. She was completely in the dark and useless as per usual.

At that moment, Leo appeared at the door to the control room with the right script for the show in his hand.

"I have it," he blurted out breathing heavily. He must have run up four flights to get it there. "I've got the right one!"

"Great. Bring it over," Brendan said. "Maybe we can go to commercial now. And Millie will put the next segment in by the time we come back."

"I need a script," Hal said immediately. "How am I supposed do anything without a script?" He threw his "correct" script up in the air to prove he was completely at sea.

Brendan then grabbed a page off the floor, turned it over, and wrote "Commercial" on the back of it in big letters and put it on the lectern in front of Hal.

"Okay. *Now!*" Hal said when he saw the page. He had a renewed confidence in his voice. "Commercial!" he ordered grandly as if responding to a precise cue. It made him feel like a director.

Brendan then tapped Millie on the shoulder again and said, "Write 'Go to Commercial.'"

"Go to commercial," Bambi repeated.

Hal cued the theme music and then faded to black. Everyone breathed a sigh of relief. There were hoots and hollers from the tech crew as they pushed their rolling chairs back from the consoles.

"We're out," Hal announced.

"Three minutes," the assistant director shouted.

Out on the set, Bradley approached the table to tell the women that the problem was being worked on.

"Did I look stupid?" Bambi wanted to know.

"Yes," Marge told her flatly.

"Can we actually do the show without a script?" Moonie asked.

"Sure," Marge replied. "Think of it as eating a meal without a menu."

"Ohhhhhhhhhh," Moonie said and understood the situation for the first time.

"Don't panic. Robert will fix it," Beverly said with quiet assurance.

"Right," Marge said. "We'll be co-host impersonators," she added.

Back in the control room, disaster had largely been avoided and a fix was in the works. Mugsy felt a strange sense of accomplishment after the incident, like a fireman after a fire.

"Well, I'd call that one of the great cluster-fucks of all time," Mugsy said leaning back in her chair. "Millie, can you really get the right script in?"

"No problem," Millie replied while she typed, "I'll have the whole script re-typed by mid break."

"Then we're good," Mugsy said checking herself out in the dark glass of the counter top and feeling as if she had just actually done something. She wrapped her hair, still damp from her morning shower, into a bun and pinned it there. Hal turned around and looked at her.

"That made 'The Hindenburg' look like 'Masterpiece Theater'", he said, "How did that happen?"

"New script software," Brendan said.

"You mean that piece of crap your boyfriend forced on us? Does he own stock in it or something?" Hal said looking at Mugsy.

Mugsy reacted immediately to the fact that someone would dare ask her anything that would indicate an intimate relationship with the executive producer. She didn't like that everyone still considered her his girlfriend when Bad Bob had definitely moved on to

Jeanie the Censor while still relying on Mugsy as a trusted confidante and an occasional "booty call".

"I dunno… And he's not my boyfriend. I don't know what he does. Why're you asking me? I had nothing to do with the new software," she said defensively.

Jeanie, for her part, was on the phone and perfectly cool in the face of any implication that she was currently involved with a married man who was also her boss. It was as if Bad Bob's sexual pursuits had nothing to do with her personally. After all, she wasn't actually *sleeping* with him. She liked being in control too much for anything that crazy or passionate. Jeanie preferred heavy petting in Bad Bob's office, Bill Clinton style. It was sort of like having sex with a seven second delay. All the offensive parts could be eliminated. Besides, it wasn't the sex she was interested in with Bad Bob anyway. It was a baby. And, with five kids to his credit, she knew he was good at that.

Hal looked at Mugsy for a long beat. He was deciding whether to get into it with her or not. But he decided not to and simply turned back and faced the monitors instead.

"*What?*" Mugsy said in full defensive mode. "We're friends. Is there some law?"

The technical personnel at their consoles looked at each other and smiled as they prepared for the next segment.

"Hey, it's all great," Brendan jumped in with, trying to diffuse the charged atmosphere. "It shook things up. It proves we're live."

"Yeah, the show's live. But our careers are dead," Hal added.

"Can't work forever, Hal," Brendan said.

"My friend, I'm a director. I believe the script came from the writers."

"It was nobody's fault. It was an accident," Mugsy said. "Like a pregnancy." With that, the entire room turned around and looked at her, waiting for more.

"*What?*" she said again.

"Chernobyl was an accident, Mugsy. Pregnancy is …," Hal began.

"...For lovers!" Brendan blurted out ingenuously, trying to diffuse the tension.

Mugsy was unsure how the exchange had gone, so she merely folded her arms across her chest instead of saying anything further and pouted until the next segment began.

Jeanie had gotten off the phone and was sitting with her hands folded and beaming like the angel she was. Then she very gently placed one hand on the "kill" button as the second segment was about to begin. She looked like a Mary Tyler Moore version of Standards and Practices. She was simply too wonderful to be dragged down by anything as inappropriate as office sex.

At the "post mortem" meeting, the women were apoplectic at being shown up as idiots by a software glitch. But Bad Bob quickly deflected it to the writers by saying that the writers had somehow not followed the specific instructions for the new software, and that's why the wrong script had come up.

"You've got to realize the new software is very powerful." Bad Bob told the assembled cast and production staff. "That's what makes it so great." Then he turned to Leo as if it was solely his fault. "Sometimes that hurts a little."

"The last time I heard that, the next words were 'open wide'," Leo said. "But to tell you the truth, I don't know how it happened."

"Made us look like damn fools," Moonie chimed in.

"And we can usually adlib that," Marge added.

The whole thing made Beverly very uncomfortable. She prided herself as being the smartest one in the room and the one with proprietary information on her teleprompter.

"Perhaps we should consider going back to the old method. The one where I know what I'm talking about," she said quietly.

"Let's give it one more chance. I want the writers to feel totally comfortable before I pull the plug," Bad Bob said.

"That's like putting a whoopee cushion on an electric chair," Brendan added. He was getting that feeling again, the feeling that something was wrong. And yet the show had gone off without a hitch after the first segment.

"Exactly!" Bad Bob said by way of ending the meeting.

Everyone liked the notion that it was somehow the writers' fault. Brendan and Leo took it in stride.

They were used to it.

CHAPTER TWO

Brendan eventually found out why he had that feeling that something was wrong, terribly wrong—that nagging, sinking feeling that something just wasn't right. It wasn't the script software glitch or the "CrossTalk" debacle after all. What was wrong was something else altogether. And he found out what it was the following day which happened to be a "dark day" in more ways than one.

He was fired.

There's a fine line between birth and death. For Brendan White, it was his career.

It was all coming to an end at the hands of the iPhoning Bad Bob Vapors, co-executive producer of "The Ladies' Room" and former defensive end from the University of Tennessee who actually had the release date of the next "Big and Tall" catalogue marked on his calendar.

Bad Bob's office, where all this was happening, was decorated like the "Bad Bob Vapors Road House" in Memphis which he had once owned. But, instead of pictures of errant Elvii, (Bad Bob's had been the watering hole for the first Elvis impersonators) he had pictures of Beverly Frost (some on black velvet) —his boss, and benefactor. Beverly had rescued Bad Bob from the motor pool of the local network affiliate in Memphis and had eventually elevated him to the position of her "partner in broadcasting".

Bad Bob's bent for vicious capitalism had caught Beverly's eye during the Elvis Presley funeral when it was brought to her attention that Bad Bob owned 100% of the broadcast-equipped vans in the City of Memphis which he then leased back to the various media entities as they needed them. She decided right then and there that Robert Vapors was exactly the man she needed to become a force of nature in television and not just a field reporter. She would become the owner of her own work product—in this case, news and information—the way Desi Arnaz had owned "I Love Lucy".

But, in truth, Bad Bob was really just Beverly's bag man— "Driving Miss Beverly"—doing her bidding in her declining years as a culture whore and a self-styled West Coast news diva. Beverly Frost would remind anyone within earshot, even though long ago most people had stopped believing a word that came out of her mouth, that she was, first and foremost, a "journalist". The only problem was she couldn't say "journalist" any better than she could say "Frost" thanks to a delicate, but persistent, lisp that had been carefully papered over with a phony mid-Atlantic accent designed to intimidate Americans and impress foreigners. How she came to be an on-air personality with a speech impediment was more a credit to her laser-guided ambition than any natural talent. She sounded less like Barbara Walters, whom she considered a phony, and more like "Baby Bear" from Sesame Street. The more she tried to convince the public of her so-called credentials, the more she reminded them of a sock puppet.

Brendan had been writing comedy at "The Ladies' Room" for fifteen years, since its inception, in what often seemed like a show business internment camp. It put him out of sight of anyone else in the entertainment industry but still qualified him for Writer's Guild pension and welfare. He was gainfully employed in "The Business" but could never actually prove it. Performers, actors, singers, comedians, producers, and directors filed past him daily, but he knew none of them, and none ever acknowledged him as anything more than a functionary along the lines of hair and make-up. What might have seemed like a glamorous job to his family and friends was more akin to that of a valet parking attendant on Rodeo Drive: show business proximity with complete anonymity.

For Brendan, working at "The Ladies' Room" had been the final installment, but also the saving grace, of a self-destructive career in television and screenwriting. Had he been Japanese, instead of Irish, he would have accepted what he'd become with perfect Zen tranquility instead of going into that good night like a maniac. Each year that passed was another reminder to him that he was comfortably going nowhere. His center would not hold. One way or another he was hell-bent on destroying what was essentially a "good thing".

His imminent dismissal had always seemed part of the show itself, like a perennial segment that was perpetually planned, and even scheduled, but never aired. His firing seemed always to be on the horizon, but nobody ever thought it would actually happen because of the shit-storm that would ensue. Only Bad Bob, as co-executive producer of the most dysfunctional show on television, would actually fire someone and then expect them to show up for work the next day.

"The network doesn't want to see you around here anymore," Bad Bob said to Brendan after he'd been summoned, "And neither do I."

Bad Bob had his own secret speech impediment—a decidedly unmanly lateral slur in his articulation that he'd swallowed with a Tennessee drawl and phony swagger. Thus, the two of them— Beverly and Bad Bob—were joined at the lisp. It probably accounted for how they found each other. Like lovers who subconsciously recognize themselves in each other's face, Bad Bob and Beverly had an affinity that ran deeper than anyone could ever guess.

Brendan had always known that this overgrown yahoo hated him, but he never thought Bad Bob had the balls to actually say it to his face. Consequently, at the moment of his dismissal, he did what any veteran, burned-out, self-destructive comedy writer, working for women in Daytime would do on the occasion of being fired for the last time in his life.

He keeled over.

Not for real, of course, but because Brendan White knew something that Bad Bob didn't.

Earlier that morning, in the Wilshire office of his cardiologist, Brendan had taken a stress test during which a slight heart anomaly had been tracked. As a result, but only after a "wallet biopsy" confirmed sufficient insurance coverage, Brendan had been fitted with a Holter monitor which was now wired to his chest with a nest of blue and red wires that made him look like either a suicide bomber or the victim of one.

In addition, after that test, but just prior to coming to the office, he had fulfilled an appointment at the UCLA fertility clinic where he had been required to leave a deposit. It was the closest Brendan would come to actual sex with his wife for several months; but, given the quality of the porn, medically supplied by the clinic, it was far better than the real thing and certainly better than the normal pornography Brendan was used to. So it was that, while jerking off for science and family, Brendan had wondered exactly how it came to pass that the good doctors of the UCLA Medical Center had gotten hold of such excellent porn. It probably made the four years of medical school almost worth it.

In fact, the experience was so enjoyable that, afterwards, Brendan had tried to shake hands with the head of the clinic to thank him but was summarily rejected by the good doctor who chose to only nod accommodatingly while keeping his arms tightly folded across his chest and his hands jammed deep into the safety of his armpits. Apparently, *nobody* shakes hands at a fertility clinic— especially within 50 feet of the "deposit" rooms.

Now, as he lay curled up on the floor in front of Bad Bob's "Playboy After Dark" velour couch, Brendan was, at once, wired and relaxed. After all, most men like to nap after sex, even if it is with themselves.

It was at that point that Brendan gradually became aware that the office carpet smelled vaguely familiar and not unlike the fertility clinic where he'd just been. It was probably what the rug in the Oval Office must have smelled like during the Clinton Administration. More specifically, it smelled like cum. It made Brendan instantly sorry he'd pulled the fainting act; but, by then, it was too late to go back. Nonetheless, the unfortunate discovery did confirm one thing: it meant Bad Bob was now definitely having sex with Jeanie the Censor just as Brendan and everyone else on the show had suspected for some time. But the virginal Jeanie would only give Bad Bob a "modified Lewinski" rather than the real thing, hence the cum smell on the rug; so the confirmation of the executive producer's affair provided only a brief moment of satisfaction for Brendan's in this, now, decidedly less than ideal situation.

Brendan glanced under the couch to see if there were any Standards and Practices panties lurking there, but there were none. Only rat shit, some AA batteries, and a toupee. He then decided that one of the benefits of merely *pretending* to pass out was that he really didn't have to do anything else. It wasn't as if he were trying to fake the Gettysburg Address. Consequently, he continued to lie there in a semi-fetal position and did nothing.

"Hey, man. You okay?" Bad Bob said trying to sound cool despite his dislike of anything hip or anyone north of Graceland.

Brendan thought about moaning but closed his eyes instead and exhaled while trying to keep the corners of his mouth under control. He could hear the concern in Bad Bob's voice now, but he knew that the concern was not for him, by any means. It was for Bad Bob's own fat ass. He'd have to explain to Beverly that the firing did not go well; that Brendan had collapsed and had to be taken by paramedics to the Emergency Room; but that, hopefully, he'd been too out of it to leak anything.

Bad Bob and Beverly had been convinced that Brendan was the source of all leaks to the press about the show. The truth of the matter, of course, was that Beverly, herself, was the biggest leaker of them all, especially given the fact that three out of four of her best friends were Hollywood gossip columnists. They all had Beverly on speed dial in case they needed some last minute dish on either Moonie Brown, the morbidly obese Native American co-host who claimed to be a full blooded Indian, but nobody had the guts to call her on it; or on Beverly's nemesis in the SBS news department, the drop-dead gorgeous shiksa icon, Delores Whitcomb, who always held her microphone as if she were holding a croissant in her elegant WASP fingers as opposed to the normal closed-fist, "cock" grip favored by Beverly and most other on-air reporters. It drove Beverly nuts because, by so doing, Delores was able to demonstrate her superior breeding and social status every time she was on camera. Beverly could not deny the effectiveness of Delores' technique and kicked herself daily for not thinking of it first.

Brendan rolled over on his back to get away from the cum smell, but he still kept his eyes closed. Bad Bob knelt down and straddled him. But now Brendan knew that this wasn't the first time Bad Bob had straddled someone on the floor of his office, the most recent being Jeanie, the Censor; and before her, Martha Muggeridge,— known as "Mugsy" to her friends and "That Crazy Fucking Lunatic" to Brendan and anyone who actually had to work with her.

"Wake up, man," Bob said.

Brendan figured it would be only a matter of seconds before Bad Bob got a load of all the wires covering his chest.

"Holy shit," Bad Bob said when he finally saw them. "What's the matter with you, man?" Brendan didn't reply. Instead, he smiled weakly while keeping his eyes closed so Bad Bob would think he really *did* have a medical emergency on is hands.

"Call the medics!" Bad Bob shouted to his secretary, Terri Shaw. Terri was a tough-as-nails Brooklyn Irish girl with perfectly formed tits that looked like you could get into art school just by drawing them. She had brought herself and her tits west in hopes of launching a film career but, so far, had only succeeded in landing a job as a receptionist. That is why Los Angeles has the best looking blue collar workers and support staff in the country.

"The SBS medics or real ones?" She asked dumbly.

"Call an ambulance," he shouted. "Now!"

Brendan regretted that he couldn't watch the desperation spread over Bad Bob's mashed potato face like a ladle of Elvis' "thickenin' gravy". But he knew that passing out in the office was definitely the right thing to do under the circumstances, so he decided it was best to go all the way with it. Besides, once in the ambulance, if he could convince the EMS medics to take him to Cedars, instead some place in the Valley, he could save on the cab fare home. But that wouldn't solve his commuting problem since his car would still be at the SBS studios in Reseda. Such is the constant "car anxiety" that pervades everything in Southern California. People are obsessed with the whereabouts and well-being of their automobiles the way new mothers are about their two year olds.

But, alas, Brendan had no such luck. He ended up at the Reseda Urgent Care on Reseda Avenue, of all places, with a sallow Paki intern attending to him as if he were a candidate for reincarnation. Then, while trying to explain that he was basically okay, Brendan saw Bad Bob arrive. He was wearing a "man" hat, for crissakes, and looking dutifully hang-dog—not because he was a Good Samaritan (You don't need to break out a clean shirt and tie just to show you care) but to absolve himself of any guilt and to certify that he hadn't actually killed Brendan. But the tables were now turned, and Brendan suddenly felt like he didn't really want to see Bad Bob around there anymore, either.

CHAPTER THREE

Anyone who's ever been loaded into a walk-in clinic in Los Angeles against their will knows the distinct feeling of, "Where the fuck *am* I? Does anyone even know this place exists?" Nothing looks real. It feels like you're on the set of a half-assed medical drama being produced, on the cheap, in a strip mall in a Valley. In fact, that's exactly what it's like since everyone in LA is an actor, and every job is temporary.

As it was, that afternoon, even the medically challenged staff at Reseda Urgent Care knew a Holter monitor when they saw one; and they quickly determined that Brendan was okay. That was great news because it meant they could roll him for as many tests as they could remember from their sunny medical school days in Guadalajara without actually hurting him. It was the perfect storm, and Brendan White was the perfect patient: absolutely healthy and insured. Brendan assumed it would all be free anyway because he had been stricken on SBS property and on the job (or, at least, in the process of losing one). Consequently, he let them poke, test, monitor, and drip to their hearts content.

"How you feelin', man?" The distinctive Tennessee drawl with the semi-redacted lisp came floating through the stanchions at back of Brendan's gurney.

Bad Bob's lame attempt to reconcile with the Hollywood liberals he loathed was to affect a goober's version of jazz hipness. Hence, he would tag the incongruous "man" onto the ends of his sentences to signify that he had come in peace. Brendan could never understand why Bad Bob had such a hard-on about liberals in general until he learned that his corn-fed wife's first marriage had been to a New York Jewish intellectual from the Upper West Side of Manhattan.

Apparently, in times of stress, and when the heavy meds were mixing with the Chardonnay, Mrs. Vapors was not above pointing out to her second husband that he was nothing more than an oversized Tennessee football meathead, and a nondescript lineman at that, with a brain that varied inversely to the size of his belly. Then she would toss off a few of the overly intellectual "New York Review of Books" put-downs she'd learned from husband "Number One" as an added twist of the knife.

"Oh. Hi." Brendan said meekly, not exactly sure how he was supposed to respond. Should he be glad that Bad Bob had come over to this hell-hole to visit him, or should he be mad that the man who had just fired him was coming back for more? Or was Brendan supposed to be too sick to know the difference?

"The docs tell me you're okay." Bad Bob had switched back to his old country ways. "Those dang things on your chest are nothin' but a Holter monitor." He pronounced "Holter monitor" as if it were a piece of farm equipment or some kind of cattle hitch.

"Yeah," Brendan said and looked up at him for the first time. "My doctor discovered an irregular heartbeat. But now there's a rapid ventricular response on top of that. I'll be okay. I guess."

There was definitely something different about Bad Bob's demeanor. He was much less comfortable in the Urgent Care Center than Brendan was. Then it dawned on Brendan that the man had actually gone all the way back home and changed into his best business suit before coming down to the walk-in. He certainly hadn't been wearing the shiny, three button, piece of shit earlier when he'd fired him. It tickled Brendan that Brendan's well-being wasn't the first thing on Bad Bob's mind during this apparent life or death crisis; his own was. He looked silly. He hadn't bothered to change the lame bowling shoes he always wore when he had changed into his suit.

"Well, I'm glad you're gonna be all right," he said again. "I wanted to make sure of that. The doctors, here, say there's nothing wrong with you. This Holter 'git-up' you're wearing is just a normal testing device."

Brendan knew what he was up to. He was absolving himself of all responsibility. You don't carry Beverly Frost's water for twenty-five years without learning how to deny, lie, and maneuver. But Brendan couldn't let him get away so easily.

"Yeah, but you never know," he said. "The heart's serious shit. My brother had his first heart attack at forty-three. That's practically late thirties."

"Yeah, but it isn't. It's early forties. We did a special on that sort of thing, and it's not as unusual as you think. Besides, with statins, now, heart attacks are almost never fatal anymore."

"Is that supposed to make me feel better?" Brendan wanted to return to their normal hostile relationship. Bad Bob only knew about hearts because Beverly had been fucking a top cardiologist at UCLA and had done a special on Dick Cheney. All of Bad Bob's knowledge was in sound bites because he oversaw the editing. That's why he was fairly effective at network meetings and cocktail parties. But get him on a "one to one", in an extended conversation, and he was completely out to lunch and a blithering idiot.

"Yeah, man. I want you to feel better," Bad Bob said, standing there stiffly in his special "bidness" suit that employed enough fabric to tent a circus.

"Well," Brendan said wanly, "I guess we'll see."

Bad Bob rocked back and forth on his god-awful bowling shoes for a few moments before shifting gears and settling into finishing what he had come to do. He was like a hit man who had botched the job and didn't want to have to report back to the "boss" that the "guy" was still alive.

"So, if I were you, I'd start looking around for another position. I'll honor your Writers Guild twenty-six week guarantee and four week notification, but that's the best I can do." Bad Bob said continuing the conversation he'd started in the office.

"All right," Brendan said matter-of-factly.

Bad Bob was firing him nonetheless. Brendan didn't know what he was supposed to do now. Argue about the particulars? He immediately started to litigate the termination in his head. He knew Bob had no real cause, so he decided to try to draw him into specifics.

"Why?" Brendan said after a beat. "Aren't the jokes funny enough?" Bad Bob knew that Brendan had nothing to do with the script software fuck-up the day before. His contributions to the show were largely separate from the actual script. His primary responsibility was to provide Marge Foley, the alleged comedian, with comedy material for her to weave into the daily "CrossTalk" discussions.

"No, man. Your material is great. I really do marvel at the way you do that every day."

"Then what's the problem?" Brendan asked knowing that the issue was purely personal and a political thing between Bad Bob and himself. Then he flashed on the possibility that, on top of everything else, maybe the problem was Brendan reminded him of his wife's first husband.

"Your intros. A lot of them are unusable." Bad Bob said with a straight face.

That caused Brendan to rise up off the gurney and sit on the side of it. The monitors attached to him went wild, and the commotion frightened Bad Bob. Brendan had suddenly warmed to the opportunity of actually having a substantive discussion over the two sentence introductions for guests that, strictly speaking, weren't even his responsibility.

"That's bullshit," Brendan said as if he were actually prepared to defend the genius of, "Please welcome, the always irrepressible, Regis Philbin".

"Well, Mugsy told me that when she gets them at the read-through they're unacceptable."

"Have you ever read them?"

"Yes, and I agree with her."

He was lying, of course, but they were now at loggerheads. Brendan understood then that the given reason for his firing was going to be his failure to write intros that would pass the highest standards of literary merit as set by this Ozark orangutan and his neurotic "Senior Producer" ball girl. He was nonplussed about how he should respond. It was beneath him to argue the relative merits of those two-line throwaways written with about as much artistic integrity as a traffic sign. But, on the other hand, Brendan did want to keep his job.

"You're wrong. They're fucking brilliant," Brendan said.

But Bad Bob shook his head. His mind was made up. No Proustian intros, no job.

"You also have failed to involve yourself in other areas of the show," he added.

"I didn't know that was my job," Brendan replied. He was getting steamed now and feeling high-minded. "Am I supposed to go up and down the halls mugging people for work?"

"You know that there is a lot to do, and you choose not to do it. It also doesn't help that you are always grousing and complaining about the way things are done around here," Bad Bob said meaning the show, of course, and not the urgent care center.

With that, Brendan felt he had enough to go on for a law suit. Now he wanted to make sure Bad Bob didn't mitigate anything by talking any further on the subject.

"I was told," Brendan added, not being able to control himself, much less Bad Bob, "That I was to write comedy intros for Marge when she had to do them. I don't want to have to explain the process to you, but if you're going to do a comedy intro, then you're going to have to push the "intro envelope", so to speak, and that means you could possibly run into trouble. It's not the same as a straight intro. You have to take a chance with the subject matter in order to get the laugh. But I always checked with the segment producer each time and got their approval, or I rewrote them until I did. And that's a fact," Brendan said sounding slightly like Brando at the pigeon coop in "On the Waterfront".

Suddenly Brendan realized he was doing it. He was actually having a serious, substantive conversation about the inane introductions for B List celebrities on a daytime talk show. Actually, Leo, the other writer, was the one who wrote most of the intros. But, for Leo, they were like math, not art. His comedy chops were not on the line when he wrote them as, obviously, Brendan felt his were.

"Whatever," Bad Bob said, "The end result is they're unusable when they get to Mugsy."

"All of them?" Brendan said getting louder.

"Enough to be a problem."

"But that isn't my fault. Fire the segment producers. Am I supposed to be smarter than they are and change the intros they approved?

"I don't know. You'll have to take that up with Mugsy. My decision's final." He said. Brendan and Bad Bob looked at each other for a few beats.

"Okay," Brendan said. "I guess that's the way it is." He found himself anticipating the legal fight that he would soon bring. He decided Bad Bob was an asshole not to throw him out on the spot and remove him from "The Ladies' Room" altogether. He was either too dumb, and/or Beverly was too cheap to understand that Brendan would spend the next twenty-six weeks gathering evidence against them.

"Sorry, man." Bad Bob said trying to re-establish his South Central "street cred" even though it was too late. "Hope you get out of this hell-hole real soon." He looked around for an exit.

"Right," Brendan said without really acknowledging him. "I think I'll go right now." With that, Brendan stood up and ripped the wires not connected to the Holter monitor off himself. Then he pulled the IV out of his arm. He knew that would scare the shit out of Bad Bob, and it did.

"Hey, take it easy, man," he said backing away thinking Brendan was preparing to slug him.

"Don't worry about it, *man*. See you later."

Then Brendan walked past Bad Bob and out the door, reveling in the fact that he was leaving the urgent care center before Bad Bob did, and now Bad Bob would have to explain to the Filipino nurses where their patient was. Brendan's macho display was all an act, of course; but, at the same time, it was a put-down to Bad Bob who ended up looking like the big baby that even he, himself, knew he was. But Bad Bob took it all as just another reason why he hated all writers—not in the least because they were liberal, usually from New York; and, most of all, because they belonged to a union.

Brendan found himself on the street outside the clinic looking like an escaped mental patient in a hospital gown holding his shoes and pants. An "off- duty" yellow cab came around the corner, but Brendan managed to flag it down which meant he had to then negotiate a trip back to the studio parking lot with a driver who was dressed worse than he was.

CHAPTER FOUR

B rendan White didn't have a completely wasted life. He did have a semi- wife. "Semi" because they lived together and had a child. "Semi" because neither of them was sure they were really, legally married. And "semi" because she was still dating.

They lived at the top of Laurel Canyon in a bungalow she bought when they moved west. He, in search of a writing gig, she in search of a law career and men with better abs. She would have preferred San Francisco.

Brendan was there for the kid. They had been "married" in Philadelphia by a local hipster and jazz poet who had called himself "Addison G. Rage" after the sign over the Addison Street Garage whose perennial missing "A" in "Garage" had thus baptized the dubious Rev. Rage. It was unclear whether the good reverend was authorized to perform marriages *or* poetry, but it had seemed fun at the time to be "married" by someone who sounded and acted like Lord Buckley.

The Wife's name was Sarah (don't call me "Sally") Davis. Her father, Brooks Davis, had been a Boston Brahmin drunk. He had fancied himself a gentleman environmentalist which meant he rode a bicycle to work in the city each day like an asshole, wearing a bowtie and tweed jacket just so he could be thought of as wonderfully eccentric. Money forgives all. The family had made their fortune in caulking, putty, glaze, and spackle. Her mother was an Irish party girl intent on trading up.

Brendan met Sarah through a friend who had gone to Harvard and who was slumming (as all Harvard grads who aren't running something consider themselves) as a reality show producer. The show was called "Eat Your Pet", or something like that, where families were given a lamb, pig, duck, or a cow to be raised from infancy as a family pet and 4-H show animal before being summarily slaughtered and eaten by the same family that had nurtured it. Disney had passed on the show because they were afraid the doomed animals looked too much like their beloved anthropomorphic characters. The Swann Company, on the other hand, thought the show would be a good way to downplay their failing "character" business in favor of an edgier "Call of Duty" feel that would come from having a 12 year old boy unceremoniously dig into "Fluffy's" flank at Sunday dinner.

The fact that Brendan and Sarah lived together as husband and wife and were having sex in no way diminished Sarah's quest for a rich husband. Brendan was good for sperm but bad for security. She wanted the best of both worlds and was currently fucking the interim Governor of California.

"It's not like he's a Kennedy," Brendan would say to her, "The guy's a sleezebag and will probably end up getting indicted one of these days."

"I don't care. He has a huge office in Sacramento, and he wants me to be in the gallery of the Capital whenever he introduces a bill."

"Sitting right next to his wife," Brendan added. One of the benefits of not being actually, or legally, married is that there are no fights. Jokes, sarcasm, and bits remain funny and appreciated instead of grounds for divorce.

"Temporarily," Sarah would say. "The man has thirteen billion dollars. That's "million" with a "B". They just bought back half his empire for him. And he's not a politician. He's from Silicon Valley where he invented the mouse or something. He gets a royalty for every 'click.' And when he leaves office, he'll be worth twenty-five billion when his so-called blind trust kicks in."

"And how much do you want?" Brendan would ask, knowing the answer.

"Just one," she'd say holding up a finger. "And I'll get it, too. The present Mrs. Governor signed an iron clad pre-nup. But not me. His last girlfriend got "50 mill" for five years. That man knows which side his pussy is buttered on."

This was the mother of Brendan's child. She was mildly psychic and would know things before she should, so Brendan always believed her predictions. She liked living with Brendan because it provided great cover for her affair without too much hindrance. It also gave the kid a semblance of normalcy that a single mom couldn't provide. But, of course, she wanted another child the way most women want another cat to stay home with the first one while they're out all day.

But since her sex life was complicated, she had opted for "in vitro" fertilization even though they didn't really have to. She wanted IVF so she could be sure the sperm for her egg was Brendan's. That way, the kids would match. She also liked the idea of having Brendan's sperm "scrubbed" or whatever they did to it in the lab to make sure it worked. It was like being impregnated with *organic* cum which was much better than ordinary jizz right out of the tap.

Unfortunately, their sex, as far as Brendan was concerned, had deteriorated once The Wife had opted out of "sales". After all, she'd gotten the "purchase order" with the first pregnancy. Their sex had become spotty at best and consisted in her always asking Brendan, at the end, to leave the room so as to not interfere with her orgasm. She wanted to enjoy that in peace. Less of *him* was definitely more exciting for *her*. She also preferred the game of "Solitaire" to any social situation that involved Brendan and would begin endlessly shuffling the cards every evening after the kid went to bed.

"Thurrrrrrrrrraaap!" he would hear from the kitchen table indicating her "Solitaire" shuffling had begun, and he would be alone for the rest of the evening.

Brendan didn't mind. It was like getting an "Early Out" at the office "provided all your work is done" as the producers of "The Ladies' Room" would announce from time to time with great beneficence even though most of the staff had already left, on their own, hours before.

The end result of their living arrangement was that Brendan got to have sex once in a while but with all the hard parts left out—like those ads on TV for "The Greatest Classical Music of All Time... with all the unfamiliar parts left out". Besides, performance didn't count once she'd determined that he was just a working stiff, and she actually had been much nicer to him after it'd been established that his sperm was more socially acceptable than he was. The Wife had actually once confessed to Brendan, as a compliment, that she loved his cock because it was so "soft and cuddly". As a result, Brendan was able to save a fortune on Viagra after the Writers Guild health plan stopped covering it. Of course, if the Guild's health plan hadn't initially covered Viagra, Brendan would still be on the street and not a father. Even so, Brendan adored the sex they had for all those reasons. The ambivalence of their marriage made the sex more "date-like" and passionate, like a series of one night stands that had no reason to ever happen again. It was only when The Wife's feet hit the floor, and reality set in, that they became mutual caregivers to the boy instead of a real couple.

There's nothing like leaving a deposit at a fertility clinic to make a man feel superfluous unless it's returning home afterwards to the so-called loving female who got him to do it in the first place. By the time Brendan got home from the hospital that night, he was late.

"What happened to you, she said.

"I got fired"

"What about the clinic? Did you at least show up at the clinic like you were supposed to?" she shot back, still pissed that Brendan was late.

"Oh yeah," he said.

"And did that go well? Did you 'do' it? Suddenly, she seemed to be taking a real interest in Brendan's day.

"Yeah, it was great"

"Good." She had moved to another room. Brendan could tell from her tone that she had returned to picking up and cleaning. "Don't worry, you'll get another job." She said as an afterthought, as if she were reassuring a child that there would always be another Kleenex.

"And I'm wearing a Holter monitor from the stress test." Brendan said. Brendan was consciously trying to load up as much information as possible about his day to see what the tipping point would be.

She stuck her head out from around the corner of Zeke's room. "Oh, my God," she said registering some apparent concern. "That didn't interfere with your 'deposit' did it?"

"Who knows? I wonder how many other patients with monitors jerk off into a cup during the day." He said. "They probably don't see that kind of spike on their read-outs very often."

"But it didn't *interfere*," she persisted, looking at him straight in the eye to indicate the seriousness of her line of questioning.

"No," he assured her. "It all went well. I guess. Who knows? All I know is I came in a cup and handed it to some stranger through a hole in the wall. Could have been a homeless, gay guy on the other side for all I know.

"Well, I doubt that. Thanks, Sweetie. Now, go kiss Zeke good-night," she said crossing into the kitchen.

"I mean, I really did get fired today," Brendan said plaintively, now standing alone in the living room.

"And I want to hear all about it," she said condescendingly. "But take care of Zeke first. He's been waiting for you."

The kid's name was officially, "Hezekiah"; and they had fought bitterly over it. Brendan wanted it because it sounded retro hip and was actually an old Yankee name his father had used in stories he'd made up for his children at the Sunday dinner table. The Wife had finally agreed when it was determined that he would be called, "Zeke" which she thought sounded Jewish enough to pass as the Governor's son when the time came.

Brendan went into Zeke's room. He was laying there holding the covers up to his chin looking all angelic and about as beautiful as a boy could look and still be called a boy. "Hiya, Champ," Brendan said.

"You're an idiot," he said matter-of-factly. The good thing was that at least Brendan knew their relationship hadn't deteriorated any further since breakfast.

"Okay." Brendan replied benignly. There was a time when Brendan would have taken that kind of statement seriously, but he knew it meant that things were the same—not good, exactly—but, at least, the same.

"Don't call your father an 'idiot'," Brendan heard from the kitchen. Zeke shrugged. Brendan dismissed it with a wave of his hand because the truth was he *was* an idiot, and so what if everyone in the house knew it. At least Zeke didn't know that his father, the literal jerk-off in the Holter monitor, had just been fired.

"Your father just got fired. Show a little respect," The Wife called out blithely.

The fact that her semi-husband had just gotten fired held about as much weight with her as if he'd just come in out of the rain. Fortunately, the concept of "being fired" did not resonate with an eight year old. Now, if she had said, "Your father has just been fired *upon*", then the kid could have related it to one of his many combat video games where the body count before breakfast each morning was probably greater than any real battle in World War II.

"Hey, wanna see something cool?" Brendan said, lifting his shirt to show Zeke the monitor wires. "Your old man's a robot."

This engaged the boy. Suddenly, the aspect of his father as a cyborg interested him far more than the idea of his father as the old guy living with his mother.

"Cool," he said fingering the red and blue wires. "Can I have it?"

"No. It's for me. It's a test to check my heart." Zeke always wanted to see everything.

"You gonna keep it on?"

"Yeah, I have to until tomorrow."

"In the morning?" he asked.

"Yeah, I gotta sleep with it. It listens to my heart continuously. And records it all here." Brendan showed him the recorder on his hip.

"Cool, Dad." Brendan was almost moved to tears. He thought how sweet it was that he was able to connect with his only son by means of heart disease. He also liked hearing the words "Cool" and "Dad" coming out of Zeke's mouth in close proximity even though he didn't mean it exactly that way. The Holter monitor was "cool", and Brendan was his "dad". They weren't really connected, but it still sounded sweet to Brendan.

"Hey, whaddya say you and me go back to the doctor together when they take this thing off, and then you can see all the equipment and maybe we can get something to eat (Brendan was piling on, now) or buy something at (the magic words) "Gamestop".

Zeke looked at his father for a beat to test whether he was serious, but only about the last "Gamestop" part. The kid could see that Brendan was scrambling and full of shit.

"Don't push it, Dad," Zeke said.

"Good night, Slugger" Brendan said. They exchanged a look that meant that Brendan knew that Zeke knew that everything was all right. The kid was smart, smarter than Brendan. And hipper, too; even though Brendan could never fully explain that, even to himself.

Brendan was an alien in his own home. Of course, he had produced that very situation quite methodically, and it was as if he'd acquired the perfect players to act out his chosen scenario. In the same way that the "Green Earth" people worry about their "carbon footprint", Brendan was determined to leave no "husband footprint" on his family. Thus, he was the only one who ever operated a camera or took video of their little trio. If archeologists ever uncovered the record of the Brendan White family, or even its immediate survivors, they might rightly surmise from the photographic and video evidence that there was no father. Pay no attention to the man behind the camera.

Brendan was living his life like the photographer on Mount Everest who took the triumphant pictures of Edmund Hillary, the so-called first man to conquer Everest—if you don't count the photographer who had to get there first to capture the moment of Hillary reaching the summit.

Brendan knew he should have legally married The Wife in front of someone with a license, but she would have none of it. He had made the mistake, late in life, of knocking up a rich feminist. Women like that who are still fertile should have a warning label tattooed on their foreheads declaring: "Danger! Dwindling eggs. Any pregnancy will result in a live birth".

The Wife was a lawyer with a large Los Angeles corporate firm. She was blindingly bright and quick. It was impossible to tell her a joke or story because she claimed to already know the punch line or ending, not by memory, but by sheer chess-like logic, algorithm, or psychic intuition. She was always ten moves ahead. Just the sort of person a stand-up comic would not want at ringside on opening night. Thus, as someone who was never surprised by even the most brilliant and spontaneous turn of wit, she was not a great laugher, either.

"So what're you going to do?" she said settling down finally with her one glass of wine for the day.

"I think I'll sue," Brendan said. I think I have a good age discrimination case, and then there is the whole defamation business about the homosexuality; and Chester, the runner, running around saying, "I hate white people" all the time. Maybe you could handle the case."

"They'll think you're crazy," she said.

"Of course they will, but it's all true. They've left themselves wide open."

"You'll come off as a crackpot," she said with wave of her hand.

"But you're a lawyer. Wouldn't you sue? I was going to ask you for someone in your office."

"As Zeke would say," she said, "Don't embarrass me *and* yourself."

"But that's what you do. I thought being married to a lawyer...."

"...Don't get me involved. Please," she said. "It's very uncomfortable. Let it go, or else you'll come off as a troublemaker."

Brendan looked at her for a beat. It was a decisive moment when he could have either pursued the subject or returned to his safe place under a rock. Marriage is about accommodation and peace. All husbands are Neville Chamberlains. All wives want Poland.

"Now tell me everything about Dr. Beecham and the clinic. Did you think of me?" she said excitedly while curling her legs under herself on the couch.

"Was that a requirement?" Brendan asked as he was immediately reminded of the incredible pornography the clinic had supplied. "Don't tell me it has something to do with how IVF works. Are you worried the kid might come out looking like Jenna Jameson?"

"Well, it would've been nice if you were thinking of me when you "did it," she said pouting slightly. All of a sudden Brendan found himself backtracking from a situation not of his design where his wife considered his thoughts at a fertility clinic a breach of the marital vows because of exactly whom he was fantasizing about when he ejaculated. It reminded him of the story of the man sitting alone in his living room who gets slapped by his wife the minute she comes home because she had just seen a woman whom, had the husband been with her, he would have ogled. Explain that to a marriage counselor who also thinks your wife is brilliant and unappreciated.

It always amazed Brendan that marriage counselors were notorious for not only always siding with the wives but also, nine times out of ten, for sleeping with them as well. Hadn't the husbands suffered enough? It proved the marriage counselor really wasn't listening, just as the husbands had always suspected. As the veteran comedy writer Harry Crane would say, after a perfectly timed puff on his cigar, "Soon as the little lady comes home and says she wants to start seein' a therapist...pack your fuckin' bags. (Of course, what Harry had *really* said was, "Soon as the little lady comes home and says she wants to start takin' courses.") But it all amounts to the same thing: "Pack your fuckin' bags". Anything outside the kitchen is "location". And they think the same rules apply.

The most prized possession The Wife had was not her jewelry, Brendan, Zeke, or her house, or anything else one would think she might hold near and dear to her heart. No, it was her collection of knives—kitchen knives. The significance of that did not dawn on Brendan until several years into the marriage. And when it did, he feared for his life as well as his balls. She would've sooner had Brendan put little Zeke in the dishwasher than one of those precious knives. The knives had their own drawer and their own little cutlery rack inside the drawer where each blade had its own little custom fitted bed. Explain that to a counselor.

"I'm jealous of the knives, counselor. They live better than I do. They have their own place; they get more respect; and they get washed lovingly and gently,—by hand in warm water—which, I think, means they also have better sex than I do."

The Wife wanted to hear all about the sperm deposit at the fertility clinic. She obviously felt she wanted to be part of the whole thing as if the collection had been done vaginally instead of on the 4th floor of a clinic in Westwood. So Brendan told her all about it and about how Dr. Beecham did not want to shake hands with him after it was over. The Wife tried to appreciate why Brendan had been offended, but she didn't really get it. After all, that man is a *doctor!*

"Oh, honey, I'm sorry," she said, trying to sound truly concerned for his hurt feelings the way a mother would talk to a child whose coloring book got slightly crumpled. For The Wife, getting fired at age 68 was a glass of water; getting stiffed by a doctor who collected sperm for a living, *that* made her feel bad for him. "I'll speak to him, if you want. I'll be seeing him this week."

"No, that's okay," Brendan said. "They'll think you're a crackpot." Brendan thought about that for a beat. "No, they'll think *I'm* a crackpot for even noticing."

"The Holter monitor wires make you look like a suicide bomber," she said changing the subject and trying to be sweet.

"It's actually quite comfortable," he said.

CHAPTER FIVE

There was a pervasive stench of death in the building where "The Ladies' Room" was broadcast, live, each day over the SBS Network. The place had once been a Ford and Subaru dealership, so most people chalked the smell up to old tires and seat covers whose aroma had never fully vacated the premises. But the lingering odor was endemic to the building in the same way that the CBS Broadcast Center in New York still smelled vaguely of milk because it'd once been a dairy; and the bungalows in Los Feliz that had once been whorehouses still smelled of pussy.

But to the connoisseur, the "nose" of the SBS building had a deep and distinct twinge of mortality and dark purpose like the sweet horror that thickens the air of an embalming room. In any event, the place was known as a "sick building", meaning that something in it, either by pathogen or karma, was making all who ventured inside either sick or dead. But then again, television is all about sickness and death, so maybe it was a good fit.

"The Ladies' Room" shared the building with a soap opera called "Living for Love" which was shot in an adjoining studio that was the mirror image of their own. The "Living" people didn't pay much attention to the staff or stars of "The Ladies' Room" because they considered what they were doing to be high art compared to the pedestrian task of producing a daily talk show. In many ways, they preferred to think "The Ladies' Room" only existed to facilitate their own mission, the way craft services took care of their stomachs. In truth, it was less about the arrogance of actors and their competitiveness and more about simply not wanting to get close to anyone else in "the business". In that, actors are like soldiers in combat who avoid intimacy in order to make the inevitable fatalities less devastating.

The "Living" people easily ignored "The Ladies'" staff because "Living for Love" had been on the air forever, and they considered themselves to be in the "theater". They also assumed that anything in the studio opposite them was going to be canceled anyway—especially a daytime talk show for women. So it was in their best interest not to associate with Brendan or anyone else across the hall. They figured any show named after a toilet was not worthy to occupy their same air space.

But Brendan always thought that, with all that young pussy traveling the elevators and stairwells with them every day, somebody would fuck *somebody*. But it never happened. Either the starlets were too busy learning their lines to hear a pickup one, or they were just too damn good looking to consider fucking anyone who worked with their hands. They never fucked "below the line", only each other.

The soap stars basically didn't like anyone at "The Ladies' Room". And neither did the production staff. Brendan had made a point of begging their casting director to throw him a part. He showed her his AFTRA card and resume', but she never considered it, even as a lark. She would've had Brendan barred from the building if he didn't have a network pass around his neck.

"Those soap people are just as cunty as the characters they play," Brendan declared to Leo one day after some perceived elevator slight. "But it's not life imitating art," he added, "They're just '*method*' cunts."

The two elevators that incessantly plied their way between the floors of the building every day were crucibles for the lives within them. At any given moment, Brendan and the rest of "The Ladies' Room" staff would find themselves riding in close quarters with either the supercilious divas from the soap opera they didn't know or the bitchy ones from their own show that they did. People might try to cop an attitude in an elevator; but, like atheists in foxholes, there are no elitists in elevators, either. For the brief span of the one or two floors they might travel together, all within are literally in the same boat. The irrefutable reality of that situation was liberating for some but a nagging irritation for others.

For Brendan, it was show time. It's what got him fired as an NBC Page back in New York when he dropped his pants one day after the elevator doors had closed without knowing that the wife of the head of the network was part of the tour he felt compelled to entertain. That was at a time when NBC pages wore stiff cardboard collars and pants with no pockets to prevent the overqualified sentries from standing around with their hands in them. Thus, by deliberately dropping his draconically doctored pants, Brendan had grossly over-stepped the dress code in an inane attempt to amuse both himself and his charges. In any event, he had been dismissed almost before the elevator doors opened again.

The elevators at "The Ladies' Room" were almost never empty. There was always someone standing there when the doors opened looking as if they had been trapped in a Diane Arbus photograph. On the rare occasion when Brendan rode the elevator alone, if a closely held fart were to be released, he could be assured that the person waiting to step in, when the doors opened, would be either Beverly, Bad Bob, or the good looking new ingénue from "Living". In fact, the occurrence was so inevitable that Brendan would often purposely fart just to see whom he could materialize at the other end of the ride.

Beverly Frost, of course, spoke to no one beneath her in the elevator and only in heavy coded pronouns to peers and above. Her middle distance stare was legendary. Every now and then Brendan would actually find himself sharing an elevator alone with this woman he'd worked intimately with on a daily basis for 15 years; but her thoughts, on those rare occasions, were always so deep, proprietary, and royal that his mere presence, only inches away, was never sufficient to jar her into acknowledgement, no matter how long the ride.

Then there were those for whom taking a public elevator was the equivalent of flying commercial. Moonie Brown would step into an empty elevator to go up to the studio to do the show, and if anyone attempted to join her before the doors closed, she would stop them, with false eyelashes batting.

"Ah *prefer* to ride alone," she would say demurely as if riding an elevator alone was some sort of status symbol.

This was always perfectly fine with "the unwashed", but if one of the stars of "Living" tried to get into the elevator to go up to their show and was told, "I prefer to ride alone", there was hell to pay. But, incredibly, she got away with it.

The whole notion of celebrity elevator etiquette harkened back to the days when Mariah Carey was married to Tommy Mottola, head of Sony Records. Supposedly a directive was issued in writing from his office to everyone in the Sony building in New York ordering that no one was to look at Mariah if they found themselves in an elevator with her. Eyes were to be averted in the presence of her celebrityness. One could only imagine the screaming matches on 1200 count sheets that would induce a CEO to write such a memo. But it worked. No one dared gaze upon at the pouty Ms. Carey in the Sony elevators for fear of losing their job. You couldn't even bring it up with HR.

So Moonie mostly rode the elevator alone, especially after she got thin. But, sometimes, when she was fat and in a gregarious mood (as opposed to her showtime diva one), she would actually tolerate having people in the elevator with her because she knew her girth would limit the total number to just a few hardy underlings who could brave the odor and her heavy breathing for the forty second ride. In addition, the few extra bodies were good cover in case the "overload" alarm sounded. But when she got thin, she considered herself too precious for any company and would only take the passenger elevator. By then she considered the freight elevator (which had always been her stand-by) or the one fitted out with the permanent industrial-grade protective pads on the walls, far beneath her station.

As far as Brendan was concerned, Beverly, on the other hand, was such an incredibly self-contained diva that she could ride with a high school football team in the elevator and not acknowledge them. It was all part of the "invisibility ray" Beverly had perfected over the years. Brendan could be standing right next to her just before show time trying to brief her or get a crucial (to the show) answer out of her, but she would decide that the person she really wanted to talk to was the "A List" celebrity or her hair stylist standing on the other side of Brendan. Then the "invisibility ray" would come out of those dead, grey eyes; and Brendan would virtually disappear. Sometimes he would try to outlast "the ray" and stand his ground without moving, being clearly closer to her than the object of her schmikeling and often directly in her line of sight. But she would never acknowledge or even see him because "the ray" had hit him, and he had disappeared.

It was possible for Beverly to have a full conversation with a celebrity while a "nobody" stood directly between them because she honestly did not see them. The "invisibility ray" was that strong. And if the person she was talking to was any sort of royalty, super rich, a war criminal, or Henry Kissinger; the "nobody" might not reappear in the normal world for several hours afterwards. Many times Brendan would return to his rabbit hole of an office after such an encounter and have to touch himself repeatedly just to make sure he still had corporal substance. The only upside of "the ray" was that, at times, Brendan occasionally would hear things he probably wasn't supposed to—like about how lubrication was the most important thing a woman had to offer—but he could never repeat it since he could never prove he had actually been in the room, in person, to hear Beverly Frost say it firsthand.

"Darling, Astroglide. Trust me. Always carry it. Just in case. I do." Beverly once said. No doubt, in case "Henry the K." showed up between hopscotch diplomacies for some "shuttlecock". Once she had even shouted to Marge across Canon Drive in Beverly Hills, "Remember, darling, lubrication!" Beverly was referring to the gratuitous sex lecture she'd just given Marge during lunch at Nate and Al's after the show. Beverly was nuts. And getting nuttier.

The other thing about the two elevators at the SBS Studios was that there always seemed to be a new death notice taped up between the cars on each floor and above the elevator buttons on what Brendan called "The Wall of Woe". People in the building were dying like flies, and all of them seemed to be connected to the "Living for Love" soap opera as if they, themselves, were "*Dying* for Love" instead. Stagehands, electricians, associate producers, and long suffering production PA's were endlessly being afflicted with an array of rare diseases and untimely deaths And when they ran out of actual employees, they would put up death notices for the relatives of stagehands, electricians, associate producers, and long suffering PA's. After a while, Brendan actually got to know the names of most of the "Living for Love" crew by their dead relatives, and he could recite the names of the leading funeral homes in the Los Angeles area from memory. None of the wakes ever seemed to occur in a town where Brendan actually knew anyone, but always in Tarzana, Sepulveda, or The City of Industry. And nobody famous or recognizable ever died. But the workers were all "taking cabs"(as they used to say on Broadway), and those "cabs" were being taken in deepest, darkest South Central or Glendale

Very rarely, one of the dead would be a worker from the maintenance company for the building, but never a relative of one. That perk was reserved only for the staff of "Living for Love". The custodial company was strangely named "Yale Maintenance", and the men and women all wore blue uniforms with "YALE" emblazoned in collegiate-size white letters on them as if they were WASP football captains posing on the Yale Fence in New Haven. But since all of the "Yalies" were actually black or Mexican and grossly mistreated, Brendan wondered if they ever knew the irony of their company's name. "Yale", in this case, was charged with picking up pieces of shit instead of graduating them. Often Brendan would hear over the building's public address system, "Raoul from Yale, to the lobby, with a mop." It always made him smile.

With all the death going on around "The Ladies' Room", it seemed inevitable that the odds would eventually catch up to them. But no one had the energy or the temerity to establish a "dead pool" to wager on who would fall first. Brendan became obsessed with the fact that no calamity had ever befallen them nor any person directly connected with "The Ladies' Room" in 15 years. He wondered if the people on "Living" ever noticed that "The Ladies' Room" was never represented in the death notices on the "Wall Of Woe".

Brendan's money was on Beverly. Even though she had never been sick or ever missed a day of the live show for any reason other than a better deal, he still thought the odds were that she would drop dead one day. Like the indestructible cockroach that she was, he imagined that one day, with no visible trauma, she would be found dead on the floor, lying on her back with her legs up in the air like some desiccated water bug. And everyone would wonder how she got there and marvel at the fact that she'd never been sick a day in her miserable life. But Brendan knew the *real* reason Beverly never got sick was because she never actually touched anyone. Germs were left stranded like everyone else. "If only the good die young," Brendan was fond of saying, "That would make Beverly a bitch of legendary proportion.

No one knew exactly how old Beverly was. Her age was indeterminate. Her birthday was celebrated like a Feast Day on "The Ladies' Room" but never with a number. She had been listed in her early seventies for the first ten years and then had popped to 77 when Mike

Wallace admitted to 88. But Beverly was just enough of a conniver to have somehow gotten her official records changed. Brendan was sure she would have fucked the head of the DMV in exchange for five or six years shaved off her age. He figured her to be somewhere around eighty-three, but the gap between Brendan's and her age was constantly shrinking as they traveled forward on the conveyor belt of death. He knew Marge had quietly turned seventy several years before, and it galled her every time Beverly would insist, on the air, that they were both in the same generation. But Beverly's true age was unknowable. Even childhood friends who had sat next to her in high school couldn't pinpoint it.

But as far as Brendan was concerned, Beverly was living that old Joe Lewis quote. She could run, but she couldn't hide. He was surprised that she was even healthy enough to be such a pain in the ass at her age since that, alone, took a certain amount of vitality. Even Miss Daisy and the Queen Mum had mellowed toward the end, but Beverly Frost was the Energizer Bitch. She was as competitive and cut-throat—especially to other women and absolutely to other female on-air talent—as if she were an ingénue with an agenda just off the bus. She was one of those people, like David Suskind before her—from whom she stole her interviewing and producing acumen—who only *gave* migraines. They didn't die, but everyone around them did. Like something seemingly benign but actually highly toxic, dealing with Beverly could be harmful to your health and definitely to your self-respect. Even though, by all actuarial tables, Brendan knew he should out-live her, he was convinced he wouldn't and that's why he specifically requested that she speak at his funeral.

Funerals were like five finger exercises for Beverly. She could eulogize her alleged best friend practically in her sleep and forget about it completely by that afternoon. An editor at Los Angeles Magazine had once told Brendan that Beverly had just spoken at her friend's funeral the day before and had been so brilliant and moving that she had reduced the entire congregation to heaving sobs and muffled blubbering. His friend had wanted Brendan to be sure and tell Beverly how comforting her brilliant eulogy had been for the family and friends of this dearly departed woman who had obviously been extremely close to Beverly and had died a terrible death at an early age.

"Beverly, I heard that your eulogy for Myrna Williams yesterday was wonderful, and a friend of mine who was there wanted me to tell you how much he appreciated it because Myrna was so important to everybody," Brendan said.

"Who, darling?" Beverly asked distractedly while thinking of her lunch that day at The Palm with the Sultan of Brunei.

"My friend or Myrna Williams?" Brendan asked. "You spoke at Myrna Williams's funeral yesterday, and apparently it was wonderful. My friend was..."

"Oh, darling," she shot back cutting Brendan off. "I do so many of those I don't know from one day to the next who it is. But thank you." Brendan stood there, not really computing that she had no idea what he was talking about.

"Myrna Williams's funeral," he said figuring it would register. "Yesterday."

"I really haven't got time right now," she said generally dismissing him while moving forward to indicate that, not only was the conversation over, but it should have never taken place in the first place. "I'm sure it was marvelous." And that was that.

What Beverly really wanted in life was to bury all the other network and local anchors. She wanted to be the last anchor standing. And no matter how much the real news heavyweights detested even the mention of her name and openly vilified her while they were alive, Beverly was always the first to respond upon their demise with a tribute bite for the Evening News and always managed to give the keynote eulogy at their funerals.

Roland Sturges had been the reigning anchor of "The Evening News" at the SBS Network, and he had long ago banned Beverly from the newsroom because he considered her a celebrity monger and not a legitimate journalist. But when Sturges went down in a helicopter in Baghdad, Beverly was front and center among the public mourners bemoaning the loss of her colleague. She even managed to lead a prayer vigil for him while privately crossing off another name on her secret anchor hit list.

But that was not to say that Beverly loved death; she was just its master. In fact, the worst thing that could happen to anyone within her sphere of necessity was to get sick, become a burden, or die. The inconvenience was simply unacceptable.

That's why, when her personal manicurist, maid, and confidante was diagnosed with terminal cancer, Beverly treated it as a liability rather than a tragedy even though the dear woman had been with her for over twenty-five years and was closer to her than even Rémy, her dog. Well, almost closer.

Beverly had originally taken the woman on as a favor to the Shah of Iran who had been fucking her royally even though she was a Saudi, and he was gay. She was that adorable. But just before the Shah got sick, the Shahness, or whatever they called Mrs. Shah, got wind of the affair; and the Peacock Throne was forced to reach out to someone who knew how to make a deal. In return for the "get" of having the last interview with the Shah before he was overthrown and sent into exile and, ultimately, to his death, Beverly agreed to take his highness' girlfriend off his hands and bring her to America. For Beverly, it was perfect fit. The girl knew how to serve unconditionally and knew only a minimal amount of English.

Sasha (that wasn't her real name but one Beverly gave her because she couldn't remember her Saudi one) had daily manicured Beverly's nails and massaged her hands and feet adoringly like a devoted saint during the twenty-five years she'd been in service. It was an indulgence Beverly allowed herself because it reminded her of her father who used to buy his mistresses expensive manicures at the Fairmont Hotel the same way other philanderers would buy their girlfriends handbags at Gucci. Manicures were harder to trace.

When Sasha got sick, Beverly felt she had to intercede and do *something* for the poor, dying woman. After all, she was practically part of the family. So Beverly decided to send Sasha back to Saudi Arabia to die among her people. And, best of all, because once in Saudi Arabia, as a woman, she would never be allowed to publish her memoirs. What Beverly had forgotten or, perhaps, remembered only too well, was that "Sasha" had been married to a prominent ambassador in the Saudi foreign ministry while she was wildly fucking the Shah; and, as such, would be executed as an adulteress when she returned home. But Beverly insisted. She ordered Janet, her stylist, to go on a special re-gifting tour of the best Rodeo Drive shops and specifically told her to demand cash this time when she returned the lovely but useless gifts that had been lavished upon Beverly during the year by her high-toned friends.

Then she told Lawrence, her manservant, to buy a one-way ticket to Saudi Arabia with the accumulated cash. When she presented the ticket to the, now, failing Sasha; the woman was all the more appreciative because she herself had been the one who had located all the foolish green leather desk sets, still in their tissues and boxes, and discarded pashminas from Neiman's.

Part of Sasha's tears of gratitude were because she had originally feared Beverly would merely direct an anonymous PA to purchase a hundred dollars worth of CD's as her parting gift as Beverly had thoughtfully done when her secretary was rendered a quadriplegic in a car accident. The CD's had arrived, useless, at Northridge Hospital while the girl was still in the emergency room sans insurance. At least Sasha's non-stop coach seat to Riyadh came with a meal.

Unfortunately, the cash payment for a one way ticket to the Middle East flagged the dying Sasha as a terrorist, and Sasha was all but water-boarded at LAX before she gave up the name of her former employer and serial re-gifter. Sasha had been afraid, not for herself, of course, but for the revelation that Beverly had returned so many of her fancy friends' gifts for cash to get Sasha's cancerous

Arab ass out of town. The matter was cleared up by Lawrence on the spot, with the help of Henry Kissinger and Maria Shriver; and Sasha was finally sent on her way out of the country. More importantly, a proposed TMZ headline reading, "Beverly Frost Returns Gifts for Cash!" was summarily quashed.

Upon Sasha's arrival in Saudi Arabia, she was immediately arrested for her 30-year-old crime of adultery and condemned to a worse death than the one she was already facing with cancer. She was sentenced to be beheaded by order of the strict Muslim high court with an additional 200 lashes to be administered beforehand just to teach her a lesson. The only mercy shown was that the Royal Executioner would hold a copy of the Koran under his whipping arm to restrict the severity of the lashes and guard against any rotator cuff injury of his own in the process.

On her way to the chopping block at half-time during a soccer match, Sasha proudly wore an Hermes scarf with Beverly Frost's initials embroidered on it along with Michael Douglas's and Catherine Zeta-Jones's birthday wishes that had been *personally* given to Sasha by Beverly when Neiman's had absolutely refused to take it back. The Douglas/Zeta-Joneses probably never imagined in their wildest dreams that their carefully thought-out birthday gift would one day end up 10,000 miles away on an executioner's chopping block in a soccer stadium in Saudi Arabia, carefully spread to the side, as the manicurist of their friend, Beverly Frost, daintily laid her head down to be severed. But then, to add insult to that indignity, when the executioner's assistant jabbed his pointed stick into Sasha's side in order to make her neck involuntarily extend and stiffen, thus thrusting her head forward to facilitate a nice clean chop, the sword that followed the poke tore a hole in the scarf and ruined a perfectly good Hermes scarf beyond repair. It was a small price to pay for justice.

Beverly was devastated when she heard the news. The Saudis, of course, assumed Sasha had stolen the scarf from her esteemed (in Saudi Arabia) former employer because they couldn't believe that anyone would give away such an expensive item of obvious personal and celebrity value. And so, Sasha died an adulteress *and* a thief.

The only redeeming news for Beverly upon hearing the details from King Abdullah himself was that, fortunately, Beverly could be comforted in the knowledge that dead manicurists write no "tell-alls".

CHAPTER SIX

Brendan's immediate task, after his termination, was to start building a case against his tormentors. He was so angry at Beverly that he was actually afraid she might die before he could sue her. Since "The Ladies' Room" never had any postings of its own on the "Wall of Woe", the odds were pretty good that *somebody* from the show would eventually expire, contract a strange disease, or, at least, be maimed. Brendan resisted the joke of putting up phony death notices from time to time because he knew it would be lost on the earnest "Living for Love" pamphleteers, SBS corporate would get involved, and it would bite him in the ass in the end.

The parent company of SBS, The Swann Company, was known to be very conservative. It had something to do with the fact that they had started out as a chain of funeral homes and parking lots and had built an empire that included all of those as well as theme parks, a television network, a movie studio, and just about every car wash on the planet. They were the Starbucks of car washes. The wags in the company referred to it as "The Swine Company", due to their unethical dealings with labor unions and minorities. Black workers would say they were working for "The Bird", and anything corporate was known as "Swann shit". And the "Swann shit" was as ubiquitous around the company as Canadian goose poop on a golf course.

The company logo was a white swan, but the swan's eye was accented with heavy black lines that made the bird look sinister rather than elegant. It probably had something to do with the fact that whenever the logo was displayed as a plaque in bas relief, the swan's glass eye always held a surveillance camera.

Because "The Ladies' Room" happened in a converted car dealership and garage building, the space was perfectly suited for a studio but less so for offices with human beings inside. Insulation had been hastily applied for the conversion, and toxic dust was still settling. On top of that, there were no windows. It was as if the whole structure was a basement. Wherever you were in the building, you were entombed. People had to literally call out to learn about the weather, and often reports would come over the PA system announcing, "It's sunny outside", which would make no sense to a normal person but was always news to those within.

Bad Bob had already left for the weekend when Brendan hit the reception desk as a "dead man walking" the morning after his firing. There were two receptionists. One was the tough Irish girl, Terri Shaw, with a killer body, and the other was Anita, an angry Latina with a Mike Tyson facial tattoo.

"Good morning, Brendan," Anita said when Brendan came into the office. "Did we sleep well last night?" That was the kind of question she would greet people with which was, at once, intimate and condescending. Everyone assumed she was a plant from PermaFrost, Beverly's production company.

"Actually, I didn't sleep at all, Anita." Brendan replied, "I got fired yesterday."

"Always the joker," she said.

"No joke, and you know it," he told her pointedly.

"Well, I'm sure it'll all work out for the best."

"I doubt it," Brendan said and walked past her. He assumed that, since he was the first one there on a non-show day, it meant he could rummage through the offices for stray swag and magazines that the show would never willingly give up to a writer. But he wasn't the first one in. Mack McLeary, one of the production managers, was already there. Mack was, by nature and by job description, obsessed with the budget for the show. That and his wife's spending habits for their house in Redondo Beach drove him nuts every day.

"Disaster!" Mack shouted when he saw Brendan pass his darkened office, purposely kept dim to cut down on electricity costs. "Absolute disaster!" He got up and walked around to the front of his desk as if making a presentation when Brendan stopped in the doorway. For a moment Brendan thought Mack was talking about Brendan's own situation, but then he realized it was just the overages on last week's musical act.

"Out of control! Skyrocketing! Completely irresponsible! I don't know what I'm supposed to do? These figures are unacceptable!"

Brendan loved Mack. He was a titular representative of the corporation, but he was also low man on that totem pole, and he knew it. He had to eat a lot of Swann shit; and, as a result, he had an automatic kinship with all writers.

"Only one thing to do" Brendan said. Mack knew what he was talking about.

"Well, of course. That goes without saying."

"Johnny Walker just came out with a Blue Label. God knows what it does."

"Probably costs a fortune," he said.

"Yeah, but you'd think, if you paid that much, you could fuck it first before you drank it."

"And you'd be justified." He laughed with a finger in the air for emphasis. "I still like my old Dewar's. It never varies, and it's kind to the old pocketbook," Mack said wistfully and returned to his chair as Brendan moved into the office and sat down.

"You can't keep drinking that cheap shit, Mack. I keep telling you, the Brits prefer Famous Grouse," Brendan said knowing the response he would get.

Mack winced with distaste, "Tried the last bottle you were kind enough to leave for me, and it was just a *little* bit too pricey and smoky for my taste. But, hey, any Scotch in a storm I always say. It'll do."

"Bad Bob fired me yesterday." Brendan said as with as little drama as possible.

"No!" Mack gasped. "Unacceptable!" he declared as if Brendan had just asked for an extra umbrella on a rain shoot. Then, more conspiratorially, "They actually did it, huh?"

"You knew?" Brendan asked.

Now Mack dropped into his professorial persona. He leaned back in his chair with his hands behind his head as if he were a Professor of Comparative Literature at Berkley who had just been asked to comment on the relative merits of Borges versus Hemmingway.

"Wellllll," he began with a flourish of his hand, "There were *allusions.* I keep my ear to the ground, as you know. And I have to say, I did hear *some* rumblings in that area," he said dubiously, "But nothing confirmed," he added quickly.

"You mean in the area of, 'they hate me'."

"Not in so many words, of course," Mack said parsing his words carefully. "But let's just say management has not been on your side for some time. It's purely a corporate decision."

"Bullshit," Brendan shot back. The 'Swine' Company doesn't get involved in who writes this shit. It was Bad Bob and Beverly. Mainly Bad Bob. Although, I think I told Beverly, one time, I wanted to fuck her.

"Oh, that could've had something to do with it," he said reassuringly.

"Do you think I should sue?"

"About wanting to fuck Beverly? Only if you could prove she was capable," Mack said and laughed. "Of *course* you should sue. Why not? How much time do you have? Why are you still here?"

"He had to give me 26 weeks, actually 30 counting the notification period; and I guess they're too cheap to eat it, so I'm here until March."

"Excellent. Just enough time to gather all the evidence you need," he said wriggling his fingers as if he were feeling his way through tall grass.

"But what I want to know, Mack my friend and confident, what I want to know is how will it end? What happens when it's over?"

"Escorted from the building!" he said as a proclamation. "Locked out! Physically barred from the premises forever."

"Can they do that at any time?"

"I believe they can, and will. Management likes to do things on their schedule, not yours. If I were you, I wouldn't go to any meetings alone that were called by them out of the blue."

"Why not?"

"That's when they lock you out of your office *and* your computer. It's purely a distraction tactic."

"And then what happens?" Brendan asked. The whole scenario was fascinating to him.

"Why, then... escorted from the building," he said grandly once more.

"By whom?"

"Could be me, if I'm called upon. Oh, and make no mistake about it. They may even call security, given that it's you."

Brendan leaned forward so Mack would know he was serious, which he actually was, although not angry or threatening.

"I'm telling you right now, Mack, if it comes to that, I'm not walking out. They'll have to carry me. I may even barricade myself in my office, nude, and live there while I call the media."

"Of course!" he said. "I'd expect nothing less."

"For weeks!" Brendan said imitating Mack's raised finger.

"That could cause some consternation," Mack said. "The Swann Company tries to avoid confrontations at all costs...:"

".....and raises," Brendan added

"Well, that goes without saying," he shot back immediately, "But it would definitely be interesting. Do you really think you have a case?"

"Who knows? But when you're an old fuck like me, everything is discrimination"

"Well, you've probably got them on that," he said

"Why? Do you know something I don't? Brendan asked.

"No-no," Mack quickly assured him. Then, "But there have been enough rumblings about your age and unionism and things like that which could probably be whipped into something actionable by a good attorney which I assume you have."

"I'm married to one."

"Well, there you go. You're home free. What could be better?"

"How about married to an attorney who actually wanted to represent me?" Brendan said smiling. "But I'll find somebody."

"Brilliant! Sue the bastards. And let me tell you," Mack now became conspiratorial. His face screwed up into an expression of pure hate, "These sons of bitches will fuck you up the ass so fast it'll make your head spin. And I've seen it done. You have to meet them with the same shit they throw at you. Be prepared. I worked for Mike Douglas in Philadelphia for eight years. He told everyone he couldn't do the show without me. But when it came time to stand up to Westinghouse when they wanted to put the CEO's son in my job, did he go to bat for me?" Mack slammed his hand down on the top of the desk. "Threw me to the wolves. Just, threw me to the wolves. That was it." He tossed his hand in the air. "Never spoke to the man again."

"Then you understand," Brendan said.

"Ha!" Mack laughed. "Like no one else." Then he stood up signaling that his work ethic was kicking in, and he had no more time for idle chitchat. "Keep it tight!" Mack said with a clenched fist in the air like a coach. "To the bone!"

"You got it, pal," Brendan said and slipped out of his office.

Brendan found his newspapers by picking through all the other publications addressed to everyone else on the staff but him. PA's, secretaries, and even Chester, the runner who *really* hated him, all got magazines, newspapers, and swag sent in daily by hopeful guests and PR firms. The writers were lucky to get the one set of newspapers between them, but only Monday through Friday, never the weekend edition. And even for that set of papers Brendan had to fight Hair and Make-up since, traditionally, they had first dibs.

"The Ladies' Room" was a daily show about current events; but Gloria, the Swann liaison to the production, could not be bothered to order extra papers or have any papers delivered on weekends. Hence, there was always a two day hole in the information flow. Gloria was known as "Madame Defarge" because she walked around the office, slightly hunched over, wringing her hands, with a constant sourpuss expression of gloom and doom on her face. It was only much later that Brendan learned that Swann had promised her a bonus based on any savings she could wring out of the budget. It accounted for the lack of decent pens and the periodic purges of personal mailings.

The office to which Brendan had been banished after the first few years on the show should have been an indication of management's animosity toward him. It was a dressing room with a sink situated in the farthest reaches of the talent area two floors above the production offices. The only thing it had going for it was the sink into which Brendan could piss while on the phone. He had been hired to provide comedy material for Marge Foley, but his office was so far away from her lavishly appointed dressing room at the other end of the floor that he would have been closer to her had he stayed at home.

Actually, his solitary cell proved to be a godsend because it took Brendan out of the line of fire compared to where he'd originally been billeted on the same floor as Bad Bob. It also put him about as far away from Beverly Frost as one could be and still be in the same building. Even so, in the 15 years they'd shared the same floor,

Brendan had never seen Beverly venture past the exit door leading to the studio or to her waiting limo in order to visit the work space containing her loyal minions. Neither curiosity nor necessity could move her to step ten feet down a hallway that offered no immediate remuneration or transportation. It was *terra incognita.* Any staff that did not directly serve her was simply not in Beverly Frost's universe.

Once, there had been an editing emergency surrounding one of her patronizingly saccharine specials, a series called "Beverly Frost's Teaching Moments". She needed something from a PermaFrost producer who had toiled devotedly for her for twenty-five years (without health insurance). His cubicle was a shrine to Ms. Frost and his life of doing her bidding. This day she needed him immediately and was screaming for him from the other end of the floor. Someone told her that he was in his office which was like saying the poor man was on Mars. She started down the hallway to find the office from which she had already extracted twenty-five years of work, but had never physically visited, and stopped short once her steps were about to take her past the ladies' room next to the exit. It was as if an invisible shield prevented her from venturing further into the unknown. She screamed so loudly that people who also worked for her, accountants and PA's, stuck their heads out of their offices. Since it was minutes before the live show, Brendan happened to be hurrying down the same hall with material for Marge.

"He's in his office, Beverly," he told her, truly trying to help.

"Where?" she asked.

"All the way to the end and take a left," Brendan said knowing how absurd that must have sounded to her. Still, she could not make herself move. Then he added pointedly, "Just past my office". Beverly gave him a look.

"Go get him," she said, "I need him now."

Brendan then mimed his dilemma of having to deliver his blue cards to Marge before the show that was about to happen—the very same show she was about to appear on as well. Fortunately, the racket had brought the sought-after associate producer out of his office, and he appeared around the corner just in time to rescue her and preserve her record of knowing nothing about anyone, or anything, except herself.

Brendan sat down at his desk and began plotting his campaign to make his exit from "The Ladies' Room" as unpleasant as possible. Bad Bob had made a crucial error in allowing his dismissal to fester for 26 weeks, and Brendan would make them rue the day they decided to fuck with him. He was going to go kicking and screaming and take as many people down with him as possible. Brendan decided he would go out with a bang, not a whimper.

He had learned long ago from a dangerous girlfriend to always take notes and keep a dossier on everyone because one never knows when it will come in handy. Brendan justified the practice as part and parcel of being a writer, but it was really merely a defense against any inevitable break up, firing, dismissal, or termination. Everyone was vulnerable, and they exposed their vulnerabilities in every instant of personal interaction. It was the sword they unwittingly placed in Brendan's hands for their own demise.

Of course, keeping "a book" on everyone the way a baseball pitcher takes notes on opposing hitters brings with it a responsibility not to employ that tool capriciously. That same girlfriend had referred to its deployment as a "nuclear holocaust" when she would do a dossier dump on someone who had merely shown up late for lunch. The devastation far outweighs the slight; and, often, the effect on the other person is irreversible. You can't go around wiping out an entire city just because someone criticizes your hat. But like those deadly martial art moves they teach suburban white women in karate class—the ones that maim, disfigure, and disable, as well as kill—there comes a time when it actually *is* appropriate to deploy them. When you're life is threatened, or you *think* it is, then it's okay to unleash all hell. It's justified, baby. Self-defense. "Stand your ground," as they say in Florida. That was the mood Brendan was in.

And seeing how he had married a lawyer, as his father had been, and grown up with five more successful siblings, his ability to gather compromising evidence bordered on genius. Or so he thought. The whole prospect of constructing a case that would bring down his adversaries and crush them like bugs was enough to keep him engaged and strangely excited about navigating the next 26 weeks. Suddenly, he had stopped being a mere writer and had become, instead, "Rambo with a Laptop".

CHAPTER SEVEN

The Make-up Room was at the very heart of "The Ladies' Room". Despite the pretentious mission statement that Beverly insisted on running as a "cold open" for every show—where she would look imperiously into the camera and proclaimed, as "Her Majesty", to all women, "I've decided to do a show about the other side of women: the serious, the funny, the intellectual, and the concerned side of who we really are. I'm Beverly Frost, and this is my show."—-despite that daily drivel, everyone knew that what really made Beverly's and the other girls' hearts pound was "hair and make-up", especially Beverly. Why else would she have a hairdresser and a make-up artist lashed to her side 24/7? Her perpetual state of painted artifice was so complete that even *she* didn't know what she really looked like any more. That's the kind of intellectual Beverly Frost was.

Only once did she make the mistake, in her degenerative mental state, of walking into the make-up room with only her "unmade-up" make-up on, at which point a security guard, thinking she was from Yale Maintenance, almost handed her a mop. She was the only celebrity, and certainly the only so-called "journalitht," who would actually order make-up that was specifically designed to make her look like a serious semi-attractive intellectual *without* make-up. This was the "career girl" make-up that she thought she needed to add gravitas to herself as a newswoman. She had various degrees of make-up depending on the celebrity she was interviewing or disaster she was attending (as opposed to "covering").

But no one, not even her Lhasa Apso, Rémy, had ever seen Beverly completely without make- up. That was a level of reality, like the underlying code at Microsoft, which no living creature could ever reach, penetrate, or gain access to. Her "preliminary make-up" was there to be built upon but never explored, plumbed, or understood. There were rumors she even wore make-up in the shower in case she happened to steal a glimpse of her natural and unpainted self out of the corner of her eye in the bathroom mirror. Beverly Frost lived with a horrible creature that just happened to be herself. A creature that was always carefully kept locked away from everyone, especially Beverly.

The Make-up Room was where the ladies came for their daily transformation from hags to Hollywood and where the topics for the daily "CrossTalk" segments were chosen. There were four barber chairs facing a mirrored wall on the make-up side and three shampoo chairs backing up to more mirrors on the hair side. In between were several high director's chairs for guest hosts and for Beverly herself who insisted on being seated above everyone else in the room whenever she deigned to do the show.

When Beverly was seated in her high chair, no one dared challenge her "Alpha" position. She sat in the center of the make-up line and spoke to no one directly other than herself in the mirror when Sydney Irving, her personal make-up girl, would silently attend to her ravaged face. At the same time, her personal hairdresser and only friend, Barry Havasu (known as "The Vicious One"—and the pair as "Syd Vicious" to the rest of the staff) would slouch in one of the shampoo chairs on the opposite side of the room and watch over Beverly like a Secret Service agent with an expression that was, at once, protective and replete with contempt.

The other hair and make-up people would arrive first and open the room up. They would then proceed to stand in front of the mirrors and do their own make-up at their designated stations in front of the corresponding empty co-host chairs while gossiping to each other even though they were separated by at least 15 feet each. It was sort of a "bus and truck" version of the "CrossTalk" meeting that would follow.

Beverly was always the first co-host in unless she had been doing the morning shows beforehand to promote one of her specials. "Syd Vicious" would enter first to do mini advance work for her. And then Beverly herself would appear walking with a slight granny shuffle, tilted forward, and always with one hand extended like a "Supreme " (as in "Stop, In the Name of Love") to protect herself from a fall or to ward off any unwanted petitioners. Her perpetual "Heisman" always preceded her. Then, the rest of the show staff would file in and sit around the periphery of the room. The line producer of the day, the "CrossTalk" producer, two writers, a researcher, and hair people all waited for the ladies to finish their "CrossTalk" topic selection and come off the make-up line so they could talk to them or attend to them about that day's show.

With the advent of HDTV, make-up was applied, not with a trowel, as it had been before, but with a small spray gun. Thus, applying makeup to the dames of "The Ladies' Room" was more akin to shooting gunite at a clay embankment in the Hollywood Hills than whisking a light brush across an aging cheek.

Brendan, as the so-called comedy writer, was not allowed to speak. But Leo, the other writer, was usually writing "continuity"; and because of his more reticent demeanor and reputation, he was allowed to comment but only if called upon. The ladies would turn to Leo for clarification of some pop culture reference as if they were consulting Yoda. The only other people allowed to speak— freely, that is, without being asked—were Mugsy Muggeridge, Jared (Lurch) the "CrossTalk" producer, Bad Bob, and the co-hosts themselves.

Mugsy Muggeridge, the Senior Producer, was a widowed single mom from Pasadena whose lifetime at the Jonathan Club and years at the Buckley School in Sherman Oaks had scarred her for life as an insufferable twit. Unfortunately, she had never managed to graduate from either one. Her semi-beloved husband had dropped dead jogging around the Hollywood reservoir leaving her alone with their baby girl of uncertain parentage in a condo on Alta Loma in West Hollywood. He had been a failed actor who died wearing a full beard that he'd grown for some half-assed modern day Irish production of "McBeth"(sic). Consequently, Mugsy's first decision as a widow was to decide whether to shave his beard for the wake or not.

She got everyone on the show to weigh in on how to groom the corpse of her late husband. Of course, it was easy for her to enlist their help since she never missed a day of work over the loss of her spouse, from his sudden death to his cremation. And the fact that her dearly departed was to be cremated had no impact on her "corpse grooming" question. In the end, she left the beard on in the open casket, because she thought it made him look less gay and definitely like someone she didn't know and would never have had sex with. That's how she wanted to remember him. She did this, she told everyone endlessly, because she didn't want to ever think of him longingly. Having him displayed in his coffin as a stranger with a beard helped her recover from the shock of suddenly being alone.

The truth of the matter was that Mugsy embraced widowhood the way most women fall in love—with her whole heart, and mind, and being. Had she shown that much emotion during the marriage, perhaps the poor guy wouldn't have dropped dead from trying to match her fitness regime. Being a young widow solved all the issues surrounding the necessity of her getting married in the first place and gave her complete control over another human being (her daughter) and a ready-made persona to which she could always retreat. One would have thought that her husband's sudden death would have re-directed, ever so slightly, Mugsy's obsession with her own body. But the truth was it only made her narcissism more dominant and twice as annoying.

Mugsy played two sets of tennis religiously every morning at the Beverly Hills Hotel with Pancho Lobo, the pro there. No one could talk her out of it. She said it was her celebration of life; but, in truth, it just got her out of the house early, leaving the kid with the Pakistani nanny. It reminded her daily that *she* was able to exercise endlessly while her sperm donating husband had dropped dead trying to do the same and was buried unrecognizable to even his own mother. *That* gave her a sense of empowerment.

After punishing Pancho for an hour and a half, Mugsy would then drive directly over Mulholland on Coldwater, still in her skimpy tennis outfit to the SBS studios in Reseda. She would then arrive for the "CrossTalk" meeting still flushed and wearing her sweat-soaked tennis whites whose skirt was short enough so that when she perched on the counter in front of the ladies and the staff to run the meeting, she would proudly expose her tennis panties that were grey with pussy sweat. The fact that she was consistently ten minutes late for the meeting drove the rest of the staff crazy, but it didn't seem to bother Mugsy, Beverly, or Bad Bob in the least. Mugsy was the daughter Beverly Frost had always wanted. Namely, just one, and living in Los Angeles, instead of the triplets she actually had who carried her name and were currently living in North Dakota. No one ever understood why Mugsy couldn't engage Pancho ten minutes earlier in order to, at least, arrive at work on time or, perhaps, even a half hour earlier to allow for a shower and proper office attire as part of her regime. But Mugsy *liked* looking like a tennis slut.

As it was, Mugsy would then disappear after the "CrossTalk" meeting to complete her stretching and ablutions for an hour before the show as if the urgency of live television didn't exist. The only executive decision she made in the morning was the standing order to her secretary to come up to the second floor from the basement to remove the sodden pile of workout clothes she had left for her in the hallway outside the shower. Her personal appearance would then progress during the day from newly showered wet hair, to towel-dried hair, to blown dried and coifed by 1:00 in the afternoon at which time she would disappear again for another round of calisthenics or, in the early days of the show, sex with Bad Bob. The only time the staff ever saw her fully clothed and dry was at the Christmas Party. The hair and make-up people probably spent more time on Mugsy than they did on the on-air guests or co-hosts. It was all because, early on, in Pasadena, Mugsy had determined that big hair would make up for an average face, and exercise would take care of the rest.

Moonie Brown would waddle into the 7:00 AM meeting roughly on time. She would look fairly presentable but only because of her habit of sleeping in her make-up from the night before so as to not have to scare herself when she woke up in the morning. Despite all her proclamations to the contrary, cleanliness was not one of Moonie's attributes. Once she got her clothes and make-up on, she would do anything not to have to remove them. Showers and baths were of such low priority that the stench coming from her was like rotten broccoli left too long in the refrigerator and just as toxic. She drove the wardrobe people crazy because of her over-use and abuse of the clothes that were on loan from Nordstrom's. It meant the show stylists were constantly making excuses for the intimate stains left by her on the borrowed designer dresses. And if the store wouldn't take them back, the clothes had to be purchased and destroyed after only one wearing.

Moonie was the only one who got her hair worked on at the same time as her make-up because two solid hours were not sufficient to accomplish each task sequentially. In the beginning she wore and endorsed wigs, and she proudly wore a different style, with an appropriate name, each day. She was a walking Frederick's of Hollywood catalogue. But once her deal with the wig company ran out, she decided she was more like Beyonce' and changed to extensions.

The staff would look on in mild disgust as wads of raw hair, undoubtedly exploited from some third world country, were fished out of sacks in the back of the room and brought over to Moonie's chair to be attached to her head. Often this resulted in hair remnants all over the floor as if the make-up room were a crime scene. But, as the transformation process with spray gun and thread took place, Moonie would transform along with it.

"Make that a little less "Shaniqua" and a little more "Barbie," she would tell Ginger, her stoic hair stylist. By that, Moonie meant she didn't want to appear "too native" anything for her public and preferred to be adorned with the golden streaked locks and bangs popular with white pop idols and African American hookers.

For Marge Foley, hair and make-up was the godsend she had discovered only with the modicum of fame she'd acquired late in life as a lounge entertainer in Las Vegas. Marge had grown up the youngest of six Foleys in the Canaryville section, near the old stockyards, on Chicago's South Side. Her father was an Irish drunk, a "Streets and San" worker, union enforcer, and a full-time crony of politicians and lowlifes and was rarely home except to impregnate his wife. The phrase "out and about" always struck a note of sadness in Marge as it was how her father, "Big Bill Foley", would always describe his day when pressed.

Marge's mother was an Italian Jew who had neglected to mention to her husband that her religion was different than her ethnicity. She had always told Marge she was descended from Finzi-Contini-type Jews in Tuscany. But the lesson was not lost on Marge who, although she had five older Irish brothers, always felt alone in the family. She completely identified with her mother and was raised virtually as an only child since her next oldest brother was almost ten years older than she was. Marge considered herself both the only girl in the family *and* the only Jew. Big Bill attributed the 10 year break in the birth order of his children to the Kelly-Nash machine when he was busy playing piano and carousing with Mayor Kelly and didn't really get back home until Daley took over from Kennelly. Marge's mother knew better, and she attributed their lack of conjugal traffic to a certain hooker named Alison McCormick, an ex (Bill would always correct her to say "former") nun who had given up one habit for a more lucrative one.

Consequently, little Margie Foley grew up with what was considered a birth defect on the South Side. She looked and acted Jewish and became the first Jewish-American princess to receive her First Holy Communion at St Gabriel's on South Wallace. She never felt Irish or Italian, and she made that point clear to all around her. She observed all the Jewish Holidays and even tried to make the Foley household kosher although with little success. When she got married, she married a fellow Jew, Lars Becker, to seal the deal on her ethnicity and was then forever considered fully Jewish by anyone who didn't know her. Of course, she was the marvel of all her adopted *mishpokeh* when she drank because her Irish/Italian DNA enabled her to drink like one of the boys. And it was only when she was drunk that she would lapse into a faint brogue and begin to sing songs of the Irish Revolution, much to the dismay of her Hebrew companions. Lars, for his part, would then load her into a cab, take her home, and fuck the shit out of her while she was still Irish knowing that the morning would bring a hangover and a return to Judaism which meant no more blowjobs, and spanking would become a thing of the far distant past.

Because Beverly insisted that her show was proudly diverse, there was always a chair for a "young one". Originally, this had been a Dominican girl named Carmen Rodriguez who, at various times, passed herself off as Puerto Rican, Cuban, Mexican, or Argentinean. She was as tough as a piñata and sexually active enough to cause Beverly to inform her that "The Ladies' Room" would not tolerate an unwanted pregnancy should she turn up with one.

"Oh, no, Beverlita," Carmen told her. "You don't understand. I only get pregnant when you want me to. Maybe during sweeps, no?"

"We'll talk," Beverly had told her. Even though she was appalled at the brass of young Carmen, Beverly knew a ratings stunt when she heard one. And if this girl wanted to ruin her life for a Neilson rating and end up getting fired anyway, baby and all, Beverly was more than willing to accommodate her. As a "journalitht", Beverly Frost believed in "free press"—not *a* free press, just "free press", as in free publicity that she didn't have to pay for.

Carmen did get pregnant and left the show to "spread her wings", according to Beverly, and become a stay at home single mom instead of a network television talk show host. Some "spread", no "wings".

"We wish her well," Beverly told the live television audience afterwards which, of course, meant she had been fired for her fecundity.

Eventually they brought in Bambi Crutchfield to fill the "Young One" chair because she looked like a Fox Anchor and would work cheap. PermaFrost ended up saving a fortune. And, as an added bonus, they didn't have to feel guilty about not providing health insurance for Carmen who had made herself, now, a *non*-working, single mother on welfare, all in the service of "The Ladies' Room".

CHAPTER EIGHT

M oonbeam P. Brown was born in Washington County, Maine. Specifically, she was born in the town of Eastport, the eastern most point of the United States. Her mother, Estelle, ran the Sunrise Diner there and became pregnant by person or persons of unknown origin or race. It became convenient for her to say the child was the result of a liaison with one of the Indians from the Pleasant Point Reservation of the Passamaquoddy Indian Nation located just outside of town on the road to Perry.

But when Moonie was born she looked more African American than Native American even though Estelle could've sworn the father was an Indian and not a musician. After all, this was Maine, not New Orleans. Even so, she named the child "Moonbeam" to lighten her up and keep her Native American bona fides. It was Moonie who later, temporarily, changed her lineage to the hipper "Cherokee" when she was old enough to figure out that nobody knew who the Passamaquoddy were; and those who did, knew that the tribe's main claim to fame was sardines in the old days (the name means "People of the Pollack") and, currently, a week-long summer celebration called "Indian Days".

Moonie always said she was "schooled" in the South. When the Passamaquoddy elders became dubious about her bloodline, her mother shipped her off to some rich white relatives in Baltimore who were happy to re-live their slave trade glory days and raise little Moonie as their own, albeit, housemaid.

It was to Moonie's credit that she was able to break free of those velvet shackles by getting herself properly educated through college and then into a marginal osteopathic medical school in Florida on affirmative action. She emerged with a D.O. after her name and a neuro-surgical residency at the most desperate ghetto hospital in East St. Louis. It was there that she discovered that she was too fat to stand close enough to an operating table to do any real good. But her street smarts and medical training, along with her commanding physical presence, stood her in good stead whenever she was asked to testify for the defense as an expert witness in serial killer cases. She actually carved out a small reputation for herself as the go-to defender of slashers, mashers, and cannibals through sound bites on the local news. Then she decided to head west to Los Angeles to conquer the white world, not just as a dark-skinned Native American doctor; but, in Brendan's words, as "the biggest Indian princess pain the in the ass that ever appeared on television."

"I'm a diva!" she announced on her first day on the job at "The Ladies' Room". "I'm sorry, but that's just me. I'm a diva, and I'm a doctor, so put the camera on *me*."

When the staff of the show met her they couldn't believe how incredibly fat she was. But in retrospect, she could have had a touch of "the AIDS" compared to the size she became as the show and her visits to Fatburger continued. Fatburgers and bacon were her downfall. No one knew if she frequented the place because she loved the taste or because she mistakenly thought it was named after her.

"Ah am hong-gray!" she would proclaim at any given moment, day or night.

People would run to protect their lunches. The limo in which she was riding would U-turn immediately with screeching tires and accelerate directly to the nearest Fatburger in a cloud of dust. Moonie's Fatburger "jones" had a GPS system of its own, and she could hone in on an "XXXL" like a dog sniffing pussy on the far side of town. The franchise at La Cienega and San Vincente was a favorite of hers because it was centrally located in the blighted landscape south of the Strip and was surrounded by a moat of urban debris and ample parking. For that particular Fatburger, Moonie Brown would call ahead and then make a point of striding in from her limo, like the queen she considered herself to be, only to re-emerge with a bag or two of her subjects clutched tightly to her bosom as she returned to her royal carriage.

Otherwise, it was the driver's duty to present himself before the pimply kid behind the counter to inform the boy in a heavily laden tone, "Ms. Brown is here for her burgers, and she would appreciate the kindness of the management." Then, after it was established that this Fatburger franchise was going to play ball and comp Moonie's order, the driver was then instructed to follow up with, "Ms. Brown would like *two*." Meaning that Ms. Brown was not satisfied with glomming only one measly Fatburger order when, by saying the magic word "two" she could turn a mere "comp" into a windfall.

The saving grace of Moonie Brown and her prestigious weight was that, originally, she was quite happy with it.

"Ah am a fine, round, Native American woman." She would proudly proclaim on the air. Marge always said she wished she had Moonie's mirror because of Moonie's absolute certainty that, whenever she looked into it, she saw Audrey Hepburn. On top of that, she had a filter on her e-mail that blocked all derogatory words and racial epithets leaving her with nothing but "good news" and compliments. Her weight wasn't the only thing that insulated her.

Despite her immense girth, which would have discouraged anyone else, Moonie was always on the make and proud to celebrate her down-and-dirty sexual appetite in the same breath as her praise of Jesus. Once, on a trip to Las Vegas with the show, Moonie

85

boarded the show's private bus to the airport and proudly displayed her collection of condoms specifically acquired for the trip to "Sin City". Everyone cringed at the sight of them, not out of embarrassment or modesty, but at the sheer Schmerber-grade "shock to the conscience" thought of Moonie buck-naked in bed and lathered up for sex. But with whom? With what? What living organism would dare approach that black hole who's event horizon, once breached, would let nothing escape —except the smell, of course. Stephen Hawkings would be hard pressed to explain the physics of a cosmic sink of such immense size, weight, and gravitational pull that light was prevented from escaping but not the odor which emanated from deep within her papoose.

Once ensconced in her Vegas hotel suite, Moonie had then demanded meetings with producers and writers while she remained splayed out on her king-size bed. On one occasion, she was holding court thusly when an unidentified male tentatively emerged from under the covers, but she carried on as if there was nothing out of the ordinary about that except, perhaps, the man's sexuality. The truth of the matter was that Moonie attracted gay men as lovers to such an extent that being identified as a boyfriend of hers was tantamount to being outed in "The Advocate."

"My new boyfriend is a preacher man," Moonie would announce to everyone on the show. The staff would then congratulate her while assuming that what this really meant was that he spent most of his time on his knees.

She was the first to rush to a friend's side when their husband or boyfriend was revealed to be on the "down low" which apparently was the uniquely African American (or, in her case, Passamaquoddian) phenomenon of a seemingly straight male who like to have a cock up his ass in his spare time. At the same time, she seemed completely impervious to the big "down low" in her own life. Her boyfriends were so "up front" about their "down low" that Brendan always assumed they liked it when she didn't wear her wigs during sex and exposed the nubby stubble on her head that looked like Tina Turner's over processed noggin. Perhaps, Moonie was better off. The "butch-colored glasses" through which she viewed the men in her life enabled her to have a rich, full, social life and never, ever, have to worry about whether she was pretty enough.

Moonie prided herself on being a pin up girl for the incarcerated. She would boast about the number of head shots she sent out to penal institutions around the world each week. Even on the air she would do a shout-out to her "boys in the can" the way some performers talked about the military. She considered it her Christian duty to perform her particular corporal work of mercy and satisfy, at least, one of the Beatitudes by "visiting the imprisoned" with her heavily Photo-shopped 8X10 glossy until Beverly reminded her, in that cold condescending way of hers, that these were rapists and murderers she was championing, not war heroes. Still, Moonie persisted in her ministry of self-glorification until a guest on "The Ladies' Room" revealed that he was so happy to meet Ms. Brown personally because he had been incarcerated at one time, and her photo had kept him company through the hard, lonely nights in the cell block.

"Why, darlin', I am humbled that I, as a good Christian woman, could offer you the succor of the Good Shepherd," she said flashing her anatomically ridiculous false eyelashes that would have blinded a lemur. "Allow me to hook you up with something a wee bit fresher." She was referring to a recent publicity shot of her morphing body that had been so highly altered through Photoshop that Michael Jackson would have rejected it.

"No," the guest had said to her earnestly. "We liked the one that was just you."

What he meant was that, because of the fatness of her face in her pre-op head shot, (there had not been enough unexposed silver oxide available in the western world to accommodate an image of Moonie Brown's full face *and* body) her 8X10 glossy had been highly sought-after among the incarcerated.

"You see, Moonie," the guest continued on live television, "All us brothers in jail preferred you to all the others because your picture worked perfectly"

Moonie then slipped into her full "Disney Bashful Hippo" mode, and she tapped the guest lightly on the knee. "Chile, you makin' this Moonie shine so bright with yo' testifyin,'" she said lapsing into the most ghetto sounding black-bonics she could muster. "Shut yo' mouth, now," she continued. This from a woman who had actually graduated from Medical School as a Native American. Brendan always wondered if she talked that way when she was wearing her surgical "greens" and was about to drill into the skull of a newborn. "Dis here hydrocephalus done swelled up in da cranium to such a degree dats necessitatin' a ventriculo-peritoneal shunt and a bilateral neurectomy wif da shiv what's in mah hand. You unnerstan' what I'm sayin'?"

But the guest, a recently released rapist who had found Jesus and a sympathetic parole board, was intent on telling Moonie, on air, exactly how much he had appreciated her photograph. He took her hand and held it like a cancer victim relating a spiritual awakening during treatment.

"You see, Moonie," he began. But no one—not Hal the director, not Bad Bob, not Liz the talent coordinator, nor Jeanie the Censor with her finger on the seven second delay button—could possibly have known where he was headed. "You see," he continued, almost in tears, "You were special to us."

"I know. That's what I try to be. That's my mission, and why I was put on this earth, praise Jesus," Moonie said softly covering his hand with hers. They looked like they were exchanging vows.

"You see, what we would do," the ex-rapist continued, "What every poor incarcerated man would do was cut the mouth out of your photo and paste your picture on the butt of his punk so when he was lovin' him in his rectum, it would be through your mouth," he said sweetly. Then blurting out rapidly, "'Cause I ain't no faggot, and I got you to thank for that, Moonie Brown."

It was a moment in live television that will live forever on YouTube. The *camera's* jaw even dropped open. There was silence. Moonie continued to look the guest deep into his watery eyes and continued patting the top of his hand. More silence. More patting. Universal paralysis. The live broadcast could have been on a seven *minute* delay by the time anyone reacted to what had just gone out over the network airwaves in the middle of the "Daypart". Jeanie the Censor's only move came when her *head* hit the "kill" button, instead of her finger.

"The Ladies' Room" went to "bars" first and then to a commercial for Charmin Bathroom Tissue featuring a bear taking a shit in the woods and in desperate need of toilet paper.

CHAPTER NINE

B everly Frost was never on vacation. Even when she was out of
town, she was on the phone from one of her glamorous, but
comped, venues. Beverly never stopped, never got sick, and never
looked back at the debris left behind her.

Beverly had always been known as a go-getter, so it was no surprise that her "distinguished" career as a journalist was most notable for her famous "gets". She had single-handedly changed the
landscape of what had once been considered hard news into what,
now, had morphed into gossip, celebrity stroking, and cross promo-
tion. It was Beverly Frost who had elevated the celebrity interview
to the status of an earth-shattering news bulletin.

To her credit, a "Beverly Frost Interview" had become the
anointing of its chosen subject even though, in actuality, it was really just a further celebration of Beverly herself regardless of whom
it was she was talking to. She invented the notion that she was as
important as her subject. Thus, Beverly was always on camera as
much as, if not more than, the notable person or world leader being interviewed—and in better close-ups as well. It was as if Beverly,
herself, were the "get". Never before in the annals of journalism, or
entertainment for that matter, did the subject of an interview—the
star, the world leader, the one with the tale to tell, the *story*, for

crissakes,—consistently take second billing to the interviewer, the person whose role it was to merely listen and bear witness. This complete inversion of story and reporter, of performer and audience, was Beverly Frost's greatest achievement.

If Jesus Christ, Himself, ever returned to earth, and Beverly secured the "get", the interview itself would contain more close-ups of Beverly asking questions than of Christ answering them. Plus, our Lord and Savior would not have the benefit of a #2 stocking from Frederick's of Hollywood covering *His* close-up lens.

The original Frederick's of Hollywood always kept a large supply of the "Number 2's" on hand per order of Bad Bob who, of course, never told Beverly he was using them. And Beverly never noticed the way her interviews would cause any normal person watching to rub their eyes thinking they had suddenly developed cataracts. When Frederick's went bankrupt, it was a blow to, not only the naughty lingerie business, but also to the celebrity interview game. Bad Bob quickly bought out their inventory of "Number 2's" and hoarded them in a safety deposit box as insurance against his ever being replaced.

Beverly Frost had learned, growing up in San Francisco—where her mother was a Davis and some sort of descendant of Captain Richardson and her father a small time Jewish gangster who ran a liquor store while on the lam from New York—that two things were necessary for success. Location was one of them and giving people what they want was the other.

Even though she was half Jewish with a checkered portfolio, she could have just as easily been considered a scion of one of the original California titans. But the only time she openly admitted she was Jewish was right after 9/11 during the mailed "Anthrax to Anchors" scare at the networks. In order to make herself, once again, the center of even *that* story, she would pull staffers aside and announce to them solemnly, as an act of bravery, "You realize, of course, I must consider myself a target. I'm the only network anchor who is Jewish," she would say as if bearing up under the great weight of being singled out by the terrorists. But it never came to pass. Beverly never got her shipment of anthrax. Apparently, the terrorists didn't know she was Jewish, either.

But Beverly had learned early on to be, at once, totally assimilated and totally other. This training would stand her in good stead when she hit New York after getting her degree from Wellesley. Her reputation of being one of JFK's earliest conquests when she was in college also helped. The fact that she was bright and beautiful was always a given in San Francisco, but her carefully constructed persona of being one of the crowd belied her resentment that she would always also be, at the same time, completely apart. She knew of no other status.

In New York, she adopted an East Coast accent she had picked up at Wellesley which ended up sounding, by her own design, more mid-Atlantic than anything truly American. It also made her seem instantly less Jewish. Her accent and timbre were perfect for broadcasting. There *was* the problem of her slight lisp, of course, but Beverly had turned that into a sexy thing. It meant her tongue was always in play, and her bosses (always men), responded immediately to the hint of intimacy and infantilism in her speech and the glimpse, every so often, of the moist red tip of her tongue. It came across in the boardrooms of Rockefeller Center as a promise of ecstasy to come. Beverly made it her business to never disappoint anyone in power. Her "gets" did not stop at mere celebrities to be interviewed, and she was Hemingway-esque in her lifelong and relentless pursuit of the elusive "Big One".

Many would call it "lisping for success". Legend had it that negotiating with Ms. Frost and her famous tongue was not unlike getting a blow job from her, albeit a virtual one. She would make it clear up front that there was no way she was going to be fucked. Therefore, anyone sitting across the table from her would do better to just lean back and enjoy themselves while Beverly did her thing. And when negotiations were over, those same executives would have the distinct feeling that *they* were the ones who had been had and not vice versa. It was the tongue wagging the dog. No man or woman could ever resist her in her prime nor dare cross her in her decline.

Beverly loved her dog, Rémy, more than any other breathing organism on the planet. And she treated him accordingly. Rémy's groomer was the only one who had Beverly's private, *private* phone number, but that was only because the dog couldn't dial a phone... yet. Beverly always claimed the pooch was gifted as well as adorable.

Of course, the fact that "Mother" held her dog in higher esteem than her own three "so-called" flesh and blood, blonde, shiksa daughters was not lost on the Frost triplets who ran a chain of aerobic studios in Minot, North Dakota. "So-called" because when Beverly had decided to have a child she opted, not only for a sperm donor from Utah, but donor eggs from a WASP clinic in Stowe, Vermont as well, and then a surrogate mother in Florida to carry it all. It was the surrogate mother who had produced the triplets when she refused to allow a reduction of the resulting fetuses in her womb. Beverly went along with it, in part, because it was "such a bargain" that she couldn't resist. She instantly made it *her* idea and declared that, besides, "the girl's getting paid, darling. It's the highpoint of her life".

Years later, Marge would often asked Beverly if she ever wished that her daughters were genetically Jewish instead of being only culturally so by virtue of their upbringing.

"Yes," Beverly would declare coldly, "They'd be smarter."

There were no secrets at "The Ladies' Room". None. Everyone knew everything, from the newest intern to the most grizzled stage hand. Through pieced-together conversations overheard in elevators, revelations blurted out in the make-up room, indiscreet phone calls made or received in the rehearsal hall, toilet stall snippets, closed door confessions, barked orders, shared gossip, jokes, and public observations of private behavior; everyone's life was an open book whether they knew it or not, and whether it was true or not.

But the resulting tales were endlessly repeated and with the certainty of legend.

"Darling, I hope everything works out between you and Robert," Beverly had said to Brendan a month before Bad Bob had fired him. It was in a rare moment when Brendan found himself both alone with Beverly and actually acknowledged by her.

"Huh?" Brendan had replied. He really didn't know, at first, what she was talking about. Beverly's constant modus was to relentlessly pretend not to own the "The Ladies' Room" outright (SBS was merely a distributor). The fact that she was not only the most celebrated and senior host of the show but also its creator, owner, and executive producer meant that, with bonuses for ratings, she probably took 10 million dollars a year out of a production that policed personal mail, forbade any writing instrument above a Bic, and flatly refused to pay any health insurance for its employees. And this was in addition to the 14 million she was getting a year from the network for her role as a "senior correspondent" even though the regular news anchors all shunned her. On top of all that, her deal (signed with a particularly "friendly" CEO of Swann) also granted her complete ownership of her "Conversations" and "Teaching Moment" specials, and they reverted to her, alone, after only one airing on the network.

"I mean, between you and the show," she clarified to Brendan as if she weren't the show itself, and nothing could be done without her knowledge and approval. She was speaking to Brendan in her pose as a "stenographer" in her own typing pool: someone who had all the knowledge of an insider but not a whiff of power.

"Right." Brendan had replied. He hadn't known that his struggles with Bad Bob over the Writers Guild union rules were even being discussed, much less that precipitous. It was a bad sign that the issue had reached Beverly's consciousness no matter how clueless she pretended to be. But Marge had warned him. She had basically told him he was on his own, and there was nothing she could do to protect him. But Brendan hadn't realized the situation had advanced to this point. So when Beverly revealed that his future was definitely in play, he feigned naiveté.

"I'm really writing well these days," he blurted out almost as a non sequitur. "Marge says the material is first rate." He suddenly sounded like a comedy writer with brain damage.

"I'm sorry." Beverly said demurely and lowered her eyes as if at a wake. Brendan could not let her know that he knew what she was talking about. He wondered in a flash whether anyone had ever "decked her", as in, punched her in the face. He had actually considered it for a fleeting second, but then he erased the thought because he knew if he *did* hit her, he would kill her.

At that moment, Beverly suddenly found herself grossly overdue in the allotted time that she would ever deign to be alone with a mere mortal,—or with someone who was neither a dictator, a royal, a celebrity, a war criminal, or a richer Jew—so she immediately turned all Bette Davis-like and pretended to see someone out in the hall with whom she simply *had* to speak.

"Darling!" she said to no one over Brendan's shoulder, and, in an instant, she was gone.

CHAPTER TEN

There were two more death notices on the "Wall of Woe" when Brendan came to work on the following Monday. This was strange. The show was dark for two weeks before the start of the new season; and, since so many people were on vacation, one might think there wouldn't be anyone left in the building to die. One of the notices was for the mother of a cameraman on "Living", and the other was for the beloved lighting director who had worked on the soap from its start. The cameraman's mother's wake was in "Occupied Glendale", as Rubin Carson used to say; and shiva for the lighting director was being sat in God-forsaken Thousand Oaks.

Brendan could tell that the lighting director's demise had been a shock to everyone because there was an additional notice put up by NABET, his union, and another by the crew of "Living for Love" to establish a college fund for his kids.

It made Brendan more and more convinced that the building was a "sick building" and that a death from "The Ladies' Room" side of the edifice was imminent. He wondered if Beverly would make it through another season.

"She could survive a nuclear holocaust," Marge always said. "The woman has not had as much as a sniffle in 15 years. She hasn't gained weight, she hasn't lost weight, even her collagen hasn't migrated. She'll bury us all! She's connected."

It was natural for Marge to think of Beverly as part of a cabal or, at least, connected to the mob, and that's what was keeping her alive. After all, Marge was born and raised on Chicago's South Side. Her father, besides being a piano playing politico, was a free-lance enforcer for "Jimmy Blue Eyes" and operated out of a social club in Bridgeport. She had always claimed that the Italians only acted vicious, that they depended on the cold blooded Irish to do their dirty work. Hence, the success of "The Westies" in New York and guys like her father who could "stick an ice pick in a guy's ear as easily as running an arpeggio on the piano."

Marge was full of death. She grew up going to mob funerals (many at the hands of her old man) and could rattle off the names of all the cemeteries in the Chicago area and the gangsters—famous or merely unlucky—buried in each one. But she didn't go to funerals, now, as an adult. She hated them. It was partly because of her upbringing and partly because of her family's intimate connection with them. And partly because, as a comedian, she was always asked to do a chunk of material at "show biz" funerals, free, as a eulogy. She found it particularly inelegant and bad for career longevity.

Beverly, on the other hand, because she thought she would never die, went to funerals like it was the gym. She honestly thought she gained something from each one and got stronger on account of it. Beverly Frost feasted on the lives of the dead the way a vampire feasts on the blood of the living. She was able to co-opt whatever the deceased had left behind in terms of acclaim, reputation, or prominence and make it her own. This was especially true of colleagues, celebrities, and news anchors.

The stench of death filled every corridor of the building. Brendan continually looked for signs of who the next dead one might be. Beverly was the obvious candidate but unlikely. Brendan was sure it would come unexpectedly from another quarter. Perhaps Bambi, the "young one" co-host, who had her life so mapped out that even her three year old daughter's menstrual onset had been penciled in for September of her twlefth year so as to not interfere with her summer fun and be well in hand for the following aquatic season. But Bambi was so organized and so confidently in command of her fate that the Grim Reaper would undoubtedly take a pass just to avoid being "finger shooked" by that little dynamo. Death was just another illegal immigrant in Bambi's scheme of things.

Moonie was a walking heart attack. But then there was the problem of what to do with the body, and even God didn't want to deal with that.

Perhaps it would be Marge. Brendan thought that might be poetic because then they would both leave the show together, the naked and the unfunny. Marge was certainly old enough, older than Brendan. The biggest secret of her life was that she was over seventy and looked every year of it in the morning.

With "The Ladies' Room" shut down, there was really no reason for the staff to be in the offices at all except for the Swann Company's special genius of treating all its employees as if they were dwarfs in a diamond mine. Brendan had come in anyway figuring he really shouldn't take a vacation after being fired. On his way to his office on the second floor, he ran into Raoul from Yale in the hallway. Raoul was carrying his trusty long-handled dustpan and broom which, in his hands, were as noble as a lance and a shield.

"Hey, Papi." Raoul cooed when he saw Brendan, "How is everything witchu? You still sweet?"

Raoul was of indeterminate nationality even though everyone and everything around him was Mexican. Raoul insisted that he was "One hundred percent "Hongareesh" and claimed to have fucked either one or all of the Gabor Sisters and their mother, Magda. But, then again, he also claimed to have fucked Goldie Hawn "who had a pooosey so big you could clap your hands in it like this," he would say demonstrating with both hands. He boasted that he had shared a hot tub with Brooke Shields whom he said had fucked Bob Hope when she was a teenager. He was a true pan sexual—equally, and completely, attracted to men, women, farm animals, and most electrical appliances. He was an electrician by trade but not by license and, as a result, was often called upon to wire the various illegal gay clubs that sprang up, pre-AIDS, in the meat packing district of New York and the back alleys of West Hollywood.

For all his sexual bravado and his overabundance of self-confidence as far as getting laid was concerned, Raoul was, in fact, remarkably successful with his cock and had had sex with more individuals at "The Ladies' Room" than anyone else. He was called "Papi Chulo" by his co-workers because of his record of insatiability and sexual success and because they considered him Puerto Rican not Mexican. But whatever his true nationality was, he had the street moves of a Dominican as he prowled the halls of the building where "Ladies'" was shot. His specialty became the interns, male and female, who considered him to be in show business and would submit themselves to him in his secret bower located in a dead space behind the generators in the basement of the building. He would take them, like a Latino Grendel dragging a stunned prey, back to his lair which was, in fact, a nest of old props and boudoir furnishings stolen from the soaps before budget cuts made those daytime drama sets look like DMV offices.

"Dead man walking" Brendan said, "Bad Bob fired me, you know."

"Oh, Sweetie," Raoul said exhibiting about as much true emotion as he could muster. "When you got to leave?"

"Twenty-six weeks," Brendan said.

"Don't go," he replied with the inflection of either a nymphet or a four year old child being left alone.

"Not my call, Raoul. When you're fucked you're fucked. You ought to know that."

"But you so beeeg, Papi," he said pursing his lips and looking Brendan up and down like a naughty coquette practicing her moves.

It would have been personally offensive to Brendan except that it was also the way "Leetle Raoulie" asked for a cup of coffee as well. But it was true. Raoul seemed to have a special thing for Brendan that bordered on obsession. Brendan had the unique distinction of being stalked by the janitor.

"They not going to fire you, he continued, "Just don't leave."

"Whaddya mean, 'don't leave'?", Brendan said.

"Stay in your office. Das all"

"Probably not a bad idea. We'll see."

"You know too much, Papi. When they think about that, they change their minds. Beverly Frost, she want you on the *inside* where you can't hurt her." His eyes got wide and all sparkly, and he affected a Cheshire Cat smile as if he'd just uncovered a treasure for Brendan's sole benefit. "Kabeesh?" He said nodding lasciviously. "Marge never let you go. She need you more than tits."

"Maybe" Brendan said sounding more like Rod Steiger in the taxi scene from "On the Waterfront" than himself.

But Brendan's attitude was appropriate. Someone was going down, that was for sure. He left Raoul to wrangle new interns interviewing for the fall session and turned around to go, instead, down to the basement where the production offices of "The Ladies' Room" were strategically placed. In the event of a nuclear attack, only "The Ladies' Room" and "Living for Love", across the hall, would survive and be up and running the next day.

The basement office of the show consisted of a warren of tiny, individual offices built around a reception area in the front and a large conference room in the back. No one could make or receive a cell phone call there. Somehow, the "Living" offices across the hall seemed more airy and normal while "The Ladies' Room" was like a bunker and had the mentality that went along with it.

The co-hosts never ventured down to the production offices but came and went from their brief dressing room stop-overs each day by way of the ramp and loading bay three floors above on the studio level. The separation of production and "talent" was perfect for

Bad Bob and Mugsy when they had been an item and even better now that he had moved on to Jeannie Murphy whose office was in the network building next door. It put some distance between his office and his work but provided the convenience of nooners when the spirit moved him.

"The Ladies' Room" and "Living" staffs rarely interacted even though they shared the basement and would merge at the elevators. The separation was like church and state, like art and commerce, like banking and trading. "Living for Love" being the equivalent of church, art, and the bank. "The Ladies' Room" was a lower species and dangerous.

The rumor mill at "The Ladies' Room" was such that you could go up to anyone, at any time, and say, "Did you hear the news?" and get an immediate audience with that person behind a closed door. Brendan was fond of doing just that in the most unlikely of situations. It never failed to get the desired response of, "No! What?" even though he had pulled the same ruse five minutes before with the same person. Such was the volatility of information and intrigue within the show. They were all like a gaggle of palace courtiers, whispering plots and scandals behind castle pillars. And the passage of information through the staff was instantaneous, faster than any electronics.

But while there may have been few, if any, secrets at "The Ladies' Room", there were layers upon layers of ulterior motives on the part of senior management. No one took any statement or act on the part of the bosses at face value. The truth always lay in the motives that were ultimately behind them. Thus, Beverly would praise a celebrity and be overly protective on air in order to achieve the "get" down the line. Bad Bob would book the show in waves of similar guests without telling anyone he was constructing a "backdoor" pilot within the daily presentation of "The Ladies' Room". Mugsy would insist that a doctor or trainer be put on the show to facilitate her own health and physical regime. Producers would ask for "review" copies of everything in order to sell them. Huge suitcases on rollers would appear on Fridays ostensibly for "weekend overnights" but really to accommodate the swag being removed from the premises that would be sold on Ebay or Hollywood Boulevard. The ruse was unnecessary. Everyone knew what was happening because everyone was doing it.

Sometimes, however, the layering of motives and hidden agendas was so dense that no one could decipher their ultimate objective. The result was that Brendan often felt he was merely a cog in someone else's much larger wheel. He would spend hours in discussions with Leo trying to parse the overlapping and interlocking secret deals whose purpose would only become evident when the *fait accompli* was finally revealed.

When Brendan walked into the reception area after his encounter with Raoul, Anita, the angry Latina receptionist greeted him with her usual friendly greeting.

"What're you doing here, Brendan? I thought you got fired."

"Not yet. Still working on it."

At that point Liz Sterling, the talent coordinator who was fond of pants suits and shoulder pads for her exquisitely tailored hunched shoulders, sidled up to him conspiratorially which, for her, was normal behavior. Lizzie had worked in the Nixon White House and probably fucked whatever was left of "the prez" when he moved to San Clamente afterwards. Consequently, *everything* was a conspiracy for Liz and "strictly on the Q.T.", "entre nous", "for your ears only," and "just between you, me and the bedpost". She must have caught her posture from her old boss, and she skulked around "The Ladies' Room" offices practically talking to the pictures of Beverly and the co-hosts on the walls like Nixon had done, drunk, to the portraits in the White House. The fact that she always walked with her hands in her jacket pockets and her feet splayed out like a tall penguin only added to her gestalt of Nixon in drag.

"You excited?" She said at Brendan's shoulder but looking away as if they were spies in a movie.

"About what?"

"You didn't hear?" She said, truly surprised that he hadn't.

"What? That I got fired?"

"Better than that, and this actually may help you."

"What?" Brendan said.

"Roberta," she said, "Or should I say, 'Bobby'".

"Roberta Monzon?" Brendan said and turned to face her. "What about her?"

"They hired her," Liz said triumphantly.

Nothing got Liz wetter than possessing some piece of information that her listener did not know, no matter how inconsequential. She would pass Brendan in the stairwell right before show time as he was running up to the studio and say, to the back of his head as if he were facing her, "I got him".

And Brendan would stop short, turn, and say, "Got who?"

"Rob Schneider. I booked him. Called him up on his private line and asked as a personal favor to *me*. Not to the show, or Beverly, but to *me*. I asked him to come on the show, and he said, I'll get right back to you. So I waited, and then I said, what the hell, and called him again. So I told him, 'Robbie, bubbie, you gotta give me an answer.' And, not for nothin', right away he wants to know what about "The Talk"? And I said that's not my problem. But if you do them you can't do us. That's just the rules. Leave me out of this. Don't kill the messenger. But we really want you. And, more to the point, *I* want you. So he says, —and you can't make this stuff up, —he says..."

At which point Brendan would have to beg off in order to try to get the material to Marge before they went on the air. It had to have been something from her West Wing experience. She always acted like she didn't know they were doing a live show but that what was happening between her and her Rolodex was the *real* drama.

Brendan immediately had to wonder, however, whether his firing had anything to do with the arrival of Roberta as a new co-host and the start of a new season. Maybe Bad Bob was re-aligning the staff to show the network that he was capable of righting this foundering ship of a show whose ratings had sunk lower than whale shit at the bottom of the ocean. But getting rid of Marge's comedy writer was certainly not the answer although it undoubtedly made Bad Bob feel better. And bringing Roberta in was like inviting Governor Christie to a Thanksgiving dinner. It might be entertaining, but you could kiss *that* turkey goodbye.

Roberta was a legendary friend of the oppressed and especially of anyone wrongfully maligned. For that reason, alone, Brendan decided her arrival bode well for him if she would just stay long enough to take up his cause. That is, unless the machinations of the show and the deadliness of the building didn't get to her first.

Having delivered her prized piece of information, Liz returned to her office to check her stock portfolio and play internet solitaire. Brendan then noticed that Norman, the head booker, was also in his office. It made him smile, and he stuck his head in the door. Norman was as crazed and apoplectic as if the show was in production, and it was sweeps, and he had no bookings. He was like Woody Allen on uppers.

"I-I-I-I can't talk to you right now, Brendan, Please! Doris Roberts missed her plane in Chicago," he would say holding his head in his hands at his desk as if Kennedy had just been shot.

"But I just want to *talk* to you, Norman. I want to hang out." Brendan loved tormenting the man with threats of frat boy hijinks. He actually could have used Norman's help, but he knew he would have to be satisfied with only the pleasure of seeing the man squirm in his own skin over the fact that Lorraine Bracco had decided to do "Good Day LA" on the same day she was booked on "The Ladies' Room" rendering her unfit for "The Ladies' Room's" consumption. The high point of their relationship had come when Brendan inadvertently spilled Norman's coffee all over his screening invitations and "house seat" orders for shows at the Taper that he would never let anyone else have. Brendan really thought the man was going to have a heart attack. Neither the death of his mother, nor the passing of his cat, had extracted as big an emotional response. The man fell on the floor in a swoon and cried. A secretary had to come in and quietly shut the door to let him quiver in private.

Brendan figured that this was as good a time as any to try to line up testimony about his "contributions to the show" before things picked up in earnest with the new season and the arrival of Roberta. After all, he wasn't planning on going to any of the funerals or wakes posted on the "Wall of Woe", and there was no show being produced, so the staff members who did wander in were all pretty relaxed and cooperative. The problem was that they were completely unaware of any problem with Brendan's performance; and, thus, thought Brendan's request for support was a set up for some sort of joke or scam.

Mugsy, of course, would take no responsibility.

"That's completely between you and Bob," she said sweeping her hair up into a pile on top of her head, checking her various looks and pouts in her desk mirror, and then letting it all fall again.

"But you're the producer, Mugs." Brendan liked making her name as unattractively unfeminine as possible. "You're my immediate superior."

"I have nothing to do with that," she said.

"But Bad Bob doesn't do the script read-throughs, you do. If he has a problem with my intros, it must have come from you. Do you have a problem with the intros?" Brendan persisted.

"I don't know what you're talking about," she said. "What intros?"

"The ones I write. Did you tell him they were unusable?" Brendan wanted to push her into a statement. He knew she would take absolutely no responsibility for anything, but he might be able to force her to sign off retroactively on the intros and anything else she had a direct hand in that had already been produced and aired.

"I can't remember. They're fine. You should take this up with Bob and leave me out of it."

"I can't leave you out because you're the one who either accepts or rejects the intros I write."

"Well, you have to admit you do write some pretty ridiculous ones."

"That's my job," Brendan said. "I was told to write Marge's intros funny."

"Yeah, I guess some of them are all right"

"So you're saying that, as far as you're concerned, the intros are fine. And if not, I always rewrite them"

"I didn't say that." Mugsy bristled. She was not about to be quoted or pinned down unless it was under a sweating English rock star or the Executive Producer. "I didn't say anything of the kind. I really don't know what you're talking about. If you have some issue with Bob, then you should take it up with him."

"Well, I'm going to tell him that you signed off on the intros, and you said they were okay."

"I didn't say that, Brendan. Don't put words in my mouth."

"Well, what do you *want* me to put in your mouth," Brendan could feel himself getting angry and destructive. "I just want the truth."

"The truth is leave me out of this. It's not my problem. All I care about is that the script is in order."

"And the intros I write are part of that, and that's okay."

"I don't know. Don't quote me. Don't try and drag me into your issues with Bob."

She looked at Brendan with her best porno kitten pout as she pulled the bottom of her tank top up so she could finger her abdominals. Then she sat down on a large exercise ball that she kept just outside her office, arched her back, and started seductively rolling back and forth on it in front of him. Her attention turned exclusively to the ridges on her stomach that she loved more than her daughter.

"But are you not the senior producer here?" Brendan persisted. Mugsy didn't answer. She was deep into her endless loop of exercise, verification, and self-adulation. Brendan made a note to secretly put a pin prick in the ball before he left so she'd think her weight was causing a slow leak.

Brendan sought out as many of the producers as he could in the days before the show geared up again. Most of them were nonplussed that he was being fired and, especially, that he was being fired over the relative merits of the intermittent intros he wrote. He couldn't get them to focus on the issue because it seemed like such a non-issue—as it did to Brendan every time he explained it. No wonder people thought it was some sort of bit.

Brendan did make a trip to the Swann Human Resources Department who informed him that, as a freelance employee, he was not really under their jurisdiction. In other words, "Get a staff job with Swann and *then* get yourself fucked over," they seemed to be saying. But somewhere, he thought, there was a case for age discrimination and retaliation for union activity. Brendan called the Writers Guild on Third Street in West Hollywood, and the executive director said she would look into it.

Marge was out in Santa Monica lunching with her collection of garmentos and aging, half-assed comedians trying to reassure herself that she had made it in Show Biz by merely surviving on 'The Ladies' Room' for fifteen years without extending any real effort. But, unfortunately, even though she'd begun as only a two-day-a-week bit player, in the course of those fifteen years, she'd traded her outsider, smart-ass persona that Brendan had carefully crafted for her for that of a cranky old lady who listened to too much talk radio.

But with Roberta coming on board, the attention shifted to the whirlwind that surrounded her in any space she occupied. (Roberta's code name around the office, and especially when uttered in public, quickly became "Tsunami"—a mixed metaphor, to be sure, but at least "Tsunami" sounded more like Roberta's overwhelming impact than the relatively pixie-like, but equally devastating, "Katrina".)

Once "Tsunami" hit, Bad Bob and the others would quickly forget about Brendan's impending demise. But, of course, Brendan wouldn't. He had become energized by trying to figure out whom he could take down with him. It was "Top of the world, Ma" time for Brendan. And as such, it was, in a way, the best of all worlds: he had been fired, but had refused to leave. He was a free agent. A man without a country. But Brendan knew it was only a small victory. Very small.

CHAPTER ELEVEN

Roberta Monzon hadn't always been "Roberta". For the first twenty-two years of her life she had been *"Robert"* Monzon, the middle child of the sprawling Monzon family of Ishpeming, Michigan in the Upper Peninsula, the hunting and incest capital of America. And true to the natural grandeur of the countryside and the proclivity of its natives, Roberta's mother had molested the young Robert nightly from infancy through his senior year in high school (or so Roberta claimed).

What had begun as normal maternal cuddling by a mother and her newborn simply continued unabated as "Baby Bobby" went from toddler to preschool, from scamp to schoolboy; and then, from teenager to young man. It was a nightly ritual of love—first on her part toward him and then on his part toward her. It had unfolded in Bobby's room which was right next to the master bedroom where Mom would then retire after she had had her way with him to sleep alongside Robert's acquiescing father. What had started as a natural embrace soon advanced to heavier shenanigans and then to full blown sexual intercourse between mother and son in the loving confines of the Monzon home. Young Robert was the first of his school friends to lose his virginity, but he could never tell them with whom. It wasn't that he was a "mamma's boy", he was a mamma's *man*.

The mother died of a gunshot wound to the back of her head in the woods behind the house when Robert was eighteen. That stopped the affair, or molestation, depending on how you looked at it. The father had had enough. It was ruled a "hunting accident" as most homicides in the U.P. are. But the damage had been done.

By that time, little Robert was so in love with his mother and so hated his father for killing her and breaking them up that he decided to become a woman in her honor; and, by so doing put a permanent speed bump between him and his father. He figured it would also insure that he would never have to go hunting with the old fuck again. And for that reason alone, transitioning for little Bobby was a lifesaver.

But the "chop" that came years later proved so successful that boys and men immediately began coming on to, the now, female Roberta who turned out to be quite attractive in an outdoorsy, Yooper way. But that was abhorrent to her. Roberta still missed her mother, and she wanted nothing to do with anyone who reminded her of her father. She wanted to *be* her mother and make love to her at the same time. Consequently, Roberta had to go one step further and become the world's biggest and meanest lesbian this side of the Timberland Outlet in Escanaba just to make her point and find the happiness she had felt as a young boy. Psychiatry was a rare commodity in the Upper Peninsula in those days.

Roberta soon became something of a sensation by going into local singing contests. She won the "Yooper Talent Parade" and also "Michigan's Got Talent" after which she scored a lucrative recording contract and inadvertently retained the publishing rights to all her music. Her biggest hit was "Girl, Girl, Give It a Whirl". Several triple platinum albums later and a song that became the Coca Cola anthem, as well as some very shrewd business moves, made Roberta Monzon a very rich and famous woman. On top of that, her lawyer had leveraged Roberta's cash flow into the purchase of the Mamas and Poppas' song book which was then rolled over into ownership of the publishing rights to Andrew Lloyd Webber before "Cats". Consequently, she soon ruled Broadway, and her imprimatur could determine whether a new musical would make it or not depending on how compliant the song writers were when Roberta's "Conundrum Productions" came calling. In relatively short order, Roberta Monzon landed on the Forbes' list of richest celebrities in the world, just behind George Foreman and just above the plummeting Rosie O'Donnell. Suddenly, this little abused boy from the Upper Peninsula had become one of the richest women in America with an influence that rivaled Oprah's.

That's when she decided to pull off a victim quadfecta and come out of four closets simultaneously: as a molested heterosexual, as a troubled gay man, as a transsexual, and as a lesbian. Her mail from the gay, lesbian and transsexual organizations quadrupled overnight. She was the most comfortable with her lesbianism since she considered lesbianism perfectly compatible with her birthright as a mostly straight man: the object of her affection remained the same, only the delivery had changed. Her celebrity was, thus, secure in the hearts of her faithful fans who could glom onto any single anomaly in her life out of the four possibilities. Make that, "five". Roberta also had a weight problem which had never bothered "Robert" before he cut his dick off, but the loss of his balls and beard aggravated an obesity that had been lurking just beneath the surface. Roberta's body, which had been perfectly fine as a heterosexual man became "super butch" as a gay female. The lesbian Roberta looked right out of Central Casting, and the gay community embraced her as the best of all worlds: a man/woman with no balls who was lousy at doing her own hair and make-up but was, strangely, great in bed, especially with older women.

It was, apparently, this "all things to all manner of men, women and dogs" aspect of Roberta Monzon that led Beverly Frost to offer her a seat at "The Ladies' Room" table so that Beverly could take time off to concentrate on the care and feeding of her legacy in what had to be her fairly short remaining time on this planet.

Roberta's reputation preceded her. There was good reason she was called "Bobby Badfinger" in most television production circles. She was known to be stark raving mad, and everyone around her was equally nuts. She was so crazy that even the story of her being molested by her mother was questioned even though it formed the cornerstone of her "victim, like you" personal marketing campaign. The only thing people never questioned was that she was a transsexual. That, at least, had been vetted by all the tabloids with many "before and after" pictures which, incidentally, were indistinguishable. One comedian even wondered what she had *really* done with the money she put aside for the operation. The big joke was that she had gone through all the trouble of having her balls cut off and her cock turned inside out when all she really needed to do was change her shirt, and she could have achieved the same effect.

Roberta had even done a stint as a commentator for Fox News but had famously blown up on air when her political passions could no longer fit into the "fair and balanced" Bloomberg Boxes at Fox. The word on the street was that she had probably left one testicle intact for old time's sake, and this was pumping just enough testosterone to make her dangerous in a fight. No one tangled with her for fear of physical harm and mental anguish from her rapier sharp tongue and dossier on everyone she met. As her Vienna Choir Boy singing voice had waned, she had ramped up her comedy chops and was now known equally for both.

The fact that she was coming to "The Ladies' Room" this late in the game was actually good for the show but problematical for the co-hosts. Marge feared her because Marge was extremely insecure around other comedians and felt she couldn't hold her own, head to head, with one. When comics were booked on the show, Marge would fall silent and grumpy rather than join the fun. Also,

Roberta was younger than Marge, much younger. And age, for Marge was the bogeyman she could not vanquish. It killed her that, with the addition of Roberta, she would be positioned even closer to Beverly's age than before.

Roberta and Marge had known each other when Marge worked at KNBC in Burbank doing warm up for Kelly Lange's midday show, and Roberta had come on to sing and talk. But talk shows now booked Roberta more for her comedy than her singing which was considered, at this point in her career, "all sell and no pipes". Roberta always liked to fancy herself as a latter day Julie Andrews, but she wasn't. She was more of a present day Rex Harrison who spoke her lyrics rather than sang them.

The real problem for "The Ladies' Room" was Moonie. She and Roberta had exchanged barbs in print, and had tangled the few times Roberta had guested on "The Ladies' Room". Now they were going to have to sit at the same table every day. Let the fireworks begin.

CHAPTER TWELVE

Moonie Brown hated Brendan. She hated him almost as much as she hated Star Jones who had appeared for years on "The View" in New York. Moonie was very competitive with Star. Star had reveled in her "fine brown frame" for years and then had gotten thin and married. Of course, Moonie was always about twice the size of Star even at her "finest", and that made Moonie hate her even more. On top of that, the only "chubby chasers" even vaguely interested in Moonie, for God only knows what ulterior motives, were continually gay. Star had found a perfectly formed, straight, black banker, no less, and had married him at St Bartholomew's on Park Avenue like a society princess, and even had a website to celebrate it. Moonie had none of that except a fat ass that hung off her backside like a fully-loaded Airstream trailer.

Moonie had two missions on "The Ladies' Room". One was to maximize the opportunity for the greater glory of Miss Moonbeam P. Brown regardless of any loyalty to the show or her co-hosts. The other was to use the show to maximize both her bank account and her girth. And she was remarkably successful at both. Even a veteran like Beverly could not figure out how she did it. And it drove her nuts.

"Darling, she plugs everything and gets away with it. The network is afraid of her," Beverly was often heard to say. "But I guess it does benefit the show, and I do own it. So, in a sense, she's doing it for *me.*" Beverly made sure she always came out on top.

So despite Moonie's relentless plugging and self-aggrandizement, Beverly felt that, ultimately, she would benefit from it more than Moonie would. At least that's what kept Beverly semi-sane. But Beverly was like a eunuch in a whore house when it came to Moonie's ability to parlay the show into real cash. She could see the trick done daily, and in all manner of ways, but she was unable to duplicate it or even to try to understand exactly how it was done. In order to keep her credentials as a journalist, Beverly had to avoid plugs, gifts, endorsements, product placements, and commercials. Beverly had to let all of that swag go down the drain; and, yet, she *still* was not allowed into the SBS network newsroom.

Moonie was not going to help Brendan even though, originally, when the show had first started, he had written a chunk of material for her motivational lectures for free. He did it as a professional courtesy. This was despite the fact that Moonie's fee for her "MoonShine For Life" lecture was a minimum of $40,000, four first class tickets, a five star hotel, and a hospitality suite stocked with enough vittles to feed Ms. Brown before and after the lecture as well as her immediate family back in Maryland and the tribe in Maine.)

Moonie's agents would submit a list of her required food for something as simple as a paid appearance at a book signing at Book Soup on Sunset where she would sign anything with pages knowing full well that a signed book was a sold book and could not be returned. After every appearance, she always left the hapless bookseller choking on more copies of "Moonbeams" by Moonie Brown than could possibly be sold, returned, or burned without violating EPA restrictions..

Even after arriving at a local venue by limo with only Maurice, the Haitian driver, onboard, Moonie demanded the following meal be placed in her dressing room before she arrived: Four orders of chicken nuggets, two magnums of Dom Perignon, two orders of chicken wings, two orders of barbecued ribs, two dozen chocolate chip cookies, two bags of Fatburger hamburgers, a case of Diet Coke (so she could feel good about herself), a case of Perrier (she didn't really like Perrier; but she liked the way it sounded, and she liked leaving the empty bottles around even though she only used it to wash her feet), twenty Dove bars on dry ice, and chocolate syrup. She claimed she needed the extra food for the "trip home" which would have made sense if "home" were in Saskatchewan and not three miles away in Westwood.

Moonie and Brendan had parted ways after he had asked her, as a favor to a dear friend, to speak at a special high school graduation ceremony; and she had told him that her fee was $30,000 for non-profit and $50,000 for profit. He then told her that this very special graduation was the first of its kind at "a school for underprivileged African American, inner city, blind children, with AIDS—who had been rescued from the wars in Sierra Leone, Rwanda, and the Congo where their fathers had been hacked to death with machetes before their children's very eyes; and the children had then been forced to watch their mothers being systematically tortured and raped by their captors and only allowed to live and remain in sexual captivity if they gave birth, as a result of the rapes, to a semi-ethnically cleansed child who was then sold at slave auctions to the highest bidder."

"Then that would be $30,000, " Moonie had replied to Brendan in the green room, straight-faced and without a beat, before going air to discuss the dating travails of a full-bodied, lusty, red/brown woman.

On another occasion, Brendan had stopped her as she was coming off the set to introduce her to a couple from Chicago who had paid $15,000 at a charity auction for the privilege of going to "The Ladies' Room" (whose tickets were free). He quickly told her that the couple had paid an exorbitant amount of money to a worthwhile cause and hoped to have their picture taken with the famous

Ms. Brown. Moonie had declined loudly, without breaking stride.
(or, rather, altering her waddle).

So it was that Brendan was glad when she killed a mouse in her
dressing room by inadvertently stepping on it (Raoul, upon hearing the news, had simply said, "Poor mouse!"). Brendan was glad
because he knew the rodent carcass would remain in the high shag
until the smell of decomposing mouse flesh rose above the stench
from her fetid pussy. And he knew that when she complained
about the odor, Yale Maintenance would not know whether to send
a cleaning crew or a douche.

No, Moonie was not going to help Brendan. Although she had
been good to some people on the staff, she was openly hostile to
him, but he had reveled in that hostility knowing that it probably
helped his reputation rather than hurt it.

Brendan couldn't believe that, fifteen years later, she was still
using the same material he'd written for her, even though she de-
spised its author. She would stand in front of her, supposedly, mo-
tivationally challenged audience and hold up a poster-sized head
shot of herself, so airbrushed and Photoshopped that it looked like
a still from "Grand Theft Auto". Then she would sing, *á capella*, "You
Are So Beautiful (To Me)" —in its entirety and at a maddening and
self-indulgent slow pace—plus a whole set of special lyrics Brendan
had written about how it's what's inside (if you could dig that deep)
that counts, and that inner beauty is what gives people her specially
branded "moonshine". The "moonshine" was her contribution, but
it was confusing. People didn't know if she was talking about inner
beauty or illegal liquor. She couldn't be persuaded to change it
to "moonlight" because she probably considered "moonlite" some
kind of diet "moonshine", and she wanted nothing to do with it.

"Hal, put the camera on *me*," Moonie would declare on the air
in the middle of a show which meant that she wanted the director
to do a single shot of her alone so that she could make some self-
serving remark.

Moonie was the best at "audience suck lines". That is, statements that were guaranteed to evoke an affirmative applause from the audience. Any time a wedding anniversary was announced, or somebody's advanced age, or even the mere fact of having more than one child, the audience, for some reason, was always moved to applaud to signal their approval.

Then there were the self-effacing and overtly modest proclamations that also produced applause. It got so that she began adding the line, "But that's just me" to even the most obvious of statements. "Mothers should take care of their children," she would pronounce fearlessly. And then, in case the audience didn't catch the heroism of her brave public proclamation, she would add with self-effacing courage, "I'm sorry, but that's just me." It always got an additional burst of applause. She would interview a guest and say, "I think your movie is wonderful," but then would add, "I'm sorry, but that's just me" to position herself as a fearless supporter of the guest and everything the guest stood for especially if there were any freebies to be had down the line. If Moonie had been hanged by British soldiers instead of Nathan Hale, she would've said, "I regret that I have but one life to give for my country. I'm sorry, but that's just me."

After a while Brendan was convinced the audience took such utterances as an order, something along the lines of the flashing "Applause" sign. Moonie would assume a "damn the torpedoes" stance on the most innocuous and unassailable positions. "I think drugs are bad." "Serial killers must be stopped." "Baby animals are cute." "All people should be free."

"I'm sorry, but that's just me."

The other reason Moonie was not going to help Brendan was because, while he was being fired, she was busy having a gastric bypass operation whereby she, essentially, had her throat tied to her asshole. It was a last ditch attempt to finally make her lose weight.

After the operation, eating for Moonie became such a straight shot, start to finish, mouth to shitter, that she probably could have put just as many calories into her system by dumping the Fatburgers directly into the toilet than by going through the trouble of eating them.

Apparently, the word was that she had raised holy hell at the lying-in facility in the Valley where she had gone for the procedure under security that hadn't been that tight since Michael Jackson's last nose job. The simultaneous breast reduction that had accompanied the stomach operation had equaled the Berlin Airlift in sheer tonnage of meat moved from one place to another while the by-pass itself was akin to re-routing the Mississippi to such an extent that St Louis would no longer be a river-front metropolis.

The problem was that she thought it was a secret; but, unfortunately, no one else did. The staff all witnessed her announcing it to the other co-hosts in a closed door session in the rehearsal hall. But the revelation made the ladies angry, not sympathetic, because they then would be forced to lie about the fact instead of legitimately being able to claim ignorance.

As the weight started to come off, Moonie would publicly attribute it only to yoga and portion control. She even went so far as to insist as much in a taped piece, produced for "The Ladies' Room", showing her yoga instructor, a stoic Indian (from India, no relation) lass working on her in a Beverly Hills yoga studio.

The raw tape of the "yoga shoot" became an instant hit in the office because of one specific sequence where the kneeling instructor serenely addresses the miraculously leotarded Moonie lying Orca-like on her back on a yoga mat. The poor instructor then makes the mistake of lifting one of Moonie's legs off the mat (probably the equivalent of a 200 pound "clean and jerk"). But when the leg gets to about twenty inches off the mat there comes a loud and lethal fart from deep within the lotus of the blissed-out Moonie. The poor yoga teacher does not react. But neither does she dare raise the leg any higher.

In true yoga-like fashion she pauses (probably checking for the nearest exit) and then, slowly and gently, lowers the leg back to the mat with the deftness of a Bomb Squad officer replacing a deadly, un-defused, explosive device. For anyone else, the incident would have been like miraculously escaping the event horizon of a massive black hole. But then, after a beat, the instructor gently raises Moonie's leg again, as if to tempt fate and certain death. But when the leg reaches approximately the same elevation, another fart is produced. This time it's slightly more insistent, a little nasty, and with just a hint of "wet". Again, the yoga instructor pauses, maintains her composure and circular breathing; and then slowly lowers the offending limb back to the mat with the finality of a grave digger. After a beat, she decides that, perhaps, a less volatile position is in order, like, maybe, the "dead pose". Then the hapless instructor excuses herself, rises up off her knees, and leaves the frame—undoubtedly to either quit the ashram or relieve herself of her lunch.

Even though the clock was ticking on Brendan's career and gainful employment, he found himself strangely relaxed. A lot of it had to do with the imminent arrival of Roberta Monzon who was joining the co-hosts as a woman but with a decidedly masculine bent. This could only mean great television as Monzon (supposedly related in some way to Carlos Monzon, the legendary prizefighter from Argentina) was not only a celebrated singer, but had become a leading female comedian after taking first place on "Last Comic Standing" (without balls), scoring a sold-out performance in Madison Square Garden, and starring in several highly successful comedy specials on HBO. And that was on top of her insanely famous Broadway career.

Roberta, ("Bobby" still to her fans and even herself), was outrageous and volatile. And now that she was a woman, she had switched her politics from bomb throwing liberal to a bomb making Libertarian. She felt she owed it to the women of America and to family values. She was also supposedly best friends with Jay C. Montgomery, a backup point guard with the Lakers. Thus, while she might not have any balls anymore, she did have two seats on the floor at Staples Center, and those were much more valuable.

Brendan felt a certain kinship with Ms. Monzon even though he had never met her. Perhaps it was merely that an aging comedy writer has more in common with a female transsexual than anyone else in show business. Their life experiences at the hands of bosses and surgeons are strikingly similar: both are left with something definitely missing. He knew he could relate to her on numerous levels except he also knew he had to keep his smoldering hostility toward women (nurtured by fifteen years of working for them) at bay lest she think he considered her equally suspect. In truth, Brendan thought of Roberta as a male spy: a man who had gone deep under cover and paid the ultimate sacrifice to infiltrate the enemy. He also knew that she was a Carol Burnett freak, and Brendan had written for Carol for several years, so he knew he could trade on that "special" relationship whenever necessary. Even so, Brendan still had no idea how to approach her. Should he flirt with her and pretend he wanted "to boldly go where no man had gone before"? (Post-surgery) Or should he treat her like a guy? He couldn't figure out if a transsexual woman hated men, and that's why she became a woman; or else she loved men because now men might want to fuck her. He forgot about the lesbian part.

CHAPTER THIRTEEN

On the first day of the new television season and what would be the dwindling weeks of his career, Brendan was surprised to see Roberta Monzon coming down the hall outside the make-up room. Usually, the co-hosts didn't arrive until just as the morning meeting was starting but always before Mugsy would roll in, ten minutes late like clockwork, breathless in her tennis sweats, straight from her morning workout, and with her tortured "Jackie O" bouffant hair smeared on her forehead and neck.

So when Brendan saw Roberta lumbering around the corner on her way to the make-up room a full half-hour early, he knew it was a sign of no good thing to come. She had a scowl on her morning face that matched the one on the Japanese warlord that was tattooed on her upper arm. She wore dark blue, cut-off sweats that looked, not as if she'd just slept in them, but that she had *lived* in them as well while sleeping in the back of a Camry. She was barefoot. Of all the things that were vile and repugnant about her, going barefoot at work was the most distasteful to Brendan. The vision of what this man/woman's fat feet probably looked like at the end of the day almost made him dry heave.

There was no avoiding her since they were the only two in the hallway. Roberta looked at him in a sort of curled-lip Elvis way as they approached each other, and she continued to eye him menacingly as the distance between them closed.

"Hi, Roberta," Brendan said. "Welcome to the show."

Roberta's gaze and demeanor did not waver. Brendan then realized she was listening to a show tune on her iPod and doing that Broadway vixen walk to whatever she was listening to. She was on stage, and Brendan was the hapless audience.

When they got close enough to where any normal person would have at least acknowledged him as a fellow human being, Roberta merely did a tough girl chin-jerk as her salutation. It was the manly nod of a cop, a coach, or a short order cook. Or maybe just the nod of a man, now woman, turned lesbian to satisfy her boy-born needs. It was a nod that was, at once, menacing and collegial. It might have even carried a wink along with it if Roberta's nature had been more benign. But all that came across to Brendan that morning was the nod of a thug who was allowing Brendan to exist on her turf, temporarily.

Roberta quickly turned and went into the empty make-up room. It would be her first time getting made-up with the other co-hosts for her first show. Brendan quickly pretended he was heading elsewhere and continued on past the door and around the corner toward Marge's dressing room. When he heard the make-up room door close, he turned around and headed back toward his office but glanced through the window of the door to see Roberta casually, but decisively, take Beverly's chair in the center of the co-host line in front of the mirrors. Then Roberta thumbed her way to a new track on her iPod, put her bare feet up on the counter which was full of cosmetics and beauty supplies, and lovingly smirked at her lumpy, unmade-up face in the mirror which, at this hour, looked as if her "man-ness" was making a comeback. Without averting her gaze, she then menacingly began to silently sing the lyrics to the Amy Winehouse tune, "Rehab" by mouthing, "They tried to make me go to rehab, but I said, 'No, no, no,'" at her image in the mirror with a knowing, defiant lip curl and an understated, ultra-cool, head and neck roll to the beat. Then she leaned back, closed her eyes, and waited for the others to arrive.

"I always show up early. That's the way I like it," Roberta said when the staff and other co-hosts started filing into the meeting. "I like to get to a new place early and get ready. Sort of like the first day of school with all my new school supplies."

"Good for you, Roberta." Marge said to her jokingly. "Just don't make it a habit". They both laughed.

Beverly arrived, already made up from a morning show appearance, and then Bambi. And then, finally, Moonie Brown. There was an unmistakable chill in the air when she came through the door since everyone knew there was already bad blood between Moonie and Roberta. Roberta did another non-committal nod as her official acknowledgement. Moonie merely sailed on by and headed to her industrial strength chair whose distressed seat cushion had to be fumigated and disinfected after each session.

Brendan took his seat in the back and picked up a newspaper so as to not have the morning be a complete waste of time. Mugsy, ten minutes late per usual, entered expounding meaninglessly on what she had seen on "Charlie Rose" the night before, and each of the co-hosts prepared to stake out their reactions to whatever issues might be raised. The long suffering researcher, Keelin Lambek took her seat next to the phone. Bad Bob sat in a chair in the front but with his back against the side wall. It was position of hoped-for power and control, but it definitely lacked conviction. Consequently, he was relegated to the role of a weak (as opposed to a "Greek") chorus while the real power in the room floated among the women.

Whenever Beverly deigned to do the show, she always began speaking the moment she sat down regardless of who else had, or had not, arrived. The meeting started when she showed up, and not a moment sooner or later. She always began with a personal story of what had happened to her the evening before or a phone call from some celebrity or war criminal. If that wasn't available it would be a performance she'd seen that had reminded her of herself or related in some way to her career. Or she might "reluctantly" share her very vaunted appearance at an unattainable venue, an award bestowed upon her, a deserved honor received, or a news story that related to an interview she'd done that scooped it and that she was in the process of promoting. In any event, it always involved a clip or prop of some kind: such as the invitation to the event, the actual letter or card, the menu, the party favor, or a stolen artifact to prove positively that she had been where no mere mortal could have gone. The prop or clip also served to deflect, although only slightly, the self-serving aspect of the story. It was as though the presence of an artifact or video clip raised her solipsism to the level of history, albeit ersatz history at best.

Thus, Beverly always presented her most self-serving anecdotes as if she were doing a service to the show, the medium of television itself, and the country as a whole by giving up the minutiae of her life which were far grander than anyone else's existence could possibly be.

"I brought you all soap with the presidential seal embossed on it from the White House ladies' room. No one saw me take it, but I wanted you to see what I was washing my hands with after using the facilities. I thought it would be fun. I'll let you pretend to wash with it on the air. And I think we have footage of me shaking hands with the president afterwards," she announced one morning, pulling off a television "trifecta" by combining celebrity, inside information, and the toilet all in one story.

On Roberta's first day, everyone was on their best behavior except, of course, Roberta who seemed hell-bent on marking her territory as the savior of the show—the one who would lift it from being a coffee klatch of mindless women talking about diets to an hour providing real relevance and life-changing information. By that, she was trying to out-Oprah Oprah with whom she was in a smoldering feud over her intimations to the press that Oprah was gay, or, at least, "gay-curious".

Bambi Crutchfield was the "young one" on the panel who had embraced her married name harder than she had her husband on their wedding night. Brendan would occasionally call her by her maiden name, "Anna Terrasovik", to remind her of her roots and let her know that he knew where she came from. He considered it his civic duty to refresh Bambi's memory of her humble origins in Father Panik Village, a desperate housing project in Bridgeport, Connecticut that she had escaped from and never looked back. As one of the few white girls in "The Vill" she was used to standing out, but she kept her naturally blonde hair jet black to pass as a Latina in order to snare an over-looked "full house" scholarship to Brown for any disadvantaged child excelling in Greek and Latin. The scholarship was so eagerly remunerative once they actually found someone who qualified, and Bambi was so incredibly pain-in-the-ass penurious, that she was able to bank $50,000 free and clear by the time she graduated. Along the way, she latched on to Ben Crutchfield who had always promoted himself as a "Kennedy", despite his name, because his mother was some sort of cousin to the clan.

Once Bambi got out of Father Panik and landed in Providence she took the name of the town as prophetic. The first thing she did was dye her hair back to golden blonde and change her major to Theater Arts. After which she proceeded to fuck every professor smart enough to give her an "A". With that kind of academic prowess proceeding her, she was quickly passed up to the head of the Drama Department who promptly proclaimed her Summa Cum Laude and would have endowed a chair in her honor, if not a bed, such was Bambi's talent for taking direction. But Bambi was a pouty "finger shaker", despite her humble origins, which made her professors feel that *they'd* been taught a lesson every time they got "finger-shooked" after sex.

Ben "Crusher" Crutchfield had been the heavyweight Ivy League wrestling champion for three years at Brown and even enjoyed a mediocre run as a professional wrestler before retiring from the ring to become an executive with the WWE. But his real job, because of his political connections, was to guide Linda (Mrs. Vince) McMahon in her bid for public office in Connecticut. When that didn't pan out, the Crutchfields moved west to spread their Kennedy magic in LA.

If nothing else, Bambi Crutchfield was lucky. Luckier than even the Kennedys she now thought she was one of. The Kennedys had always wanted to be in show business but had settled for politics because politics was easier to pull off despite the fact that their particular dedication to public service had ended up killing more people, including themselves, than a small war.

Bambi had landed on "The Ladies' Room" mainly because, as her luck would have it, she looked exactly like the shiksa dolls that Beverly Frost had played with as a little girl in San Francisco and whose make-believe lives of ease and acceptance she had fantasized about until she got her period at age 9. (Beverly's mother had always told her that she was the youngest girl in the Northern California to get her period; and Beverly, confused but proud, had always taken this as an achievement.)

Bambi was perfectly formed, just like those dolls, and her Ukrainian hair had been bleached out to the exact Kennedy girlfriend hue (roughly within the blonde spectrum of Mary Jo Kopechne, Paige Lee Hufty, Marilyn Monroe, Daryl Hannah, and that straight-haired ice queen from "The West Wing" who went with the Lawford boy) in order to net the only "Kennedy" on the Brown campus at the time, Ben Crutchfield. It had worked almost too easily. Blonde was a bait that no Kennedy could resist. It was better than DNA in establishing a true Kennedy blood line. Little did she know, as her luck would have it, that little half-Jewish Beverly Frost from San Francisco would fall for the same ever-retreating vision of American perfection that the Kennedys promised. And of course, Beverly, being one of the greatest Kennedy sniffers of all time (after Lorne Michaels), was perfectly set up to discover Bambi working as a part time food stylist on "Good Morning, LA" when Beverly appeared there to promote her flirtatious softball interview with Slobodan Milosevic, the "Butcher of Belgrade" whom she found to be "a *most* fascinating world leader and ethnic cleanser".

Bambi Crutchfield went from holiday food stylist (her special-ty was food that looked like flags) to network co-host in one fell swoop. Along the way, she also became the official spokesperson for OPEC thanks to the fact that she thought Aramco was a big box dis-count store. Bambi loved oil and especially Persians, as she called all Arab derivatives who arrived in this country with money and a Kennedy sized lust for blondes. She would defend the oil compa-nies to her last day. After all, they were just like her: all energy and no conscience.

On that first morning with Roberta, Bambi walked into a buzz saw completely oblivious to the shredding that Roberta was capable of inflicting. The subject of teenage abortion was brought up for "CrossTalk" because of an article arguing that teenage girls should be able to get one without parental consent.

"I just think that is way out of line," Bambi began, automatically taking a hard line. She didn't even lift her head up from the news digest she was reading when she said it. "I mean, what's this world coming to when kids can just run out and get an abortion, like a piercing? It promotes promiscuity. It even rewards teenage sex. Because these girls probably wear their little abortions around like badges of honor. I mean, that's just what I think. Abortion. It isn't right. For teens. Or parents."

Bambi had a way of running on with little bites of declarative prattle that made her self-satisfied "Tinker Bell" voice feel like a tin spoon being drummed on the top of your head. Her scattered thoughts at the end of her sentences sputtered on like the engine of an old car after the ignition has been turned off.

"It's a little more complicated than that, dear," Roberta replied in a low rumble that attempted to smother her automatic rage at Bambi's seemingly charmed Kennedy life. Roberta kept her chin on her chest contemplating her stubby, fingernail-bitten, mannish fingers that the sex change had failed to alter.

"That's great. Don't do it here. Save it for the show," Bad Bob piped up from the side.

"I think it's ridiculous to give kids that kind of freedom. To do whatever they want. Where are the parents?" Bambi went on. "They're nowhere. The parents. Nowhere."

"You don't know," Roberta growled. But Bambi didn't hear her.

"You get all these kids. Having sex willy-nilly. And then not taking responsibility for it and just pulling the plug. Or whatever they do when they kill the baby. And everybody just walks away happy as a clam. Or something."

The room fell silent. Roberta's shoulders got bigger and rounder and, from the back where Brendan was sitting, her head was almost overtaken by the back of her neck which swelled with rage.

"That's bullshit!" Roberta exploded while doing a "dinosaur take". "Bullshit, bullshit, bullshit!"

Roberta turned in her chair to face Bambi. She looked like a Brontosaurus who had just lifted its head, mid-gulp, up out of a swamp at the sound of an intruder, with weeds and shit streaming down from its mouth. As "dinosaur takes" ran, it was better than Gleason's on "The Honeymooners". Bambi, however, was oblivious to how close she was sitting to her own destruction. She smiled sweetly at Roberta and blinked several times as if that sparkle, alone, could diffuse whatever kind of bad day Roberta was having.

"What?" Bambi said crisply, like a ditsy teenager hiding a baby bump. "Why should teenage girls have free reign? To kill fetuses after school," she said quoting a Scientology hand-out she'd read on the toilet and been converted on the spot—as long as she could still be known as a Kennedy-type, *Catholic* Scientologist, like Katie Holmes.

This caused Roberta to rise out of her chair, stand up, and take a step closer to Bambi's chair. Brendan would later learn that this was always an indication, on Roberta's part, that the conversation was not going well.

"If you were sucked off every night of your life, from age eight to eighteen, by your mother while your father slept in the next room with his ear to the wall, and you felt powerless to do anything about

Andrew Smith

it or say anything until after your father killed your mother in front of you; not to stop her from fucking you but because she blew the family nest egg at the track, maybe you'd feel differently about what some teenagers have to do after school to survive," Roberta said taking the argument from A to Z.

Bambi did not back down. But her steadfastness was more out of genuine curiosity than any moral conviction or courage. She blinked benignly several times at Roberta's gnarled up face like a hostage sending a secret message.

"But wasn't that when you were a boy?" Bambi chirped.

"I fucked *her*!" Roberta bellowed. "My mother taught me how to have sex...with *her*! And I thought it was because she loved me."

"Oh." Bambi said with a twinkle, registering only mild shock. "Well, maybe she did. In her way. But that's not very nice. I'm sorry for you. And for her," she parsed out thoughtfully in little cheerful spurts. "But at least you couldn't get pregnant," she said as an afterthought.

"But *she* did," Roberta said. "And I went to three abortions with her because the babies were *mine*. But what I *really* needed was an abortion for my brain," Roberta spit out, tapping the side of her head, "But I couldn't get one. Because of people like you."

Now they were both way off base. The staff in the room was frozen in time like the baked citizens of Pompei after *their* eruption.

"Darlings," Beverly broke in, "My triplets live in North Dakota. They're really not interested. It's too local. Let's move on," she said as if responding to a perfectly normal exchange. "I have a story about a cab ride I took last night. Now, I haven't been in a yellow cab in years, but my regular driver had a heart attack while waiting for me outside of Bouchon and had to be taken to the emergency room at Cedars where he eventually died. So when I came out of the restaurant after dinner, there I was, left with nothing but his illegally parked town car. Well, thank God I'd taken my purse. But dear Barry flagged down a cab as if nothing happened, and the next thing you know, there I was in one of those Yellow Cabs that

130

people go to the airport in for the first time in *ages*. Now, here's what's interesting. On that little television screen they have now in the back seat, the next thing I know; there I was, talking to *me*. I couldn't believe it. I was fascinated. I mean, what are the chances? And I watched myself the whole way home. So I think what the discussion might be is have any of you ever seen yourself in a strange situation like the back seat of a cab, or maybe in Dodgers Stadium on the Jumbotron where, incidentally, I was the first female anchor to ever be displayed there and have been seen on that Jumbotron and the one in Times Square more times and by more people than any other news anchor *or* celebrity, for that matter, of any kind. I think we have footage of the last time they had me up on the one at Staples Center." She turned to Bad Bob, "Robert? Could you.....?"

"I'll get right on it." Bob said bouncing out of his high director's chair and heading for the phone, arms flapping, to order up footage of, not only Beverly's last Jumbotron appearance, but also the so-called ambush taxi performance which, of course, she had taped months ago with full hair and make-up after intense negotiations in which she insisted on owning the taxi tape outright after a window of only three weeks. Bringing it up as part of "CrossTalk" on "The Ladies' Room" was a good way to promote both it and herself. Beverly always had an angle.

In fact, virtually unknown and unannounced to anyone on "The Ladies' Room", Beverly and Bad Bob had made a deal with the Los Angeles Department of Transportation to produce an original and exclusive weekly clip for taxi cabs featuring Beverly and, later on, Bad Bob in a sort of home-style chat show like the old radio breakfast shows direct from their "living room." Beverly wanted to be the first person to produce original content for "TaxiTV" which is what the backseat broadcast came to be called. The venture, which included taxis in Chicago and New York soon became competitive to "The Ladies' Room" merely because Beverly could not help winning a "get" even if it meant scooping herself. She would poach celebrity guests from her own network show to appear with her on her taxi cab vanity production, and often she would withhold information during an interview on "The Ladies' Room" in order to "break" the story in the back seat of a cab to the one or two bored passengers on their way to LAX. No-one really cared since "TaxiTV" would never be competitive with the network, but the segment producers of "The Ladies' Room" resented Beverly's "PermaFrost" retainer/ producer trolling the production offices for research and pre-interview packets for stars that were slated to appear on both shows. Remuneration to anyone but herself was like healthcare to her PermaFrost micro-staff: nonexistent. But Beverly treated this minor backseat start-up and star-turn as if it were the roll-out of a prime-time series. She had lost the ability to distinguish between the real and the bullshit just as long as the star and central figure, in either case, was herself.

"Wha?" said Marge as if she had just woken up when the taxi story appeared to be a foregone conclusion as a "CrossTalk" topic.

"Okay. So it's a pass on the kids and abortion, but we've got Beverly's wild taxi ride, and did anyone see what happened last night on 'Charlie Rose'?" Mugsy pressed on.

The room fell silent since no one, especially in that crowd, ever bothered to watch the latest installment of "Charlie Rose" except Mugsy for whom it was the Rosetta stone of all knowledge. She also knew Charlie was perennially single and thus available to be snared and paraded around in front of Bad Bob to teach him a lesson.

Of course, Mugsy was oblivious to the resounding non-reaction because she had momentarily lapsed into a deep pose, hair-poof, and pout in the mirrors on the opposite wall in mid-sentence like some addled post-traumatic stress victim. (Mugsy had "post-traumatic *tress* syndrome"). It was the only reason she chose to sit on top of the counter during the meetings. It enabled her to get a clear shot of herself in the multitude of mirrors over the heads of the co-hosts. For that brief shining moment in the morning, Mugsy Muggeridge was the star of "The Ladies' Room", all by herself, as it should be.

"I wanna give a shout-out to my main man, Lebron, who was with me at the openin' of my new celebrity nail salon last night." Moonie chimed in.

"Whaddya mean *your* nail salon?" Roberta quickly shot back. "You have a nail salon now?"

"The Moonie Brown Celebrity Nail Salon and Massage Center—-worldwide," she said proudly.

"Why not throw in "weight loss" while you're at it." Roberta tossed out while shifting her own considerable ass in her chair. The air in the room became electric again. The two were at it already, and they hadn't even debuted together "on air" yet.

Moonie looked down at her lap which was easy to do since it occupied everything visible from her throat to her swollen feet. She thought long and hard about how to respond, smoothing out the creases in the house painter's drop cloth they had to throw over her to do her make-up.

"Why that's a good idea, Miss Roberta." She said sounding like a southern belle. "I think I will do just that. It would diversify the venture capital exposure and increase return on first quarter earnings while improving the business plan and balance sheet projections." There was a pause. All eyes were on Roberta.

"Hell, even *I* might show up at one then." She said, making a joke of the confrontation and releasing the tension.

"I won't have you two going at each other on my show," Beverly said. "It's the first day of the new season and our new co-host, so let's all try to get along."

"Ladies it's getting late," Mugsy said trying to change all the subjects at once. "Can we move on?"

"How about something with some laughs?" Roberta ventured. "Enough with the heavy stuff."

At that moment the door to the make-up room opened, and a woman who looked like Eva Braun's personal trainer walked in.

"Ladies and gentlemen, this is Jet, my make-up artist and hair stylist." Roberta said grandly.

Jet gave a wave to the room like Richard Nixon's goodbye in the door of the helicopter. She appeared to be half woman, half android. The geometric haircut she wore looked like a Nazi helmet. She was thin, fit, and, had it been a James Bond movie instead of a daytime women's talk show, she would have been easily recognizable as the fun new villain: over the top, but deadly. But at 7:00 in the morning in the make-up room, the menace was palatable; and everyone instinctively felt intimidated and uncomfortable.

"Can we try to wrap this up?" Mugsy's sweat was coagulating in her workout pants, and she had exhausted her "looks" and hair style combinations. She longed for a new mirror, new lighting, and a shower.

"I like this one about the black teenagers objecting to the "white sale" at the local department store. Any time Al Sharpton gets involved it's good for us." Moonie said looking over the list of news stories for that day.

"What's the discussion?" Marge wanted to know. "Linens N' Things or Al Sharpton? You're not going to tell me 'White sales' are racist?"

"No more racist than goin' to the 'dark side' or the black keys on the piano not soundin' as good as the white ones. Shoot. You even stole chocolate from us and made white chocolate the more expensive one."

"Let's do it." Bad Bob said taking his seat again. "Save it for the show."

"Okay, we've got Beverly and the taxi, the Jumbotron and your face in Dodgers Stadium, Chocolate..."

"And 'white sales'," Moonie added

"They're the same thing. The whole 'are white sales racist?' leading into a 'black is bad' discussion, a shout out to Lebron, Moonie's new store on La Cienega...We have three segments, so we could use something else."

"Does anyone realize that Queen Elizabeth still has 'Ladies in Waiting'?" Beverly began. "I would have never imagined." Nobody reacted. They had had enough Beverly for the morning. "Does anyone care anymore? I mean what would you do if you had a 'Lady in Waiting'?" Beverly persisted.

"I'd make her retain for me," Roberta quipped.

Everyone laughed and took the laugh as an excuse to forget Beverly's topic altogether.

"I was reading this morning about the situation in the Congo where they're making women perform their own clitoral circumcisions. It's a total human rights disaster, and no one cares," Marge said.

"Self-circumcision. That smarts. You think the men have to do it, too?" Mugsy said pouting at herself.

"I doubt it," Marge said. "They're too busy trying on mud for the big dance.

"Allow me to say something interesting about that," Beverly said. "When I first interviewed Nelson Mandela, who by the way, was *very* sexy; and his aides told me he was interested in me, but I would have nothing to do with him..."

"...Once you go Black, BF....." Moonie teased.

"Well, of course, I kick myself now, because I think he was the *most* handsome man and had such charisma that you can't imagine him being under house arrest for twenty-five years. What a waste!"

"Unless you were under house arrest with him," Marge added.

"Please. I'll tell you all the whole story later," Beverly said enjoying the notion that she actually might have a sexual appetite. She glanced around the room indicating that the rest of the staff, although necessary to put on the actual show, were completely unworthy to hear her confidences. "Anyway, one of the things that Mandela brought up was the fact that Africa is superfluous to the rest of the world even though it's an entire continent. He felt that if he had been imprisoned in Europe or the United States he would have been out in eighteen months." Then she turned to Bad Bob again, "Robert...?"

Bad Bob jumped up immediately and headed for the phone, "We can get the quote," he said.

His chair really should have been near the phone, but then he would not have been positioned on the same "power plane" as Beverly and the other co-hosts. To remedy this, he had wedged his chair sideways into the corner which put him, technically, in front of Beverly and the other co-host's chairs but, alas, still superfluous. Only Mugsy seated on the counter facing them all was ahead of him, but she didn't count because she was completely under his control, and had sucked his cock at one time, so it was okay.

"Well, if we're going to talk about that, then I'd like to bring up this whole thing about children's work shoes," Roberta said. "There's this company in Indiana that makes children's work shoes and is actually selling them."

"To whom? Kathy Lee?" Marge quipped.

"No, to China. Really. Isn't that a hoot?" Roberta said. The tension in the room was back to where it should be. Everyone loved the work shoe story and immediately wanted to riff on it in the "CrossTalk" segment.

"Explain to me again about the children and their shoes," Beverly said who had zoned out thinking about exactly which Mandela sound bite showcased her the best.

"It's a crazy item about somebody making work shoes in children's sizes and selling them to China," Mugsy told her.

"Oh," Beverly said, "I see. And the next thing you know they'll have the same thing for toddlers."

"Right," Marge said as if humoring her grandmother, "Booties with union toes."

"Whatever. But I'm from North Dakota. What do I care about unions?"

It was Beverly's standard "kill" for any topic that didn't relate directly to her. Her idea was that "North Dakota", where her triplet daughters lived, was the archetypal "Heartland" of America, the non-New York.

"Anyway, I'm sure you'll make it funny," Beverly said signing off on a topic she still didn't get, "I'll just laugh." It was Beverly's version of being a "team player".

"And this being Roberta's first day...." Mugsy continued. But most of the staff assumed the meeting was over and had signaled as much by standing and checking each other's list. "Listen up, everyone," she shouted over the din. "We're giving away milk and cookies today, thanks to Roberta...."

"...And Nabisco...," Roberta added.

"Right. Roberta will do the plug, and also Roberta will do our first give- away which is," she had to look at her notes, "Steak knives from Brookstone's in the Beverly Center."

Roberta loved giving stuff away whether it was her own money or somebody else's. Part of her deal for coming on the show was that the audience would be treated as her personal guests as if they were there for a massive slumber party. Roberta would have had them all dressed in "jammies" if she could have and seated in the round. It was widely attributed to her magnanimous "down-home" anti-celebrity nature; but, in truth, her generosity was compensation for her insecurity and the deep insatiable feeling inside her that she, by herself alone, was never sufficient for anyone to care about (other than her mother). Hence, the over the top gifts to staff and strangers and the gift of sex to her mother in order to secure the attention and love that a normal son should have freely enjoyed.

Brendan rose out of his chair in the back of the room and approached Marge to find out her specific take on each of the topics. It was a pro forma meeting since Marge was already deep into her hair and its configuration and was already miffed at the hijacking of the "CrossTalk" segments, once again, by Beverly.

After fifteen years of doing the show each morning, Marge didn't really care about the material as much as she cared about how she looked. She was at a time in her life and career where the preservation of looks trumped all else including the very thing, comedy, which had brought her to that point in the first place. Vanity was "Job Number One". It was no longer as important to be funny as it was to look like the person who *once* was funny. She was hoping that the momentum of the audience's memory would carry her further than any new comedy material could, the way people would laugh at Bob Hope the minute he walked into a room, before he even uttered a word, just because they were reminded of how funny he was, or was supposed to be, just by him showing up.

"What?" Marge said slightly annoyed as her head descended backwards into the sink to get her hair washed. "How do you like our new "girl?" she said with a perfect comic arch of her eyebrows. Then she closed her eyes and shook her head as if rejecting a product sample she'd been hired to taste.

"She's great. Good television," Brendan said dutifully standing by her wet head like a male nurse or else Tom Hagen in "The Godfather", lethally armed but with a quiet patience that only underscored his deadly capabilities.

"What-ever," Marge said with her eyes now closed against the water. "And how about the 'Me Generation'?" It was her code word for Beverly's solipsism.

"Yeah, the beat goes on. She's a journalist, you know." Brendan said facetiously. "Do you think they'll *ever* be able to pull that Mandela tape in time for the show?" He was being sarcastic as well.

"*Please.*" Marge said in disgust. "'The Examiner' is in full force today. I'm not going to fight it. I plan to 'sit heavily'."

Sometimes Marge often referred to Beverly as "The Examiner" which was short for "The Medical Examiner" which was short for the inscription over the door of the New York City Morgue which begins, "Let all laughter cease..." That's what Marge claimed happened any time Beverly came around. She was a comedian's worst nightmare: a comedy killer; a person who lit up a room by leaving it. "Sitting heavily" was a phrase taught to Marge by a beloved nun to describe the act of "remaining"—sitting in a group without comment or visible reaction but being, at the same time, fully aware of the resulting negative impact.

Marge's decision to "sit heavily" or "remain" meant Brendan was on his own to come up with an attitude for her and the lines she would nonetheless demand, be critical of, but never use. It was a morning ritual and charade, endlessly repeated, with nothing to show for it but a pay check at the end of the week and file boxes bursting with fifteen years of unused and unseen material that Brendan studiously kept in order to have, at least, some physical evidence of his existence and labor upon this earth. He needed the files piling up year after year because he was too lazy and offended to witness much of the very same material in Marge's comedy act which she plied each weekend, at fifty grand a pop, and which could have equally validated his efforts.

CHAPTER FOURTEEN

"Where have you *been*?" The Wife demanded when Brendan got home after his first day with Roberta. "What happened to you?" she continued as if he'd just entered their Laurel Canyon bungalow wearing a South Pole parka and sporting a beard embedded with icicles.

It stopped Brendan in his tracks. Was she really in a quandary over his whereabouts, or was it just a bad reading of an otherwise benign greeting?

"Just working," he said finally. "It was Roberta's first show. I thought I should stick around."

"Oh. How was it?" She was genuinely interested now. She mostly saw his life as street theater, diverting but utterly disposable; and certainly not anything with any real content like the Governor's.

"Hold onto your hat," Brendan said taking his shoes and pants off and putting them in the closet, per her orders, and where she would have had him sleep, as well, if there had been room. It was the husband "footprint" thing.

"What's that supposed to mean?" she said actually looking at him for the first time.

"Roberta is all about fireworks. That's why she's great. But I don't think the show is big enough for all of them."

"You mean, Moonie?"

"Moonie, Beverly, Bambi, and Marge. There's a lot of shit flying around. Lot of turfing going on. Even Liz, the booker, is repositioning herself so she can be closer to Roberta than Norman is. She patrols the halls all hunched over. Everything she says is cautionary and conspiratorial. But nothing is attributable to her because she ends every statement with the caveat, 'Don't shoot the messenger' or 'don't quote me' which is supposed to mean that a) she she's on your side, but b) she can't help you."

"Oh, how exciting. But they still need you."

"For what?" Brendan said candidly.

"Is Roberta nice to you? Are you writing for her?"

"She's hard to get to. I offered to, but she doesn't want anything. Least of all, a man with a dick. She's got anger from two sex changes ago," Brendan said and laughed so that at least he'd give himself some acknowledgement. "I think she's afraid I'll try to fuck her."

The Wife dropped her dish towel and held Brendan by the shoulders like a concerned father.

"Now, Brendan, I don't want you to do that. Don't even kid around. Trust me on this."

"On what?"

"I've been a woman longer than she has, so I know more about how she feels than she does."

"She doesn't like heterosexual men."

"Of course not. Who does?" The Wife said without realizing the implication.

"I don't know if I can break through to her. She's a tough nut."

"Used to be," The Wife said. "Now she's a tough 'you know what'."

"Cunt? In her dreams. God knows what hell she's got down there. She probably had a vagina tattooed on her crotch. She's got dragons crawling up her fat calves. I caught a glimpse of them this morning. She looks like a biker, only with shaved legs. But it'll all be interesting, and she can really stir the pot. You know what she told us today? She said you can always tell a lesbian because lesbians have well-trimmed fingernails. They keep them short for sex, so they don't hurt each other when they stick their fingers up inside themselves. Then she showed us hers. She says she and Lois, her wife, take a weekend off once a month to just fuck. I was impressed. I'll have to ask Rosie O'Donnell about that the next time she comes on the show. Rosie must be freaking out. I don't know if Roberta is good for lesbians or bad. I know Rosie wouldn't be interested because Roberta's too ugly, and she still has that "man" thing about her. That would turn Rosie off. But on the other hand she *has* got a story, if it's true. And that would immediately endear her to her.

"But the whole thing would be so confusing. Like that scene from 'Chinatown'". Brendan started slapping himself on alternate sides of his face, "Man-woman-man-woman. Rosie wouldn't know whether to hug her or kick her in her nonexistent balls."

Brendan had lapsed into a stand-up routine, and this had ended the conversation with The Wife.

She had left the room after the "well-trimmed fingernails"

"I think we should get a dog," he shouted after her, apropos of nothing.

"No!" came the answer from Zeke's room. Zeke came out of his room in his pajamas and addressed his father.

"Are we really getting a dog, Dad?

"No!" said The Wife following the kid out. "There will be no dogs in my house."

"But I'll take care of it," Brendan said.

"I get enough dogs with the Governor. He has two Goldens, and they jump all over me like a piece of meat."

"There, see? They like you, they really like you." Brendan said.

"He has handlers who take care of them, bathe them, walk them, and feed them," she said. "All he does is show up on the weekends like a hero. They smell better than I do."

"That'll be our secret, I swear," Brendan said smiling.

"Come on, mom. Let's get a dog," Zeke persisted.

"We'll talk about it, but not while we're living here. I'm not going to go to that stupid dog park over on Beverly Glen."

"How about we get one on Memorial Day when you and Zeke move out to the beach for the summer," Brendan said.

"And what happens when we move back to Hollywood on Labor Day?"

"We kill it," Brendan said. "It's a dog."

"Dad!" Zeke shouted sounding like "Tommy" from the "Lassie" movies. But Tommy was acting. Zeke was serious.

"All right. Then maybe I just take the dog for a ride. Just me and the dog—out for a little "spin", if you get my drift," Brendan dropped into his mobster voice for effect. "But out of consideration for you, my friend, I shall make sure we stop in a good neighborhood. No stray nothin' ever starved to death on Roxberry in Beverly Hills. You can go to sleep on that."

"No more dog talk. We're not getting a dog, and that's it," The Wife said.

"Can Zeke and I at least look through a book?"

"All right. But I'll get the book," she said exerting control over all reading material in the house like a Soviet Bloc commissar.

"Right, because if I got it, it might be a dog porno book."

"Cool," said Zeke.

"See? Thanks a lot," The Wife said seriously glaring at Brendan as if he really did have a copy of "Bitches Gone Wild".

"The trouble with you is you didn't grow up with a dog."

"And who do you think will end up taking care of it?" she said.

"I will ...and Zeke"

"Dad," Zeke warned again.

"Okay, "I'll take care of it and give Zeke the credit. A boy and his dog. It'll be like having a brother with a collar...and a license."

"No", The Wife said. "We're already getting a new baby." Brendan had forgotten about the IVF. Apparently, his sperm was still in play.

"How 'bout a fur coat?" Brendan said. "And I'll take care of that, too. I'll walk it around the neighborhood twice a day. We can practice with a coat. You'll see. It'll become part of the family. Zeke can pet it and sleep with it at night."

"A fur coat doesn't eat." The Wife said.

"Oh yeah?" Brendan said, "Ever been to The Ivy on Thursday nights?"

"What's he talking about?" Zeke said.

"Daddy's doing material. You go to bed."

"Does that mean we're not getting a dog? Ever?" Zeke said.

"Not right now, Sweetie" The Wife told him. "Maybe when your father grows up."

Zeke looked at his father. Brendan was standing in his boxer shorts with his baseball cap still on and still holding his gym bag full of papers that made him look like a homeless plumber.

"You're not like other dads," Zeke proclaimed, and he didn't mean it as a compliment for Brendan's individuality.

"I'm not?" Brendan said in mock horror.

"Zeke's right." The Wife added, "There's something seriously wrong with you. You're not like other men."

"Gee, I guess that means me coming to your school for career day is definitely out," Brendan said facetiously with a fist pump like a "Little Rascal".

"You don't make enough money." Zeke told him. "Why don't you write for a hedge fund?"

"I'll look into it," Brendan told him. Zeke and his mother had already turned away and were heading down the hall. "I mean it. I'll really look into that. Those guys always think they're the funniest guys in the room. Like advertising fucks in the sixties. Maybe I can punch up some of their e-mails, so they'll come off funny when they're indicted."

Brendan was now talking to no one. The Wife and Zeke had disappeared into the master bedroom where he was no longer welcome without a pass. Brendan continued on to Zeke's room and lay down on the bed that was already occupied by a menagerie of stuffed animals too cherished to throw away and too important to give their bed up to the man of the house. Brendan fell asleep on top of them nonetheless. The lumps felt familiar.

CHAPTER FIFTEEN

Since Beverly had alluded to his firing weeks before the fact, Brendan figured his first step in trying to amend the decision was to go back and deal directly with her; but he couldn't figure out exactly what the best way to approach her about it was. But then, in October, the show traveled to Las Vegas for a week; and Beverly Frost brought herself to him, instead.

Any man worth his dating "jones" knows in the first minute after meeting a woman at the beginning of a date if he is going to get laid at the end of it. Brendan remembered a long ago girlfriend who would signal her readiness by loosening her newly-washed and blown-dried blonde hair, piled luxuriously on top of her head, at the exact moment she opened the door to her apartment. The effect was stunning and always took his breath away as if, suddenly, he had found himself in the middle of a shampoo commercial. The fact that he knew it meant he would soon be having sex with her and could shove that hair up his ass if he wanted to only added to the expression of joy and gratitude on his face which, of course, the girl took merely as an appropriate response for her deigning to open the door for him in the first place.

So it was, when Brendan was suddenly summoned to Beverly Frost's suite at Caesar's Palace because "Beverly needed some lines for a charity roast" that he found himself strangely elated when a uniformed maid answered the door with an overly welcoming smile and graciously ushered him into a sitting room off the foyer of the main suite which was big enough to have hosted an orgy and probably had.

Rather than think he might fuck the agreeable maid, the thought immediately came to Brendan that he was, instead, going to fuck Beverly Frost that night. The suite *smelled* like he was. And Brendan was not opposed. It was the opening he was looking for. Besides, the idea of sticking his dick where Kissinger, Castro, and Geraldo Rivera had already been made him feel that some sort of fame was, at last, going to be thrust upon him. It was like finally getting his star on the Hollywood Walk of Fame.

"Oh, Mr. White. Señora Frost expecting you, yes," the maid said.

One wouldn't think that a perfunctory greeting such as that would indicate the promise (or demand) of sex, but since Beverly had never acknowledged Brendan before as anything other than a mere subject; and given the way the suite had been expensively perfumed for his benefit, the thought of sex with her immediately leapt into his head. On top of that, the place was lit as dim as a church, so he figured something was up.

"I was told Beverly wanted to see me."

"Oh yes!" the maid said.

Beverly Frost was one of those stars who traveled with a decorator—like Prince or Sandy Gallin. A single evening in a hotel or even a dressing room, much less a week, would necessitate a complete overhaul of the premises to accommodate her mood. Thus, the lavish Vegas suite that came replete with spitting dolphins, ceiling mirrors, a wet bar, and wetter hookers had been transformed by Ralphie the set guy into a Pacific Heights mansion. Brendan almost expected to see the Golden Gate Bridge rising majestically in the mist out of the windows instead of the ersatz Eiffel Tower in the hotel parking lot across the strip. Of course, this paroxysm of decorating indulgence was another lie in Beverly's life since she had officially grown up in the Lower Haight District; and closer to the Tenderloin than Pacific Heights or, especially, Woodside. The closest she ever got to a hunting lodge was when she lost her virginity in the back of Bill's Sporting Goods in Oakland where she worked as "Miss Ammo", dressed in a bandolier of shotgun shells, during deer season.

"You sit, no?" the maid said motioning to a table and two chairs that had been set up there. Brendan sat down and dutifully took out a small spiral notebook on which to, supposedly, take notes for whatever Beverly allegedly had in mind.

"You like drink?" the maid said nodding enthusiastically and smiling with wide eyes like she was about to witness an execution.

"Yeah, sure," he said. "That'd be nice."

"What kind?"

"Scotch," he told her. The maid then turned and took a new bottle of "Macallan Single Malt" out of a credenza. It had been bought especially for this occasion and was, thoughtfully, Brendan's brand. She opened it and generously poured out a full highball glass of the liquor without any ice as if it were apple juice.

"Whoa, easy there," he said and tried to stop her, but the maid thought he was just being polite and filled the large glass right to the brim as if she wanted to show him how generous she was.

"For you," she said offering it to him.

"Thank you. That's very nice." Brendan had to take a small sip before putting it down on the table so he wouldn't spill it.

"You want some more, it's right here," she said gesturing grandly toward the liquor bottle like Vanna White toward a vowel.

"Right," Brendan said. "Thank you," Obviously, this was not going to be your average story meeting.

Brendan looked around. There was no sign of Beverly, but he could hear some faint Frank Sinatra playing somewhere in the bowels of the suite. The place did smell great, though. No cheap Airwick "Stick-ups" for Beverly Frost. The place smelled like those wonderful dress shops Brendan's mother had often taken him to as a young boy, with rich old ladies' perfume mixing with laundered linen and the tart ping of undergarments. It was immediately exciting.

It reminded him of the time he gone to one of those lingerie joints on La Cienega with a hot, but unfamiliar, girl where the air inside bristled with static sexual electricity; and the girl, now given license, suddenly began to present herself to him in a parade of garter belts and teddies as if both of them were suddenly allowed to play out their separate sexual fantasies. It's the secret of upscale titty bars. Incredibly beautiful, but very proper looking, young women with clean flowing hair who cheerfully and willingly drop their one piece halter tops to expose their naked breasts without the slightest bit of urging on your part—exactly the way all men wish that all female encounters should be.

"Miss Beverly be right here. You stay." The maid said sweetly.

"Fine," Brendan said raising his hand to indicate that he was perfectly taken care of. She disappeared. There was silence. The room seemed to get dimmer, but Brendan decided he was imagining it. He looked around. Ralphie the set guy had out-done himself this time, he thought. The place was draped in browns and wine-colored reds. Only occasionally did the blare of Las Vegas hustle break through the tasteful, but hasty, re-decoration.

Brendan didn't know quite what to do sitting alone at the table. He took a sip out of the highball of straight Scotch. It was unfamiliarly tepid and harsh, but soothing nonetheless. There was silence except for the faint Sinatra playing non-stop. He looked around, unsure of exactly what he was supposed to do. He stood up momentarily and then sat down again. Then he took another sip of pure Scotch. He felt stupid and out of place.

Suddenly she was there. Beverly had somehow entered the room as if she had simply materialized within it. Her expensive perfume preceded her as she swept around the table, running her fingers along the tops of the lamp shades and then turning and sitting down dramatically into a primly seductive pose on the edge of the chair across from Brendan's. It was pure theater, and he was impressed.

Beverly looked great. Forget about her age; her people had put her together in spectacular fashion. She was made up as he had never seen her before. He could imagine her sitting before "Syd Vicious", saying, "Darlings, we're doing *sex*, tonight, not news. Pretend it's Colin Powell." She had a huge crush on the former Five Star General, Chairman of the Joint Chiefs of Staff, and Secretary of State and had openly told friends, "I wish Alma would O.D. on her anti-depressants so I could have him."

Brendan had no idea why she fancied him this particular evening unless it was something that happened to her whenever she went on location, and he hadn't known about it. "Location" does strange things to even the most disciplined players. And, best of all, everyone concerned knows "location doesn't count". Beverly must have picked that up from her first days doing "continuity" for Roger Corman at AIP after graduation. It was a job secured for her by an operative of the West Coast mob as a favor to her father. There had been no horse's head necessary in that transaction. Beverly *was* the horse, and she gave great head.

"How *are* you, darling," she said after sitting down as if Brendan were a long lost friend. He couldn't help recoil slightly and was unable to hide the somewhat shocked look on his face.

"Oh come, now, dear Brendan. Don't get all WASPy on me all of a sudden. We're in Las Vegas!" she said with a flourish.

She waved her hands above her head like a show girl. She wore a tight sleeveless turtleneck with a little extra "turtle" to take care of her ravaged neck. It was an old trick she'd learned from Katherine Hepburn to hide the neck wattles that had been missed in surgery. She'd learned that and to always have your hand at your chin for any portrait past the age of forty-five. And from Pamela Harriman she'd learned to open her mouth slightly for all "candids" at parties, red carpets, and casual meetings. Consequently, all pictures of Beverly Frost looked exactly alike: a slightly surprised, open mouthed smile as if inhaling a mouthful of rarified air, and just a girlish hint of that famous tongue. On anyone else it would've looked daffy.

"This is quite a set up you've got for yourself, Beverly," Brendan said, "It's *good* to be a star."

"Oh, darling, I never think of myself like that. You know me better than that." Then, in her best, faintly southern, coquette, "I'm just a little old townie from Pacific Heights where my daddy runs the liquor store."

"I didn't know your father did that," Brendan said, but of course, he did know. "No wonder you were so popular."

"I was *very* popular," she said with a look. At that point the maid reappeared silently with a glass of white wine on a silver tray. Beverly took it without acknowledging her and swung it over to clink with Brendan's tumbler of Scotch.

"Cheers, darling," she said and took a long, overly eager sip that would have been a gulp by anyone else and then put the glass back down on the table. The sip seemed to trigger a tipsiness that had been lurking just beneath the surface.

"You know something about you, Brendan? She went on, "You *get* it," she said leaning forward and making a grabbing motion in the air with her hand as if she were catching a fly. "You. Get. *It*."

"I try to," Brendan replied making sure he stayed with her suddenly drunken bullshit.

He had never been this close to her face before. Her lips were dry and cracked and slightly ajar exposing the tip of that famous, accommodating tongue. He could see the exquisite make-up job, the eye liner, and the faint outline of the two, small, shoulder pad-shaped implants her plastic surgeon had inserted just beneath her cheek bones to preserve the architecture of her face. During the years that Brendan had worked for her, the sunken recesses at the center of each cheek would deepen when the contents of whatever fix had been injected there would wear off. She would begin to age and dissolve right before the staff's eyes as she made her entrance into the make-up room each morning. The outline of those "pads" in her face would grow more distinct until it was thought she would finally have to admit to the plastic surgery, Botox, or monkey glands she always denied using but eagerly reported in everyone else. Then she would remove herself from the show for a week and return wearing sunglasses for a day or two, and everything would be like the old, or "new", Beverly again. As a result, with all those nooks and crannies so diligently attended to for so many years, Brendan figured her face, at this point, probably had a shelf life of close to 500 years. About the same as a Hostess Twinkie.

"Well, darling, we all must do what we must do," she said. Brendan wondered if that included firing him. "But this is Vegas, and I am determined to have fun in Las Vegas."

"Me, too," he said feeling that he'd just agreed to some heavily coded sexual contract. "Nice shirt." Brendan liked to treat Beverly like the "dame" he knew she was at heart. The slightly rough speech thrilled her.

"Why, thank you. It's just something fun."

She presented herself to him ever so slightly and crossed her legendary legs which looked like they belonged to somebody fifty years younger. If it had been anyone else, Brendan would have leaned over and kissed on the spot and then fucked her right there on the floor. But he was a long way from being in his element, and the whiff of sexuality made him realize he hadn't dropped any Viagra for this historic occasion. He didn't want Beverly to have gone through all this trouble and then have him show up with a cock that looked like one of her tits. But for this particular occasion, Brendan would probably need a Viagra drip—maybe even Viagra dialysis. But since neither was available, he reached into his shirt pocket and extracted two of the magic pills he'd saved to jerk off with later and quickly downed 200 milligrams of "Blue" as if they were a couple of aspirin for a headache.

"Are you well, darling?" she asked. Not because she was honestly concerned; but, given what she had in mind, she didn't want to catch anything.

"Yeah, I'm great. Feel good." He took a big sip of the Scotch. "Raring to go. Whaddya need?" He returned to the originally stated purpose of this visit. She stared at him for an extra-long beat.

"Just you. For now," she said smiling and blinked several times in mock naïveté. Then she opened her mouth slightly to moisten her lips with the tip of her tongue and kissed the air sensuously for his benefit without ever taking her eyes off of him. "Work can always wait."

The whole thing would have been ludicrous except that Brendan felt he was being entertained by an obvious pro. Sex with an older icon had always been something he was open to. He had been prepared to bed Zsa Zsa Gabor had she demanded it of him when he worked on the Cavett Show. And walking around New York in the 80's Brendan always thought he would run into Jackie Kennedy and be taken home to 1040 Fifth Avenue by her as had happened once to a friend of his. But Jackie died too soon for the odds to bring her to him. Nevertheless, Brendan loved the fact that Jackie had been embalmed right there at 1040 up in her own kitchen by the Frank Campbell homos in order to specifically frustrate any other post mortem paramours like himself. He was sure that Beverly, upon hearing of Jackie's private in-home embalming, had already set the wheels in motion for her to be similarly accommodated by Forest Lawn despite the laws against it and the affront to her neighbors should they, as they say, get "wind" of it.

As it was, having his face closer than normal to Beverly's made Brendan think about the missed possibility of fucking poor, dead "Jackie O" and whether he would've actually done it if given the chance. The answer was "probably", but whom could he tell about it afterwards? But now, with the corpse of Beverly Frost in front of him for real, his mission was to stall long enough for the Viagra to kick in. Once that happened he hoped that thoughts of immortality and Henry Kissinger would prove sufficiently arousing.

"Have you ever been to England, Brendan, darling?"

"Yeah, once," he said. "When I was working at Forbes. I was there for about twenty-four hours with Mr. Forbes for some meetings about the magazine."

"Did you fuck Malcolm?" she said bluntly, but she really wanted to know. It was the whole sanitary thing again rather than the scandal aspect of it.

"Not as far as I know," Brendan said. "I know you and Bad Bob think I did because Bad Bob's been ragging me about working for him ever since I started on the show. And I know where it came from, too. Gloria. And I don't appreciate him spreading his opinion all over the office. So now I get it from Mugsy, and Marge, and anyone else who wants to call me a 'faggot'." He put his glass down and was about to get up to leave when she placed her hand on his knee.

"This is a very difficult business," she said, "*Very* difficult." He took a beat because he wasn't sure whether he wanted to blow the whole sexual defamation and age discrimination case he was building against them. But Beverly was smart enough to realize that Brendan was loaded for bear on the subject, and it would undoubtedly get back to Bad Bob.

"Sometimes you can't control these things," she said looking at him meaningfully. Brendan didn't know exactly what she was talking about, the rumors or the reality.

"And now your partner's actually fired me, you know," he said without really meaning to.

"Oh, darling, I don't know anything about that. You'll have to take that up with Robert."

Beverly had slipped into her pose, once again, of being at the secretarial level in her own company. She would often retreat behind the fiction that she didn't know anyone's salary or any of the deals or business permutations of PermaFrost Productions—that it was all too, too complicated and/or mundane for her to concern herself with. She really thought she could pull off the conceit that she was just one of the girls with the other co-hosts as well, and she would make statements to that effect on the air so that the audience really thought she worked for someone other than herself. The truth was that she was a micro manager just like her buddy, Chet Young, the head of the network, who would fuss over the hors d'oeuvres being served at the "Up Front" presentations in New York and insist on personally sampling all of them first even though the radiation for his throat cancer had obliterated his taste buds. Everything he put in his mouth tasted like Styrofoam.

"Well, now you know. I'm outta here in a couple of months."

"I am sad to hear of the decision. I'm fond of you and will miss you," she said flatly. Then, brightening, she added cheerfully. "But there must be *something*...The show needs you."

"Apparently not."

"Well, *I* need you." She said trying to lighten things up.

"Then why did he fire me"

"Oh, Brendan, he didn't fire you, I'm sure he was just doing what he thought needed to be done. The network can be just impossible sometimes," she said revealing that, of course, she knew everything.

"So am I fired?"

"Darling, you'll really have to straighten that out with Robert. That's completely between you and him. I stay out of it."

Beverly and Brendan regarded each other. This was not the foreplay she had intended, but she was too far down the road to retreat gracefully now. Brendan could feel the Viagra kicking in. His face was becoming flushed with the side effect of the drug. Beverly, of course, took it as a compliment. She put her hand on his cheek instinctively.

"You're burning up. Are you well?"

"Yes," he said, still slightly combative.

"Is it the liquor? Or is this the way you are all the time?"

"I'm fine," Brendan said.

Then she leaned over and gently kissed him on the cheek. He did not move his head or respond when she did. He thought it very cool that he hadn't.

"Brendan White, you are such a dear, sweet boy."

Brendan didn't know quite how to respond, so he did his best Steve McQueen, thin, stoic smile. Then, after a beat, Beverly stood up abruptly.

"I think I shall retire," she said with a slightly more mid-Atlantic accent than usual.

And then she was gone—like a quick-change artist making an exit through an opening in a curtain. There was no sense of a door or wall. One moment she was standing in front of him, and the next she had disappeared. Of course, when Beverly Frost says she wants to "retire", Brendan could rest assured she wasn't talking "Social Security". She was either headed for bed or leaving the building. He couldn't tell which. He sat there, having not stood when she left because of the abruptness of the exit. He took a sip of Scotch and waited to see if she would return. Instead, the maid reappeared again. She was carrying a stack of towels and a folded plush terry cloth bathrobe.

"You take shower, yes?"

"No, that's okay," he said shaking her off. But she persisted.

"Shower good for you now," she said benignly.

Brendan really didn't get it. He thought the maid thought that for some reason he had come for a shower, and he couldn't convince her otherwise. But then it dawned on him. This was part of the "Sex with Beverly" ritual. This was the shower phase. The *cleansing*. Beverly required absolute assurances that the men she ordered up, like so much take-out, be lathered and scrubbed clean of any offending odors or trace aromas from their own unfortunate lives. She insisted they smell like her.

"Oh," Brendan said finally getting it. "Thank you. Okay. You want me to take a shower first?"

The maid was overjoyed at his cooperation and led him out of the small dining area, across the grand living room to a small guest bedroom with its own bathroom and shower. He half expected her to get in the shower with him to make sure he washed everything. But instead, she went in and laid the towels and a bathrobe out for him on the bed and then stood at the door smiling at him.

"I come get you," she said. "Twenty minutes."

Brendan took his time in the shower and actually enjoyed the appointments. Talent always got better accommodations than writers. Usually, writers were relegated to bad hotels on the wrong side of the strip, the ones that had "Fat Elvis" appearing in the lounge and rooms decorated with red flocking and sperm. You practically had to grease yourself with Ortho Novo just to lie down in the bed without waking up pregnant or with a bad taste in your mouth.

The shower filled the room with sweet steam and lavender. Brendan even took one of the shampoo vials for later. He dried himself off and put on the lush terry cloth robe. He felt like either a fighter or Fernando Lamas. Then he sat on the bed and waited. There were no magazines around, and he dared not explore. So he waited. Presently, there was a soft knock on the door. It was a different maid. She was very pleased that he had apparently completed his "pre-schtupp mikveh".

"Come with me, now," she said.

But first she looked past him into the room to make sure Brendan's boxer shorts were on the bed where they should be and not on him. They walked down the length of the living room to what he assumed was the master bedroom. She opened the door. The area inside was even darker than the rest of the apartment. Beverly had applied a different "love perfume" for the occasion, and it came wafting out of the actual sleeping area. The maid led Brendan to a little dressing area where there was a small couch next to a make-up table. She motioned for him to sit down there and then left him alone once again. He looked around at the various dresses hanging there. He tried to peer into the actual bedroom but couldn't see much beyond the door. Brendan smiled to himself at the thought that everyone seemed to know the routine but him. At first he self-consciously crossed his legs, but then he decided that was un-cool, so he uncrossed them and sat there, instead, like a benched football player waiting to go in.

Suddenly from another door, probably the toilet for all he knew, Beverly appeared. She was also in a dressing gown now. It was silk and Chinese looking. The freckled skin of her chest above her tits announced that she was also nude underneath. Brendan's heart started to pound, not out of sexual excitement, but out of the sheer terror that this was actually going to happen.

She sat down beside him on the little couch and purposely jammed her hip into his. Then she turned, and suddenly her face was all over his. He could smell her breath which was sweet and not a bit old as he had feared. The billowing perfume effectively enveloped them in an intoxicating floral cloud as if they were in some magical bower and not in a penthouse suite overlooking the Las Vegas strip.

"I want you to kiss me, darling." She said with her mouth only inches from Brendan's. "Don't be afraid."

He kissed her the way an employee is not supposed to kiss his boss, even when ordered. The whole thing came apart immediately. Her mouth, either because of the surgery, botox, collagen, or all three, had no embouchure. It spread out all over her face. Brendan couldn't contain it. And her tongue, unexpectedly thick and sinewy, filled his mouth like a python trying to extract a tooth. He instantly realized that his job, now, was to work around this unbridled hunger in such a way as to never let her know how unattractive it made her and how ultimately un-sexy she was being. He flashed on how Henry Kissinger, Geraldo, and, probably, even Eubie Blake must have come to the same realization, and he wondered how they dealt with it.

Brendan broke away from the embrace as if overwhelmed by the intensity of her passion when, in fact, he simply had to get her goddamn tongue out of his mouth before he gagged. He pretended to be shy and tentative. Shades of "Tea and Sympathy" or "Summer of 42". He pushed her away and held her at arm's length and looked into her face which was, even now, starting to disassemble like a cubist painting.

"What's the matter?" She asked. "Surprised?"

"By you? Never. I just want to enjoy this moment. I want to savor you."

With that statement, he thought he was going to gag on his *own* tongue. But now it was time for him to kiss *her*, or else she'd think something was up. He moved his lips toward hers very slowly as if they were doing a tight "two shot" in a "coming of age" film. It was the only chance he had of getting the thing under control and back on track.

But as soon as their lips touched, it set her off again; and she started devouring him as she had done the first time around. This time he shoved her tongue back into her mouth with his own tongue and kept a reasonable amount of pressure on her lips. But even so, it was a disaster as far as kissing goes. One good thing about growing up Catholic in the fifties, Brendan thought, was that you learned to be a great kisser since that was all there was going to be—for *hours*—and you had to make the most of it. In the present case, there was spit all over his face, and Beverly's face was melting before his eyes like something out of "The House of Wax"; but she was totally into it.

There was a real hunger at work here. Brendan couldn't imagine Henry Kissinger handling the situation any better than he was. The Middle East was probably nothing compared to fending off a rampant and rutting Beverly Frost. He tried a few more seconds of tongue control but quickly ascertained that she was not going to learn. It was decidedly un-sexy—for him. *She*, on the other hand, was heaving like a cow being artificially inseminated by a ham-fisted vet. Brendan pulled away once again. Now *she* held him at arm's length but with a wild look in her eye that told him she had found what she was looking for.

"We must…" she began breathlessly, "…We must do something about this."

"I hope so," he replied looking deep into her sad, surgically en-hanced eyes.

Brendan didn't want her to think he wasn't into it. Although, by now, the situation was losing its freak appeal; and he knew he was facing what can only be described as: "The Job of Sex."

She continued to hold him, stiff-armed; searching his face for God knows what. Then, abruptly, she stood up and disappeared again but not into the bedroom.

Brendan sat there dutifully in the half light, again not knowing exactly what to do or what was expected of him. After a few beats he heard the tinkling of glasses and a *third* maid appeared with a silver tray and two glasses of champagne. He took one when the tray was offered to him. Then the maid turned and headed into the bedroom.

"This way," she said as if it was a doctor's office, and he was next. He then followed her into the actual bedroom section of the suite.

The bed was freshly made with the bed covers neatly turned down on each side like an envelope. The maid led him over to what he could only assume was his side. He lay down, but the maid didn't move.

"Shall I take your robe, Mr. White?" she asked.

At that point, like a Jewish girl on her third date finally agree-ing to have sex, Brendan pulled the covers up to his chin and took the robe off underneath them. Then he bunched the robe up, extracted it from under the covers, and handed it to the maid. She was quite pleased. She then proceeded over to the other side of the bed where she place the other glass of champagne on the bedside table there and left the room carrying his bathrobe.

Brendan eagerly drained his glass of champagne. The combination of the Viagra kicking in with booze on top gave him a comfortable buzz. He actually relaxed for the first time. It was a great bed, he thought. Too bad it was about to be ruined by Beverly Frost getting into it.

At first he thought it was his imagination, but he slowly became aware that the lights in the bedroom were being silently dimmed even lower. It was not unlike a play about to begin. Then, with a rustle somewhat like a turkey crossing an open field, Beverly swept into the room, dropped her peignoir, and got into the bed all in one motion. Then the lights then went down completely. Or perhaps it only seemed that way because Brendan's eyes could not adapt fast enough to the lack of illumination. He was now naked in bed with Beverly Frost. He rolled over on his side to face her.

Beverly, balls-ass naked, was actually much smaller than anyone would have ever thought—the result of eighty-three years of four inch heels and coiffed hair, no matter what. Brendan made the mistake of cupping one hand around her ass to draw her closer. It was not like any ass he had ever known. It had the consistency of a bean bag that was suffering some serious loss of bean. He deftly moved his hand up to her waist so as not to call attention to it.

"Oh, darling," she breathed into his face. "Take me. Do with me what you will."

She threw her head back dramatically with the back of her hand pressed damsel-like on her forehead as he'd seen her do "on-air" so many times when she was feigning shock or trying to be funny. But it was a good thing because it meant Brendan could kiss her neck and trace the plastic surgery scars there with his tongue. It was much sexier than kissing her on the mouth by a long shot.

"You *know!*" she said as if he were some sort of sexual psychic. "You *know!* You *know!*" she repeated. Brendan couldn't tell whether she thought he was clairvoyant or she just couldn't think of anything else to say and was stalling like an empty-headed schoolgirl.

"I'm going to fuck you, Beverly," Brendan said in his best alpha male, "dom" growl.

It was such a porno lick that it even turned *him* on. He said it with full dramatic and cinematic import as if, arms akimbo, he was standing astride her while she groveled on the floor. Brendan had learned from bedding feminists during the 70's that successful business women all wanted to be dominated in the sack in the most abject way possible as if to make up for the balls they broke during the day at the office. Secretaries and wardrobe girls, on the other hand, were to be treated like spoiled princesses.

"Yes, *yes.* I'm just a little girl," she whimpered. This coming from an eighty-three year old diva/mogul pulling in thirty million a year who considered herself nothing less than the long-lost cousin of the British Royal family. At that moment Brendan had just enough of a hard-on for his cock to be serviceable. Nothing like the old days, of course, when it would get hard enough to drive a nail with, but it was sufficiently aroused out of some sense memory so that, highly confused at the moment; it at least *looked* like a hard-on even if it definitely wasn't the stiffest thing in the room.

"You are so hot," he said to her figuring that spoken passion would do them both a world of good. He moved his lower body over on top of hers and held the upper part of himself up at arm's length so that he could look at her. Big mistake. She was deteriorating rapidly like a decomposing corpse. Her face had fallen, and the creases in it had become so pronounced that he could now see the actual outline of her cheek implants, and the deep depression in the center of each cheek was cavernous. She suddenly looked like one of those God-awful, villainous witches that Disney trots out for their animated features. In addition, her overly red lipstick had smeared so disastrously across her mouth that she looked like a *drunken* Disney villainous witch.

Resting on top of her, Brendan became aware that her body felt as if it was all bones. It was as if there was no actual flesh on her at all. He could feel her ample bush against his belly; and he was grateful for that, if for no other reason, than to use it as a book-mark for where he was headed. Brendan closed his eyes as if in a swoon of passion; but, in truth, it was more like averting his gaze at the scene of an accident or coming upon someone deformed on the street. Something was not right.

She looked up at him again with a wild, frightened look as if she thought he was going to hit her. Then he noticed that one of her false eyelashes had come loose and was stuck on her cheek like a centipede. He reached down with one hand and gently flicked it away. She took it as a sign of affection rather than an act of emergency grooming. Then he reached down and grabbed his semi-hard cock and squeezed it tight in order get it into her before it, too, collapsed like her face.

"Please, darling. Just one moment." She spoke very matter-of-factly. It was the tone a woman sixty years younger might use when reaching for birth control. He rolled back off her. She reached over to the bedside table and picked up a small plastic bottle.

"Astroglide, darling. It's the secret of life." She took a beat and then explained further. "Lubrication is *so* important at times like this."

"Oh," Brendan said, "Right. That's great. I love that stuff. I'll take a little myself," and he held out his hand to show how perfectly down he was with the whole thing.

"Lubrication," she said again. "Always remember." He figured that she must have momentarily thought she was back on television doing a segment on marital aids.

The small plastic bottle disappeared beneath the covers, and there was a little "bottle fart" sound from her pussy area as she applied the juice. It meant that, obviously, it had not been a full bottle. This wasn't the first time she'd used it. Brendan flashed on "Henry the K" again and wondered how he liked Beverly's little "jet assist", compliments of Astroglide, when he had fucked her.

"There," she said with finality, very satisfied and relaxed as if, now fully lubricated, she had just gotten a tune-up and wheel alignment as well. Brendan had this vision of Beverly Frost up on a car rack with men in overalls underneath working on her with grease guns and pneumatic wrenches.

"There," she said again, "I'm all yours, darling,"

By this time Brendan had lost his hard-on and knew that, unfortunately, the "moment of strange" that all men have, when they could fuck a stump if they had to, had passed. Of course, sometimes that "moment of strange" can last a lifetime, and that's called a happy marriage. But when you are trying to answer a booty call from an eighty-three year old pain in the ass, it is as fleeting as a whiff of grilled meat from a fast food exhaust fan: the anticipation of something tasty is spontaneously triggered within you even though, intellectually, you know its source is disgusting and inedible.

"You're going to have to help me, Beverly," Brendan said rolling over on his back. He threw back the covers to expose his cock lying limp in his lap—perfectly formed, but dead as a doornail, like one of those British guardsmen who faint in the reviewing line. Not scary or dire, just useless and sad.

"I'm *very* good at that, darling. Leave it to me." She moved down and took a position next to his crotch as if she were going to do a little sewing. She picked up his cock with those perfectly manicured nails (the same color as Paris Hilton's whom she'd interviewed after her sex tape) and placed the head of it on her tongue as if it were a lozenge.

"Oh, yeah." Brendan moaned trying to punch it up by adding a porn sound track. "Oh, *yeah.*" (He'd always wanted to write a porno flick called "Oh, Yeah" where that was the only dialogue.)

Beverly then moved the head of his cock off her tongue and looked at it as if she were going to admonish it. Brendan watched her not knowing exactly what she was up to. Then she shook her finger at the cock and touched its head.

"You be good!" she said to it as if she were talking to "Rémy", her dog.

It suddenly occurred to Brendan that maybe she had no idea what to do with a cock but was afraid to tell him. He was about to take it away from her and try something else when she took the entire penis into her mouth so completely that her lips threatened to swallow his balls as well.

"Whoa!" he shouted and arched impulsively. He looked down at her mouth with no cock showing and realized that if, in fact, he had actually *had* a righteous hard-on; he would have choked her to death on the spot or at least pierced her lungs. Not because his cock was that big, of course, but because she had inhaled the thing as opposed to swallowing it. She then began sucking it in a manner unlike any way Brendan had ever been sucked before. She was sucking it with her throat, or tonsils, or uvula, or something other than whatever is in a woman's mouth that she's supposed to suck a cock with. Needless to say, it was exciting, and best of all Brendan only had to look at the top of her head. But then he saw the join where a hair piece had been laced into whatever natural hair she had left. He made a mental note to not grab it if he came, or else she might think she was getting fucked at Little Bighorn.

Brendan decided it was time to seize the moment and his erection. He tried to gently lift her head off his cock while she knelt on the bed. She would not let go. But at least now she was moving up and down the shaft like a normal person. He slipped his feet off of the bed and onto the floor while still attached to her so that he could stand while she knelt on the bed and sucked him.

"Show me your eyes," he said standing over her. Brendan had learned that line from the cock-sucking clips on PornHub, and, also, from a famous Stallone story; so he figured it was probably demeaning enough to excite her. He was right. She obliged, and he watched as this creature, looking like something out of "Clockwork Orange", gazed up at him with her Cocker Spaniel eyes—and only one eyelash—while she continued to suck his cock.

The deterioration of her make-up was moving as inexorably as the shadow of an eclipse across her face. Brendan realized he had to proceed sooner than later, or else there would be nothing left to fuck. He grabbed his cock on one of her up strokes and lifted her mouth off the head. There was an audible slurping sound when the contact was broken. The expression on her face looked like she had just been punished. He gently pushed her back down on the bed, and sprung her legs out from under her. Then he slid her torso toward him so that he had one of her legs under each arm and her pussy at the edge of the mattress. She bit the back of her bony knuckle in wild expectation like a child fearfully anticipating another thunder-clap from a storm, a look of mild terror on her face.

Brendan couldn't get over how much slighter Beverly seemed than he would've thought. On top of that, her desiccated body indicated that she was well past her "fuck by" date. Calling Beverly nothing but skin and bones would've been a compliment. He started to slide his cock into what he assumed was her vagina.

"Oh, *GOD!*" She blurted out in a smoky growl. The trouble was he couldn't tell if he was in or not. It wasn't that her vagina was big; it was the complete lack of muscle tone within it that Brendan was unaccustomed to. She had a flabby pussy that was devoid of any articulation. He withdrew and looked down to reconnoiter the lay of the land (so to speak). Her vagina looked not unlike her mouth, but without the lipstick. He could feel his hard-on receding, so he turned her over with about as much ceremony as a butcher flipping a side of beef.

She went completely limp when this happened as if she had given up any hope or desire of being an active partner in this enterprise. She lay on her stomach with her face buried in the bed covers. He easily bent her legs up underneath her to make her present her ass to him. It was a mess. Brendan entered her from behind this time, and it felt much better. She made little whiny sounds into the covers with each thrust. He had to work hard and fast in order to trick his cock into thinking it was actually somewhere where it wanted to be. His mission, now, was to cum and be finished with it. Of course, given that she *was* a senior citizen, it would've been helpful if there'd been a "grab bar" or two on her ass; but, instead, Brendan had to bunch up some loose skin from around her waist in order to have something to hold on to.

There was Astroglide squirting out all over the place as he doubled up on his rhythm in order to get where he had to be as quickly as possible. This ship was going to land come hell or high water. He went deep, in hopes of touching even just a hint of new pussy

"Oh, my God! You *know*!" she shouted when she came up for air.

"Say you love me!" he demanded incongruously in a low, throaty voice.

Despite the strangeness of the request, Beverly responded as if she knew it was coming.

"I love you," she said almost tearfully. He fucked her harder. "I *adore* you," she added gratuitously. "My...*Champion!*"

Giving it up like that made her swoon again. Her eyes rolled back in her head, and she went dramatically limp. What had started as a gambit of domination on Brendan's part had touched her deeper than the sex she had ordered up from him. He was momentarily embarrassed he had pushed her into that secret place.

Her pussy suddenly took shape and formed around his cock. And, as he thrust deeper, his cock grew harder and meaner. The wimpy sounds from Beverly became guttural groans and then full-throated shouts of ecstasy. He was surprised at the transformation, and easily came in her with a final thrust that went as deep as he could drive it. Brendan's cock was still throbbing, and it glistened in whatever stray light had entered the room when he withdrew it from her. It was only then that he realized that he'd been fucking her in the ass most of the time, having inadvertently made the switch in mid-stroke. The abundance of Astroglide had facilitated the anal sex; and, apparently, she was no stranger to it. But it had not been what he had in mind.

"Oh-oh" Brendan said as if, by apologizing, he could take back the violation. "I think we just had anal sex. I'm sorry. That's not what..."

"But, you *knew,*" she said in a little voice with her head still flat on the bed and her ass in the air. There was Astroglide, and sweat, and cum all over the place.

"No, I didn't," he told her. "I don't know what to say."

"Say, 'Thank you, Beverly,'" she said regaining some of her customary dismissiveness. Then she rolled over on her side and drew her legs up into a fetal position. Her eyes were closed. Brendan assumed cuddling was not called for in this situation. He stood there catching his breath while she cuddled with herself. Then she sighed a very self-satisfied sigh signaling that she was comfortable, and he had become superfluous. She didn't move or attempt to acknowledge him, so he merely turned and walked into the dressing room to find his robe.

"Your things are in the other room, darling," she called to him without ever raising her head from where it had ended up on the bed. He took this to mean that, perhaps, this was not the right time to continue their discussion about his employment.

Brendan put the bathrobe on and walked alone through the darkened suite to the small bedroom where his clothes had been neatly laid out as if they'd just been laundered. He put them on and let himself out. The maids were nowhere to be seen or heard. He imagined them silently descending upon Beverly and attending to her as she lay curled up on the master bed awash in lubricant and sex.

The next day Brendan saw Beverly getting mic'd just before they were about to start the show. She walked right past him with that singularly motivated, obliterating gaze while trying to get the attention of a PA who had worked intimately with her on a daily basis for 15 years.

"Person!" she called to the P.A. even though the girl was standing only a few feet away but with her back turned, "Oh, Person! Hello! *He-llo*!" She had no idea what the girl's name was. "Excuse me. Person. I said, *Person*!"

Brendan knew then that everything was the same. Beverly had risen from her own hauled ashes. He also knew that their little "encounter" would change nothing. He was still fired.

CHAPTER SIXTEEN

Moonie Brown loved swag. She would do anything to get it. Even when she actually paid for something, she liked to pretend she got it for free. That's why the only people she was really nice to were sales girls. Even if she'd just bought, and actually paid cash for, a $7500 simulated diamond-encrusted cowboy belt (about the size of a rope ladder) at Neiman's in Beverly Hills, when the sales girl appeared with it all done up in a high-end shopping bag, with sweet smelling tissue erupting from it, Moonie was all smiles and teeth.

"Why, *thank* you, darlin'" she'd say with an overly appreciative curtsy, making the sales girl look at her as though Moonie were crazy *and* fat. Then, once back in her Escalade, she would open the bag and fish through the tissue for her "present" like a birthday girl.

Like Billy Crystal with air time, Moonie Brown was insatiable. There was never enough, and there was never anything too small or too inexpensive that wasn't better if it could be had for free.

It all got out of hand at "The Ladies' Room", and her cupidity ruined it for everyone else, especially the other co-hosts who were much less obvious but just as eager to get anything free. Even Beverly. Especially Beverly. This *grand dame* of news, a "serious journalist" and former editor of the LA Times could never figure out how Moonie, immediately upon getting the gig on "The Ladies' Room", was able to score the amount of goods and services that Beverly had never even dreamed of getting for free. Beverly Frost had always been resigned to fucking for her supper—or her 18 million dollar "bungalow" in Malibu Colony. It never occurred to her that a person could actually gain such treasures without taking their clothes off first.

Moonie was already fat when she came to "The Ladies' Room", but the opportunities that opened up from being on a network show redoubled her acquisitive nature as soon as she arrived. So it wasn't only food she accumulated, it was swag and freebies. Her dressing room was awash with products, props, and demos that had been lifted directly off the stage before the Sean, the prop man, could pry them from her fat, red fingers.

Moonie was proudly "single" and had also proudly announced that she wanted nothing to do with having children of her own. (Another mouth to feed would be too much competition). Nevertheless, when a baby theme show featured the latest and greatest infant and baby products and furniture, Moonie ordered a van, with a U-Haul trailer attached, to back up to the stage entrance on the ramp in order to receive all of the products that had been brought onto the show. This included many doubles of the items that had never even been unpacked that were supplied as spares should something fail to operate correctly. It was a legendary moment in the Moonie Brown story only because no one else on the show got so much as a pacifier after Ms. Brown had instructed Desireé, her assistant of the hour, to stand guard over the items as soon as the show went off the air and personally shepherd them down to the loading bay and into the waiting U-Haul.

As a result, close to $20,000 worth of baby furniture and accessories including a year's supply of Pampers, was heading south on the San Diego Freeway before the post mortem meeting was over. Apparently, the feeding frenzy that day was prompted by Moonie's desire to "bless" her cousin Alison who was having a baby out of wedlock in Long Beach. However, that particular haul taught Moonie a valuable lesson. Hard goods were no different than food-stuffs. So, from then on, Desireé's swag calls on Moonie's behalf were inflated to, "Ms. Brown would prefer *three* Sony Bravara XPS, 52 inch, 1080 dpi, HDTV's to be delivered to her residence as soon as possible." Thus, she was able to provide for her family, the condo on Wilshire, and her house in "Malibu adjacent" at the same time. And she would kick herself for not having asked for three of every-thing sooner.

"Where do you think *you're* goin'?" Moonie said to Ray Ray Kennedy, a smooth ex-NFL corner back when he tried to squeeze past her at her party in Malibu Heights above the beach. "You're not gonna just walk past me without saying nothin', are you?"

The fact that she was standing in, and completely obliterating, the doorway in question did not faze her. And, of course, only a former professional football player, accustomed to running for daylight on the other side of a mountain of flesh, would be un-daunted by the challenge of getting past a woman who's weight and girth rivaled the combined tonnage of the Green Bay Packers' front four. Onlookers at this historic meeting were surprised that Ray Ray hadn't given her a forearm shiver out of instinct.

"I don't think we've been introduced," Ray Ray had said in his phony courtly manner.

"We haven't," Moonie said extending her bejeweled hand com-pliments of "Murray, The Maven", the only Jew west of the Mississippi who truly understood that jewelry, not crack, was the drug of choice in the "hood". "But I know who *you* are."

This got Ray Ray's attention since cornerbacks always feel un-sung. He took her hand and kissed it so he could smell if there was any formaldehyde coming off a Zircon setting on her so-called "diamond" ring. Instead, all he got was the faint whiff of barbecued ribs. At this point in his life, Ray Ray, a degenerate gambler from way back in his college days, was worse than broke. He was into shylocks for over $500 grand. But, here, suddenly, he found himself face to face with a new line of credit.

"And I know that you are the Superdome of women," he said sounding more like a late night disc jockey than an ex-football player who didn't know where he was going to sleep that night. Referring to Moonie as the "Superdome of women" as an opening line was about as on the nose as going to Hershey, Pennsylvania for anal sex, but Ray Ray hadn't caught his subconscious insult in time.

"Am I supposed to take that as a compliment, Ray Ray?"

"You would if I was playin' inside you."

This sort of metaphor trading goes on endlessly between African, and semi-African, Americans who, for some reason, believe it to be the affect of polite society—sort of the Court of King James as interpreted by Amos 'n Andy. But this time it was, in fact, merely one hustler meeting another. They recognized each other immediately and sized each other up accordingly. It was one of those legendary meetings where the earth moved and not just from Ms. Brown's fat ass landing on double stools at Fatburger. ("Ms Brown would prefer to sit on *two* stools while dining in your establishment. Otherwise, one stool might be in serious danger of becoming an elephantine suppository.")

"Why don't you and me share this champagne," Moonie offered in a tone that signaled to Ray Ray that a deal might be in the offing.

It was at a Champagne Brunch at her home in Malibu Hills, where the Freixenet cheap champagne people had assembled a hundred of the biggest hangers-on, connivers, and fakers on the West Side for Champagne, Mimosa's, Aunt Jemima pancakes, and heated knishes (another sponsor). And it hadn't cost Moonie a nickel. In fact, she even got the house cleaned before and after, the rugs shampooed, the back fence fixed, and even the roof on the garage done over—all to make the place presentable. That and fifteen cases of the bubbly delivered to the basement sealed the deal.

Moonie was more than happy to entertain her dear "country" friends. But she could never quite get her brain around the difference between what "country" meant to her people and what "*the* country" meant to white folk. She aspired to be "country" as in "Town and Country" when she was in Malibu, but it always seemed to come off as "cun-tray" to her black and minority friends and slightly nouveau to even her "C" list white ones. She would have preferred to call it "the beach" except that the seashore was a five minute drive away.

At four hundred and eighty pounds, Moonie didn't have time to play the waiting game. She was used to identifying her prey and pouncing on it like a wading Hippo on an otter. Her over the top flirtations were the stuff of urban legend.

Moonie had once enticed a struggling white comedian, Link Millerton, to come up to her apartment on Wilshire Boulevard in Westwood. Link did so out of sheer curiosity and a desire for fresh material, no doubt. But once she got him in the door she started with her romance novel version of seduction.

"I think I shall go change into something more comfortable," she said all a flutter. "Would you care to join me?"

Link declined. Shortly thereafter, Moonie reappeared wearing the largest negligée in the Western world. Rather than a "sweet nothing" from Victoria's Secret, this negligée was more of a "big-ass somethin'" from "Victoria's Blabbermouth". Katrina refugees would gladly have moved into it over a FEMA trailer any day.

Moonie sashayed into the living room where Link was sitting stiffly at one end of the double-wide couch and proceeded to plunk herself down at the other end by backing up to it like a semi to a loading dock and then falling backwards and hoping for the best. The only thing missing was the "beep-beep-beep" warning signal. There was a huge "Harumpff" from the cushions as if the down feathers inside had breathed their last. Then she kicked off her Jimmy Choo's and snuggled her stocking feet into the comedian's lap.

"I like to have my feet rubbed," she said as if answering his question.

"Huh?" Link said, not sure if he wanted to get that close to her bratwurst-size toes.

"It makes me wet," she admitted with a girlish giggle. "Puts me in the mood."

Now Link was scared. He tentatively held the ball of one of foot between his thumb and forefinger like a soiled Kleenex while trying to explain that he was not interested in having (shudder) sex with her.

"C'mon, baby," Moonie cooed. "Just a little. Stir the sugar in my bowl."

Link waved off the invitation and tried to get up, but the weight of even Moonie's feet in his lap pinned him to the couch like a rat in a trap; of course, not without a little added pressure from Moonie herself.

"That's okay, honey," she said. "Then just rub my feet before you go. For me"

Link reluctantly obliged. Moonie threw her head back in sheer ecstasy. It was then that the comedian looked to his right and saw the immense, Native American pussy that Moonie was displaying for him willingly as she got herself off from the foot massage. It did, indeed, make her wet. Really wet. So much so that a trickle of pussy juice began to spread through the bottom of her negligée and onto the satin cushions underneath. Link felt guilty, as if he were spilling something. He felt he should stop, but she would have none of it. She reached out her hand for his. And he took it, thinking she was going to sit up; but, instead, she grabbed his hand and jammed it down into her vagina. Now he had one hand on her foot and the other in her pussy, and all he really wanted to do was get the fuck out of there and go home.

Fortunately, Moonie had no trouble climaxing right then and there. It was like in one of those submarine movies where depth charges are shot off the stern of a destroyer with unassuming "clicks".

Then, moments later, deep, muffled explosions occur somewhere far beneath the surface. Then those explosions are followed by violent eruptions of spray, foam, and debris thrown high into the air. In fact, it was *exactly* like depth charges being shot off the back of a destroyer. Moonie announced she was "coming" in a quiet matter-of-fact tone as if nothing physical was going to happen. But then, a few moments later, her back arched silently only to be followed by the eruption of her pelvis that heaved up and down like a tectonic plate shifting in an earthquake as she moaned, shrieked, and spit enough to make even the tchotchkes on her glass shelves and table tops rattle throughout the apartment. And then it was over.

Link gingerly withdrew his hand from her pussy as if from a bear trap, thankful that it had not been mangled like something in an industrial accident. But then, being a comedian, he couldn't help but wipe it unceremoniously on Moonie's negligee as a punch line because the drapes were all the way across the room.

"I think I should be going" he said.

"You don't have to," she said cheerfully as if she were ready for more.

"I know, but I have a cruise leaving in the morning."

"Really?" Moonie said. I love cruises. Which one?

"The Pacific Rim."

"That's a Gay and Lesbian cruise," she said

"Right," Link replied. "You know, I'm gay," he added. It was one of the few times he was really grateful to admit he was gay because now he was gay and saved as well.

"Oh," she said because she did not know he was gay.

"Gay as a goose," he said sounding very gay now. "I thought you knew. It's no secret."

"It's all right with me, baby. You know Jesus loves you."

"I know that," the comedian said.

Moonie was reverting to her "Christian ways" out of her guilt for the sex and as a protection from being rejected. Jesus was her douche. Praying after an orgasm made her feel clean as a whistle.

"Well, praise God" Moonie said. She was sitting upright on the couch now and took a large sip of the champagne and returned the glass to the coffee table. There was an awkward moment. Link was obviously leaving, but Moonie, at the same time, was obviously not going to let him see her try to get up from her extra plush couch.

"You go along now, baby" and give my best to Ellen or Rosie or whosever cruise it is."

With that, Link bounded up from the couch, overjoyed at being released. He bent over and tried to kiss Moonie on the lips, but now she turned her head aside and offered her cheek.

"Don't know where that's been" she said as if eating her pussy would have been any cleaner than a rim job.

At this point Link didn't care, and he literally ran out of the apartment. Moonie lay back down on the couch and fell asleep, not because she was too tired to move, but because her make-up had been done at the studio that day, and she didn't want to disturb it. She simply couldn't resist the fact that she had gotten it free; and, by God, she was going to make it last as long as she could.

Back at the Freixenet garden party, Ray Ray Kennedy had another problem. He needed a place to stay that night, and if Moonie's Malibu Hills "Love Shack" was going to be it, at least he wouldn't have to move his car.

"Did you think I was going to let you get away?" Moonie said when they had retired to the sun porch which, like the rest of her house, was done in white on white on white.

Moonie had gotten hold of P. Diddy's decorator and told him she wanted to do Sean Jean one better. As a result, a person could go snow blind in the place if it weren't for Moonie herself. And that was the point, of course. Guests were forced to look at her just to avoid a "white out". Like her constant on-air charge to Hal of "Put the camera on me", the lack of any color scheme in the house demanded that you "Put your eyes on Moonie!" in order to forestall any macular degeneration from the total absence of pigmentation in the room itself.

"I wasn't leaving without you." Ray Ray said sipping the god-awful ersatz champagne for which Moonie had signed a three year 1.5 million dollar endorsement contract. "I kinda figured *you* were gonna be my 'goodie bag'."

Moonie feigned modesty and touched his knee with a limp-wristed pat despite the fact that Ray Ray had just called her a "bag". They were speaking the same language now, the lingua franca of red carpet poseurs whose nose for available swag at an event far out-stripped any knowledge of the event itself.

Moonie raised her glass to his. "I actually *do* have a "goodie bag" for this event. And it's a damn good one, too, if I do say so my-self." She leaned in slightly bringing her mouth close to his cheek. "But I'm not in it. I'm stayin' right here."

Ray Ray touched his glass to hers with a deft "clink", made by a man who is used to sealing deals and bets this way. "Well, goodie, goodie for me," he said and laughed loudly triggering Moonie's laugh as well which he immediately took as a "buy". Mission Accomplished.

Now Ray Ray could relax and enjoy himself. He shifted in his seat as a result and became instantly familiar with her. He raised a finger to one of Moonie's extensions and twirled it seductively.

"You live around here?" He said invitingly.

"I *do*," Moonie said. Suddenly, Moonie felt like she could marry this rascal of a man who seemed to be actually paying attention to her without Moonie having to put his head in a hammerlock first. They stared at each other for a long quiet moment. Both wanted to let the moment sink in so there would be no mistaking the deal. Ray Ray began a slow smile of understanding and recognition. Moonie merely nodded once as if confirming a bid at an auction.

It was at that moment that one of Moonie's white pool boys, stripped-to-the-waist, found them with his tray of hot potato knish-es compliments of Aunt Jemima.

"Hot knish, Ms. Brown?"

"You bet. Uh-huh," she replied emphatically while taking one and biting into it without taking her eyes off Ray Ray. The filling inside ejaculated out onto the couch between them. They both looked at it, then at each other, and then burst out laughing while the pool boy responded feverishly with the towel he carried over his arm.

"Was it good for you?" Ray Ray said sweetly.

"These are the *best*," Moonie replied licking the underside of the knish seductively and then the back of her hand. "I could eat 'em all night."

The pool boy finished wiping and then looked from Moonie to Ray Ray for either punishment or thanks. But the two fakers were deep into each other's eyes, and the pool boy had become an intrusion. He turned around and left without another word.

Now all that had to be done to seal the deal was that Ray Ray would have to tell Ronnie, his male lover, that he would be otherwise engaged for a spell or, at least, until after the ceremony.

CHAPTER SEVENTEEN

Brendan's friend, Joe Finnegan, had always told him that you go along in life trying to do the right thing, and then one day your doctor says, "I don't like the looks of that"; and your whole life changes. The first time Brendan heard that phrase, his doctor's finger was up his ass during Brendan's yearly physical.

"I don't like the looks of that," Dr. Kenneth Benjamin said. He kept his finger up Brendan's ass just long enough to make it almost a social call as Brendan knelt on the examining table.

"Whaddya mean, *'looks'*? Are you looking out the window or do you feel something?"

"Sorry, my friend," Doctor Benjamin said as he pulled his finger out. "Just a figure of speech."

"So?"

"So, what?"

"So what don't you like the looks of? You found something."

"No big deal. Your prostate's got a little ridge on it that wasn't there before." he said.

"How do you know?" Brendan said, "You haven't been up there in a year. What're you, some kinda elephant?"

"This is what I do," Dr. Benjamin said as he took the glove off with a slightly angry snap. "Clean yourself up and see me in the office. You just ruined my weekend." Then he turned and left, leaving Brendan to hobble over to get some tissue, wipe his ass, and pull up his pants.

"*Your* weekend?" Brendan shouted at the closed door. He followed Benjamin down to his office for the "sit-down" after the exam that was usually a jolly affair where he could score some Viagra samples. But this time, the mood was somber.

"I hate when this happens," Kenny said avoiding Brendan's gaze. "You got a urologist? Or shall I send you to my buddy, Rich Sandler."

Brendan's head began to swim. There was a surreal quality to all this. He was use to one perfect check-up after another. Suddenly, there was a train leaving for old age, and he was being hustled through security to make it.

"I think I went to a guy over on Bedford Drive once. But that was when I was out here doing a pilot a long time ago. His name was Sykes, and he had a place in Santa Barbara.

"Michael Sykes is my urologist." Dr. Benjamin said. "He examined me once in a broom closet at UCLA."

"He stuck his finger up your ass in a closet? Isn't that a felony in California?"

"It was a hernia. Nothing wet." Benjamin shot back while writing Sykes's name and number on a piece of paper. "Go see him and get this checked out so we can both relax. Thanks for ruining my weekend." He handed the slip of paper across the desk to Brendan.

"Do you think he'll remember me?" Brendan asked.

"Once he examines you he will. He has great hands. I know." Kenny said wiggling his fingers.

"Really."

"Yeah." Kenny wanted Brendan out of his office fast. Doctors hate having sick people around. It gives them the "willies."

A week later Brendan found himself in front of one of the great assholes of California Medicine, Michael Sykes, the WASP urologist. The guy maintained a broad country club smile on his face as he sat on a rolling stool, like a mechanic going under a car, and examined Brendan's balls as if they were Christmas tree ornaments.

Why is this man smiling? Brendan thought. His face is three inches from my cock, and his un-gloved fingers are playing with my balls in a style that's more "fondle" than "medical". Brendan was confused but not uncomfortable. Either I'm used to this, or he is, Brendan thought. Maybe the guy studied to become a priest before he went into medicine.

It wasn't a homosexual thing that Brendan suspected; it was that Sykes made the whole thing seem like a play-date rather than an examination. He jiggled Brendan's balls and then ran his hands up and down his thighs.

"Nice quads." Sykes said.

"Really?" Brendan said. Rather than be embarrassed by the compliment, Brendan found himself instantly, but strangely, proud of himself.

"Oh yes," Sykes said. Suddenly the muscles in Brendan' legs were of more interest than his prostate. Much more. Brendan tightened his quads automatically the way he would flex his bicep whenever anyone touched his arm which always elicited an automatic compliment. Or he would silently tighten his stomach should anyone, or anything, come near.

"Do you work out?" Sykes wanted to know.

"Some, but not much," Brendan told him. It was true. Brendan secretly considered himself some kind of natural specimen.

"Okay. Let's see if I can feel what Kenny felt," Sykes said getting up off his stool and patting the examining table as if Brendan were a Golden Retriever. "I specifically told him not to describe it to me," he added with child-like glee.

Suddenly, this had become some sort of game of "Hide and Go Feel". Brendan could tell that Dr. Sykes was into it. He got up on the table and assumed the same position that his son, Zeke, used to do after a bowel movement, waiting for someone to wipe him. Brendan almost yelled, "I'm all finished!" in Zeke's honor.

For this exam, Sykes strapped on a rubber glove, but still with the same shit-eating grin that, now, was a little too close to home. Brendan had no problem with traditional prostate digital exams. Some men found it abhorrent, but Brendan simply filed it in the same place as other health-related pains in the ass: getting teeth drilled, having blood taken, colonoscopies. For Brendan they were the price you paid for living. So you might as well be a man about it even though it involved having a stranger stick his finger up your ass looking for something.

"Nope, feels normal," Sykes said withdrawing his finger, peeling off the glove, and dropping it into a trash can in one move. "But we'll take some blood just to be sure."

"But I just had my PSA done, and it was declining," Brendan said.

"We do a special PSA. Much more sophisticated and sensitive. And another test beside that." Sykes told him.

Brendan could hear the disappointment in Sykes' s voice. He felt mildly guilty. Being in the entertainment business, he instinctively wanted to please his audience. He felt as if his material had bombed.

"I can do better," Brendan blurted out as if reacting to one of Marge's dismissive scowls at a joke he'd just written.

Dr. Sykes put his hand (thankfully, now, without the soiled glove on it) on Brendan's shoulder like a scout master reassuring a tenderfoot. "You don't have to do a thing," he said smiling broadly, no doubt in anticipation of the next time. "Call me in a week."

The trip out of the office, through Sykes's waiting room, was better than the one coming in. Walking through a sea of jowly old men with middle-distance stares and the dank aroma of stale urine rarely encountered outside of a nursing home, is guaranteed to make anyone who can move faster than a shuffle feel at the top of their game.

Brendan averted his eyes from his future and crossed "The Room of Sighs" quickly to get to the outer door of the office and the eternal sunlight of Southern California. The prostate scare had clearly been an anomaly; but, now, it was a new source of material for bits with the girls on staff at "The Ladies' Room".

He would tell them that he'd learned how to do a prostate exam on himself and then ask them if they wanted to watch.

CHAPTER EIGHTEEN

L ittle did anyone realize, Brendan included, that Roberta's arrival at "The Ladies' Room" was the first step of a comeback
plan that the world's most famous transgender had secretly been
plotting in her Venice decoupage studio for years. Of course, since
she never bothered to make the distinction, there was very little
difference, in Roberta's mind, between a "comeback" and a "coup".

Beverly always thought she was "re-discovering" Roberta when
she had tapped her to join "our little gathering in the morning".
But Roberta's reputation as a poacher was well known in certain
circles. She had tried to take over the Late Show when Letterman
had his heart bypass under the guise of professional courtesy, but
the producers there were hip to her and would have none of it.
They wouldn't even book her on the show as a guest for fear that,
somehow, she would sit in the host's chair by "mistake" and never
leave. Most producers regarded Roberta with the same apprehen-
sion that landlords reserve for Gypsies. She was a Trojan horse full
of trouble.

Roberta was suspicious and ambivalent about straight women
because they liked men better than her, and they reminded her of
her molesting mother. But since Brendan found himself in a similar state toward women—albeit from a different perspective—it

prompted him to think that, just possibly, he and Roberta would get along famously: like two Army buddies or kindred spirits in a strange land which, in this case, just happened to be Daytime Television. Just a couple of guys—only one of them had implants and no cock. Brendan secretly harbored the thought that this would be the turning point in his wasted career where he would plug into Roberta's source of funding and access and become the powerhouse he had always thought he should have been.

"Howya doin', Roberta?" Brendan would say when they would meet outside the make-up room in the morning, making sure to get enough familiarity across in his delivery to signify that he considered them secret kinfolk. But, alas, Brendan never got more than that truck driver's head jerk as if she were acknowledging a new load of fill being dumped in the bed of her Mack D27 Vari-axle 14 Speed Super Haul.

The funny thing about Roberta was that, as remote and impenetrable as she was to the bulk of the staff, she could be, at the same time, incredibly responsive to their private needs—much more, certainly, than the other co-hosts who had worked intimately on a daily basis with them for 15 years without ever knowing their names, birthdays, marital status, talents, or even existence. The only thing that would rise above the quotidian anonymity of the staff and crew for the co-hosts was extreme tragedy, but that was only for its story quality not the actual suffering. Thus, there would be an outpouring of grief, attentiveness, and faux familial concern over some unspeakable personal horror that might befall the audio guy whose name they didn't know except that he was the one with the beard and bad breath that made them do the alphabet instead of numbers for "testing" after putting his lavaliere mic up their dress. Then they would traipse out to some non-descript funeral home in Woodland Hills to attend the wake of the incinerated grandmother of a man whose name they never bothered to learn. It was "The Ladies' Room's" version of "The Wall of Woe"(which they never graced) —a burst of instant concern and momentary deviation from their celebrity routine followed by an abrupt return to facelessness as if nothing had happened. The next day they would stand backstage, oblivious to the audio guy's groping hand, head turned away from his bad breath, skimming their blue cards; and then walk away, without comment, to do the show.

Roberta was different in many ways. It mirrored her schizoid psyche and equally schizoid body. For instance, while actively trying to ruin Sean, the prop guy's career by insisting he be banned from the studio in favor of a female one, she would, at the same time, turn around and reward him with an unannounced gift of a pair of $10,000 Koi Goldfish for his personal collection and commercial Koi breeding business. Of course, like Roberta herself, the Koi would turn out to be a mixed blessing. Queer and infertile, they raised havoc in the tanks, and the prop guy eventually had to destroy them before they could infect and kill off his entire life's work. But despite that slight flaw in the fish, Roberta's generosity had seemed real enough and worthy of adulation and credit. But the prop guy, even though he managed to keep his job, always had the nagging feeling that, rather than a peace offering, it was, in fact, the *coup de grace* of his television career, compliments of Roberta Monzon: the head of a fish instead of a horse.

"Hey, Beautiful!" Roberta yelled at the top of her voice to the obscure Broadway actress whom she insisted be booked despite the fact that the hapless dolly couldn't get arrested in a dinner theater production of "Cats" much less network daytime television. But there she was, wearing her Broadway uber make-up with lipstick applied like the signature of a serial killer.

"Ladies' and gentlemen, the fabulous Ginger Ramone," Roberta continued, pointing to her but not advancing towards her an inch. "Welcome to my show, honey."

The operative word there, of course, for everyone to hear, was "*my*" show. Hearts behind closed dressing room doors leapt at the sound of it. Roberta's voice was as distinctive as it was loud—unashamedly crass and unmistakably Upper Peninsula trash—which became all the more unpleasant once Brendan found out that she currently also considered herself an Israeli after fucking an El Al female pilot and was studying Kabbalah with Madonna—another obnoxious convert.

"Great to be here, Bobby," Ginger shot back. Her dressing room looked as if she thought her three minute number under closing credits was going to be an extended run.

"I'll come visit after the show," Roberta said, "It's an honor to have you with us." That was for the benefit of the naysayers, and especially Bad Bob, who had fought her tooth and nail on the booking. But it was typical of Roberta's modus operandi. She would create holy hell with everyone and everything and then coolly step back as if she had had nothing to do with it and was merely an observer. That was it. She freely alternated between perpetrator and observer, and neither persona seemed to know anything of the other.

Roberta then retreated back into her dressing room, leaving the diminutive and, now, confused Ms. Ramone to fend for herself among the philistines of television. She had been anointed and then abandoned in a matter of seconds by her champion who was, already, thinking about something entirely different.

Roberta took care of everything but the show in the hour leading up to air time. Of course, so did the other co-hosts; but they, at least, were veterans of the fray. And it wasn't so much that they ignored pre-show prep as they focused on things that were ancillary to its content.

Thus, Marge would fuss endlessly about her hair and her shoulder pads while texting on her cellphone and iPad as if the people who could help her were far flung instead of standing right in front of her with blue cards for her to ignore. It became a staff joke that she literally wouldn't read anything unless a stage manager was counting down in her ear and the show's opening theme was playing on the other side of the set wall. But that wasn't enough. Marge was the only co-host who would leave the table during the commercial breaks to go back into the hosts' green room to have her hair attended to rather than do anything as radical as prepare for the next segment or read the new lines Brendan had rushed upstairs to give her. And it was a standing admonition that anything put on the teleprompter was Sanskrit to Marge Foley.

Beverly spent her time before the show constantly on the phone arranging her manufactured life in an endless pursuit of the ultimate "get" that would secure her legendary status once and for all and vanquish all others, not just from the business, but from the collective memory of the public as a whole. Beverly's attitude was that "The Ladies' Room" was far beneath her and not worthy of even her partial attention. Her pose was that she did it because she was a "good sport".

"The Ladies' Room" merely added to Beverly's drive to be ubiquitous beyond any constraints of the time/space continuum or the dictates of social/professional obligations. Brendan once saw pictures of Beverly Frost in *jeans*, for God's sake, at some Topanga Canyon "hoedown". But wait. Hadn't she also been with Queen Noor in Paris that same afternoon? Or was she on tape? Or was she, impossibly, "live" in both places?

Once Beverly had once flown from Los Angeles to South Africa and back over the weekend without ever missing a minute of the Friday or Monday live shows of "The Ladies' Room" just to interview the ten year old daughter of a beloved actor who'd been mauled to death by a herd of sheep. Her Einsteinian ability to warp time and space gave her a scoop on the unexpected death of John F. Kennedy Jr. because she had divined an early demise of the scion and had actual footage of family and friends speaking of him on camera in the past tense. A pre-need obituary. It had been a ratings bonanza… although calling a Kennedy obit a "scoop" is bit of a stretch given their proclivities. But after being forced to cover Princess Diana's death as a mere correspondent doing mop up (even though she had an actual hand written note to her from Di), and after the Concorde was taken out of service, she vowed never to let a "close celebrity friend and colleague" let her down again by dying unexpectedly.

Moonie Brown's pre-show ritual consisted of her divine consultation with her laptop computer. She was so incredibly proud to not only own a computer but also know how to turn it on that she would sit in front of it for hours, like John Tesh in First Class on a commercial flight stroking his chin and pretending to work as if it were a Large Hadron Collider, and he was looking for the Higgs boson. Brendan would pass Moonie's open dressing room door before the show and see only her massive bare back that looked like a leather couch hunched over the small machine as if she were going to eat it. Where she went on the internet, or with whom she consulted, was unknown; but "on air" she would proudly reference her cyber travels with the same reverence and wonder that a recently abducted farmer might use when talking about anal probes at the hands of aliens.

Only Bambi Crutchfield would actually study. But that was because Bad Bob was always trying to cram a century of religious fundamentalism down the throat of this 24 year old idiot who thought the Bible had been written by someone named Gideon. She never did get it all straight and on the air would come out with laughable and quotable gaffes about Jesus and the Dinosaurs or how the earth used to be flat.

Roberta's dressing room became her cave, and she would retreat to it, like a beast in exile, to wallow in her half man/half woman; half saint/half monster; half health nut/half invalid; half pro/half amateur; half true artist/half poseur; schizoid world. The place was full of the knick-knacks of a troubled mind and life. Childish toys and icons standing next to religious talismans and political mementos. It was here that Brendan learned that, despite her improvised and free-range body, Roberta was, in fact, a finger wagging conservative which just made her bifurcated life as disjointed and contradictory as that thing in her vagina that used to be a cock.

"Come on in," Roberta would say to Brendan as long as he appeared at her door with some other (preferably lesbian) staff member. She had vowed to never trust a man under any circumstances after her father had facilitated her mother's transgressions. "The weather's fine." This referred to the fact that, in an exercise of her power on the show, she had insisted that the air conditioning in her office be increased exponentially to combat her hormone induced hot flashes. Of course, no one had the temerity to question whether a transsexual was even capable of menopause. But the word had gone down to Mack McCleary, the long suffering production manager, who immediately ordered a separate air duct be run directly from the 2500 ton air conditioner atop the building straight to the 10' x 12' dressing room of Ms. Monzon. Consequently, whenever Brendan was admitted to her chamber, he studiously avoided the gaping air conditioning maw in the center of her ceiling that emitted enough cold air to make even David Letterman shiver. As Brendan's mother would've said, "You could hang meat," it was so cold.

It was as if Roberta was running an alternate show in her dressing room. She was doing "The Ladies' Room" as it ought to be done, according to her. In fact, Roberta's crew of neo Nazi lesbians would gather together each morning while the rest of the staff feverishly prepared the live show in order to perform Roberta's own webcam edition of "Talky-Talk with the "Robertii" ("Robertii" as in the plural of "Roberta" since she fancied her faithful followers as mere clones or impersonators of herself—like the "Elvii" of Bad Bob Vapors' Roadhouse). Roberta would sit in the center with the others hovering around her head in order to squeeze into the webcam frame, and they would simply talk and giggle into the computer like a bunch of pre-adolescent girls making crank calls on a rainy afternoon—each of them, but especially Roberta, eying the camera with a self-referential sneer as if they were looking at themselves in their bedroom mirrors and privately practicing their "street 'tudes".

"So what's up?" Roberta would say to Brendan moments before the lower half of a sandwich would go into her mouth.

She never held a meeting nor spoke to anyone in power that she did not eat at the same time, making it abundantly clear that the food being stuffed into her mouth by her fat fingers was vastly more important to her than the person in front of her or the subject being discussed. In that, she was not unlike Mugsy who always brought a paper cup half-filled with "bird seed" to all meetings. Mugsy would then proceed to extract the seeds and grains from the bottom of the cup with the tips of her long fingers in slow motion and then distractedly place the morsel on the tip of her extended, lizard-like tongue while reading a gossip magazine or the script. She looked like Richard Pryor doing his "gazelles at the waterhole" bit.

But Roberta's food was always messy, wet, and oozing with contempt; and she would attack it in the worst way possible in order to exaggerate its distasteful attributes and her disdain for the person in front of her. Thus, a sandwich was eaten from the bottom, a piece of pie from the center, an éclair broken in half, or a broiled chicken eviscerated first. This insured that there would be as much food on her chin as on her fingers establishing an even lower rank of importance to anyone else in the room. Brendan decided the only way anyone could get Roberta's full attention was to allow her to eat *them* during her meetings.

"Whaddya got for me?"

The maddening thing about Roberta was that she *was* good. And in the brief flashes of clarity between the roast beef and the barbecue dip, she could identify the core of a guest's relevance or rearrange an interview in one fell swoop, making it suddenly exciting and pertinent. It almost made watching her rescue an errant slice of tomato with her prehensile tongue worth it. But then she would dash all that brilliance with delusions of talk show grandeur by saying, thirty minutes before air, "Why don't we get Zubin Mehta and the Los Angeles Philharmonic to play them on? The pit manager's a friend of mine."

"That's a cute kid you got there," she said to Brendan one day after Zeke had visited the show the day before when the nanny had called in sick.

"Thanks," Brendan said. "He really liked you." Brendan lied. Zeke couldn't differentiate between anyone on the show other than the one or two producers who gave him swag in the form of toys and promotional materials. But Roberta was now eye-balling Brendan with a look that said, "What're you doing with something as good as that? *I* want him". It's probably the same feeling the citizens of Malawi get when Madonna gets off a plane.

"He gets pushed around a lot at his school. More than I would like," Brendan continued, "That's why it's a great confidence boost for him to come here once in a while."

"One of my kids is a foster kid," Roberta said referring the menagerie of children she had assembled with a succession of live-in lovers at her compound in Venice. "We haven't adopted him yet; but we let him stay, so he's understandably a little insecure," she snorted a half-chuckle out of the side of her mouth as if doing a routine. "He always thinks he's going back. Ha!"

Then her face dropped into serious lesbo gravitas. "So there was this kid at his school who was bullying him about it. About being a foster child. And I saw it with my own eyes. So I waited for the kid in the playground very patiently until I could get him alone. Then I looked him straight in the eye and said, 'If you ever mess with my boy again, I will hurt you.'" Roberta paused slightly without altering her cold-blooded deadpan. "'And if you ever say anything about this, I will hurt you more,'" she added holding her killer stare as if Brendan were the bully. Then she turned away.

But Brendan knew that what she had really been saying was "If you mess with my boy, I will hurt myself. And then, I will hurt myself more"—such was Roberta's Christ-like assumption of all pain and suffering unto herself. She was both punisher and the punished, but always the spotless victim willingly sacrificing herself for the sins of the world.

"Zeke really liked those little characters you invented," Brendan went on, hoping to lighten the mood and, maybe, score an animation deal.

"Here," Roberta said getting up and moving like John Wayne over to a shelf above her sink. "Take these for the little guy." She gave Brendan three little fantasy figures that Roberta claimed to have created and designed for young minds. Brendan doubted it, yet there could be a cartoon coming out of it, or maybe a children's book he could write. "Disney's very interested," she added. Brendan inspected the minimalist figures as if they were ancient artifacts from a dig to demonstrate that he was taking her seriously.

"These are incredible" he said getting deeper into her shit than he wanted to. "You really ought to do something with them."

Now Roberta knew that Brendan was bullshitting her since she'd just told him what was happening. She took a step back and eye-balled him with her head slightly cocked, suddenly suspicious of everything. Brendan had seen that look before. If Roberta had still been a man it would've meant that the next thing out of Brendan's mouth would've gotten a punch in return. But, instead, now that Roberta was a woman, the look just signaled a deep resentment, alienation, and anger that she no longer had the "punch" option. Brendan knew it was time for him to get the hell out of there.

"Thanks for these," he said holding up the figures. "Zeke'll love them." He backed out of her dressing room holding the little rubber figures high as if they were some hot tickets he'd just scored. Roberta continued to eye him skeptically without forgiveness. Then she simply, and silently, closed the door without averting her stare. Brendan heard the small, but deafening, "click" of the latch and knew, once again, he'd blown it with the mercurial Roberta Monzon.

As Brendan retreated to his office, he had to remind himself one more time that the best strategy with Roberta was to stay *under* her radar. Roberta was always loaded for bear and looking for any man with power she could knock off. Fortunately for Brendan, on "The Ladies' Room", where hair and make-up had seventy-two Emmys between them, there *was* no one lower than a writer. Even cable pullers and prop girls got more respect and a better table at the foolish "Technical Emmys", held each year like a porn convention or Tuba Conference at the god-awful Hollywood Palladium on Sunset. Thus, keeping under Roberta's radar for Brendan would be no problem.

But Bad Bob, as the largest and most visible male target that any man-hating tranny had ever met, was another problem altogether. Even though Roberta was vocal about her desire to be part of "The Ladies' Room" crew and a "real team player", her arrival each morning a full hour before the "CrossTalk" meeting should have been recognized for what it really was: the harbinger of a coup and not even remotely connected to an alleged desire to contribute. Great Whites are not known for their teamwork. In a war between a pair of tortured balls (Bad Bob's) and a transgender woman mean enough to cut her own off, the first casualty is self-respect.

Bad Bob immediately was cast as the "Father" who had willingly allowed little Robert to be compromised each night by his wife, and Beverly unwittingly became the marauding mother, sweet but deadly in her co-opting of her son's sexuality. The stage was set. Of course, the kicker was that no one knew if the "My mother, my lover" story was even remotely true. The "mother" had brazenly had sex with her son in full view of the rest of the family. And equally brazen, in the story, was young Robert who apparently became an able enough lover to knock her up three times. Night after night this went until the mother was shot dead by the father. Then, Roberta reports, everything went back to normal. Or did the father pick up where the mother had left off? And what was "normal" in that household? Or was the whole thing the oedipal fantasy of a troubled boy, in love with his mother but released by her death to become her once and for all. Nobody dared ever ask Roberta whether becoming transgender was the boy's punishment for his own role in the violation. Cutting off the offending organ was almost biblical in its symbolic retribution. Listeners to the story always nodded sympathetically instead of asking the obvious question. Why did the father allow the situation to flourish? Or was he also a deviate? It ultimately didn't make sense, and it led Brendan to conclude that Roberta's "abuse" story was just that: a story woven by a lonely and angry kid with issues. But it worked. As an abuse story it was a beaut, and it provided celebrity *bona fides*. And Roberta never failed to recount it, coughing it up at the drop of a hat, as if she'd never divulged it before. Except that the listener always found it vaguely familiar because she had, in fact, told it many times to whoever would listen. Apparently, it was too good a tale to keep to one's self or in the confessional.

Bad Bob's response to this surgically altered fox that he and Beverly had willingly ushered into their chicken coop of a show was to become a male anorexic. Unable, or unwilling, to combat her effectively, Bad Bob stopped eating. Maybe it was his transgender way of fighting fire with fire. He would out-bitch the bitch. Whatever the reason, the staff watched him melt away the pounds and his pot belly before their very eyes. And, perhaps, as a means of cementing her dominance over him, every pound of lard that Bob took off, Roberta put on. Not only were their first names linked forever, but their bodies seemed to have a strange symbiosis. Nothing was lost between them, like energy and matter. Bad Bob was just another expression of Roberta who, in turn, was really Robert. And they were both equally abused/loved by Beverly, the mother. They were all the same substance, just existing in different unstable forms.

At the same time, the show's obsession with dieting meant that there were at least two segments a week on the subject, but neither the staff nor the co-hosts were able to practice what they produced. Everyone was overweight. Except Beverly who maintained herself like a cockroach petrified in amber. But everyone else had become so addicted to the calories they were daily talking about controlling that more and more food segments crept into the grid for no other reason than to give the co-hosts tasting privileges and the staff left-overs. The very fingers that were wagged at the public about the "obesity epidemic in America" were then licked clean of pudding in the following segment.

Thus, the endless food segments made Bad Bob's physical turn-around and wasting away all the more startling. But rather than become a cause of concern for Roberta's bleeding heart, it was merely a daily reminder that she was winning. She was gaining what Bad Bob was losing.

"I want a private toilet," Roberta said to Bad Bob one day as he passed her in the hall after the show. "There's no toilet in my dressing room." Roberta had stopped when she said it which meant that Bad Bob had to stop, also.

"There aren't any bathrooms in any of the dressing rooms," he said. "Just a sink."

"You want me to pee in the sink, Robert? I can't do that anymore."

"No." Bad Bob said trying to remain calm. "There's nothing I can do about it. Everyone uses the ladies' room down the hall."

"You see, that's just the point." Roberta went on, "I've always had a private bathroom on all my shows. I can't hold it until I go home. Whaddya think I am, a camel?"

Bad Bob really didn't want to get into this discussion standing there in the middle of the hallway. He knew he didn't have a solution, and he knew she was going to humiliate him in some way. His face began to glow red as it did when he was embarrassed, mad, lying, or being put down by Beverly.

"I'll see what I can do," he said.

"What the hell does that mean?" Roberta persisted. "Do I get a private bathroom or not?"

"Look, Roberta, even Beverly doesn't have a private bathroom. She uses the ladies' room like everyone else. All the cohosts, all the celebrities, all the stars, and me."

"But not *me*. I don't know if I can work this way."

"Beverly does."

"Beverly doesn't *go* to the bathroom. Everyone knows that. She doesn't get sick, and she never pees." Roberta said. "She's not like a normal person. I am. I need a private toilet."

Bad Bob almost told her to "use the men's room, then". It would remind her of her youth, and she could do everything standing up. Of course, he figured she probably did piss standing up, dick or no dick. Old habits die hard, and a man never loses his ability to aim.

"Do you want me to *make* a bathroom?" Bad Bob said exasperated.

"Yeah," Roberta said looking up at him. "And the air conditioning still sucks. I'm flashing like crazy and sweatin' like a pig in there."

"That I can fix," he said seizing on something he actually could attend to.

"Get on it," she said dismissing him and turning back toward her, still, too-warm and toilet-deprived dressing room.

Bad Bob could do nothing but stand there, nonplussed. Red faced, hungry, and completely undone, once again, by Roberta. But Roberta, for her part, had already forgotten about the exchange two seconds after leaving him hapless and at sea in the same way that her off-hand complaints would get stage hands fired and executives' offices moved. She was one of those people whose shit rolled off their back but stuck wherever it landed. Roberta was on to the next.

She never did get her toilet. But, per order of the executive producer of "The Ladies' Room", and much to the consternation of Mack, who had to find the money in the budget for it, a second dedicated duct was dropped directly from the main frame air conditioning compressor on the roof, through three floors of the building, to the ceiling of Roberta's dressing room where it blew forced cold air across the beads of sweat on her upper lip. She would sit under the, now, double vent as if it were dispensing indulgence from on high during the "post mortem" meetings which she insisted be held in her room rather than the rehearsal hall. Anyone standing near her would then be treated to the cool effluent down-wind coming off Roberta and smelling of Roberta's sweat, sour perfume, and the faint odor of balls.

The ultra-cool of Roberta's dressing room confirmed it as a mini studio over which she could maintain the complete control she lusted for in the actual studio above her. Roberta's webcast each morning expanded to demonstrate just that and also to rub it in. "Talky Talk" (Roberta's nod to "South Pacific") quickly grew from a prankish gaggle to a legitimate webcast presence. Roberta and her crew—her hair dresser, make-up artist and personal assistant—would do their own show which would often scoop the show Roberta was actually getting paid to do an hour hence. Not even Bad Bob realized the ramifications of this, nor, if he had realized them, did he have the balls to stop her. By the time "The Ladies' Room" went on the air, "Talky Talk" with "The Robertii" had already been aired on the Web. No wonder "The Ladies' Room", presented "live" on the SBS network, felt like an anticlimax. By the time Roberta went on the air each day, she had "been there and done that" which accounted for her slightly bored demeanor on the show and her impatience with the co-hosts and guests around her. It also accounted for the fact that when Roberta went live on the network she felt she had to up the ante from the mini show she'd just done in her dressing room. And this led to her demise, in that, the one thing she hated as a performer was to repeat herself. If she had been a sweetheart on "Talky Talk" she would be a bitch on the same subject fifteen minutes later on the air.

"Whaddya mean I can't have a private toilet in my room? I've always had a private toilet on all my other shows. It's absurd," Roberta said again the next day to Bad Bob, bringing up the topic in the make-up room this time in front of everyone as if she were continuing their conversation from the day before in the hallway.

"Beverly uses the ladies' room on the floor. So did Carol Channing when she got sick." he whined back.

"That's their problem," Roberta said. "I never heard of such a thing. What am I supposed to do?"

"That's *your* problem" Bad Bob said without realizing that he had just trumped a comedian and a deeply disturbed transsexual. He knew in an instant from the look on Roberta's face that he would pay dearly for the laugh he got.

"Bob," she said carefully and looking straight at him, "You couldn't produce a pile of shit if you ate an elephant."

That ended the discussion.

But Bad Bob was telling the truth. Beverly, for all her faux royalty, did use the common ladies' room and every female staff member had been treated to her long wet farts that emanated from her stall each time she urinated.

Despite Roberta's seemingly unsolvable "Mountain to Mohammed" toilet situation, (The AC ducts could be jerry-rigged, the plumbing could not) Roberta did actually concoct a plan for her use of the public ladies' room if ever an absolute emergency presented itself. She would have Jet, her scary make-up artist in combat boots and Nazi haircut, stand guard outside the ladies' room like a member of a rock star posse so that no one would hear *her* farts nor, more importantly, be able to check out her surgically enhanced genitalia. The secret of what hung, or didn't hang, between Roberta's legs would remain one of the great unsolved mysteries of the world.

CHAPTER NINETEEN

D r. Sykes called to happily tell Brendan that he would need a biopsy on his prostate.

"One of your tests came back normal, but the other one--the "special" one we do—was inconclusive. So you must have a biopsy," the doctor said with a certain breathlessness in his voice.

Brendan got the message on the same day another notice went up on the "Wall of Woe". This time, a boom operator on "Living" had been stricken with multiple, mysterious, but terminal ailments. Not only that, his house had burned down while he was in the hospital. The single piece of typewriter paper—with a "compassionate" font, that made it look like a greeting card—stayed up on The Wall for a full week. Brendan would read the page each time he took the elevator as if there might be an update. But the message was always the same. The guy was hopeless, alone, and needed money—the stuff of the soaps themselves. Then Brendan started reading the notice half expecting to see his name there, too. But no one "above the line" ever seemed to be afflicted. It was always an unknown crew member, laboring in the dark, beloved but invisible, except for a burst of illumination at death like the last puff of a cheap firework, and then nothing.

For Brendan, the entire biopsy process was nothing more than another small adventure. The hardest part was maintaining a full bladder in Sykes' waiting room while the other elderly patients, in their soiled plaid shirts, padded in and out of the examining rooms ahead of him. The procedure itself was akin to a visit to the dentist, except upside down. Sykes even almost said, "Open wide" when he inserted the various probes up Brendan's ass.

At the time, Brendan never connected the beginning of his own medical journey with those notices pasted on the "Wall of Woe". It had begun so routinely and had proceeded like nothing more than another due diligence test. So when his cell phone rang while he was driving to work a week later, he answered it with no foreboding even though it was too early for a normal call.

"You definitely have cancer," the happy Dr. Sykes said. "I want you to get a bone scan and an abdominal cavity MRI and then come see me to discuss your options. I'm going on vacation. So, in the meantime, get the tests; and then we can talk."

"Oh," Brendan said, "Great." But he wasn't being sarcastic. His first response was to congratulate the doctor on the success of his tests.

"I'll be back in a week, and then you'll come in and see me."

"Absolutely," Brendan said as he pulled into the parking lot at the studio. "Okay. I'll get everything done and see you when you get back."

"That's great. See you then," the doctor said cheerily and hung up.

Brendan sat in the car for several beats and then got out and walked into the SBS building. As he stood waiting for the elevator, he noticed that the sheet of paper about the man whose house had burned down while in the hospital had finally been taken down. But, thankfully, another one with Brendan's name on it had not replaced it. He felt curiously safe.

Usually, when Brendan got to his office, he liked to hustle through his e-mail and other computer housekeeping chores until the "CrossTalk" meeting began at 7:00. But this day he sat silently with his hands in his lap. He realized that he was now fired *and* possibly dying. It was all drawing to a close. What he needed now was a doctor to take care of the cancer and Marge to take care of the firing. Strangely, he had more faith in getting rid of the cancer than the pink slip. But he was determined to bring it directly to Marge because he was sure that there was no way she would allow them to mess with her *cancer-ridden* writer. He would couch it in fascist terms to appeal to her Commie patina. He would lay the cancer on her and remind her of the firing at the same time. A one-two punch that could not be denied. He mentally rehearsed how he would break the news. With any luck, she would blame Bad Bob for causing the cancer.

Brendan walked into the meeting early. Roberta was already there sitting in her barber chair with her dirty bare feet up on the counter and her linebacker practice sweats hitched up exposing the blue dragon tattoo around her calf. Brendan couldn't help but notice that the sex change had not reached her feet, and her toenails were still decidedly male: unpainted and gnarled, and each toe had a five o'clock shadow on top from being shaved.

"Morning, Roberta," Brendan said as he entered. She looked up from her Jet Ski Magazine and nodded again like a garage mechanic up to his elbows in an engine block. Brendan continued on and took his seat in an empty barber chair in the back of the room.

Because of cutbacks at The Swann Company, not only was everything suddenly printed on both sides of the paper now, but the newspapers for the writers had been reduced to one set. "You can share!" Madame Defarge had cheerfully offered when Brendan pointed out that there were *two* writers on the show. But she was too pleased with the bottom-line savings to care. Swann was famous for cutting off its beak to spite its face.

Since the "writers set" of newspapers was automatically delivered directly to Leo's office, merely because his name came first in the credits, it meant Brendan had to forage for the papers issued for the talent in the make-up room which the hair and make-up people naturally assumed were meant for them. The only perk for arriving early for the "CrossTalk" meeting was that Brendan could secure a fresh set of papers before the hair and make-up people had descended upon them and ruined them. Brendan was like the legendary baseball catcher/spy, Moe Berg, who was also fanatic about his papers and considered newspapers that had already been opened and read to be "dead".

Brendan hadn't really processed the fact that he had just been told he had cancer. It didn't exactly rock him as he thought it should have. Rather, he seemed to deal with it as just another production problem. There wasn't any enormity to it, just one more chore to be checked off. The event seemed mundane and pedestrian.

The ladies entered one at a time in various degrees of undress looking like the delusional losers of a "The Ladies' Room" look-alike contest. Beverly usually arrived wearing pre make-up make-up so as to not scare anyone. She would shuffle in with one hand extended in her modified "Heisman" even when there was no one around as if she were trying to make her way through a crowded room even when it was empty. By the time anyone else arrived Beverly usually had her head slung back in a shampoo sink. This solved two problems. It prevented anyone from speaking directly to her and also avoided the horror of being seen without her full panoply of make-up and coif. She would allow her curlers to be observed but only after her make-up had been applied so that she looked like a 1940's glamour queen in repose. It was her "dressing room Vegas showgirl" look which constituted her only true memory of her father.

Marge, without hair and make-up, looked as if she'd just been given a "beatin'" the night before. The roots of her dyed hair and her Irish heritage were clearly visible. Her unpainted face looked tough and combative. If she'd had a fish in her hand, it would not have looked out of place. In order to tame her Irish curls they had to apply measures that made even Moonie Brown look askance. Moonie chose wigs over having her hair literally baked and flattened with a tool that looked as if it could tame rebar. The result, on Marge, was a clown-like display of feathered hair wings that stuck out like the branches of a paper Christmas tree before it was mercifully combed into something that resembled a hairstyle. Her "aggressive woman's bald spot" presented another problem. She would admit to many things in her act but never anything to do with her looks.

Of course, Moonie came into work having slept in her hair, make-up, and underwear from the night before, and she smelled like it, too.

Roberta was late for once but quickly explained why. "I want everyone to know that I am now wearing Pampers to work." Roberta announced when everyone else had arrived, but the meeting had not started.

"I'm sure you mean 'Depends', darling," Beverly said. "Pampers are for babies." Leave it to Beverly to get, at least, one dig in per every exchange.

"Whatever." Roberta replied. "It's because they won't put a toilet in my dressing room."

"I thought your dressing room *was* a toilet." Marge shot back unable to pass up a straight line.

"Only when you open your mouth in it, Babe," Roberta said with her hand on Marge's forearm to indicate it was just comedy jousting. They both laughed. The rest of the room kept their heads down.

Sometimes the ladies' would forget that more than half the room was filled with staff members who had never been out to the Malibu Colony or to Ivy at the Shore. In this way, the co-hosts were like porn stars or reality show players. They really did forget that the cameras were always rolling. And sometimes the sex and fights were actually real, even though most times they were not. The ladies had the same problem with onstage vs. offstage, real vs. not real, bitch vs. sweetheart. Brendan and the others never knew whom or what they would meet in the halls or the elevator. Beverly and Moonie were the worst offenders.

Moonie was always playing out her private fantasy of being a legitimate celebrity which, in fact, worked for a while. On airplanes she would travel with her "slave of the month"; and, when the flight attendant would come by and inquire about her meal choice or a cocktail, Moonie would whisper her order to her assistant seated protectively next to her on the aisle who would then relay the message to the attendant that "Ms. Brown would like a glass of champagne." And when the flight attendant didn't quite get it and would continue speaking directly to the obese half-breed sitting in the window seat, the assistant would then be prompted to reply with even more insistence, "*And* Ms. Brown will have the chicken."

After the meeting, but before he returned to his office to write the jokes for Marge to ignore, Brendan decided there could be an upside to his cancer. Now that he could honestly claim that "I have cancer", the trick would be to maximize the effect of that revelation to serve his own purposes. He would tell Marge in the same way that he told her he'd been fired. The combo would release a mother's rage in Marge to surround and protect her writer like those stories of 90 pound women lifting cars off their fallen toddlers. Then he would tell Bad Bob, just to watch him squirm for having terminated a cancer victim. Then he would tell Beverly.

Brendan knew that, in truth, he really *wasn't* dying, but he liked to fantasize about Beverly being the main speaker at his funeral. She would be brilliant and faux sincere exactly as she was on television when eulogizing an underling whom she'd just fired. "Rachael wanted to spread her wings and fly. We wish her well. She will be dearly missed."

"We wish her well," was Beverly-speak for "Fuck you."

In short, Brendan knew that, if anything could save his job, it was the cancer. He had been with "The Ladies Room" for 15 years, since its inception. He had written his jokes for Marge day in and day out and contributed countless additional material for her appearances on Leno and other venues. He estimated that half her stand-up act consisted of material she hadn't used on the show but saved for herself. He had even gladly provided material on demand for her best friend Moira Monahan, a relentlessly foul-mouthed anti Semite who, at her best, looked like a wet cat—a wet rabid cat. Brendan knew that Marge was his ace in the hole, and the "hole", in this case, was the show. A comedian always protected her source like a junkie his connection. Unless they were too stupid, arrogant, angry, and fatally lazy to realize where it all came from.

"I can't help you." Marge had said when Brendan first told her he'd been fired. "I've done as much as I can do."

Brendan was shocked at her response. Together they had fashioned her presence on the show to be integral to its success and, in most people's minds, its only saving grace.

"I told you to keep your mouth shut, but you wouldn't do that. So now I can't help you."

"All I was doing was following union rules," Brendan said.

"But you knew it makes them crazy." Marge shot back while alternately worrying over her hair and her cellphone.

"You mean, I should have just rolled over and allowed them to make up their own rules. They don't treat the stage hands that way."

"NABET and the Teamsters can shut the place down. You're a writer. The WGA is a bunch of pussies. They don't give a damn about you. You have to live in reality, Brendan."

"Look," Brendan said, "I don't want to get into a union measuring contest here, but the fact is that Bad Bob's firing me at the end of this cycle. And I wanted you to know about it."

"Well, I can't save you. They told me. There's nothing I can do. It's out of my hands. Keep your mouth shut, do your job, and maybe they'll change their minds." She began fussing with a hair band, putting it on and off. "Whaddya think? Hair band or no hair band? They don't know how to do my hair here. When I do Conan, I look a thousand times better."

But for some reason, Brendan thought that *this* time around it would be different—that the mere mention of the world "cancer" would move Marge to action. He was wrong.

"I just found out I have cancer," Brendan said as flatly as he could when he was finally alone with her in her dressing room. The unexpected harshness of the words made him choke slightly. He could feel his throat constrict with emotion even though he hadn't planned on it. Marge looked up from the iPhone she was holding in her lap along with two shoulder pads she desperately wanted to insert.

"Where?"

"Prostate."

"That's very treatable," she said. "You'll be fine." It would be the first of thousands of "You'll be fine" diagnoses pronounced by friends and strangers upon hearing that he had cancer. It was "French" for, "I really don't want to deal with this." People love saying, "You'll be fine". It gets them off the hook by declaring that the conversation is over. They probably said it to Jesus Christ on the Cross. "You'll be fine, JC," and changed the subject to more pleasant things.

"Yeah, I know I'll be fine, but I wanted you to know first."

"You haven't told Bad Bob? Maybe you should do that. Cancer's good for job security," she said with a smile.

"Until it isn't," Brendan said looking her straight in the eye.

"I don't want to think about it. All my friends are sick. It's getting so I'm afraid to answer the phone. I can't stand it. Just take care of it, okay? So I don't have to think about it." Brendan stood there for a beat. Yeah, that's the ticket, he thought. Take care of your cancer so Marge can feel better.

Marge continued to look into her dressing room mirror and endlessly poke and primp her hair as if her hair had a life of its own and had to be cajoled into going on stage with her.

"It's all about the hair," Marge said into the mirror with a sly smile of victory and smug pride knowing that, fortunately, her hair didn't have cancer.

Brendan realized he had done all he could do. There wasn't going to be any call to arms by Marge on any front, no marshaling of forces, no application of leverage on his behalf. He knew then that she was not the friend, nor even the colleague, he thought she was. Brendan turned and walked out of the dressing room to finish writing jokes for her. She didn't even notice that he'd left until he was half way down the hall.

"Brendan!" Marge yelled standing at the doorway to her dressing room, "Hurry. It's almost 8:15." Brendan kept walking and raised his hand in silent acknowledgement without stopping to look back.

Back in his office, Brendan sat down and logged onto his computer. He opened "Word" and centered the prompt by clicking the "centered text" icon on the format bar. Then he hit "Caps Lock" and typed in the date as a heading—New Times Roman, 18 point (so Marge could read it without her glasses) bold, all caps. He looked at his notes from the meeting to decide which topic would probably go first. Then he typed the headline of that topic in the same style as the centered date at the top of the page. Then Brendan stopped. He stared at the screen impassively with the small, vertical line of the prompt blinking in readiness. Then, instead of trying to forge for the millionth time, another laugh based on the lifeless, male bashing topics he'd been given, he reached for the phone. He dialed The Wife's number and waited.

"Hi," she said when she finally picked up having already determined through "Caller I.D." that it was him.

"This is Brendan White," he said. He always started phone conversations with her by using his full name. It was as if he was on the radio, not the phone.

"What's up?" she said with a tone that told him she was busy.

"Sykes called and says I've got cancer."

"Oh," she said. "I'm so sorry, Sweetie." He imagined the wheels turning in her head parsing all the permutations that that piece of information carried. "But it's not *bad* cancer, right?"

"No. It's the *good* cancer," Brendan said as if they were suddenly thrust into an episode of "Curb Your Enthusiasm". "I have to get a CAT scan and an MRI to see if it's spread."

"Well, I'm sure it hasn't. You'll be fine." Brendan winced at those words again. "Are you coming home tonight?"

"Yeah, I guess so. Where else am I going to go? —A guy with cancer." Brendan felt the particular rush that accompanied the opening of a new comedy vein. It was edgy, blasphemous, and applicable. This is how crazy anybody in comedy is. They will welcome any calamity as long as it can be funny; as if actually being hanged is worth the "gallows humor".

"Just come home. Zeke needs you."

That's it, Brendan thought, she thinks I'm terminal.

CHAPTER TWENTY

W hen he finally did get home that night, Brendan half expected a hero's welcome. Instead, Zeke and The Wife were
watching an interview being given by the Governor. Unable to rouse
them, Brendan dutifully sat down on the couch next to The Wife.
She took his arm in her lap and squeezed it without averting her
gaze from the television where the pasty, but precisely coifed, political fuck was explaining his position on health care.

"He really does care," she said finally turning to Brendan when
Jon Stewart came back on. "He cares so much."

Of course, the fact that the only place she could see her boyfriend "care so much" was on the "Daily Show" where he was a
"go-to" punchline, didn't seem to bother her. She didn't really see
the difference between "fake news" and the real thing. Brendan
wondered what special kind of idiot would willingly sit for an interview with a "Daily Show" correspondent. But, apparently, ego
trumped discretion; and The Wife was thrilled that the Governor
looked so "presidential" when he was ambush interviewed in front
of the Sacramento State Capitol. The lighting there dampened his
chronic forehead sweat, and his lips didn't look so much like the
lizard's in the Geico ads. The fact that he was making a fool of
himself was secondary.

Brendan had half-expected that the news of his cancer and the possibility of a sex-ending procedure as treatment would trigger a paroxysm of sexual interest by The Wife. He fantasized that, for once; he might even get more sex, pro rata, than the Governor. But it was not to be. Instinctively, he knew that even if he did make a pass at her that night, in the sanctity of their marital bed, she would undoubtedly say, "Please, Brendan, not here."

It wasn't that she was afraid that Zeke might discover them *in flagrante* if she consented; it was that Zeke needed his sleep more than she needed sex, and Brendan was in the boy's spot. Brendan had recently taken to going up to bed early in order to establish a beachhead in the king-size bed, but even then he would be nudged off when Zeke decided it was his time to turn in. Often Brendan would wander, not thinking, into the master bedroom after coming home late only to see the happy couple already entwined. "Get a room," he'd say to the blissfully sleeping pair. And then, after their somnolent non response, "Oh. Right. You already have," he'd say extricating a pillow so he wouldn't have to sleep with his head on a stuffed frog that night.

"I will be going to see all doctors with you from now on," The Wife said making herself seem taller by her new sense of mission.

"That's really not necessary. I can handle it."

"No, you can't. You're a goofball. You'll think it's a joke. You don't know what to ask. You forget. I've worked with Human Resources all my life."

"And this is like an 'exit interview'?"

"No, not necessarily. But I do know how to process information in a short period of time, under trying circumstances. I'm coming whether you like it or not."

"I don't like it."

"Good. Then let's not argue."

Brendan looked at her for several beats. And then they both turned back to the television where the Governor was smirking because he thought he'd beaten the smart-aleck comedy kid when, in fact, they were able to edit the cut-aways and random listening shots into a complete hatchet job. But Brendan could tell from the Governor's expression that he had convinced himself he'd won. Harry Crane was right. "Nobody wins an interview." Especially when somebody else owns the camera.

That night Brendan offered himself to The Wife for sex. After all, it was in the contract. But she was having none of it. In fact, it annoyed her.

"That is so annoying when you do that," she said without looking up from her book. She was rolled away from him facing the lamp on her side of the bed.

"How could you find it annoying? It's a 'reaching out' from a cancer victim."

"It's pawing, and it's a turn off."

"All foreplay is pawing. Ever been to a zoo?"

"Animals are much more loving than you are."

"They're faking," Brendan said "Except, maybe, the sheep." He was falling asleep and decided to replace his quest for sex with material.

"I need to be romanced not ravaged," The Wife said, still with her back to him as if her cold shoulder was a come on.

"We used to ravage," Brendan said. "I bet the Governor is big on ravaging. It's probably right behind raping and pillaging on his list of fun things." This got her attention. Brendan knew that any mention of the Governor as a lover would bring out the protector in her. She leapt to the Governor's defense. The book thudded shut, and she turned back to face him.

"When are you going to stop bringing up Carlton's name? It's really inappropriate, and it makes me mad."

"But it turns me on to think of you fucking on the Capitol steps in broad daylight." Brendan was telling the truth. Imagining The Wife as a raucous lover excited him, even with the Governor, because he knew, at least with that simpering poseur, she was the aggressor which was so unlike her in her "mommy" mode with him.

The Capitol steps incident in Sacremento that Brendan was referring to had been widely reported and undoubtedly leaked by the Governor himself who thought it made him seem more like a robust Kennedy than just a geek from Palo Alto who got lucky.

"Now that *really* turns me off."

"Which? Me or the thought of you and the Governor?

"Just shut up," she shot back sternly. "Do it for your son."

"Are you going to tell him I have cancer?"

"He already knows. He wants to discuss it in 'meeting' at school. He's decided something like that makes him more popular because all the kids will want to know about it. "

"Cute," Brendan said sarcastically. "Glad I could be of service."

"It's his way. He's 'processing' it. At least give him the space to do that. "

"Hey, my cancer's an open book. Just promise me you'll get Beverly to speak."

"There isn't going to be any funeral," she said rolling back to her position with the book under the lamp. Brendan didn't know if she had just made a "pre-need" decision or was being optimistic.

At that point, Zeke walked in, having finished the model boat he was building.

"Dad," he said in his flat, slightly admonishing, almost "HAL-like" voice.

He didn't elaborate, but just stood there looking at his father as if Brendan should know his place. It's the same inflection dog owners use when they see their dog on the couch. He waited for Brendan to react. When Brendan didn't move, Zeke climbed into bed and wedged himself, in full Freudian display, between Brendan and his mother. The boy then nestled and expanded his sleeping space until Brendan was left teetering at the edge of the bed. When it was clear that the sleeping arrangement had been irrevocably determined for the night, Brendan acquiesced and got up.

Then he removed a pillow from under Zeke's head and went into his son's room to sleep in peace.

In the days following, Brendan noticed that The Wife talked more about his cancer than he did. While he used it as a comic watershed, she wrapped herself in it like a new coat. She told all of her friends and used it in fights with valet parkers and at the dry cleaners. She was even able to negotiate a lower fee from the gardener because "my husband has cancer, and I really don't know what we're going to do." All in all, it seemed to be working well for her and Zeke.

One afternoon, before the nanny had brought Zeke home from his interpretive dance class ("He loves it," The Wife would say. "And his body is so beautiful in simple black."), Brendan found her weeping on the bed. He stood at the door for several beats and actually felt sorry for her. Undoubtedly, the reality of the cancer had caught up to her and had overwhelmed her. For a moment he didn't know whether to console her or leave her alone. He decided an upbeat attitude on his part was what she needed, so he quietly came into the room and lay down on the bed next to her. She was not startled by his arrival and reached out to him as if he had been summoned.

"I'm so afraid," she sobbed into his chest,

"I'll be fine." Brendan said sweetly, echoing the words that plagued him.

"I guess," she said. He could sense her thoughts shifting like the transmission of a Ferrari. "But he won't touch me. He's afraid." Now her tone turned clear and indignant, "And that man is chair of the Governor's Catastrophic Illness Committee."

Brendan actually relaxed and smiled. It was okay. The Wife was dealing with his cancer, and Brendan was dealing with his cancer. But it was the Governor who was a little fucked up over it.

"Doesn't he know it isn't catching?" Brendan said.

"You'd think," she said, "But it creeps him out. So I told him that we don't.... you know...."

"....Fuck."

"Well, if you must. I told him there was no way it could spread to me. I don't even have a prostate."

"Right." Brendan said, "So there's absolutely no way. Maybe you should get a doctor to talk to him."

"There are two of them on his committee. He knows. He's just using this." Now she was finished crying and was clearly angry. "Your goddamn cancer is ruining my relationship," she said in a pissed-off voice.

Finally, Brendan had come up with the one thing that might win her back to him exclusively: cancer. She abruptly turned her face to his even though it was only inches away.

"Oh darling," she said. There was a slight beat of hesitation and then, "Go medicate." It was the two magic words he'd been waiting to hear.

"I'll be right back." Brendan said.

He got up and went into the bathroom hoping he could find the bottle of Viagra without having to tear the place apart. "Go medicate" had become their foreplay, and he didn't want to be clumsy about it. "Go medicate" was the married version of "Let's fuck".

He found the plastic pill bottle immediately. The expiration date wasn't even in the same century, so he took three pills to make up for it. If it was still halfway potent, his face would flush within 30 minutes, and he'd be ready. If the dosage killed him, at least he'd die with a hard on, and it'd be the funeral director's problem.

The great thing about modern "assisted sex" is that, because of the lag time in the medication, the man taking it has plenty of time to finish up whatever he was doing *before* the opportunity for sex arose. It's not exactly "multi-tasking"; it's more like "pre-tasking": deciding to do something and then doing something totally different beforehand. In Brendan's case, it was opening the box that his new pitching wedge had come in. Thus, while The Wife lay smoldering on her bed, Brendan was doing his best to prepare for her by gently chipping golf balls into the living room fireplace while waiting for the Viagra to kick in. It was the only effective foreplay that worked any more. Now, if only Viagra could replace cuddling.

When Brendan heard a quiet buzzing coming from the bedroom, he knew she wasn't shaving. The Wife's version of assisted sex was the vibrator. She was starting without him. After stealing some batteries out of Zeke's old "Tickle Me Elmo" doll, she had begun to tickle herself with her Pocket Rocket in one hand and her Astroglide in the other.

After a few more chip shots, and when he heard the buzzing getting muffled, he knew he had to make an appearance whether he was fully ready or not. He carefully laid the beloved wedge back in its satin coffin with a caress that should have been reserved for The Wife, and turned toward the bedroom. Then he stripped down to his undershorts and t-shirt.

At the door, he paused momentarily, and then, instead of entering the room like a normal person, Brendan snuck in, moving silently and rapidly along the wall opposite the bed. It was unclear whether The Wife even noticed the man who had stealthily joined her in her chamber, but Brendan moved knowingly past the bureau and chair until he was at the window. Then he disappeared behind the hanging drapes and stopped. The buzzing from the bed got louder when The Wife brought the vibrator up for air in order to tighten the battery compartment which was threatening to spill its Energizer double "A's" into her pussy. Had the batteries been the weight and girth of flashlight-size "D" batteries, she might not have stopped. But there was no way she was going to tolerate a measly double A anywhere near her pooch. The Wife had her standards. The muffled buzzing continued and became more rhythmic. The Wife let out a sweet moan.

Behind the drapes, Brendan checked his watch. The timing was working out after all. He could feel himself respond. Thank you, Pfizer. "Better fucking through chemistry". He began to rustle the

curtains that hid him. Then he took his cock out the fly of his undershorts and began to fondle it with little attention to the effect of
open masturbation on the integrity of his hiding place.

Brendan's cock looked like an earthworm with goiter. It no longer got hard uniformly. Tumescence, for Brendan's penis, happened
like a gopher passing through a snake. Fortunately, the women in
his life only saw the finished product. Had they ever gazed upon
the "work in progress" they would have refused to touch it, much
less suck it or allow it inside their bodies. But now, past his fucking
prime, Brendan appreciated all the help he could get. A morning
erection was no longer something to hang his underpants on. Like
a spoiled child, each erection needed to be constantly amused and
cajoled in order to perform at all. The key was a launch code of
specific input: something old, something new, something vaguely
twisted, and something blue (Viagra). He missed that look on a
woman's face that signaled sexual desire, sexual desire for *him*. In
his present situation, however, a soft buzzing that was alternately
muffled and then free would have to do since he, and the vibrator,
both needed to come up for air during sex.

Brendan began to rustle the drapes more deliberately. The
bobs at the ends of the pull cords rattled against the molding of the
window. The Wife opened her eyes and raised her head slightly off
the pillow.

"Hello?" she said but made a point of not looking directly at the
bulging curtain that held her husband. "Is anyone there?" Then
she put her head back on the pillow, closed her eyes, and pressed
"Resume" on her fantasy.

Then Brendan made his move. He came out in full from behind the curtain. He was now an exposed intruder in the bedroom. Of course, he also knew that, in her mind, the difference
between a "real" intruder and the one she was married to was mea-
ger, at best. Brendan walked stealthily across the bedroom and
stood at the foot of the bed. The Wife continued to masturbate

softly with her eyes closed. She looked beautiful in her semi-ecstasy. Her lips slightly parted, her throat presented forward, her neck long and creamy. Her luxurious brown hair was spread lovingly on the pillow as if she were posing for a Wamsutta ad. Did she lay her locks out purposely, knowing that it was a special turn-on of Brendan's? She turned her face to the side as the passion within her mounted and lightly bit the corner of her lower lip. Even her tooth was sexy as it hung on the soft flesh of her mouth. Brendan was momentarily overcome by her beauty and sexuality and his love for her and his desire to be inside her all at once. He almost forgot his role and his mission.

But the moment was not wasted. Brendan's cock was heavy and full now as he dropped his boxer shorts and slowly brought a knee up onto the foot of the bed. As he did, The Wife writhed slightly, exposing a breast. The nipple was erect and inviting. Brendan brought the other knee up onto the bed. He crouched there studying her like a cat as the buzzing became a drone beneath the covers.

Then he pounced like feral animal. His hand covered her mouth; and her wide, wild eyes met his as he brought his face close to hers. Without removing his hand he shifted his head to the side and his mouth down to her ear. He could smell her special "fuck me" perfume that she saved for these occasions.

"Don't make a sound" he whispered hoarsely, "I won't hurt you."

She shook her head in immediate acquiescence. Her eyes were terrified. Brendan was in complete control. He kept his hand over her mouth while he searched under the covers with the other. The vibrator was still buzzing, and he located it immediately, throbbing next to her thigh. He couldn't turn it off with only one hand, so he brushed it aside, deeper into the bed to dampen the hum.

The Wife's pussy was wet and inviting. He played with it with his fingers but did not enter. Arching his head down to her chest he began to suck on her erect left nipple, the one over her pounding heart. He could feel her mouth relax under his hand and her body undulate ever so slightly. Her vagina became liquid, and she placed her hand on top of his to push his fingers inside.

Brendan was now kneeling astride her. His cock was as erect as it was ever going to be. He guided the tip of it into the lips of her vagina and stopped. The Wife moaned. Her head thrashed uncontrollably beneath his hand. He lowered himself and straightened his legs along hers as her hands grabbed his back to pull him inside her. He lifted his hand away from her mouth for the first time.

"Fuck me," she whispered in a low "Exorcist" voice he'd rarely heard from her.

"This is what you want, isn't it?" he said menacingly into her ear.

"Don't talk" she said signaling that their little playlet was finished, and she didn't want to hear any ad-libbing.

They made love silently for several minutes. Brendan kept himself on the edge of orgasm, waiting for her to cum. At one point, he pulled out and scrunched down to eat her. One of the benefits of marriage, Brendan liked to think, was that you don't have to wear a hat when you perform oral sex. Who cares if you have a bald spot? And wives probably find it somewhat exciting being eaten by a monk.

"Please. Don't," she said. He stopped somewhere around her navel. "Don't spoil it. Come here." She pulled him back up to her face and kissed him deeply and placed his cock back inside her. It was warm and slick as she hooked her legs behind his knees to hold him in. The uncharacteristic hunger excited him, and he drew closer to orgasm. "I want you to cum," she said.

"You first."

"No, you. Cum in me, now." Her tone was slightly demanding, and it was all that Brendan needed to release himself to his orgasm.

He couldn't tell if it was the ejaculation that excited her or the fact that she could produce it by edict. He came fully and then relaxed on top of her. He was more out of breath than he expected to be, and his first thought was about how out of shape he was rather

220

than anything to do with the moment or the woman beneath him. The Wife, also, had other thoughts.

"I love you," she said, but then added, "What did you do with the thing?"

Brendan had momentarily forgotten that he and The Wife were actually in a three-way. He could faintly hear the Pocket Rocket humming deep within the bedcovers. He located the little sucker with his foot first and then reached down to retrieve it for the woman he'd just made love to. He tried to turn off again but finally just handed it to her still buzzing.

"Thank you," she said as if he had just returned her wallet. "That was great." Then she turned it off. Brendan smiled. But then she turned it on again.

Brendan thought he should be offended. Did she realize what she was doing? But then he thought he didn't want to start an argument right there in bed. And besides, it did fall within the parameters of him wanting to please her and give her a satisfying sexual experience. The vibrator disappeared under the covers. He stayed for a beat, kissing her lightly on the neck and cheek. He half thought he might be part of the "after sex", but he could feel her attention shifting to something else that did not include him.

"Do you want me to leave?" he said.

"Would you?" she said quickly indicating that she thought he'd never ask. But even The Wife knew she was testing the bounds of marital intimacy. "You understand," she said sweetly. He could hear the vibrator already entering her.

"Absolutely," Brendan said getting up, and out of bed, and pulling on his shorts. He wanted to show that he was secure enough to allow all permutations of passion. Specifically, even those not involving him. "Have fun," he said leaving. She didn't answer, but the buzzing seemed to get louder and more aggressive as he quietly closed the door.

Brendan wondered if he should be jealous. But then he decided that the Pocket Rocket was less of an insult than the Governor, and at least he was the one who'd actually bought it for her. Yeah, that was *his* vibrator in there finishing the job. That's the ticket. He was instantly assuaged by the realization that he didn't have to cuddle and could get back to his golf club. The gift of a vibrator was brilliant. Less work for Daddy.

Zeke came out of his room as Brendan came around the corner.

"Where's mom?" he asked.

"Asleep. Leave her alone."

CHAPTER TWENTY-ONE

"The Ladies' Room" chugged along, as daily shows do, oblivious of the drama of any of its participants. Beverly became more and more personally involved in the selection of topics for "CrossTalk" whenever she appeared on the show while, at the same time, her appearances in the News Department became less and less frequent.

"Darlings," she had originally announced to no one because no one had asked, "You must understand, 'The Ladies' Room' is my 'dessert'. I'm involved in far too many projects and assignments to devote all my time and energy to it."

But then, the silent artillery of time began to find its mark both on the aging anchor and her news credibility. Portraits of younger and perkier anchors started showing up along the escalator wall in the news building—with Beverly at the bottom and Delores Whitcomb at the top. Her stint as the first female editor of the Los Angeles Times had faded in everyone's memory. Suddenly, "The Ladies' Room" as "dessert" began to move up on the menu until it became the "main course" on Beverly Frost's plate of life. At that point, the staff, and even Bad Bob, experienced what long-suffering wives go through when their "captains of industry retire: "For better or for worse, but not for lunch." For the staff at "The

Ladies' Room" it was, "Two times a week, but, please God, not every day".

But Beverly was relentless in her quest for permanence and indestructibility. Of course, since Beverly never touched another living being other than her dog, Rémy, the only ailments she could *possibly* contract were distemper, rabies, and, maybe, worms.

The staff knew she was a relentless doctor groupie, but once a person hits 80, even the best doctors in the world can't keep someone out of harm's way. But with "Syd Vicious" toiling around the clock, and with the advances in micro surgical adjustments, hair pieces, and shots of God knows what, Beverly actually looked *better* as she aged. The real threat then became the possibility that Barry or Sydney might die first and leave her bereft of her special hair and make-up. But God wouldn't be that cruel. Beverly Frost was God's favorite, right after Ryan Seacrest. And knowing Beverly, she undoubtedly had a replacement hair and make-up team all warmed up and ready to go, like understudies in a hit show, should disaster befall her regular team. Leo even surmised that she probably also had some deluded fourteen year-old girl on retainer in case she ever needed a new body part or heart transplant.

But as Beverly clamped down harder and harder on "The Ladies' Room", she set an inevitable course straight for Roberta who had joined the show thinking *she* was the moderator. For the staff, it was like watching two trains hurtling toward each other on the same track. It was frightening; but it was also great theater, and the audience picked up on it as well. Ratings soared because of Roberta's notoriety, sex change, and her collision course with Beverly and everybody else on the panel. Basically, no one knew, on any given day, what Roberta would say or do on the air. Not even Roberta herself.

Roberta would have openly and gladly locked horns with Bambi, but that confrontation, which even the audience knew was overly ripe, didn't happen right away because Roberta wanted to fuck her so bad that it clouded her mind to the inane statements that regularly came out of that perfectly formed mouth with the infantile lower lip knowingly double-glossed. Instead, Roberta sent her kids to do her dirty work, and they were magnificent. Bambi didn't know what hit her until Roberta's leg did one night in the hot tub during a "family" weekend while their kids romped in the "Neverland"-type back yard that Roberta had constructed on her compound in Venice. However, in true sitcom fashion, Bambi knew exactly what was up, despite her apparent wide-eyed stupidity. She'd engineered the perfect "frustrated fuck" scenario that was just "hot" enough to keep Roberta coming back for more.

Brendan watched this real-life daytime drama unfold on air but mostly in the make-up room during the morning "CrossTalk" discussions. Seated behind the women and out of mirror shot, he could monitor the push and pull between Roberta and the rest of the co-hosts with impunity. Besides the obvious "street theater" it provided, he was convinced that eventually Roberta would reveal an opening that he could capitalize on. But her commitment to derailing the show in order to make it her own, whether conscious or not, was so entrenched that it left little room for any hustle from the outside on Brendan's part.

"That's the trouble with a train wreck," Brendan said to Leo out of the corner of his mouth one morning while Roberta picked her bare feet and complained about the audio level in the studio, "In the end, it's a train wreck."

"The audience can't hear anything I say," Roberta said ostensibly to her fungus-encrusted big toe. "They're looking at the monitors and not at the set. They might as well not even be there. It affects the laugh." She stopped and turned in her seat and looked directly at Beverly who was staring into the mirror while Sydney reconstructed her face. "They can't hear me...or even, God forbid, you, Beverly." Roberta slumped back into her barber chair. There were several beats of silence while Sydney continued to apply mascara to Beverly in a vain attempt to "un-beady" her eyes.

225

"Well, darling, we'll certainly work on it. I know Hal is doing everything he can to get you heard. After all, the studio was completely redesigned just before you joined us... especially for you."

Roberta had sunk into her petulant child mode. "Hal Jennings couldn't adjust his ass on a toilet seat, Beverly, and you know it."

Hal had become a target for Roberta. She would dress him down by name "on air" every time there was a missed shot or a stage managing lapse. In fact, Hal had become so paranoid about being fired by the raging tranny he was trying to placate that he would hide in his office after each show and make Bradley, the stage manager, run interference for him by checking the halls and then giving an "all clear" signal after which Hal would then skulk out of his office and into a waiting elevator, assured that he wouldn't bump into Roberta, by mistake, on the way.

"Well, I'm sure he's doing the best he can," Beverly said.

Bad Bob would have preferred to have stayed out of this mini-confrontation, but now he realized his silence as co-executive producer was looking like a set up.

"The audio has been a problem we've been aware of from day one, Roberta. I think right now, they know what the trouble is, but it's only a question of money."

"Then spend it" Roberta said fearlessly.

"Talk to Swann," Bad Bob came back, happy to lay it off on corporate. "If you can get them to spend it, we'll do it."

"Bob, that's not my job. It's yours."

The refusal of Roberta to back down made the "red" rise on Bad Bob's neck and continue all the way up until his whole head looked like a tomato.

As soon as Roberta had arrived, not only as a co-host on the show, but as its moderator; there was not enough oxygen in the make-up room, and especially on-air, for the three of them: Roberta, Moonie, and Beverly. But since it had been Beverly herself who had orchestrated it all in an eleventh hour effort to save the show from cancellation, it was she who was left the most breathless.

"The Ladies' Room" became a demolition derby that was broadcast, "live", every morning, and the audience picked up on it immediately. Marge and Bambi were largely kept out of the melee mainly because both had come along for the ride not for the contest. They were spectators and got along with everyone, but only out of their own laziness. The other three were committed, each to their own agenda. Moonie's was to use "The Ladies' Room" as a money making machine and launching pad that would set her in the firmament as the next Oprah, Beyonce', and Maria Tallchief combined. Roberta's short term goal was to fuck Bambi, but immediately beyond that she wanted to re-establish herself as not just the Queen of Daytime but as a hydra-headed talent monster that could control all phases of life, not just entertainment. Like her bifurcated sexuality, she wanted to be all things to all men, women, and children. If she could have done it with another transforming operation, she would have. But short of that, she was left to her own devices on the show. First things first: gain control of the soap box.

Beverly had not survived fifty-five years of banging her head against the glass ceiling--- and the headboards of the rich and famous--- to be out-maneuvered by a couple of newbies. Her trump card was that she *did* own the show. Even though her pose was that the show was merely her "dessert", it was her creation. It was the "dessert" of her career, and she was determined to end that banquet in style. Besides, she wanted the money. It made her feel royal.

The three of them were like eels in a bucket. They became so intertwined that you couldn't tell whose agenda was whose, which *bête noir* belonged to whom, or which subtext informed whose every statement.

"I would like to thank The Lord for the blessings he bestowed on me over the weekend," Moonie threw out. Roberta rolled her eyes, knowing what was coming. "That tsunami in Bora Bora that killed all those people? Ray Ray and I were right there only three months ago. God's takin' care of me. He didn't want me to be there this weekend."

"What?????" Roberta shouted at Moonie's reflection in the mirror that ran the length of the wall in front of them.

"It was a natural disaster that would have been even worse if Ray Ray and I had been there like we were. That's all. Praise God."

The CrossTalk group had heard it all before. She also thought Jesus had spared her on 9/11 because she'd once had breakfast at Windows of the World.

Roberta chose not to even engage the issue but, instead, raised herself halfway out of her barber chair and twisted around to look incredulously at the assembled staff behind her.

"Darling, I think the tsunami's really only a "mention" at best," Beverly said.

"Three hundred thousand people were killed," Moonie said.

"I know, darling. It's a terrible tragedy. But I live in North Dakota; it means nothing to me. I think "tsunami" is lunch meat or some place in Florida. I really can't be bothered."

"Let's move on," Mugsy said.

"However, I *would* like to say something about my evening with Princess Stephanie of Monaco," Beverly began.

The word "however" was Beverly-speak for "Now I'm going to tell you what's *really* important...according to, *me!*" The word sent chills down the spines of veteran Beverly watchers because it meant that everything that'd been said previous to it had been bullshit in her mind even though it was what everyone else_thought was pertinent.

"I mean, I really don't have to mention Stephanie by name, but if you think you'd like to, I have pictures from the affair, and we can show a clip from my interview several years ago where she says something very prophetic about and me and her mother, Princess Grace. In case none of you were aware of it, Princess Grace and I were very close. I also have the table linen, the special instructions in the Ladies' room, which I will read and which are very amusing and which no one else knows about; and a scarf of her mother's that the princess personally brought all the way from Monaco to give to me which I will wear, and you can ask me about it or make fun of it or whatever. But that's only if you want to do it. I think it would be fun." She finished in her best "Executive Producer" voice.

"Okay, we've got that," Mugsy said. The tape coordinators and PA's immediately began to scramble to pull and assemble all the clips, "still-stores", and props that Beverly had casually mentioned. "We're picking for three segments. How was everyone's break? Any stories there?"

Somewhere a focus group had declared that the audience loved to hear about the personal lives of the co-hosts. Consequently, there were endless self-serving taped pieces about the co-hosts buying dresses, working out, learning to bowl, hanging with professional athletes or movie stars, and, especially, re-decorating their apartments and homes because of the attendant swag.

Thus, it was perfectly natural for Mugsy to call for any personal stories and events no matter how mundane and trivial and self-serving. And the co-hosts willingly obliged with inflated accounts of meals, gaffes, child rearing dilemmas, spousal mishaps, movies, and faux family disasters as if they were all living in some elaborate sitcom where every move they made had a laugh track. Except Roberta. Her issues were real and crucial to her world. Her neuroses were on her sleeve. Demons and enemies were everywhere. She could hear her mother's footsteps coming up the stairs for "bedtime" every day. Her life was a bad reality show, not a sitcom.

Roberta's current beef was with the blowhard LA Times columnist and television personality, Conrad Conroy. It had started with him calling her a "Isolationist idiot". When Roberta responded by holding him responsible for the deaths of American soldiers in Iraq because of his jingoism, the battle quickly escalated to name calling and personal attacks. This was normal "Battle of the Network Stars" stuff except that the insults got pointed and specific with an underpinning of treachery courtesy of Beverly and Bad Bob.

In an effort to undermine Roberta's take-over of their show (which they had willingly enabled) Bad Bob and Beverly had been feeding Conroy incriminating leaks about Roberta almost from her first day. Roberta knew this and hated Bad Bob for doing it and Beverly for allowing it, and she set out to remove Bad Bob from the show altogether. Beverly, who avoided accountability as if it were an intern seeking an autograph, was a close social friend of Conroy's. They often dined at Bouchon within air kiss of each other. Thus, when Conroy recklessly began to specifically quote Beverly in his put-downs of Roberta, the feud circled back on itself, and Roberta was not about to let it lie.

"My vacation was just ducky," Roberta spat out. "How was yours, Beverly?" She twisted emphatically in her chair to face Beverly squarely.

"Well, darling, we know you've had a difficult time recently, but hopefully that's all been put to rest."

"NOT!" Roberta shouted loudly. She easily reverted to a ten year old when it suited her.

"Well, I don't think we should talk about Mr. Conroy on the show. It'll only encourage him. Why give that poor man the publicity?

"That's not the point, Beverly." Roberta said as she rose out of her barber chair on just her arms at first but then actually took her bare feet down off the counter and planted them firmly on the linoleum floor. Then she actually stood.

Brendan, seated at the back of the room in a shampoo chair, actually looked up from the "Style" section of the LA Times he was reading while the women prattled on about what they would talk about. Suddenly, the air in the room had changed. Roberta was *standing.* No co-host had ever moved from her chair before the meeting was over. The sight of a free-ranging Roberta was, at once, disturbing and fascinating. For Beverly, it was terrifying.

The room froze. "This is interesting," Brendan quietly said to Leo out of the side of his mouth.

Roberta stood in front of her chair for a beat and looked down. She pulled at the crotch of her sweat pants as if setting her nonexistent balls like a ballplayer coming to bat. Then she turned and took a step toward Beverly's chair and put both of her hands on the black porcelain arm rest. Beverly knew enough to stare straight ahead and deal with Roberta only through their reflection in the mirror.

"Why didn't you answer my call? Why didn't you defend me? Why were you silent while I was being taken to the cleaners every day by that man? I reached out to you and you did…. NOTHING!" Roberta ended on a loud accusatory note, like a crusading defense attorney making a summation. She was inches from Beverly's immobile face.

Roberta had not only gotten out of her chair, which was a signal of deep distress, but she had now made a hostile move toward Beverly, *the* Beverly Frost—icon, diva, and beloved national treasure. It was like crossing into the personal space of the President or the Pope except there were no Secret Service Agents to throw themselves on her body nor Swiss Guards to surround the suddenly frail old lady at the center of the storm. Beverly was exposed and threatened. No one in the room moved—either out of shock, or their long-standing history of being repelled by Beverly at every turn, or, perhaps, even a desire to see the physical denouement of Roberta's threat which now seemed imminent. Roberta did not touch the elderly anchor, however, but leaned her face in toward Beverly's cheek. Another beat passed. No one moved. The eighty-three year old woman at the center of the maelstrom was as alone as she had made those around her feel every day.

Brendan could appreciate Roberta's beef. Conroy had issued a barrage of *ad hominem* remarks to the press about Roberta, her transgender status, and her waning talent for weeks before and while the show had been on hiatus. Roberta had answered him by mentioning the unmentionable: Mr. Conroy's very public sexual harassment of a co-worker about which there were answering machine recordings of him proclaiming his desire to either wash the girl's body with a sponge or *be* the sponge (like Prince Charles wanting to be Camilla Parker Bowles' tampon). And to make matters worse, Conroy had then referred to the sponge as a "falafel", the street venders' mystery meat, instead of a "loofah" which is what the torpedo-shaped natural sponge is actually called.

The horror of Roberta's mentioning this well-known, but suppressed, fact came from the tacit understanding that, during all of Conroy's appearances on "The Ladies' Room", this one subject was never to be mentioned, even in the face of his constant bloviating, lies, and put-downs. This implicit agreement had never been breached, or even its subject hinted at, on any show. It was a little piece of media back scratching that proved that celebrities are celebrities first and ideologues next.

But, in truth, the bad blood between Roberta and Conroy actually went deeper than anyone knew. It turned out they had both been in love with the same knock-out Ralph Lauren model. She had fancied Conroy at first, but then Roberta stole her away from him and fucked her for about a year and a half. It made Conroy not just a blowhard but a spurned blowhard and one that had been cuckolded by a hybrid lesbian. And that's what was *really* fueling the feud.

So, when Roberta escalated the name calling, and started referring to Conroy as a "falafel eating sex deviate", Conroy first threatened to sue and then began directly quoting conversations he had had with Beverly where she had called Roberta "the ugliest castrato on the face of the earth" and a "daily nightmare" and a "botched transsexual with one testicle and half a vagina". Conroy was careful to always quote Beverly directly on these statements; but Beverly, over the span of the feud, had carefully never directly refuted nor challenged their veracity. Instead, she had merely issued a string of vague policy statements of continued support and affection for the beleaguered Roberta who, even in Beverley's public support, came off as marginalized beyond Beverly's reach.

The culmination of Roberta's feelings of betrayal during the Conroy dust up came when Roberta put a call in to Beverly, vacationing on an arms dealer's private yacht anchored outside the Great Barrier Reef, which Beverly had never returned until she had reached Hawaii before flying home. This "unreachable" excuse would have held were it not of for the fact that she and Bad Bob had been in constant touch, Great Barrier Reef or no Great Barrier Reef.

For Roberta it was a replay of her life as molested boy. The marauding mother, the abandonment of an enabling but distant father, the isolation, the shame, the self-disgust and the self-mutilation. It was all there playing out for Roberta and brilliantly cast by Beverly Frost and Bad Bob Vapors. Even her "siblings" on "The Ladies' Room" played their part perfectly as a mute chorus to her daily tragedy. This was what lay behind Roberta's unthinkable and unprecedented move of physically threatening, by mere proximity, the inviolate Beverly Frost.

"Hold on there, Roberta. I think you're out of line," Bad Bob finally said from his chair on the side.

Bad Bob had not moved or spoken throughout Roberta's tirade and assault. He had stayed glued to his chair while his partner/boss was left to withstand the attack alone. If Roberta had had a weapon, Beverly would have been lying in a pool of blood like Robert Kennedy on the floor of the Ambassador Hotel kitchen.

"Let's deal with this later," he added while still not moving out of his chair.

Roberta had said her piece and had testified in front of Beverly. There was a show to do, and Beverly, a trooper throughout, hastily went through the news compilations to find something, *anything*, to move the agenda along. The rest of the staff sat there, eyes wide, as if, by remaining motionless, they might also render themselves invisible as well.

"What's this whole deal about prostate cancer all of a sudden?" Bambi blurted out. "It seems everyone's dying of prostate cancer these days. I think we should do that,"

Bambi's words fell on a hushed room. She took the silence as a sign that they hadn't heard her or didn't understand. Roberta sunk lower in her barber chair as if her outburst had sucked everything out of her.

"I mean, it's ridiculous. Prostate cancer. It's like an epidemic. Everybody's dying. I don't even know what a prostate is. And where the cancer's supposed to be. It's crazy."

Bad Bob coughed loudly. Brendan, upon hearing this suggestion for a topic, was strangely detached from its relationship to himself. He continued to read his paper although it suddenly seemed interesting that, while his specific diagnosis was already known to everyone on the staff, it had, apparently, not penetrated Bambi's dim consciousness yet. As far as Bad Bob was concerned, Bambi had no idea she was hitting so close to home, and he tried to head it off.

"I don't want to do that," Bad Bob said.

"But it's happening. Prostate cancer. Killing everybody. And nobody's saying anything. I know three men who..."

"We're not going to do it," he repeated emphatically, "I'll explain later. Let's move on," Bad Bob said with new-found authority. Brendan was enjoying the exchange. He wished that Bad Bob had allowed Bambi to dig a deeper hole for herself.

"It's crazy. All of a sudden," she said as a parting shot, "Prostate cancer. Everywhere. The prostate. Who knew?" She wasn't going to fight for the topic, but obviously she had not been apprised of the ongoing cancer issue with one of the writers.

Two other topics were chosen before the meeting broke up. One was whether "Pork, the other white meat" was racist, and the other was a lawsuit charging that a gay softball team had been unjustly disqualified from the Gay Softball World Series because three of its players were only bi-sexual. The women were foursquare against racism and sexual discrimination of any kind and felt compelled to demonstrate that daily along with their devotion to whatever television program had won in the ratings the night before, and, of course, dieting. Politics and international affairs were only reluctant add-ons. The "North Dakota" demographic prevailed.

Marge found a story about a man who could play Mozart on a duck call, and she thought that would be fun as a topic and also as a guest if they could get him.

"I don't understand, darlings. What is a duck call?" Beverly asked the room.

Leo felt obliged to explain. "It's a thing that makes a quacking sound when you blow into it."

"And that's a musical instrument?" She really had no idea and had never heard of such a thing.

"No, not usually," Leo said, "Hunters use them to attract ducks because it makes them sound like one."

"But why would anyone want to sound like a duck? It doesn't make any sense."

"So they can shoot them," Leo told her. "That's why it's called a 'duck call'".

"Darlings, I live in North Dakota. I don't care about any of this."

Leo was too far into it, now, to retreat. He had taken complete ownership of the exchange.

"No, Beverly. In fact, North Dakota is one of the places where you actually *would* care about a duck call. Trust me," Leo persisted.

"I'm sorry. I don't think it's for us," she said putting the final kibosh on an otherwise lighthearted story because she felt anything but lighthearted after the flare up with Roberta. "Besides, ducks don't have anything to do with Mozart. So it doesn't make any sense."

But the damage had already been done. Roberta had sealed her fate as surely as the original "young one" from New Jersey who had done herself in when she gave an interview in which she extolled Beverly's extraordinarily preserved breasts, ass, and other gravity defying attributes thinking she was complimenting the surgically enhanced Editor in Chief instead of damning her with actress-like attributes.

The truth of the matter was that Roberta had caught Beverly red-handed and had called her out on the comments that Conroy had directly attributed to her. Beverly had coyly never actually denied the Conroy's quotes because she knew he was a better newsman than she was and could probably cite names, places, times, and even surveillance video if he had to, to substantiate his report. She was protecting herself first at all costs. It was the type of abandonment that Roberta had experienced when her father left her twisting in her bedroom under the alcoholic breath of her mother after which both of them would then proudly lead the family to the Communion rail at Sunday Mass. Both Beverly and Roberta's mother were smug in their blamelessness. The sin was the child's. The adults were above reproach. It was a Catholic tradition.

And as far as the issue of Beverly not answering her calls, Roberta knew that Beverly was never out of touch in case a sizable "get" surfaced that needed immediate attention. She had been in touch with Bad Bob by ship to shore, satellite, or army field radio about how they would spin the Conrad Conroy feud. Thus, Beverly had carefully chosen not to be in direct contact with Roberta until the morning of the show. The sense memory of exploitation and abandonment was all too familiar, and Roberta couldn't stand it.

And Beverly, stung in public, immediately retreated to the recesses of her "mobbed up" origins. There was no forgetting. There was no going back. Roberta was now a "dead (semi) man talking". And no manner of transgender operations could change that.

CHAPTER TWENTY-TWO

Moonie Brown was laying low. Unlike Roberta, she didn't want to fuck Bambi as much as she wanted to eat her like the trifle she was. Moonie had her own problems. She had maneuvered Ray Ray, her dashing boyfriend, into a proposal.

"I knew it. I knew he was the one, the moment I laid eyes on him," Moonie gushed.

Apparently, he had reminded her of a rack of lamb. She wasn't that good at men, but she did know food, and when she had stopped Ray Ray at that party and said, "Where you think *you're* goin' ?" she knew that she bumped into Mr. Right.

Of course, Mr. Right was simply trying to get himself through the doorway and knew there surely wasn't room for both of them. In fact, there really wasn't enough doorway for one of Moonie, and he was just trying to be polite. But, instead, he had lingered long enough for her to enmesh him in her sticky web.

"Cuz, I believe I know where *I'm* goin'. But do you know where you're gonna be in fifteen minutes?" Moonie had said, flashing her teeth (her most prized attribute) and her false eyelashes made out of mink (her most indulgent beauty secret).

That was the start of it. Later that night she had talked him into massaging her feet (for the load they had to carry, God knows, they deserved it), and she obliged him with a perfect blow job. But because Moonie's back looked like a field of volcanic ash, and the rolls on the back of her neck made him think he was being sucked off by a Sharpei, Ray Ray had plenty of time to survey the strategically displayed objects of her success in the room while he waited for his cum to rise.

When Moonie's slobbering eventually reminded him of the last time he'd stuck his cock through a glory hole at "Numbers" on Santa Monica, he came in her mouth, not because he was that excited, but because he wanted to make sure he wouldn't have to fuck her. Besides, the sheer size of her on her knees made it easier for him to fantasize about who the fellatist might be: An NFL interior lineman or, perhaps, a leather-suspendered dude in a motorcycle cap looking like a cross between a Nazi and Ken Norton in "Mandingo".

But "sales" was Moonie's forte, and she knew how to close a deal. She would serve him blowjobs, and "blow", and big-ass celebrities that he could hit on for the Rapper Hedge Fund he pretended to front. Eventually, she would make him fuck her, but right now she was in no hurry because of her religion and because she knew his "down low" was a little too "up front" on Saturday nights. And neither was he in a hurry, for that matter, because, big and black as his dick might be, it still wasn't big enough to get past her ass cheeks and her panis to the booty below. He would need the equivalent of an off-shore drilling platform for that and a rig that only British Petroleum might possess.

In order for Moonie to properly vet Ray Ray, she went back to her roots. She got in touch with a Cherokee elder in Ojai and paid him handsomely to serve as medicine man and meat inspector for six months of counseling and celibacy, just long enough for any residual H.I.V. to incubate. If Ray Ray wanted to score Moonie's celebrity money connections, he would have to go to a "lodge" in Ventura County once a week and sweat it out with John "Big Bear" Pappas and his Cherokee wranglers who would remind him that his "down low" better be "outta sight" if he knew what was good for him.

The end result was that Moonie had her hands full. Her impending nuptials presented a whole new venue for schnorring that had hitherto been denied. She was like a pig in shit, a sow in slop, a wading hippo in a warm effluent of merchandise and services. In other words, she didn't have time for Roberta's daily dramas.

Roberta was constantly baiting Moonie "on air" to expose her true self the way Roberta had made a career of doing so herself. But Moonie would have none of it. She hadn't spent 38 years putting layers of fat between herself and the world for nothing. Besides, Moonie had a lot to hide.

The standard gastric bypass or lap-band surgery that Star Jones of "The View" had denied at first, and then dined out on when it suited her, had not worked for Moonie. Moonie's obese body and equally obese eating habits had frustrated the, now, routine procedure for these cases. Her follow-up intervention was far more direct and even more controversial. Basically, the new procedure diverted 90 percent of what she ate into a pouch taped to her hip. The operation consisted of sewing a section from her own intestines to her upper stomach just below the esophagus that allowed only a fraction of what she put in her mouth to actually reach her lower stomach and be metabolized. Thus, she could continue to be the life of the buffet while suffering none of the consequences. The system was purely mechanical, like adding a spur to the main line on a heavily trafficked railroad. As a result, while her mouth might be gorging, her stomach was on a starvation diet. But as a bonus, the colostomy-type bag on her hip was clear plastic so that she could revisit all the food she had consumed, but not digested, at the end of the day like a tourist pouring over snapshots of a trip.

For Moonie it was the perfect answer, and she didn't want Star Jones, or Carnie Wilson, or Al Roker, or any of the other celebrity fatties to know how she was eating her cake and having her diet, too. The only problem, and it was perfectly counter intuitive, was that, by the end of the day, she actually did, indeed, look fatter than when she had started because the pouch was, by then, the size of a basketball. But the pleasure of throwing away pounds of fat food out-weighed the late night embarrassment. It was instant lipo in the privacy of her home. Moonie would go to sleep and wake up visibly thinner only to spend another day eating everything in sight like a swarm of those African ants that can devour a water buffalo in twenty minutes.

With Moonie not taking the bait that Roberta snidely dragged in front of her every day like a piece of bacon, Roberta turned to Bambi whom she cast as the younger sibling who had not come to her rescue when she was being raped by their mother. Bambi, for her part, saw Roberta as a transgender freak. But she was determined to prove to herself and the world that she was an open-minded bigot who could embrace all kinds and disapprove of them equally. And she wanted to prove that her children *liked* playing with freaks.

To accomplish this, she continued to drive down to Venice for play-dates with Roberta's kids at her compound. But the rough and tumble adopted urchins, rescued from foster care and juvi half-way houses, didn't exactly mesh with a pair of Beverly Hills dandies with their bowl haircuts and fish belly flesh. In fact, Bambi's two boys were so stunned, confused, and nonplussed by what they encountered that Roberta immediately diagnosed the oldest as brain damaged and then reported back to everyone on the show that she was sure the younger one was probably either autistic or certainly on the Asperger's spectrum. When Bambi got wind of this, it was the end of the happy beach trips and her personal relationship with Roberta. Instead, they began to fight on air over everything. The public took it seriously and assumed it was political, but Brendan knew it all went back to Roberta's curb-side diagnosis of Bambi's children. It re-affirmed Bambi's mission in life as a self-proclaimed "goodie two shoes" and protective mother. But Brendan also knew she would have reacted the same way if Roberta had criticized her children's choice of penny loafers as beach wear.

Meanwhile, Brendan found himself reading the weekly "Wall of Woe" sick and death notices with more care and attention to specifics. "The Ladies' Room's" soap opera neighbors seemed to be hit with a new death every week. Of course, in typical theatrical fashion, they upped the ante by expanding their grief to include ex-staffers and long-gone retirees. Like the soap itself, they cast a wide net in search of trouble.

Then the building staff, security, and Yale Maintenance personnel began to lose people as well. But there would be few, if any, announcements posted between the elevators for any of them. There would be only a silent "missing airman"-type configuration among the janitors and porters to mark any of their passings.

"What happened to Miguel? I haven't seen him for weeks."

"He died."

"Oh. He seemed nice." And the elevator doors would close.

If the building people always seemed sad and downtrodden, it was because they were. A death to any one of one of them was a wash. Only "The Ladies' Room" seemed strangely immune to any personal calamity as if Beverly Frost could ward off even death with a flutter of her cockroach wings. The building was killing everyone but them. "The Ladies' Room" was long overdue. It defied the odds and all reason. But every time Brendan read that another stalwart and beloved crew member of "Living for Love" had bitten the dust; he took it as *good* news. It meant "The Ladies' Room's" immunity was still intact. He was bulletproof.

But Raoul was becoming weird. He began following Brendan around the SBS building. Brendan didn't notice it at first, but then he realized Raoul seemed to show up no matter where Brendan went. It took a while before he put it all together, but then he finally realized he was being stalked by the janitor. He did not take it as a compliment. Because of Raoul's relationship to the building, it was like being stalked by the Angel of Death.

Brendan didn't know whom he should complain to. He doubted whether he could he use it in the law suit. It sounded too creepy, and it would undoubtedly be chalked up as a case of paranoia on the part of a dismissed employee. Brendan decided to confront Raoul on it directly.

"Hey, man. Why am I suddenly running into you all over the place?" Brendan said when he found himself, once again, alone with Raoul outside the studio. "Are you following me or something?"

"No, Papi. Why would I follow you? That's what strangers do. You're my friend. I have to look out for you."

"I appreciate that. But, listen pal, you really don't have to. I think I've got this thing under control" Brendan said, noting that Raoul never once took his eyes off him when they spoke.

"Yes, you do," Raoul said. "It's okay."

"Right," Brendan said. He didn't know how to proceed with the conversation. Suddenly he didn't know what he was complaining about or exactly what bothered him. "Anyway, I'm fine. Everything's okay."

"Das right," Raoul said as if he already had all the answers and had thought the whole thing through. Brendan felt creepy, like he was in the middle of something he hadn't bargained for. It wasn't homosexual. He didn't think Raoul wanted to take him back to his room like some wide-eyed intern, but there was something else going on. Some kind of power struggle between him and this building maintenance lothario. And yet, Brendan had never really paid that much attention to Raoul. In that way, Brendan was no different than anyone else in the building whose relationship to the Yale Maintenance people was minimal at best. The "Yalies" were ultimately invisible to Brendan just as they were invisible to just about everyone else. The only difference was that, at least, Brendan felt bad about his neglect. It didn't seem to bother anyone else.

"Okay. Well, then, I'll see you around, I guess. Brendan said somewhat nervously.

"Any time, Papi. I always here for you."

"Thanks," Brendan ended with, but then he immediately felt bad about it. He didn't want to give Raoul any gratuitous encouragement.

Brendan turned and walked away knowing that nothing had really been solved. But then he made the mistake of looking back at Raoul which immediately indicated that Raoul was still on his mind. Raoul, for his part, had not moved and was standing there still smiling at him, almost as if he *knew* that Brendan was going to look back. Brendan then smiled wanly and gave a little wave before turning back and walking away.

"Happy Friday," Lucy, the Yale Security girl said to Brendan, as she did each Friday when he passed her booth. She sounded like a cross between Aunt Jemima and Minnie Pearl. Her cackling good cheer probably set the NAACP back fifty years every time she opened her mouth. "Whatchu up to now, Bren-Dan?" she asked. It was one of those questions that begged no answer.

"Nuttin', honey," he said when she buzzed him in.

"Dat's jes' like you." Lucy shot back. "You always up to *somethin'.*"

Brendan had just come from the urologist's office where the ever-smiling Dr. Sykes had pushed a folder across the desk to him and The Wife telling them it was apparently an aggressive prostate cancer, a T2C with a full Gleason 8 and peri-migration in one lobe; and he recommended Brendan do something about it. But that was as far as he was willing to go except to give Brendan the phone number of every practitioner he'd heard of in the prostate cancer business in Southern California. The only definitive opinion he gave was not to go out of the country or to Canada because insurance wouldn't cover it. The Wife was reeling when they left the office.

"Maybe you could ask your friend," Brendan posited archly, referring to the Governor.

"I can't bother him with a call that's not about him or his last press conference. And I really don't want to have to have phone sex just to get my husband an appointment with the Head of Urology at Sloan Kettering in New York. I'm sorry. That's just me."

"You sound like Moonie Brown."

"Really?" she said taking it as a compliment. They walked silently toward the parking garage—he thinking about her phone sex with the Governor, and she thinking about how the cancer would impact her wardrobe. As a former actress she always wanted to dress the part.

Brendan brought his prostate file with him to work and had almost memorized the doctors' names that The Wife had scrawled on it while Brendan had beamed back at Doctor Doom. He decided he would start calling as soon as the monologue was written and the show had started.

After the "CrossTalk" meeting, Brendan went into the men's room to relieve himself and take a look at his poor cock. As he came through the door, the lights were out which he always took as a good sign because it meant the room hadn't been used recently enough to keep the automatic lights on. The room seemed fresher that way. Unfortunately, the second floor men's room had become "The Ladies' Room's" staff bathroom of choice either because the "Living" staff and building workers had trashed the larger facility on the basement floor or because everyone knew that the celebrity guests of the show used the second floor one, and you might be pissing alongside a rock star if you were lucky. Even Bad Bob came all the way upstairs to unceremoniously take his daily dump as if the second stall there was his alone.

But this time, when Brendan came into the bathroom, he stopped short as he passed in front of the sinks on the way to the urinals. The automatic lights hadn't come on. Somehow he had not triggered the motion sensor sufficiently to activate them. Brendan stopped. Then he backed up and made his entrance again. Still no lights. He spread his arms and twirled around to make sure the sensor saw him. Nothing. Then, very slowly, Brendan turned toward the mirrors above the sinks to see if his reflection was at least registering. It was too dark to see.

Brendan turned back and opened the door. He was sufficiently disturbed that he didn't even bother grabbing a quick handful of paper towels to insulate his hand from the "cock cooties" on the door handle. Once back outside in the hall he ran into Raoul again.

"Hi, Papi," Raoul oozed, his tongue lingering on his lips like a hooker's. "You okay?" Only Raoul could make "hello" sound like a proposition.

"Raoul, the lights don't work. Nothing goes on." Brendan said with slightly overblown urgency.

"Where, Papi? Raoul's body was now weaving as if in anticipation. He batted his eyes at Brendan. The stub of the finger he'd lost in a blender in the commissary gently massaged his lower lip.

"In the bathroom. The lights don't go on when I go in. What's that all about?

"I take care of it....for *you*." He kept his eyes on Brendan while he opened the door and reached deep into the room with one arm and waved it. "You got to have the good motion, like me," he said. Brendan couldn't see what he was doing exactly, if anything, but the lights in the bathroom flickered on silently.

"Is there a switch? I thought they were automatic? I thought they came on automatically when you went in, right?" Brendan was much more concerned about this than he had to be.

"You have to turn them on with your body. Just like you do to me."

"Yeah, but most of the time, they're on. But it's automatic, right? I mean, I've never had to actually turn the lights on before. Ever. They just turned on whenever I went in there. When did they change the system?

"They didn't, Papi. They always been like that. But I always can do it for you. You never have to worry."

"You mean, they're automatic."

"Das right. "Raoul purred. "Like you and me. Automatic."
"But...."
"You still got a job, right?" Raoul said.
"Not for long, my friend." Brendan replied still distracted by the lavatory light problem.
"Don't worry. I make sure you never leave," Raoul said somewhat ominously. "No one touch you...," then he added, "...But me."
"Thanks, Raoul. But I'm afraid it's out of our hands."
"Don't worry. And don't worry about the lights, either. I take care of everything."
"Thanks," Brendan said, not sure exactly what he was thanking him for. He looked at Raoul for a beat and was struck by what he assumed was Raoul's unfettered loyalty to him "I appreciate your help."
Brendan realized he was being crazy. The fact that for the first time in his life the automatic men's room lights didn't go on when he entered had no existential meaning. It was a malfunction. A glitch. It meant nothing. It wasn't that Brendan hadn't triggered the lights. There were simply no lights at that specific moment to be triggered. That's all. Brendan knew all this intellectually, but he still took it as a sign. The building was rearing its head. The building could sense his cancer and wanted a piece of him now. His existence was suddenly not even sufficient to trigger the automatic men's room lights. The building was ignoring him just like Beverly did, and now Marge. He had become superfluous to them and the building. The episode with the lights ruined Brendan's day worse than the doctor's visit. He returned to his windowless office.
The monologue went spectacularly that day. It was like automatic writing. Brendan would start a sentence not knowing where the joke was, and the punch line would follow automatically, as if from God. It made him high. Writing was like that, and comedy writing was especially like that. When the writing was going well, Brendan enjoyed a "runner's high", or whatever it was that fuels marathoners and sex addicts to persist beyond normal limits. This day the comedy gods

were generous, and the words flowed magically. Gambits, references, associations, and tangents emerged that were never anticipated. It reminded him of that speech in "The Hustler" when Fast Eddie talked about being "hot" and making shots that had never been made before. The speech always resonated with Brendan because he often experienced, as a writer, what Fast Eddie talked about as a pool shark. Fast Eddie's pool was Brendan's jokes. When Brendan was in that zone, no one was better than him, at that moment, on that day. It was linguistic joy.

But then he knew that he would have to hand the joke cards to Marge who would skim them between her game of solitaire on her iPad and her hair. Marge's "cursory" look was done scowling and dismissively. She would complain and scold him about missing material that was literally, word for word, before her very eyes and which she ostensibly had just read but, somehow, had been too preoccupied to notice.

"Marge couldn't recognize a joke if it bit her in the twat," Brendan would say to Leo more than once on his way back after his daily ritual of offering his pearls to her swine. After fifteen years of sandbagging it on the show, she had forfeited her comedy chops. He purposely never stayed around to see Marge deposit the joke cards unceremoniously into the wastepaper basket before the show as if they were junk mail or the wrappers of her ever present chewing gum.

"You wouldn't want anyone to know that I don't really need you," she said to Brendan once just before the show.

"No, I wouldn't want *that*," Brendan had replied facetiously, only too mindful that the charade of "Marge's special material" that went on each morning kept him employed.

Then, the worst thing that could ever happen to Marge Foley— and "The Ladies' Room" for that matter—came to pass. It was the day some Washington Post columnist likened Marge to Walter Cronkite because she had changed her mind on euthanasia as Cronkite had done on Vietnam. The fact that the columnist was actually making an arch joke that Marge's views had more to do with stray cats than with people was all but obscured by the mere juxtaposition of her name and Cronkite's. From that day on, she forfeited her comedy persona for the *bête noir* of all comedians: legitimacy. But it was a legitimacy that Marge could not pull off intellectually. She didn't have any knowledge base, only bites of info. Instead, she became just another posturing comic who had discovered that earnestness was easier than laughs. All you had to do was *act* like you were telling the truth, as if the truth were just another "bit".

During the actual show, Marge would sit at the table with a scowl on her face. On the rare occasions that she would actually avail herself of one of Brendan's jokes, she would invariably get a laugh. But then, unlike a *true* comedian, she would stop—as if fearful that further hilarity would undermine her credentials as a newly-minted pundit. There was no fun or silliness in her delivery any more, only smart-ass reactions, obvious dismissals, and an iconoclastic attitude left over from when she was mildly funny. She rarely did self-deprecating material; and, as she became more famous and a star in her own right, she would do less and less material aimed at fellow celebrities. Like so many before her, (Marty Short, Billy Crystal, and Adam Sandler, etc) she became the person she used to make fun of. The only thing that kept her semi-human was the constant frustration that her agents were unable to get her a show of her own as Joy Behar's managers had done for her. Marge wanted to do Behar one better. She thought she should be on NBC on Sunday mornings doing an all-female version of "Meet the Press", except, as Brendan pointed out upon hearing of that fantasy, Marge's version of inane breaking news on the "red carpet" would more properly be called, "Meet the Dress".

Beverly and Bad Bob had become kings of "TaxiTV" and had maneuvered themselves into complete control of the annoying backseat theater in most taxis across the country through Beverly's relentless flirtation and courtship of the Governor. It didn't matter that he was very politically married with two kids and had a girlfriend (Brendan's wife). Her appropriation of him stemmed from the fact that she had always assumed he "had issues". It wasn't that he was homosexual, but she was pretty sure he was "half a fag"; a "mezzo finocch" as her father's friends would say. And that thrilled her almost as much as his power and money in the same way it had thrilled her when she had, incredibly, almost married J Edgar Hoover. The nexus of homosexuality and power was an elixir that Beverly could not resist. Hollywood moguls were too obvious, and movie stars too silly. Fashion designers only qualified if they were listed on the New York Stock Exchange, and European royalty only if the gross national product of their country exceeded 3 trillion. The Governor of California was perfect, and she wouldn't have to travel across any time zones to fuck him if he called.

The incredible thing was how excited Beverly and Bad Bob got about their TaxiTV shows. Between them, they were producing and/or appearing on a daily network television show, prime time specials, and breaking news exclusives; and Bad Bob, on his own, was selling game shows directly to syndication. But, somehow, the small-time bullshit of their taxicast show generated more heat and excitement for both of them. It was as if they were getting away with something, and that made it all the more delicious.

Beverly's mob pedigree stood her in good stead. While her father had been known as a man who would "steal a hot stove", Beverly was a woman who would gladly cook on it merely because she loved getting something for free. She and Bob made a nice piece of change off the "TaxiTV" show; and, best of all, it put Bad Bob on camera—even if it was in the back seat of a careening taxicab. But it was on someone *else's* camera instead of his own iPhone. And *that* made him a true celebrity in his own mind. They had plans to go global and put their pixilated faces in Haitian buggy busses, Venetian gondolas, and Chinese rickshaws before they were through. And Beverly had actually let Bob share in the ownership of the venture because deep down she knew it was silly and would amount to nothing. But it kept his fat fingers away from the real prize which were her network shows for which she had connived mightily, and submitted her once desirable body, in order to own them outright. Bad Bob would never get a piece of that pie nor a percentage of "The Ladies' Room's" profits. It was all hers. And, in the end, that was her only real trump card versus the blonde and flawless Delores Whitcomb.

CHAPTER TWENTY-THREE

"Ah am going to be married at the Cathedral of Our Lady of the Angels," Moonie proclaimed on the air one morning.

"But you're not even Catholic," Marge shot back. You're Native American...sort of. Don't your people get married in the forest or somewhere?"

"My sweet Ray Ray is very close to the hierarchy over at that church." Moonie beamed, "In fact, he has all his papers and everything a natural born Catholic has."

"Like a rap sheet as a pedophile," Roberta said immediately without thinking. She couldn't help channeling her stand-up days when it came to Moonie.

"I think that's awesome," Bambi said trying to stay on the right side of both of them.

"Bambi and I will be flower girls," Roberta said winking visibly at Bambi which made Bambi shudder as if she'd just been touched by the town pervert.

"Darling, I think it's wonderful. You should get married. It will do wonders for you," Beverly said.

"Like it did for you, Beverly, five times" Marge said. She didn't really want to join in this conversation since it undermined her new status. "Anyway, good luck, but just remember," Marge added dismissively, "Marriage is a 'mind' field." Marge got phrases and sayings wrong all the time, but no one had the balls to correct her.

Then Beverly asked the question that spelled doom for them all.

"Now Ms. Moonbeam, you know we love you, and, in fact, I shall give you away. And, darling, I'm sure it will be a grand wedding in the style of "Trump" or "Liza", but who, darling, will pay for it?"

"Already taken care of as we speak," Moonie said smugly. "You got nothin' to worry 'bout. This is going to be bigger than Donald Trump..."

"And gayer than Liza Minnelli." Roberta put in.

"If that's what you want, that's what you'll get. There'll be something for everybody, even you, Roberta. You can sit up front with the newly converted," Moonie said through her teeth.

The audience went wild. They were getting tabloid info with tabloid bitchiness.

Moonie never finished the business plan for her wedding on air, but as soon as the segment was over, Beverly grabbed her and pulled her back into the co-hosts' green room.

"I assume we should have a meeting about this," she said.

"Most Definitely, Miss B."

Moonie was proud that she had gotten Beverly's attention rather than just Beverly's customary cool acknowledgement. Beverly, for her part, had to constantly remind herself that Moonie was a network personality in her own right, with a career in broadcasting and a degree in medicine...and not a maid.

"All right, then," Beverly said, "Why don't you, Robert, and I sit down and see what this wedding is all about. We definitely want to be part of it."

"I wouldn't make a move without you, B.F. You know that. Without you, this would not be happening. "

That reassured Beverly and her shoulders relaxed under her double-wide shoulder pads. She always told Janet, her wardrobe girl, that she preferred to be more Joan Crawford than Donna Reed. It was better for business and added to her news cred.

"Maybe we should get the network involved. No, not yet. Let's just us figure this out ourselves before we call Sandy," she said thinking aloud. The wheels were turning. The monster was loose.

It was Sandy Abrumpkin's thankless job to be the point man for SBS in all matters having to do with Moonie Brown and her various schemes, deals, endorsements, plugs, and co-ventures. And somewhere, in all that, was her actual daily appearance on "The Ladies' Room" for which she had been hired. The network would be horrified by the 'roll-out" of Moonie Brown's Nuptuals. Horrified at what the extravaganza would entail production-wise, and horrified at the jeopardy in which it would place them in respect to the FCC. Gaining a few ratings points was not worth a hefty fine from the Feds. Or was it? A "wardrobe malfunction" on Moonie Brown, like the one that sank CBS when Janet Jackson took her breast out at the Super Bowl, could turn the SBS studio back into a Ford and Subaru dealership; or it could go "viral" and live forever on YouTube as a reminder that SBS was definitely "the place to be". If it was bare tit, "live", that the public wanted, SBS would give them enough boob to feed a small nation.

During that same show, Brendan had been trying to calculate how his cancer was affecting his impending termination. He couldn't tell from the actions of Bad Bob. The only indication that he was still toast came when Beverly actually looked him in the eye that day when they found themselves alone backstage during a commercial break. It was terrifying. Not being alone with her, but being held in her gaze as if that alone could vaporize Brendan right then and there.

"How is everything going?" she said completely out of nowhere in her crisp, demure, "Audrey Hepburn", little girl voice.

"Great," Brendan had replied. He figured she was just making conversation.

"I heard you were sick."

Then Brendan realized exactly what she was doing. Beverly was inoculating herself against any incriminations or responsibility for firing a sick man. Suddenly, Beverly Frost, the queen of the Swann Company and the SBS network was again acting like a file clerk who had overheard that he was fired *and* had cancer. Both of which were nothing *she* could do anything about. It was part of the "precocious little girl" act that had propelled her to the top faster than her pussy. But Brendan chose not to acknowledge that he knew she could order up the finest medical team in the country for his benefit if she so desired. She simply didn't want to.

"Yeah. I'll probably have to have an operation." Brendan replied. He was determined to either push her to confront the fact that she was firing a sick man; or, short of that, he would make her feel guilty that she was doing nothing to help him as a fellow human being and co-worker.

Beverly was silent for a long beat, touching the tips of her fingers together at her waist like a diplomat. Then she smiled for no apparent reason other than to cover her panic that she suddenly was alone with a writer who was between her and her entrance.

"Good. Just get better," she finally said.

"Yup," Brendan continued. He clapped his hands together like a fraternity doofus. Then, realizing that Beverly had nothing more to say now that she had assuaged herself of any guilt in his firing *or* his cancer, he stepped aside so that she could slither out the door and go onstage. After she left, he laughed at her innocent pose and her brief moment of internal conflict. But what Beverly's volunteered concern *had* established was that not only was the firing still active, but she was not going to volunteer any of her extensive medical connections to help him with the cancer, either.

But, on the other hand, at least she hadn't offered to buy him a ticket to Saudi Arabia.

It occurred to Brendan that, perhaps, he should delay any cancer surgery until after he was fired. Nobody seemed in any hurry about it. They called it "watchful waiting" and recently that course of action had become preferred. The doctors had all told him that prostate cancer was usually slow-growing and self-contained; even though real enough to eventually kill. And real enough to keep a job, Brendan thought. He immediately recognized the leverage it gave him at work. Thank you, God, for the cancer. You do work in mysterious ways, you Fucker.

When the show ended that day, Beverly stormed offstage.

"We have to talk," she barked at Bad Bob as she passed him where he was standing in his key light by the edge of the audience risers. "Now!"

Instead of going to her dressing room Beverly turned and walked into the empty Green Room and sat down, alone. She wasn't angry as much as she was disappointed in herself for being blindsided by the wedding deal. She was determined to get control of the situation. Moonie had long been the mistress of schnorr. From the first day that Beverly had snatched her from the dust heap of failed television personalities, Moonie had set out to make this shot pay. Fully aware that she had no discernable talent other than the fact that she was a semi-Native American who looked African American and was fat enough to be both, Moonie saw her ascendency to co-host of a network show as her 401K, set up by Jesus Christ himself. She knew in her heart that if she were to ever move on from "The Ladies' Room", it would be as an entrepreneur and not as an on-air talent. The audience can only take so much, even in Daytime.

Beverly arrived first in the Green Room, but then Moonie stormed in right after her, loaded for bear as if she had anticipated and prepared for this meeting for weeks, which, of course, she had, and in spades.

"I'm so happy for you." Beverly began through her frozen mouth, the corners of which never moved when she spoke. Because of her secret surgery, the only part of her mouth that moved any more was that little section of her lips in the center, directly under her nose. It made her look as if she were speaking through a key hole.

"Why thank you, BF," Moonie replied as if she were there for a fitting. "It's going to be the most wonderful day of my life." She plunked several folders down on the coffee table in front of them. "And yours."

"Darling, this is *your* wedding. Been there done that."

Then Bad Bob lumbered in, oblivious to exactly what was up. But, when he saw Moonie and Beverly seated opposite each other, squared off as if at a deposition, he knew not to waste time with pleasantries.

"I take it this is about your wedding," he said.

"Why thank you, Bad Bob," Moonie said with her best Aunt Jemima flutter and smile as if he had congratulated her. "We just got to go over a few things."

"I think we should be part of this, Robert. It'll be good for the show. After all, a member of our family is getting married. How can we not be?"

"Right," Bad Bob said sitting down. His huge frame looked bigger sitting than it did standing. Nothing fit. He looked as if he'd just entered his daughter's play house, and he acted that way; overly careful not to break anything or disturb what the girls had set out.

"Whatcha got?" he said metaphorically licking his chops as if back in his Memphis road house.

If there was anyone who knew how to beat a dealer, it was Bad Bob. He could turn a dollar in any situation. In a way, he reminded Beverly of her father even though their backgrounds were about as opposite as you could get. But both men had come from nothing and had survived solely by their wits and their ability to always have something else going simultaneously in any relationship or transaction.

In fact, there was no difference between her father and Bad Bob. Relationships were transactional in both men's minds. But while Bad Bob only thought of money and deals, Bernard Frost (aka "Benny Ice" or "The Iceman") only thought of pussy and staying alive. His secret deals that constantly ran in the background always involved a broad, a horse, a fighter, or a show. He broke the Broadway hipster's cardinal rule; "Never put your money into anything that eats." As it was, "Bennie Ice" lost a fortune on show girls and prizefighters; and his daughters never knew who was going to be at the door: a cop, a bill collector, a hit man, or the undertaker. It made for a childhood of uncertainty and excitement. But Beverly had transmogrified it all into, "Daddy was a producer, not just the owner of a liquor store", when, in actuality, Daddy was a schnook with a dream who was addicted to long shots. The only thing that kept him alive was that he had a better way with numbers than he did with women. But in the end, all those long shots with appetites devoured him long before the mob got around to it.

"The roll-out is divided into two thirteen week segments covering the fourth quarter of this year and first one of next, culminating in the wedding ceremony the week before the close of the first quarter, week twelve, enabling a recap segment of the reception, at no additional cost, for the thirteenth and final week of March. I always wanted to be a June Bride, but I'll settle for February sweeps," Moonie said in one breath as she unfolded her flow charts, graphs, overlays and individual segment presentations complete with product illustrations and set design sketches for production possibilities.

"I *am* drawin' the line at the church door. I cannot grant anyone, even "The Ladies' Room", access to my Sacrament of Holy Matrimony. That is between me, Ray Ray, and Jesus. But everything else is wide open and available. Just like I used to be before my lover Ray Ray came into my life."

Bad Bob and Beverly sat back on their couches, stunned. They had never seen anything like what Moonie had laid before them. Network series, specials, inaugurations, coronations, and state funerals had never produced this amount of preparation and attention to detail. There was even a check-in desk at the Cathedral to collect all cell phones and cameras from the guests which would then be returned only after the reception, held at the ultra-exclusive

Jonathon Club on Figueroa, in order to forestall any unauthorized pictures or simulcasts. Security would be tighter than an Obama visit to Dallas.

"Why Darling, you've thought of everything," Beverly began.

"It's my medical training. Checklists. There ain't gonna be no sponges left behind in this operation."

"No, it's definitely sponge-free," Beverly said leaning forward, gently lifting some of the pastel plastic overlays with her exquisitely manicured fingernail.

"This is one hell of a job, Moonie. You could be a production manager," Bad Bob said finally, figuring he had to say something.

"I *have* production managers," Moonie shot back."

"But how much will all this cost us, Darling?" Beverly asked.

"That's the beauty part. Nothin'. It's all product placements, endorsements, and plugs. That's my gift to "The Ladies' Room" and you, BF."

Beverly shot a look at Bad Bob. She was losing control of a situation that should be completely *under* her control.

"Well, I just don't know if we can devote an entire half year to your nuptials. It seems unfair to the other girls."

"There's plenty for them in there if they want to participate. Look," she said leafing through the pages, "Right here." She pointed to some architectural drawings of a shaded deck, "Home Depot will remodel Marge's patio for my "surprise" shower. That's all for her."

"I don't know if we can shoot that," Bob said trying to find a foothold for himself in the negotiations. "The sight lines look a little...."

"...Please" Beverly stopped him. "It'll be fine. The bigger question is *should* we do it. Can we turn all these months of the show over to Ms. Moonbeam P. Brown? I'm worried that the network won't like it, and then where are we? Darling, is there a modified plan? Something a little more manageable in the context of our daily show?"

"BF, you know I love you, and I owe you everything, but this boat is fully loaded and ready to leave. If you and "The Ladies' Room" want to be part of it, then, c'mon, jump on. 'Cause I'm gonna sail this sucker over to ABC, Oxygen, WE, Lifetime, or Bravo. Hell, I'll go to the Home Shopping Network if I have to. Miss Moonie is pre-pared. I just wanted to give you and Bob first crack at it 'cause I love you. But the boat's leaving, everybody. Jump on while there's still time."

The meeting was over. Bad Bob knew it because Beverly sat upright, gazed at the documents before her, and then placed her hands palm down on the tops of her thighs.

"We shall discuss this at a later date." she said

"When?" Moonie said a little too quickly for a subordinate.

Beverly did her best approximation of a "slowly I turn" take, and turned her head, very deliberately, to look at Moonie full in the face. "Later," she said simply and coolly. Then she stood up. "I'm having lunch in twenty minutes with Angela Lansbury in Encino."

The network initially turned down Moonie's master plan. First of all, they were afraid of anything associated with the still gargan-tuan Moonie that was ominously described as a "roll out". Secondly, what she was proposing was essentially hijacking the network to turn the entire operation into "Moonievision" for the Holidays and February sweeps. The binder mapped out a series of weekly epi-sodes highlighting every aspect of her nuptials and the sponsors that went along with it. The sales department was jealous. Moonie had accomplished by herself what the entire 5th and 6th floors of SBS headquarters had been unable to do with a staff of a hundred and fifty. It was all there, every last plug of it. Moonie would be the only bride who would actually make more money getting married than if she had picked Donald Trump as the groom rather than the willing gay man she'd actually chosen.

When the network turned it down, it was okay with Moonie be-cause it gave her license, then, to sell the wedding market-by-mar-ket through a syndicator. That was when Beverly *really* stepped in.

Even though Moonie's plan violated every known tenet of the FCC code, Beverly personally signed off on it and indemnified enough of the plan to prevent Moonie from marketing the television rights beyond "The Ladies' Room" and SBS. Moonie had won, and it made Beverly furious that she had been beaten by an employee. But Beverly's own self-aggrandizement had made it imperative that Moonie merchandize herself on "The Ladies' Room" rather than on any other show. Of course, it galled Beverly that her only remuneration in all of all this was on the back end, and Beverly Frost hated the "back end" in business as much as she *claimed* she hated it in sex.

CHAPTER TWENTY-FOUR

When it finally sank in that Moonie was getting married at the main altar of the Cathedral of Our Lady of the Angels in downtown Los Angeles, Marge went ballistic. West Coast Catholics consider the Cathedral their front porch, and they don't like anyone else sitting there. They especially don't like it when Hollywood Jews or politicians show up for Midnight Mass, or when they take Communion during funerals. The Cathedral is the visible triumph of modern Catholicism in California even more than the early missions or the election of John F. Kennedy. It may be open to the public, but not really.

"Moonie's getting married at the *Cathedral!*" shrieked Marge loud enough so that Ms. Brown could hear her in her dressing room. "And who's going to perform the ceremony?"

"I believe that would be an Indian chief and former cattle wrangler from Ventura County," Brendan said quietly.

"What? If I were still a Catholic, I'd file a complaint. My cousin, Bridget, was denied the Sacraments all her adult life because she'd married a Lutheran and was considered living in sin. They had to get divorced on her death bed so she could go to Confession and get Extreme Unction. Those bastards. Indian Chief? Is that even legal?"

"Special dispensation," Brendan told her. "The ceremony will be concelebrated."

He was actually enjoying her anguish because he knew what it was about. Marge and the others were upset, not because Moonie had hijacked the show with her nuptials, but because she was in the process of choking the golden goose of perks and comps. The co-hosts knew instinctively that Moonie's wedding would prove to be a "schnorr too far", and it would queer all their various sweet deals in one fell swoop.

"I'm having my media room in Sherman Oaks remodeled," Marge said. "Mark my words. This is going to be bad for all of us, especially Moonie. The network isn't stupid. If I have to actually pay for that flat screen and total sound, I'm going to be pissed. It's just not fair."

Brendan nodded in dutiful appreciation of her predicament. Marge had a tin ear when it came to the "Beverly Hills Blues". She had little empathy for the plight of the rank and file whom she really considered should be happy to be working at all. Consequently, staff members and PA's had to regularly listen to her salary laments like being docked a day's pay at "The Ladies' Room" because she had scheduled a two and a half million dollar female Viagra commercial instead. The injustice of it all! Then she would listen heedfully while a production assistant or wardrobe mistress, making $500.00 a week, would feel her pain but try and make her see that, even after taxes and the ten percent for her agent, the two and a half million dollar pharmaceutical deal as a day's pay was worth it even counting the lost residual when the missed show was repeated. But then, when they all went to dinner afterwards, and the bill came, all bets were off. Marge would pay only for herself after grilling everyone at the table as to who had the tuna fish. Suddenly, she was like Ellie Wiesel dining with Nazis.

Moonie's deal rippled through the show like a boulder dropped in a puddle. Suddenly, everybody had a stake in her marriage. As parts of the proposal leaked out, the segment producers lamented the fact that there would be pods of highly produced pieces that would require Moonie, herself, hovering over them. And no one—man, woman, nor dressing room mouse—wanted a hovering Moonie anywhere near them.

However, Beverly had asserted her rightful control over her show and had actually agreed, ultimately, along with the network, to a modified version of the plan. "Modified", meaning basically the same plan but without the "Moonie Brown" brand superseding "The Ladies' Room's". The show and the co-hosts would celebrate their sister's happiest of days, but for 8 weeks not 26. Moonie moved her wedding up as a gesture of good faith for services rendered. That's when the trouble started.

Roberta would have none of it.

"She's a liar. A dirty, filthy, rotten liar. Her pants are not only on fire, but they stink, too," Roberta said in the make-up room a few days later before Moonie had arrived. She was doing material, but she was truly pissed. The staff and the other co-hosts might chuckle to themselves, but they knew better than to go up against the Moonie juggernaut, even in her absence. It was like getting between a rhino and her young, only, in this case, it was between a rhino and her swag.

"Darling, she's entitled," Beverly said.

"Ha!" Roberta said with a cruller in her mouth. Flakes of pastry flew out onto the make-up counter and stuck to the mirror. This made Roberta convulse in laughter. She had just done the first re-corded "cruller take" in comic history.

"I read where that church was built to withstand an earthquake of 8.4 on the Richter Scale," Roberta said. Then she held a finger up for the punch line. "Not strong enough!" she added.

"It's all a mystery," Beverly lamented again. "The girl must make a million dollars from all her plugs. Of course, the news department would never let me take even so much as a nickel. What's her secret?

"Bourgeois guilt," Marge chimed in. "Nobody wants to fuck the Indians *again*. I'm surprised she hasn't opened a casino."

"Oh, darling, please," Beverly said.

Beverly had doubted Moonie's Native American claims from the beginning, but it had worked for the diversity of the co-hosts. When she was selling "The Ladies' Room" to the affiliates she would proudly intone, "We have a newly-minted woman, an Indian princess, a bit o' the fightin' Irish, a young WASP who's not afraid to sting, and me, a journalitht." Beverly hit every stereotype but her own.

"Well, I'm not going to put up with it. I *can't* put up with it. The whole thing is a lie and that includes her weight loss," Roberta said folding her arms defiantly across her implanted chest.

"I, for one, am really proud of her for at least trying to lose some of the weight, Bambi offered. "I know I struggled after my baby was born, and it took me almost a week, well, actually, almost two whole weeks to get back in shape." Bambi may have been the only woman to have ever produced a baby without gaining *any* weight. For every pound the baby in her pristine uterus gained, Bambi made sure she took one off somewhere else on her perfectly sculpted body. Her little girl fetus was the lucky one, however. She was able to develop her eating disorder *in utero*.

"Oh stuff it, Sweetie. You don't know what you're talking about. You're young and terribly misinformed," Roberta said turning on the love of her life in a particularly patronizing way. "Moonie is a disaster. But when she tells lies in front of me, I have to do something about it. I'm sorry, Beverly, but as Moonie herself would say, 'Dat's jes' me'." Roberta leaned heavily on the black accent just to make her point.

"Well, try to restrain yourself, darling, for my sake," Beverly said while secretly agreeing with everything Roberta said. She was still pissed at the amount Moonie was able score right under the nose of the Network and the FCC's payola rules. But Beverly's insistence had indemnified the network, and they were confident that she knew enough of the right people to beat down even a federal challenge to Moonie's shenanigans.

"It's your show, Beverly, but the lying is going to bite everyone in the ass" Roberta went on. Roberta was a nasty tranny, but an uncanny truth teller. "I have to sit here and listen to her talk about how her love of Jesus and aroma therapy made her lose the weight when we all know it's that goat dick inside her that's siphoning it all off into a colostomy bag." Roberta turned and saw a dark shadow fill the small psycho ward-type re-enforced glass window in the make-up room door. "And speak of the by-pass, here she is." Roberta knew that the door was such that no sound could travel through it. She had tested that thoroughly after her first day on the show.

After a beat, the door opened; and Moonie Brown swept into the room. Everyone instinctively bowed their heads or looked away either out of chagrin for what had just been discussed or to avoid the cloud of smell that preceded her like a thunderhead. She arrived in full evening make-up which meant that, once again, she hadn't showered.

"Morning, everyone," Moonie said in apparent good cheer. "Sorry, I'm late, but I was *busy* at home." She leaned on "busy" to indicate a sexual event. It could have been anything, intercourse being the least likely. And she *was* late. Even later than Mugsy who was still toweling off after her come-to-work tennis game. Moonie didn't wait for even a perfunctory reply or salutation but launched into her story for the morning.

"I had the most wonderful birthday," she said lowering herself into her barber chair like a twenty ton containment dome on an oil spill in the Gulf.

Moonie always hesitated slightly before the final descent as if to allow observers in the room to catch their breath. Then, when her "wide load" finally landed, there was an almost audible sigh of relief/disappointment that nothing had broken. Even so, the barber chair looked decidedly squatter for all its trouble.

In the beginning of the show, Moonie's size was such that Ralphie, the "Ladies' Room" set designer, had feared that one day, live and "on air", she would collapse whatever chair she was sitting on. Consequently, he had ordered a specially built chair for her that was essentially a column of solid, reinforced concrete with a cushion on top and the frame of a normal chair built around it. It was the only way he could sleep at night.

"When I got home from my Dom Perignon Champagne birthday reception in my honor at the Beverly Hills Hotel," Moonie continued, "My Ray Ray gave me the most wonderful birthday present in the world."

"He left some food on his plate," Roberta blurted out. But Moonie's manufactured euphoria was bigger than a mere jibe.

"I came home, and my Ray Ray had prepared a love snack for me," Moonie began.

"You mean, a whole buffet?" Marge said.

"That came much later. First, there was a note from him informing me that he would probably be still at the gym and that I was to follow the path made out of nothin' but rose petals that he'd done strewed on the floor."

"If you'd had an Irish maid, she would've quit." Marge interjected. Moonie was not to be sidetracked. She was in full fantasy mode.

"So I put down my things and followed those lovely rose petals. They must've come from five dozen roses or more. And they led me right into the bathroom where there was a perfumed bubble bath already drawn and an open bottle of Dom Perignon chilled in its own silver bucket and lit candles everywhere. And those petals led right up to the bath, and there was another note saying that I should slip into the tub and then slip into something comfortable before Ray Ray came home and slipped into *me*. Now, isn't that the sweetest?"

The room was silent. The operative word in that whole story was the word, "bath". Roberta shot Marge a look and arched one very dubious eyebrow. Marge stifled a laugh.

"Well, as my Aunt Alison used to say, 'I bet they could've knocked you "ovah" with a "feathah"'", Marge said in her family's best Irish parish priest accent familiar to any church-going Catholic alive in the Fifties.

Roberta immediately twisted around in her chair to face Marge. "A *feathah?*" Roberta mouthed silently.

"Wasn't that just the sweetest?" Moonie said when no one volunteered.

"Well, I think it was more than sweet. This man is your true love. And he's not afraid to show it. All men should be like that," Bambi said, "All men."

Roberta looked visibly disappointed that her girlfriend had stepped up so eagerly to join Moonie in her fictional romance.

"So what did you do?" Bambi went on eagerly and very publically interested in a minority whose personal habits she didn't want to even think about. "I wouldn't have touched a thing. I would've kept everything just the way it was for weeks. Or maybe a month. I don't know. I would've done something. But I don't know. What I would've done. But something."

"I just took my time to savor that delicious moment." This prompted another look from Roberta to Marge. This time she didn't have to mouth, "savor something delicious". Marge couldn't look at her. For a comic, there's nothing better than a repressed laugh, a "church" laugh.

"I put down my things and followed that rose petal road right into my bathroom, removed my clothes, and didn't even bother to hang them up. Then I poured myself some of that fine $200 champagne, stepped into that tub with the floatin' rose petals, took a sip, and leaned back and thanked Jesus with all my heart."

Marge had, by then, controlled herself enough to turn back to Roberta and pantomime, "What happened to the water in the tub?"

"What about the water?" Roberta evilly blurted out. Marge was aghast that it got repeated. Fortunately Moonie was in deep reverie about the moment.

"Ray Ray had fixed it to exactly the right temperature. It was heaven." Marge breathed a visible sigh of relief.

"That's really sweet," Mugsy said. "But we have to pick some talking points here. Do you want to talk about your birthday, Moon?"

"I prefer not to. It's really so private." She said demurely. Then she brightened up. "But do we still have the confetti cannons and balloon drop?"

Moonie was referring to celebratory devices once available during "The Lavender Period" of "The Ladies' Room" when Lance Lussier, a famously gay coordinating producer, had insisted that four confetti cannons be installed on the set along with a perpetually loaded balloon drop in the event that a "Ladies' Room Moment" might happen that would trigger their deployment. Moonie obviously felt that her birthday was one of them. But, alas, the cannons had been instantly dismantled and mothballed upon Lance's dismissal for fucking a boy intern on the Xerox machine. Since then, even the word "confetti" sent shivers down Bad Bob's spine, and the cannons themselves became an object lesson for the horrors of creeping gayness that was supposedly, in the confidential words of Liz Sterling, "Not our show". The balloon drop, however, remained because it was considered a legitimate Daytime game show staple. But its deployment was strictly reserved for only monumental events in Beverly's life such as another lifetime achievement award, an appearance by the Governor of California, or the death of another anchor. Bad Bob was not about to have the cotton farmers in Desoto County, Mississippi accuse him of running "some kinda homo show" out in Hollywood.

That was the day Roberta walked off the show.

It was during the second segment of "CrossTalk", so the feelings stirred up in the make-up room were still hot, and the arctic blast from her personal air conditioning shaft had not been sufficient to cool down Roberta's "hard-on equivalent". They had been talking about gender issues because Roberta, as moderator, was able to steer any conversation, no matter how far afield, to a discussion about herself. But then she made an abrupt turn to international politics.

"The Chinese own all our debt," Roberta had begun.

"Let 'em have it," Marge parried getting a light laugh. Marge was adept at the "wisecrack dismissal". It was really just a well-worn and familiar attitude line instead of a joke, but it would hopefully end the discussion and falsely indicate that she knew something about the subject, which she did not. But Roberta was not to be deterred.

"What I mean is, what if the Chinese suddenly decided to do 'take out'? We're merrily rolling along, and one day the guy doing the news starts going 'Ching chong, ching chong' because it's *their* show now, and we can't do anything about it." Roberta said, effectively offending 2 billion Chinese.

"It's because of spending," Bambi said. "The money has to come from somewhere. Our future's being mortgaged. There's no end in sight. It's crushing."

"You are very young and very wrong," Roberta said touching Bambi's forearm. "The Chinese need us as much as we need them. They're like Lesbians. You may not like that they exist, but they do, and we all need each other. The global economy is no different than being on Fire Island back East in the summer. We're all trying to survive until Labor Day."

"And we all have to pull those stupid little wagons around like six year olds." Marge put in. The audience laughed because it had the rhythm of a joke even though it wasn't. Marge had become all rhythm and no humor.

"I don't think you can really compare the Chinese government to lesbians," Bambi waded in with. The conversation was about to go over her saucy little head.

"What?" Roberta shot back, slapping her hand on the table and getting a laugh on her delivery and her take.

"Lesbianism is a choice. The Chinese are communists. All of them. And they love taking our money. And doing whatever they want with it."

"Let's go back to that thing about the mice," Marge said referring to a topic that had been bill-boarded but not discussed yet in an attempt to make the conversation, at least, somewhat entertaining. "Did you know that they can make a mouse a lesbian by just removing a gene?" Marge continued.

"Really!" Roberta said turning her face to her in mock interest and placing her chin in her hand with her elbow on the table.

"Yeah," Marge went on trying to divert what felt like trouble that might step on her faux punditry. "Look. Right here in the research. And do you know what that gene is called that makes female rats hetero? The FUKm gene. Now you know why I think Stephen Hawking is sexy." Roberta's eyes glazed over. She did not want to do bits with Marge. She wanted to fuck Bambi at that moment worse than ever.

"All I know is when I get *my* jeans on, every man I meet wants to take them off," Moonie added.

Moonie got a huge laugh on that mainly because of the image of her getting her jeans on and the absurdity of anyone willingly wanting to remove them.

"Ladies', I think we should move on." Beverly finally chimed in. And then, just to make sure she'd killed any comedy or sense of play, she added yet another self-serving, self-referential comment. "But that's why we all love this show. So many different opinions. Some we can't control. But we all get along."

Roberta turned and faced Bambi squarely. "Let me just get this straight. You hate lesbians and the Chinese."

"Wrong. I didn't say that." Bambi had her back up now because she knew Roberta was after something. What she didn't know was that it was her pussy. "I said we shouldn't be so in debt to the Chinese. They're not our friends. The Chinese"

"And Lesbians?" Roberta said benignly.

"They're...they...I don't know...They're lesbians...They like women."

"Exactly!" Roberta said slamming her hand down on the table for emphasis again. The audience went wild. The laugh was so big that even Marge briefly considered doing comedy again, but just not anywhere near Roberta who still knew how to get a laugh.

Beverly smiled at the audience patronizingly as if the laugh was hers. She pretended to start a sentence several times but stopped open-mouthed and each time turned to the audience in mock shock as if Bambi were a precocious child who had blurted out some perfectly apt, but shocking, obscenity.

But all eyes were on Roberta who all but winked at the audience to signify that she had more in store for Bambi. She took Bambi's hand. It seemed like a sisterly thing to do, but for Roberta it was sheer heaven just to feel that young, smooth, white, virgin skin. It took her aback for a beat.

"Bambi, my little doe," Roberta began. And she meant it, too. "Are we talking about the national debt or sexual orientation?"

Bambi giggled. "I don't know. Maybe...sexual debt?"

That got a ripple laugh mainly because the audience didn't really tolerate big guffaws from Bambi. She thought she could be funny, but she wasn't, and the audience laughed out of pity, not merriment.

"Have you ever met a Chinese Lesbian?" Roberta said calmly. Now she was *really* fucking with her.

Bambi burst into a cascade of narcissistic laughter that only women who consider themselves beautiful ever have the balls to indulge in. They're not really laughing at all. It's just a device to buy time while they figure out how to charm their way around a subject without the conversation going any deeper.

Roberta continued to hold her hand and look at her intently like a doctor breaking some bad news. "Here's the deal," she said. "Lesbians are like the Chinese. They're everywhere, and sometimes you have a craving for a lesbian just like on Sunday nights or Christmas when Jewish people want to eat Chinese."

"Huh?" Bambi said.

"But have you ever tried to eat a lesbian with chopsticks." Marge said 'a la Groucho, proving that, once upon a time, she really was truly funny. The line came out of nowhere and even took Jeanie, the Censor, by such surprise that it eluded her mute button on the seven second delay.

The laugh that Marge got lasted longer than normal. It was one of those laughs that comedians live for. It literally nourishes them and allows them to endure those inevitable performances where there is nothing but "crickets" while they sweat in front of a hostile audience for whom nothing works. When she was just breaking into stand-up comedy, Marge would have all her friends come to her appearances no matter how late or random. Those were the days when the audience eagerly wanted to laugh for Marge, they just didn't know where to do it, or when to start. Every beginning comedian has those moments before the persona kicks in. In a sense, the audience and the comedian both have to learn to trust each other and relax. But the laugh that Marge got that morning on the show was unique and legendary. It seemed to feed upon itself like a wave gathering more and more volume before finally breaking and dissipating on the shore. The audience laughed and then seemed to laugh at itself laughing. The bad news was that Marge then sat back and refused to open her mouth again for almost a week afterwards, having assumed she had earned her keep and didn't have to.

Roberta took the laugh time to gather her forces. She never shifted her gaze from Bambi; and, even though Bambi laughed along with the audience (although she wasn't quite sure what was so funny), she knew that she had not yet been released from Roberta's cat-like clutches.

"Thank you, Marge, for that enlightenment," Roberta began. "And the answer is, 'yes, but it's tricky'. Especially, the Egg Fu Yung".

Jeanie was ready for that one so the viewing audience never heard it, and the studio audience only laughed politely despite Roberta's Borscht Belt delivery. An audience is often exhausted after a big laugh. And furthermore, they hate it when someone else tries to climb onto another comedian's joke train.

"But I want to get back to what we were talking about before we were so rudely interrupted," Roberta went on in mock high dudgeon. "Bambi, my sweet, I was stunned by what I think you said which was that somehow lesbians are un-American. Is that what you really think?"

"I thought we were talking about the Chinese and the debt." Bambi said nervously.

She was like a squirrel standing frozen in the middle of a country road with a cement truck bearing down on her. She couldn't decide fast enough whether to go right, left, or just stand perfectly still. The only thing Bambi (and the squirrel) knew for sure was that somehow, out of nowhere, she was about to become "roadkill".

"You're the one who brought up lesbians. Why did you do that?" Bambi said defensively.

The audience chuckled, but they were feeling Bambi's nervousness. Her attempt to push back, even in the slightest way, triggered the killer instinct in Roberta like a cat who can't believe the mouse in her claws is still bothering to struggle.

"I was making a point, my dear. And you chose to take that point and turn it against me like a spear." Roberta's speech was redolent with symbolism.

Suddenly, everything in her life was coming into focus: her childhood as an abused boy at the hands of her mother, the complicity of her father, her self-inflicted wounds, her sexual terror and confusion. Deep down she didn't care about lesbians, but like any man, their sex turned her on. But then her operation had made her one by default. She was now as hell-bent on destroying her tenure on "The Ladies' Room" as she had been in obliterating her offending penis. And she was determined to take Bambi with her

"Just tell me that you don't think I'm a terrible person merely for who, or what, I am."

Roberta couldn't have been more clear. All she was saying was, "Just tell me you love me." And Bambi instinctively knew it. Bambi's back was against the thin wall between her past as an idiot and her present as a *famous* idiot. Roberta's question was clear and direct; but, of course, her intention was not. The circuits in Bambi's head jammed.

"I don't know what you are saying? How did we get onto this?"

"It's called, 'conversation,' Bams," Roberta said meanly.

"Are you trying to put words in my mouth? I just think we have too much debt."

"And in all the wrong places, I know. But that's not what I'm asking you. Do you think I am a bad person because of who I am?"

Now Bambi was legitimately confused.

"I...I don't know what you're asking" she stammered.

Beverly would have jumped in and put an end to it, but she looked up at the monitor and saw that Hal had split the screen into two boxes because Roberta and Bambi were sitting at opposite ends of the table, and he couldn't get a decent "two-shot" of them with one camera. Suddenly, the show had a "News" look to it, and Beverly couldn't decide if this was a good thing or a bad thing. The audience had pushed back in their seats, riveted by the grilling going on before them and even more by its subtext.

"Why don't we go to commercial and wrap this up in the next segment.....or next season?" Marge said.

She had been out of the conversation for most of the segment and figured she ought to say something. Moonie fidgeted in her chair making the stage hands catch their breath over the imminent collapse of the furniture beneath her. It was as terrifying as watching a five ton boulder teeter on a precipice.

"No!" Roberta insisted "We are *not* going to commercial until I get an answer." She then turned again to the young co-host that she loved so deeply. "Bambi, you know me. You know my children, our children have played together; we've visited each other's homes. We work together every day. Do you approve of me? Or do you think that what I am is something bad?"

Roberta's need was palpable now. She desperately needed something from Bambi that only Bambi could give, but Bambi was unable, or unwilling, to relinquish it. Had Bambi been the least bit human or truly caring instead of living within her own reality show and her 24/7 camera-ready persona, she would have recognized the simple act of kindness that Roberta so achingly sought. But Bambi was neither human nor kind. Her heart was as blonde as her head. That, and she truly did not understand what was going on. She basically did not understand the question.

"Just tell me to my face that you accept me." Roberta said once more. Bambi's double-white teeth flashed to indicate that she was trying to think.

"Well, this has nothing to do with you, but I can't say that."

"Can't say what?"

"I don't know. You're asking me to say that "anything goes" no matter what. Spending, sex, whatever. I think there have to be limits. Even personal ones. You're a wonderful person inside, but...but please don't make me say I agree with everything you do. Or have done. That's your business, and you're welcome to it. You and I are not on the same side. That's all."

"You can't accept me."

"If you put it that way...No!" Bambi finally said without fully realizing that she had just driven a stake through Roberta's heart.

Then Roberta looked up, and saw the split screen. But it wasn't the split screen, separating them as if in two cages, that stopped her. It was the glint of a tear in her own eye that the camera, in Roberta's split, had caught. She had known the tears were there, she just didn't think they were visible and about to declare themselves on her cheek.

"Commercial!" Roberta ordered slamming her palm down on the table again. Then she rose from her chair and walked off the set.

Everyone knew that something major had happened, but they weren't sure exactly what. Bambi sat there with her hands in her lap looking around and smiling her white, toothy smile with her lower lip protruding ever so slightly. She looked like an admonished toddler with great legs.

The tabloids would say later that Roberta had "stormed off" the set, but, in truth, she had only "drizzled off", sort of in a fog. There was a moment of indecision in the Green Room when she lingered alone and off to the side, eyeing everyone and everything with the sidelong glance she had perfected as an outcast boy-child, lonely and suspicious of what life had next in store for him. Then, in an instant, she was gone. Nobody followed her because nobody actually saw her leave the floor. She had bolted down the rear stairwell, the stairs next to the third floor men's room that was in a constant state of foulness, beyond any industrial cleaning, after years of use and abuse by stage hands and male celebrities.

Once on the floor below, she turned down the empty hall toward the dressing rooms. But first she had to pass Lucy at the security booth to get buzzed in.

"Wahatchu doin'_down here, Miss Bobby?" Lucy said punctuating her salutation with the buzzer. "You 'sposed to be up there right now." She looked at the monitor in her security cubicle. "They comin' out of commercial any second."

Roberta glanced at the monitor as she pulled the door opened, but she no longer cared. "The Ladies' Room" logo was up full before dissolving to a jib shot of the audience applauding, sweeping to a wide shot of the set and then a cut to the table where the co-hosts sat like school girls saying "Grace" with their hands politely folded in front of them on top of the table. Roberta's seat was empty. Then, for once, Hal put the camera on Moonie without her asking.

"Welcome back," Moonie said in her best "white" anchor voice, barely hiding the victory she had just scored without lifting a fat finger.

Meanwhile, on the floor below, Roberta continued past the security booth into the warren of dressing rooms until she got to Bambi's. The door was open, as opposed to Moonie's whose door was always, not only locked, but with an additional special anti-theft "boot" on the knob that she had insisted Security place there. It made the room look fortified and forbidding. The staff assumed there must have been a ham sandwich inside.

Bambi 's dressing room was a lot like herself: pastel, corny, boring, and lethally non-threatening. There were piles of stuffed animals in the corners that she had snared from the show for her kids but had never given to them. It was more valuable for her to have them on display, poised for motherly dispersal, than to have them actually played with. In addition to the mute menagerie of plush creatures, there were stacks of self-help books on the floor, pink dumbbells, an actual pom-pom, a humidifier, and several rows of lip gloss along the mirror over the counter. The sink had been covered over to accommodate a close up mirror the size of the Hubble Telescope that rested on top and whose rim lights were perpetually lit. If Roberta still had a dick she would have jerked off in the pom-pom. As it was, she did the next best thing.

First she kicked everything into the center of the small room. Then she hoisted her hefty man-ass up onto the counter, pulled her slacks down, and peed all over everything on the floor holding the little stub of her cock, which was supposed to function as a tranny clit, to direct the stream of her urine.

It was at that precise moment that Lucy, who had wandered back to take advantage of a private moment with a star, appeared at the door. Her jaw dropped open at the particular private moment she had happened upon.

"Now that jes ain't right, Miss Bobby. I knew you was up to *somethin'*!" Lucy turned back toward the security booth. "I better get somebody up here right away to take care of that."

Roberta didn't answer her; but when she was finished, she shook her "clit" out of habit, wedged it back into her "pussy", got down from the counter, and pulled up her pants. Then she went next door to her own dressing room to grab her tote bag, happy that, although she had just taken a piss at the office for the first time since joining "The Ladies' Room", she *still* had not used the public Ladies' room.

Lucy had the PA mic in her hand, after having had no luck raising anyone on the phone, when Roberta rounded the far corner of the hall on her way out.

"Raoul? Raoul?" Lucy began on the PA that spread the word through the entire building, "Raoul to the second floor with a mop." Then she added, but still on the PA, with a more personal touch, "Raoul, you needs to come up here to the second floor right away and bring everything you got." All announcements made on the PA had to be repeated twice as if the person making the announcement knew that no one listened to those public address declarations anyway.

Roberta paused outside Lucy's office where the large 20X24 publicity shots of the co-hosts were hung. She stood in front of Bambi's portrait for a beat. Then, she took a Sharpie pen out of her pocket and carefully drew a Hitler moustache on Bambi's upper lip. Then she turned to her own portrait and drew a large X over her face.

"And bring an eraser, too." Lucy added on the PA. She stood dumbfounded with the PA mic in her hand and her mouth agape watching the soon to be former co-host deface SBS property. "Now, what am I supposed to do with *that*, Miss Bobby?" Lucy said to Roberta.

Roberta stepped back and admired the image of the love of her life as Hitler. It all made sense. Roberta felt good for the first time in months.

"Enjoy," she said.

Then Roberta went out the door to the dressing room area for the last time and strode down the hall to the elevators that took her out of the building—just steps ahead of the security detail that had been gladly summoned by Bad Bob to escort her.

CHAPTER TWENTY-FIVE

B rendan didn't feel one way or the other about the departure of Roberta. She had remained enigmatic, distant, and wary of him no matter how hard he'd tried to ingratiate himself to her with either personal gifts or comedy material. Nothing seemed to stick with her; and, although she could be randomly generous, it was always at arm's length.

Raoul, on the other hand, was openly pleased about the turn of events.

"See, Papi? Bobby fire herself. That leaves more room for you and me."

Raoul 's voice came from behind Brendan and startled him as he was waiting for the elevator the next morning and staring absent-mindedly at the latest postings on "Wall of Woe".

"I doubt it," Brendan said without turning around. "But I always thought she would save me. In fact, I was counting on it."

"Das *my* job," Raoul said with a smile. But it wasn't the smile of a joke.

"I appreciate that, Pal. But only if Yale Maintenance needs a comedy writer," Brendan said heading into the elevator.

"See? You're funny," Raoul said as Brendan turned around and watched the doors silently close between them like a curtain.

With the departure of Roberta, the show was minus a moderator. There was much speculation as to who the replacement would be and what sort of person would be able to fill Roberta's Timberland boots. No mention was made of the fact that the building had claimed, yet, another soul, and this one didn't even get a final notice posted on the "Wall of Woe". Beverly gladly increased her appearance schedule and ascended to what she considered was her rightful place on any panel—and especially one that she owned.

"Sandy, I'm back in the game!" she proclaimed triumphantly to Sandy Abrumpkin the day after Roberta left.

The more interesting aspect of the rise and fall of Roberta Monzon was her possible interaction with the SBS killer building. Could it be that the structure had exacted its mysterious deadly toll on the otherwise healthy and vibrant Roberta, reducing her to a broken man/woman with a dwindling career and fewer friends than when she had walked in? Brendan wondered if Roberta's departure would turn up on the "Wall of Woe", sadly marking the untimely passing of yet another victim. It was as if the building had an animus that was growing stronger as its inhabitants grew weaker. Roberta's insistence on the special AC duct may have been the structural insult that brought on her demise. Brendan began to wonder about his own health in view of the recent events. Only Beverly, it seemed, was immune. Had she made a pact? Were she and the building in some kind of satanic architectural cahoots? Brendan began to think about all the guests of "The Ladies' Room" who had also died, divorced, or dropped out of the business in the fifteen years he'd been there.

Marge had walked into the building a saucy, smart, fresh comedian and had been reduced to a tabloid-spouting hag in the course of her 15 year tenure. Even her Christmas card in her fifteenth year raised more eyebrows than laughs among the staff who were dumfounded when they received it. The card consisted of a Renaissance painting of the Incarnation of The Blessed Virgin Mary with Mary standing opposite a strapping Michael, the Archangel, while the

Holy Ghost, in the form of a dove, descended upon her. Then, inside the card, the headline declared, "The Virgin Mary Was Raped! A donation to Abortion Rights has been made in your name. Merry Fuckin' Christmas, Marge Foley".

It took Brendan's breath away. Not only because of its unnecessary and unfunny blasphemy, but because someone might think he actually had something to do with it. But fortunately, as a Christmas greeting, it was so "not funny" and so indicative of Marge's drift away from comedy and being funny at all, that no one, not even for an instant, thought Brendan was in any way responsible. For once, her reputation for not doing his material worked in his favor. Even the Jews who received the card were offended, but they were also slightly consoled by the fact that at least she hadn't said, "Happy Fuckin' Hanukkah!"

Bambi's perfect life and perfect physical form were a thin veneer that covered the migraine headaches that turned her face blue, a husband who was caught face down on the nanny, and a child whose only source of protein was her own hair which had to be removed from her stomach as a bezoar once every six months.

Moonie had initially gained weight after she joined the show. She had gone from obese to morbidly obese before finally getting the intestinal resection bypass and colostomy bag.

Only Beverly had remained the same, but then again, she probably *was* the building, or its avatar. Soon they might even be putting up death notices between her legs. On top of that, Beverly had somehow managed to beat Google, Wikipedia, and the DMV by having her age recede during the years she had been on the show. Beverly Frost *was* the "Wall of Woe". If the show continued another ten years she would achieve the Einsteinian feat of retiring at a younger age than the one at which she'd started.

But even Beverly wasn't completely immune to the corrupting power of the building. Shortly after Roberta left, there arrived on Brendan's desk a late Christmas gift from Beverly Frost. But what it really was was a trophy to remind everyone that she'd prevailed in the "Roberta Wars". The object itself was a clear plastic obelisk with a barometer inside which merely proved that it been offered to her as some sort of promotional giveaway and hadn't cost a nickel. It made no sense in terms of the show, the season, or her.

But then, just to make sure the object would be ridiculed rather than cherished, (like the previous Christmas gift of a cheap blanket with "The Ladies' Room" embroidered on it which some of the stage hands cut a hole in the center of and wore as a poncho rather than be bothered to even put it on Ebay), the barometer came with Beverly's "personal", hand-written signature engraved into the fake silver base. The only problem was that even this personal touch was obviously far beneath Beverly's consciousness; and she could not be bothered to have actually signed something meant for her employees. Thus, the signature engraved there, for all time, was clearly in her assistant's handwriting and looked like a school girl's practice signature on a notebook—slanted upward, with letters too carefully drawn and too perfectly formed to be a diva's. On top of that, the "Beverly" was spelled wrong. It read, "Bevely"—most likely phonetically rendered.

But the aspect of the gift that made Brendan's heart sing was that the inscription read, (again, proving that Beverly had nothing to do with it) *"Love Bevely Frost"*. No comma. Thus, instead of a blessing or her loving wish, it became an order. And anytime someone gazed upon the foolish object, Beverly, like the "Red Queen", in her own words and by her own alleged hand, would be commanding all to love her unconditionally or suffer the consequences. In the end, it reminded everyone of Roberta.

Holiday gift giving at "The Ladies' Room" had always been an ersatz affair, at best, in terms of its questionable sense of good cheer and its illusion of largesse. The universal present chosen for the staff was always handed out the week before Christmas by either Madame Defarge or Chester without any pretense whatsoever of sincerity or generosity. Everyone had become a doorman ("Take that, motherfucker. It's your Christmas bonus, you fuck!").

They would go from office to office as if settling an account or paying off a gambling debt. And the gift itself, each year, was always some "irregular" or remaindered catalogue item, or a "second" in airport-grade merchandise. Thus, the item, although embroidered with "The Ladies' Room", always had the feel and the smell of a bad mall. If it was an article of clothing, the measurements were off. If it was luggage it couldn't be trusted. And if it was anything else, it was just plain useless…like Beverly's barometer.

But by the fifteenth year, Beverly had tired of the whole ritual. In addition, she found out that she had actually been personally paying for all those Christmas parties and not the network as she had been led to believe all along. Thus, in the 15th year, the party itself became the present; and all tangible gifts, except to her favorites, disappeared.

Since it was now coming out of the owner's pocketbook, the location of the party was immediately reduced to the back of an Irish bar in Burbank. And when Beverly did her "drop in" for the event, exquisitely over-dressed for a much fancier venue and an infinitely better guest list somewhere else, she insisted on over-explaining everything to the staff as if she were "on air" and explaining the metric system, once again, to the audience she considered intellectually challenged. "For those of you who don't know what the metric system is, or have never heard of it, the metric system is a system of measurements based on …" Bu this evening, for this Christmas, she decided to be extra generous with a gift she thought everyone truly wanted.

"Oprah gives out cash bonuses at Christmas time," Beverly began her speech at the Christmas Party, "And she takes her staff on fabulous trips. 'The Talk' gives Caribbean Cruises. 'The View' hands out panini makers, espresso machines, and gift cards from Apple to their hard working staff."

She held the mic in both hands before her as if it were an Easter candle. This was going to be a special moment for all her worker bees.

"But we at 'The Ladies' Room'", she continued as if what she was about to bestow upon everyone would trump them all. "We at 'The Ladies' Room' give… only our thanks," she paused dramatically, "…From *here*."

With that she pointed to the place on her chest where a normal person's heart would be.

The thing that made the moment all the more memorable was that she said it without a hint of irony, self- awareness, or humor. In fact, it was obvious that she really and truly believed that thanking the staff from the bottom of her heart was far better and more valuable than any amount of trips, gift cards, raises, bonuses, healthcare, or, even, outright cash. In fact, it was *much* better; and wasn't the staff of "The Ladies' Room" singularly lucky and fortunate that she had thought of thanking them that way. But she wasn't finished.

"I know all of you have worked very hard, some from the very beginning of the show; and I wish I could thank each and every one of you personally so that you would know how much I appreciate your contributions to our success. But since that's not really possible, I am now going to look at each one of you and make eye contact with you as my way of saying, 'Thank you'."

With that, she actually turned her head to the side in order to begin her gaze at a point slightly behind her left shoulder. Then, like a lighthouse beacon or a prison searchlight, she swept her eyes very slowly and deliberately around the room in a 180 degrees arc until she finished her beneficent gaze over her right shoulder. All in the room had been thusly touched and blest and could now return to their normal lives knowing that, at least, once in 15 years, Beverly Frost had actually looked them in the eye. Whether she had had any idea who the people were that she was sweeping with her regal gaze was another thing altogether. The gift of Beverly's personal acknowledgement had thus been dispensed.

Then, Beverly simply turned and walked out of the bar to her waiting town car which took her to a place where there were better people whom she actually knew and cared about.

It was around this time that Brendan started smelling like shit in the morning. At first he thought it was the cat that woke him up each day by pouncing on his chest and purring there until he got up to feed her. Brendan was convinced that the purring was just a cover for the cat's farting which was then captured by his t-shirt. When he mentioned this to The Wife, she immediately took the cat's side and berated Brendan for impugning the integrity of her pet's bowels.

"It's definitely coming from inside you," she said sniffing him, "Are you having an affair?"

"With whom? A sanitation worker?" Brendan said. "It's something else. The building, our house, my life, the marriage...."

"That's not funny, and it's not fun" she said quoting Billy Crystal on "Howard Stern". "Maybe it's your prostate. You should call Dr. Benjamin and ask him. Are you sure you're not eating something or swallowing something that's breaking down in your stomach?"

"You mean like that big turd I pigged out on the other day?"

"Maybe," she said seriously. "You forget a lot of things."

"Well, eating shit isn't one of them. Except, maybe, when I'm home."

"Is that supposed to be a comment? I'm trying to help you. I want you to make an appointment with 'Benji' right away."

Brendan agreed. The shit smell had become morning theater for The Wife and Zeke.

"Daddy stinks," Zeke would declare after sniffing Brendan's shirt. The truth of the matter was that Brendan couldn't exactly refute the conclusion, but the origin was still up for discussion.

A week later he went to see Dr. Benjamin but only because he was due for a check-up anyhow. Brendan hadn't been able to bring himself to make a separate appointment for a stink. Just explaining it to the receptionist was above and beyond the call of medicine.

"There's nothing wrong with you," Dr. Benjamin told him. "It could be the cat or even Mr. Katz, the Jewish gentleman living next door."

"Is it the prostate?" Brendan asked, "Maybe I'm rotting from the cancer."

"It's a good metaphor, but cancer only stinks in the last stages. My mother-in-law stank just before she died."

"So what're you trying to tell me?" Brendan asked

"Don't get married. Ooops, too late." Kenny Benjamin considered himself a comedian among doctors. He was one of the few medical practitioners outside of vaudeville who actually wore that silver reflector thing on his head but only because he thought it made him funny.

"Speaking of that, I can't get a straight answer out of anyone about the cancer. I have organic friends in Topanga who tell me you can cure it with diet. Another guy says they have a giant ray gun down in Long Beach that does the trick. I bet even Gwyneth Paltrow has something very 'special-special' for it."

"Stay away from laymen and the internet. And fuck Gwyneth Paltrow. Too much unverified information. It *is* true that one of the remedies is 'watchful waiting'."

"Like for a train?" Brendan said.

"A late train. One that may never come."

"And that's a piece of medical advice?' Brendan asked

"No, I read it on the internet." Kenny laughed at his own joke. Brendan was getting nervous.

"And what's the internet say about the shit smell in the morning?

"How would I know? I'm a doctor not a blogger. You want me to tweet this and see if anyone out there has the same thing? You could form a support group."

"Hey, Groucho, I got problem here." Brendan interjected, stopping the monologue. "I smell like shit, and I can't get a straight answer out of anyone about my cancer."

Kenny wrote a name and address on a piece of paper. "Go see Sid Kolodny over at UCLA. He's a real mensch. I guarantee you'll feel better. No matter what."

"But will he fix the shit smell?" Brendan said

"He won't even notice. His finger's been up the ass of more strangers than Charlie Sheen's. Your particular shit smell is coming from something outside you, not inside, no matter what your wife tells you. I'm your doctor. All wives think their husbands smell like shit. It makes them feel *and* smell superior. If you want a serious diagnosis, I would check the cat and anything else you do in the morning that might make you smell like shit, including taking one. It could be a wash cloth. Wet clothes smell like shit if they're left out too long. Broccoli gone bad in the fridge really smells like shit. Sour milk smells like shit. And then there's the old standby, shit. That smells *exactly* like shit. It is not inside you; it's outside you. Your prostate only smells like shit after somebody examines it, okay?"

"That's pretty good," Brendan said smiling.

"And that's why, next to my name in LA Magazine's Best Doctors issue, it says "Complex diagnoses". I wish I had a nickel for every shit smell diagnosis I've done in my day."

"And you'd have what? A dime?"

"Something like that. Maybe five cents," he said smiling. "This is the first. Seriously, you're fine except for the prostate which you'll take care of in due course. And if you can't figure out where the shit smell is coming from, move."

Brendan left the office feeling better.

Unfortunately, the consult with the famed prostate surgeon, Dr. Kolodny, made him feel worse. The UCLA offices where Kolodny had his little kingdom looked like a Westwood methadone center. There was peeling paint in the halls and missing light bulbs. Someone had even stolen the clinic's sign and left two big scabs on the wall where it used to be.

The Wife insisted on coming along for the consultation after seeing Kolodny's video on YouTube. She automatically considered him a celebrity on account of it and secretly wanted to be able to recommend him when the Governor's prostate went south. But as soon as she saw the state of the offices that Kolodny worked out of she was sorry she had come. The entrance wasn't even on Wilshire but through some non-descript doorway on a side street. It reminded her of one of her abortions. She vowed never again to venture west of Lambert Drive again for health care.

After the nurse had shown Brendan and The Wife to a large examining room, another nurse came in carrying three Naugahyde-bound, padded albums, each one the size of the old Manhattan telephone directory.

"The doctor would like you to look at these before he sees you," she said and left.

Brendan assumed they were a complete set of "What to Expect From Your Prostate" articles written by the good doctor. But as soon as he opened the first one he saw that it was actually an endless collection of photographs of smiling, curly-haired Jewish men extolling the virtues of getting their prostates removed by that genius, Dr. Kolodny. For some reason the former patients of the doctor felt compelled to have their post-surgical pictures taken with their shirts off. As a result, there was much grey, curly chest hair in evidence. One after another happy Jew smiled heartily into the camera with his arm around a usually much younger, blonde, shicksa girlfriend. And each photo was accompanied by a time stamp indicating how long it'd been since the operation (sometimes just hours). At the bottom was always a heartfelt "Thank you, Dr. Kolodny" for getting them back in the saddle in such short order. They were all so happy.

Brendan showed the albums to The Wife. She couldn't believe what she saw, and it just confirmed what she already felt about the place and Dr. Kolodny. Besides that, the photos upset her because the men all looked sleazy and vaguely like the Governor. It only served to remind her how fragile love is and how much cancer survivors like younger women with straight hair. To The Wife, the albums looked like Tiger Woods' date book.

When the doctor finally came in, he revealed himself to be basically a miniature version of his patients. But the most startling thing about him was the size of his feet. They were unnaturally small. They looked to be about the size of a doll's or, perhaps, a small ballerina's. He wore tasseled loafers, but their diminutive size made them look like slippers.

"Did you get a chance to look at my books?" he said eagerly right off the bat.

"Books?" Brendan said not having the slightest idea what he was talking about.

"Didn't the nurse bring in our photo albums? I told her specifically,..."

"Oh, you mean, the photographs," Brendan said. "Of course."

"I can give you more time if you'd like to examine them more fully or spend a few moments. They're quite impressive."

"Yes, they are," Brendan told him, "Very impressive. Lots of happy customers"

"I have more books, but I don't like to boast," Kolodny said.

Kolodny had arrived with a medical team in white coats consisting of another doctor and a young Iranian woman who looked like a Kardashian. "These are my associates," he said introducing them, "Doctor Schimmel from Jordan and Betsy Ghadimi who is a third year medical student interested in urology," he said with a certain twinkle, "I hope you don't mind. They're going to assist me today."

"Not at all," Brendan said, "And this is my wife."

Kolodney sprang to address The Wife. He took her hand and patted it with a gentlemanly flourish. He was obviously in a sales mode; he knew how important it was to get close to the wife. The doctor from Jordan also shook hands with her.

"Dr. Kolodny is the finest surgeon in the entire world when it comes to your husband's prostate," Dr. Schimmel told her earnestly. He looked and sounded like Dick Libertini in "The In-Laws". The Wife smiled wanly and nodded. She didn't like strangers talking about one of her husband's organs. "I have come all the way from my country just to observe this man. He is, how do you say, *magnifique!*" The doctor kissed the tips of his fingers for emphasis as if he were talking about fine wine and not someone who cut people's balls off for a living. He was obviously a shill.

Brendan knew what was coming next. He knew that everyone in the room was going to stick their finger up his ass, including The Wife, if he could convince her, because that's what the prostate business is all about, and they just can't wait. In fact, at this point in his cancer Brendan had had so many fingers up his ass that he had learned to relax rectally as a convenience and as a courtesy to those who had to do it. Of course, he had no idea if they actually enjoyed it. But then he worried that the anus control he was so proud of might make his examiner think he was gay and had taken a lot more up there than just a finger, so he went back to feigning discomfort just to be butch about it.

This morning was to be no different. Kolodny went into his sales pitch for the radical post pubic prostatectomy. It was like he was selling encyclopedias not surgery. The ease of his delivery indicated it was a necessary part of his job. If he wanted to cut people open, then he would have to sell them on the idea first. The lack of no presenting physical problem in the customer, of course, made his sales pitch for surgery all the more important. But when he glossed over the fact that he, personally, would not be doing the actual opening cut, nor would he be on hand to remove the sperm sacks himself, he lost Brendan. Apparently, the good doctor would still be in his car on the way in from Pacific Palisades. That part of the surgery was so routine and such a piece of cake that a surgical resident would be performing those honors. In other words, on the job training.

Unfortunately, the prospective removal of his sperm sacks by an amateur was far more disconcerting to Brendan than the more complicated, and dicey, removal of his prostate. And learning that some pimply faced med student who had just scrubbed in before class was actually going to be pulling out his "happy plumbing" did not exactly reassure Brendan.

When Kolodny finished his presentation, he nodded to the nurse who silently picked up the prized photo albums and removed them as if the books shouldn't have to witness what was coming next or get splattered with anything. Then there remained only the *coup de grace* everyone had been waiting for.

"I'd liked to examine you now if you don't mind." Kolodny said as he started to pull the wraparound curtain across the room in order to separate The Wife from the exam.

"That's okay." Brendan said stopping him with a smile, "We do this all the time." Kolodny paused and thought about this.

"Your call," he replied with a shrug and left the curtain only half way pulled so that The Wife had to move her chair to the side to watch.

Brendan dropped his pants and bent over the examining table with his forearms resting on the white paper. In the beginning, Brendan's prostate exams were usually done on top of the examining table, on his hands and knees, with his face pressed against the paper and his ass in the air like a porn shot or occasionally on his back with his knees pulled up to his chest and equally porn-like. But the real pros did it standing up, probably because Patrick Walsh, the father of radical prostatectomy, did it that way. First up was Kolodny because it was his gig. He probably also went first at gang bangs and latrine line-ups, too. He had already snapped a glove on; and, with his left hand on the small of Brendan's back to steady himself, he entered Brendan's asshole and reached up for the bulge of the prostate on the other side of the colon wall. He made two quick passes at the gland and withdrew his finger in one seamless, very professional, motion. He'd had done it thousands of times before.

Next was the sleazy Jordanian doctor with dyed black hair and a cap job that made his mouth look like Walt Disney was his dentist. He was suddenly tentative, and Brendan could tell he was a complete faker despite the resume that Kolodny had spouted when introducing him, as if having a foreigner with an advanced degree stick a finger up your ass is some kind of gift. Brendan had become something of a connoisseur about rectal exams and could tell that the so-called doctor hadn`t a clue as to what he was looking for and didn't really want to find out, either. His finger barely penetrated the rectum and never reached anywhere close to the prostate. But like a true con artist, he nodded knowingly to Kolodny after withdrawing his finger as if to confirm the diagnosis.

Lastly, it was time for the semi-good looking alleged med student. She was probably some hot lab assistant Kolodny was fucking or wanted to. It even crossed Brendan's mind that she wasn't even connected to medicine at all but was just some broad Kolodny had picked up and was showing off to by letting her pretend to be a doctor. Brendan used to do the same thing with women he wanted to fuck who considered show business an aphrodisiac. He would bring them around to whatever show he was working on and introduce them as a "gag writer from The Coast". If they were good looking enough, no one ever questioned him. Only if she were unattractive would they test her. But Brendan had better taste than Kolodny; and, besides, Kolodny's broad couldn't quite pull the scam off.

Brendan knew she was going to be trouble when he looked back over his shoulder and saw her struggling with the rubber glove like O.J. at his trial. Her problem was getting the fingers of the glove over her hooker-length fingernails with their white-tipped French manicure. Brendan had jerked off to enough internet porn to recognize the white polish under the extended nails was solid proof that the girl was a professional and not a babysitter. The porn category could be "Amateur Teen Coed" but if the nymphet had that white-tipped French manicure and a Harley Davidson size tattoo across the small of her back, she was a working girl.

The glove was finally pulled on over her nails. Neither Kolodny nor his faker friend made a move to help her but waited patiently for her to prepare herself. The girl was not attractive enough to make this interesting, and her perfume, as she drew close to Brendan, was suffocating. Brendan assumed the position once more and looked straight ahead as she gently spread his cheeks and gingerly began to explore and probe his asshole area with her finger.

This whole thing has really gone too far, Brendan thought to himself but said nothing. If you guys are fucking her, you should just do it. She's not especially enjoying this part, and I'll bet the whole sham doctor thing has ceased to be a turn-on for everybody.

The girl poked around tentatively a few times, and Brendan could feel the sharp hooker nail of her forefinger digging into his taint.

"Are you looking for the hole or trying to make one?" he said out loud, thinking it would break the tension. The girl drew back instinctively.

"Sorry," she said and changed her stance as if that was going to guide her finger better.

Finally, her finger entered Brendan's rectum and began to push up very unprofessionally into his colon. Brendan wondered if, perhaps, this was the first time she had ever done this sort of thing —with an actual glove on, that is. Maybe that was the problem. Either that or she wasn't used to doing it while standing up or without a cock in her mouth. Once inside, the girl was much more aggressive than the phony doctor had been; and Brendan actually thought he felt her wrist watch against his ass before she began to retreat. She had run past the prostate bulge, so there was nothing for her to feel. She had gotten about as far up the colon as any human being could get without stepping into it. Brendan was grateful she hadn't made a fist first. She paused there for a beat to show her boyfriends that she was game and did not want to embarrass them. Then she withdrew her finger and removed the glove all in one motion as Kolodny had done, but the way she did it signified that she wanted nothing more to do with any of this nonsense.

"Thank you," said Kolodny when it was over. "Any questions?"

Brendan had none. The Wife was nodding off in her chair.

Then the crack medical team turned and left the room, checking first to make sure that the nurse had truly removed all the precious photo albums.

Brendan looked at The Wife, and she returned his glance as if to say, "Losers". Then they both silently made their way out of the building feeling somewhat dirtier than when they had arrived.

CHAPTER TWENTY-SIX

The problem with Brendan's prostate cancer was that he really didn't feel anything he could identify as a disease or a disorder. He didn't feel sick. Thus, all the talk about removing the mysterious gland hidden behind his colon and underneath his bladder seemed more like elective surgery than anything life threatening. It would have been much easier to talk to the knife boys if there had been at least some presenting problem. Certainly, Sykes, the urologist, didn't feel any urgency when he left Brendan to his own devices. Appendicitis is an easy choice. Radical post pubic prostatectomy is an act of the will.

Suddenly, there was prostate cancer everywhere in the same way pregnancies seem to become omnipresent when a girlfriend is knocked up or counting the days after her missed period. Suddenly, everyone had prostate cancer. Neighbors, friends, Don Imus, Senators Kerry and Dodd, probably even Ellen Degeneris if she looked hard enough. Brendan had to stop using the mention of his cancer as a comedy bit for its shock value because, instead of sympathy or a laugh, all he got was a story about Uncle Harry or somebody's father or brother. Everybody had a prostate story. Not only that, it was usually better than Brendan's.

Marge completely forgot that her writer had been diagnosed with a life threatening disease. As Brendan would lean over her while she got her hair washed in order to glean some indication of how she wanted him to slant the jokes that day, Marge would close her eyes during the final rinse and repeat her mantra, "This show is so over," as a response to all inquiries. It was her way of avoiding even thinking about the show at hand. Then, opening her eyes she would add, "I can't deal with these topics. Write whatever you want." Then she would return to the only thing that concerned her every minute, of every hour, of every day: her hair.

"It's all about the hair," she would even proclaim on air to congratulate the hair and make-up people on their annual Emmys while never mentioning the Writing Emmy that had also been won. Nor would she ever mention any of the show's writers by name. Once, while Brendan was waiting to speak to her, he was forced to listen while she related to Bambi how she had been asked in an interview, point blank, if she had any writers; and how she had proudly denied even knowing any, except a couple of semi-famous novelists in San Francisco. Marge was upholding the long tradition of comedians and kings and their love/hate relationship with their writers and fools who were clearly better off dead once they'd done their job.

Even when Brendan and Leo won their second Emmy, Beverly specifically went on the air, looked into the camera, and told the world, "Of course our show is never written, and we are always spontaneous and live. But apparently we have won an Emmy for the writing of some snappy intros and announcements. Things like that."

It must have stung Marge in her atrophied heart that whenever she was quoted for some *bon mot* or world class witticism, it was always something that had been written for her. But in her darker moments she could be heard screaming to whoever was attending to her, "I have the power! I can get people fired!" It was as if this weighty responsibility of being able to irrevocably alter people's lives, at will, was the real burden she bore and not the ubiquitous shoulder pads she insisted on wearing because she thought they made her look taller.

"This show is so over," Marge sighed once again as she lowered her head into the sink to be shampooed

"Maybe," Brendan said, more as a marker than a response.

He couldn't figure out if she was talking literally about the show, or him, or his career, or hers, or life in general. She was probably right on all counts. Only the building and Beverly Frost would survive in the end. Marge never elaborated on her pronouncement of the show being "so over". And it didn't really make specific sense until Brendan found out that she had exercised a loophole in her contract that allowed her to do a reality show. In Marge's case, it would be a political one. She would make a mock run for public office on Comedy Central with cameras rolling nonstop. It meant she could get her hair done almost as many times a day as Beverly.

And so it came to pass that Little Margie Foley, born and bred in Canaryville, in the shadow of the stockyards on Chicago's South Side, on national television one day, announced her "candidacy" for President of the United States, not because she thought it would be a good idea for "The Ladies' Room" in an election year, but because she had just signed with Comedy Central to be the subject of a reality show consisting of a mock political campaign that would culminate in her "inauguration". Then she would segue into her own political talk show that would follow "The Daily Show" on the channel. Beverly, Bad Bob, the SBS network, and Swann were completely blindsided by the announcement, and their public congratulations hid a feverish flurry of legal gyrations that resulted in their being unable to find anything in her contract to stop her because it was considered "reality", and there had been no clause in her contract that had specifically prevented it. Her original contract had pre-dated "reality" television. The corporate lawyers at Swann should have been fired on the spot for such a glaring lapse; but, instead, they laid off the legal research personnel instead.

The problem quickly became that, even though Marge had obviously arrived at this juncture because of her reputation as a comedian (it was, after all, *Comedy* Central), she began to believe her own press. In short order, she secretly began to believe that she really *should* be President or, at least a senator, like Al Franken. She wanted to be taken seriously.

Viacom, the parent of Comedy Central, grabbed onto their sly foray into news with an over-the-top promotional campaign that stunned even the mighty Swann Company. Viacom saw this as bigger than even "Jersey Shore" in that it would move them closer to the news cred of Time Warner and the crumbling CNN. What Marge didn't realize was that she had become a pawn in the corporate turf wars.

Suddenly, there were huge presidential campaign posters up all over LA, Chicago, and New York and even mock political commercials that featured her ample tits and proclaimed her the "Breast Person for the Job". What had started out as a joke and a comedy gambit quickly became the darling of the elite; and all the attendant "late night" jokes curdled into something very real in Marge's mind. Unlike Beverly, who merely dated politicians, Marge was now going to become one. She was making news instead of just lampooning it. Marge became a "straight line" for the first time in her life, and she liked it. It was easier than being funny.

Brendan had briefly thought he would be swept along as both the enabler and co-creator of the entity that she had become and a necessary element for its perpetuation. But she dropped him along with her allegiance to "The Ladies' Room" in favor of her new found "brain trust" consisting of quasi-political Harvard prigs, star fuckers, and Santa Monica intellectuals.

"I don't *need* you," she snarled at him with a viciousness he had never seen before.

Marge had pulled Brendan into her dressing room at "The Ladies' Room" for a confrontation the day after her first "Marginally Presidential" show aired on Comedy Central. She'd heard that he thought she might be using material written for "The Ladies' Room" in her "campaign" and on her own show. Which, of course, she had been, and continued to use, in spades, whether unwittingly or not.

"I don't *need* you," she repeated with her nose scrunched up in abject disgust, "I've got Mark Solomon."

She said it with a sense of triumph that comes with being able to lord one writer over another. It was the only fight she and Brendan had ever had. She was clearly making the break from her past and from the comedy that had made her what she was.

Mark Solomon was a vicious right wing columnist and writer who had recently decided to call himself a Libertarian to broaden his base. He knew his politics, and he was funny in a slashing, bitchy way. It is often possible to get laughs by merely saying the unmentionable regardless of any inherent comic construction. His efforts on Marge's behalf enabled her to replace her comedy with pure snark. As a closeted gay, he was doubly angry; probably more at his sexual situation than any political scenario he could conjure. As a result, Marge positioned herself more as a "truth teller" than a mere humorist. And, as such, she could camouflage all of her baser leanings under a mantel of phony courageous honesty. The problem was that what she gained in the nihilistic landscape of Comedy Central and cable; she lost in the more mainstream network version of herself. She began to call herself a "fundit", as opposed to a political "pundit" in the flurry of interviews that followed; but, in truth, she should have re-christened herself a "dumbdit" to reflect the shallowness of her knowledge. She really didn't have the brain power to parse anything deeper than a punch line; and, like a phantom limb, her comedy became a figment of the real thing—a sense memory with nothing to back it up in reality.

Marge's newly minted incarnation made her go virtually silent on "The Ladies' Room" when she found she could neither speak out effectively nor entertain comically. In her own words, her former comic self was "so over"; but her new persona never quite fit, despite its popularity. She woke up each morning to see her face plastered on Billboards on Sunset as a faux candidate for president. But her manufactured popularity took its psychological toll, as well. In short order, she didn't know who she was, what she wanted, or which job defined her. On top of that, she secretly harbored the wild notion that she actually *could* become President through some populist fluke. And certainly should be. Of course, she didn't know what she would actually *do* if that happened, but she liked the house that came with the job.

"What a gorgeous place to live," she said to Brendan one morning while he was trying to get her attention. She was referring, seriously, to the White House. "And those lawns. Too bad it's in the middle of Washington. Do you realize what that place would be worth in Beverly Hills? Now that would be something."

Several days later, when Brendan walked into the show, a mini crisis was in progress; and Lucy, the security guard, was beside herself.

"I ain't seen Raoul for days, and everybody's been lookin' for him," she cackled.

Raoul lived in his office in the sub-basement of the studio building. The place was a huge cave-like space he had carved out that had become the repository of all the cast-off furniture, props, costumes, gags, and swag he'd collected or stolen from the various shows that had been produced in the building over the years. Brendan had never actually ever been inside this Hieronymus Bosch garden of klieg lights, and he only vaguely knew where it was in the labyrinth of the sub-basement. But he knew it to be the Sargasso Sea of the building. Everything ended up there, including several cute boy interns.

"He's probably dead," Brendan said.

"Das exactly what I am afraid of," Lucy said. "And if he's dead, that would explain the smell."

"What smell?" This got Brendan's attention.

"They been complainin' about some smell comin' from the basement recently. But I went down there, and there was no smell as far as I was concerned."

"And you don't smell it here?"

"Nuh-uh." Lucy shook her head definitively "Only in the basement where the smell's at. Why don't you go down there and tell me what you smell?"

"Just call him," Brendan said. "If he answers, then he's not dead, and the smell's not him."

"I ain't callin' nobody that could be dead. Dat's the "haints", and I ain't goin' nowhere near dat. I'm jes tryin' to do them a favor."

"Then get an intern to do it. They don't know any better."

"Maybe I'll do just that." Lucy declared, happy that she had a course of action. "Those interns'll do anything. Even let someone like you ha-rass them, Bren-dan." This produced her signature cackle and yelp that she reserved for perceived sexual advances and her own jokes.

Brendan continued on to his office. There had been another death notice on the "Wall of Woe". This one had been the life partner of a female cable puller on "Living for Love" who had succumbed to uterine cancer after a long illness. There would be a wake at Gallagher's Funeral Home in Tarzana and a funeral Mass at St Mary, the Virgin. In lieu of flowers, donations could be made to GLAAD. Brendan took the notice down and crumpled it but did not throw it away. The funeral was that morning so the notice was already out of date. Anyone watching him do it would assume it was out of grief, not annoyance. He balled the paper up and stuck it in his pocket.

The issue of the building smell troubled Brendan as he sat down behind his desk, and he thought about going down to the basement to check it out. He hadn't the slightest idea what a dead person was supposed to smell like, but he'd always heard it was unmistakable. But once inside his office, and with the door closed, he threw away the death notice and smelled himself. But he could discern nothing but deodorant and sweat—nothing that could vaguely be described as a decomposing body, even to someone who had never smelled one before. So it wasn't him because he didn't smell like shit that day.

Lucy eventually forced one of the interns to make the call to Raoul in his office. He had picked up after just one ring. The intern had then hung up immediately, happy that she was calling from Lucy's extension and not one that Raoul could trace back to her. Raoul's predatory nature was one of those truths learned immediately by all who came to work in the building, like which bathroom was the cleanest and the best shortcut to the "half-cafe" so named because the food was half-assed and the facility was a poor substation of the main cafeteria in the executive wing.

"That'll be me," Brendan said to The Wife that night after re-telling the story. "That's how it'll be with me. People will start calling me to see if I'm dead or not."

"No, Brendan," The Wife said. "That will never happen. You're married. You have a family. And a wife. You have *me*."

"Yeah, I guess you're right"

"*I'll* make the phone call. *I'll* be the one call to see if you're dead or not, not some intern."

Brendan didn't know if that was supposed to make him feel better. The scenario was the same. He would still be dead and rotting, alone, in his office. Brendan wondered where exactly The Wife would be making her heroic phone call from. Probably the Governor's vacation *palazzo* in Cabo.

CHAPTER TWENTY-SEVEN

L ove was in the air. Bad Bob traveled to Memphis to run his annual Elvis Impersonator contest at "The Vapors". He brought
Jeanie the Censor along with him ostensibly to determine if any
of the gyrating impersonators were appropriate for "The Ladies'
Room"; or, at least, that's what he told his long-suffering wife. She
was safely stashed away in Sarasota, Florida with her brand new
Hummer where she spent her days trying to download every song
in the world to her iPod from the various illegal free sites she'd discovered. Every time Brendan ran into her, she would proudly quote
him a new total.   Brendan had thought about turning her in just
to see this middle-aged woman led away in handcuffs like some errant teenager apprehended as an object lesson to her peers. But he
never did.

The trip to Memphis for the weekend was enough to seal the
deal for Jeannie. She teased and seduced Bad Bob continually and
even insisted on separate rooms to satisfy the expense account and
to make him commute for his blowjob. But by the time they returned to LA to do the show on Monday, she had made up her
mind up that time was right.

Jeanie Murphy loved being a network censor, not only because
of the power she had to intervene and interdict SBS programming

with a "bleep" that would replace something she'd instantly decided was inappropriate; she loved it because of the endless march of salacious material that was laid at her feet each day for her consideration. She loved smut but could tell no one of her delight. Her life was one of quiet fascination with the lewd, dirty, outrageous, libelous, and nasty side of life.

Jeanie lived that staple of primetime television known as the "frustrated fuck". Her life was a litany of frustrated fucks—of others yearning for the unattainable, of men getting close but never achieving what they relentlessly sought. But she longed to be, just once, that which she censored. This war of ying and yang within her, this yearning for climax in the face of restraint, gave her an appeal to men and women that went far beyond her classic good looks and unassuming demeanor. She was "The One". She was the sweetheart that everyone wanted to embrace, protect, and fuck at the same time. It was why writers didn't mind when she pre-emptively rejected a turn of phrase or premise, and producers willingly accepted her emasculation of an intricately crafted segment. Jeanie Murphy was that nice. She looked and acted like a Daytime version of an idealized sitcom star—straight, long back, adorable bangs, and a winning, toothy smile

Thus, Jeanie's whole life was one of making men ache. It was the only real power she'd ever achieved, and she was a master at it. She had identified Bad Bob as a lover long before he, himself, ever realized he was in play. Even while he was having his affair with Mugsy in the early days of the show, Jeanie had earmarked him for herself. Bad Bob was everything she wanted in a man: straight, older, successful, powerful, married, and, most importantly, fertile. He had five kids, and contrary to what one might expect, this turned women squishy at the thought of all that potent sperm swimming around inside. Jeanie wanted him in the worst way: while he was still married and her boss. She wanted him because she wanted a baby more. She had once, half-jokingly, even begged Brendan for his sperm after she'd met Zeke. Brendan had declined. He would have enjoyed the deposit but not the interest.

It really was no secret that Jeanie had singled Bad Bob out at practically the first meeting of the production staff. Even the stage crew knew what she was up to since they had worked with her on other shows and had seen her in action. The way gay men liked to boast about their conquest of unattainable straight men, Jeanie was proud that she could make any married man desire her to the point of obsession without ever having to consummate it. It was her own private genius. She was the perfect girl that no one could have.

In the early days of "The Ladies' Room", Jeanie insisted on being at all rehearsals with Bad Bob. She would then deliberately ignore him while endlessly conferring with stage managers at home base, standing in heels in profile, leaning on the table as if in deep discussions with her ass, in perfect yoga pants, deliciously raised and presented to him while the stage hands set up a food demo. Those were the days when Bad Bob was still seeing Mugsy. But that didn't deter nor distress Jeanie in the least. She knew what she wanted, and she knew her customers.

Of course, everyone on the studio floor knew exactly what was going on from the start. There was a pool run by Sean, the outside prop man, on how long the seduction would take. And in typical fashion, Bad Bob was the last one to figure it out. He vaguely knew of Jeanie's reputation as the Holy Grail of women, but his southern formalism prevented him from ever thinking he might be the object of her interest. Before he became aware of his seduction, the crew would smile knowingly behind him as they readied shots and moved furniture. But then, once Jeanie's chaste vamping became too obvious for even an oaf like Bad Bob to ignore, the fun went out of it for the crew. Now they were forced to ignore it and pretend to concentrate on their work as the two circled each other like zoo animals. The only good news was that their sex dance (suddenly tedious rather than titillating) usually added an extra hour, and sometimes more, to the time sheet. And since Swann had imperiously switched the entire crew of "The Ladies' Room" from "staff" to "freelance" in order to avoid paying health benefits, that wasn't an entirely bad thing. But leave it to Bad Bob to make a public display of forbidden sex actually boring to behold. The problem was that the crew knew Jeanie was an unattainable tease even though Bad Bob suddenly thought he might actually have a shot. So the whole thing had become tedious and a nonstarter for years.

"That's a wrap, guys," Bradley, the stage manager, said with a "good ol' boy" clap on Bad Bob's shoulder after Monday's rehearsal. The loving couple hardly noticed him as they sat murmuring to each other at home base. Jeanie had fixed her prey with a long stare of adorableness designed to undress his will before she, supposedly, would undress herself. "We're going home. Lock up when you're finished." Bradley continued into Bad Bob's deaf ears.

Bradley didn't wait for an answer, nor did he want one. He turned immediately and walked off the set whistling a Beatles tune as the lights were "killed" with a heavy, muffled "thump", leaving only several work lights and safety lamps illuminating the cavernous studio.

"Thanks, Brad. Nice show today, man." Bad Bob called after him with a manly wave and an upraised clenched fist. Bob remained transfixed, his hard-on filling his pants. Jeanie feigned being deeply concerned with the script in her hand just to intensify his passion.

Bradley knew better than to answer. He kept walking toward the exit acknowledging the couple with only a half wave, without looking back. The rest of the crew had already tip-toed out when the inevitable had become obvious: the "inevitable" being Bad Bob making an overt sexual move only to be left twisting in the wind when Jeanie drew back in innocent, chaste horror.

There was silence. Jeanie returned her gaze to Bad Bob, and smiled shyly at him as if she were a child and he was playfully withholding a present for her. Her mouth opened slightly and her jaw skewed as she ran the tip of her tongue around the back of her teeth as if she were thinking about something devious. Even merely opening her mouth was enough to drive a man wild. Bad Bob felt more like Elvis, at that moment, than any impersonator he'd ever showcased at his Memphis roadhouse.

Finally, the door to the studio thudded shut when Bradley left.

"I'll be right back," Bob said unnecessarily. He got up from his chair without realizing the full extent of the erection he'd produced during their little *tête-à-tête*. He was suddenly overcome with a Tennessee gentleman's modesty that white folk in Memphis liked to affect in order to differentiate themselves from the freed slaves. Unlike the black man, Bad Bob preferred to hide his erection rather than parade it around like a symbol of emancipation.

He turned away from Jeanie and went quickly to the main door of the studio and slid the top grey bolt across, locking it. Then he proceeded to the back entrance, by the green room, and bolted that one shut as well. Secure in his privacy, he turned back toward the set where Jeanie sat with the script. She'd even put her glasses on to reinforce her bona fides as the nicest girl in the world. Bad Bob moved more slowly now and unzipped his fly as he approached the riser that held the home base table and chairs. Jeanie's back was to him so he could reach inside his pants and feel his heavy cock for reassurance. He had done this before with all of his conquests. It gave him confidence.

"There," he said as he sat down beside her. "You were saying?"

Jeanie pouted slightly and tucked her perfect chin down almost to her chest because she knew it accentuated her eyes. She looked at him pleadingly, a look that was, at once, innocent and knowing. She had practiced that look in her bedroom mirror since she was ten and repeated it automatically whenever she was in public and in the company of men.

Jeanie's attractiveness was an idealized beauty that had the gestalt of being the most desirable woman in the world. She was one of those iconic women who seem to have it all and in just the right proportions. Like Ali McGraw and Natalie Wood in their day or Jackie Kennedy, Grace Kelly, Kate Middleton, or Jennifer Lawrence. Men can never get enough of them, nor could they of Jeanie. She was truly attractive but in an imperfect and accessible way, but that wasn't all. She represented a promise. A promise that any man who might possess her would be complete. She would fulfill all his yearnings for greatness for all time. Her real power rested in the fact that she knew it. And this was the dance she'd done with men all her life. She was the ever-retreating Fitzgeraldian heroine. Powerful in all that she embodied but impossible in her attainability. The fact that she worked as an unassuming network censor just added to her mystique. It inspired men to discover her and be the one who would uncover her beauty, intelligence, and sweetness. They wanted to be the one to remove her glasses and reveal her swan-like perfection and desirability. It appealed to their egos that they, alone, would be the one to realize the gifts that even she had seemingly overlooked. But what men didn't know was that Jeanie Murphy was way ahead of them. They forgot that her job was saying, "No". That is, until she said. "Yes".

Jeanie knew what she wanted this afternoon. And she had decided that the way to get it was to do what Mugsy would've done and undoubtedly had. Unaccustomed as she was of actually realizing any of her seductions, today she relied, instead, on channeling the supervising producer even as tawdry as she knew Mugsy was. She reached up and removed the elastic band that kept her hair tied back in a folded ponytail in the semblance of a work mode. Her hair tumbled down to her shoulders. She shook it once and lifted it off the back of her collar. Then she flipped it entirely over to one side exposing her neck and shoulder, exactly the way she'd watched Mugsy do a hundred times a day for 15 years. The censor had suddenly become uncensored.

"You don't really want to discuss the cold open, do you?" she said looking straight at Bad Bob.

"No, I don't." Bob said trying to match her apparent coolness.

"Well then," she said and took an extra-long beat. "Ain't nobody here but us chipmunks." It didn't matter that what she had said made no sense. What mattered was that Bad Bob took it as an invitation. But it was also obvious—even though the button on her blouse had now mysteriously come undone, and the milky curve and fullness of her right breast was clearly visible—that she was not going to make the first move.

Bad Bob could feel himself being transported. His head filled with as much blood as his cock, the vein on his forehead began to throb pleasantly in time with his engorged penis. Was this finally going to be it? After all the months of cock teasing and masturbation in his office?

"I..." Suddenly, his tongue was in her mouth and her breast in his hand. Jeanie's delicately manicured fingers reached inside his pants and gently removed his cock. She kissed it once, but only once. Then she stood up abruptly, walked around the back of his chair while drawing her hand past his neck and face like a silk scarf. She lost her yoga pants effortlessly, revealing that she wore no panties. She was that confident of the shape her ass was in. Then she turned around and bent over, with her forearms resting on "The Ladies' Room" table so that her incredibly tight bare ass was in his face. She turned her head back to him and smiled sweetly. The sudden sighting of the network censor's asshole and swollen pussy at the same time was like the observance of a double eclipse for Bad Bob.

Bad Bob scrambled up from his chair and came around behind her. His cock entered her seamlessly in one liquid motion. He couldn't believe she was as wet as she was without the obligatory forty-five minutes of foreplay necessary to get his wife to even audibly inhale.

His wife's breathing problems were such that Bad Bob had come to view her inhaler as a sex toy. He would work on her lifeless body until she reached over to the bedside table for her inhaler. Then he knew he was getting somewhere, and she was actually feeling something. The whistle-wheeze of the inhaler was Pavlovian for Bad Bob, and it would always make him come. Mrs. Vapors never had the heart to tell him that it was just cat dander that made her wheeze and not the passion. Often, in-between his passionate kisses, she would move her mouth to the side and take a hit off the inhaler, but, fortunately, he always took it as a compliment about his technique. Only she and the cat knew the truth.

The sex continued from behind longer than Bad Bob had ever imagined it would, mainly because Jeanie was able to see herself in the grey glass of the teleprompter mounted on Camera Three. In fact, she was quite comfortable resting on her forearms while he pounded away behind her, her eyes glued to her own image as if watching late night porn.

"Oh, baby," she moaned and felt him engorge even more. She "Kegelled" him once but then stopped because she didn't want him to cum before she'd drawn all of his sperm up from the depths of his balls. Jeanie saw her ass as a drilling platform designed specifically for the extraction of that sweet crude lying deep within a man that no one had been able to reach or exploit before. His cock was her cock now; she was probing *him* not the other way around; deeper and deeper she went as he fucked her.

"Oh, baby....Oh, baby... Oh, *baby*," she repeated, getting more emphatic each time. Her shadowy face in the teleprompter glass was contorted by the sex, and she became fascinated by her ability to observe herself being licentious. She thrashed her head forward so that her hair covered her face and then back again knowing that it would fall in wanton curls on either side of her head, framing her face just so. She pouted at herself and cocked her head slightly askance, as if she were checking out another angle in a store window rather than being fucked from behind by her boss. And she very much liked what she saw.

"Oh, baby; oh, baby; oh, baby," she repeated like a mantra. And then, "OH, BABY!" She screamed, confident that she was, after all, on a sound stage and no one could hear

But only Jeanie knew that she wasn't speaking figuratively. It wasn't a spontaneous expression of unbridled passion. It was a mission statement.

Bad Bob hadn't felt this good since his gang banging days with the University of Tennessee football team. He mistakenly thought that Jeanie's moans and shouts had something to do with his technique when, in fact, what sounded like passion was merely her single-minded intent. And when she finally let him cum by milking his cock with the muscles of her pussy, he thought he would explode right through the top his head.

"Oh, sweet Jesus!" he shouted and slapped her ass as if he were breaking a horse. Bad Bob had never cum like that, and he kept coming longer than he thought a man was capable of; the way blood spurts out of the neck of a chicken after its head has been chopped off—in descending jerks until it falls over dead. The image of himself as a boy with an axe on a Tennessee farm flashed in Bad Bob's mind.

Jeanie had watched her expression go from that of a pouty tramp to that of a cold-blooded hit man as she felt Bad Bob's cock stiffen within her, with its head engorging in expectation. Then, when his warm sperm had risen from his depths and finally exploded into the well of her vagina, only then did she relax her grip on his cock and smile sweetly into the monitor.

She got what she came for.

Bob withdrew himself and sat down heavily on a chair next to the couch. Fortunately, it was Moonie's column of reinforced concrete, so it could take the sudden weight. His wet cock still quivered happily in his lap like a fish that had been freshly landed. He'd broken a sweat, and his face was as flushed as when he lied in public.

It was then that Jeanie noticed the red light on Camera Two.

They were live. Or, at least, "live to tape". The first thing Jeanie thought of was the "kill" button that would excise what had just happened before it could be sent out over the airwaves. But then, still in her "Mugsy mode" she checked herself again in the teleprompter glass on Camera Three to make sure her hair was right. Then, instead of outrage at the horror of being recorded on tape, she smiled ever so slightly at the knowledge that she, too, would have an uncensored sex tape just like Paris Hilton or Kim Kardashian. She then turned and knelt beside Bad Bob and took his semi-hard cock into her mouth, being careful to remain in profile and on her good side which meant that she had to suck it over his thigh which proved slightly uncomfortable. The blow job confirmed to Bad Bob that he had done the right thing, and he turned in his seat to face her and make it easier for both of them. Now he, too, was in profile to the hot camera.

Jeanie could taste herself as well as his cum on his dick. She wondered if she was good enough to get him hard again as she had done so often on her knees in his office. Bad Bob's unbridled amazement at her oral dexterity was the only blowjob review she'd ever gotten. She flipped her hair over to the upstage side of her head so as to not obscure her face by the camera angle.

"Oh baby, you're so hot," she said woodenly as she sucked him and screwed her hand up and down his cock.

She was happy that, as luck would have it, her best hand for the shot, the furthest from the camera, was her right hand; and she was right-handed.

"I've wanted you so badly." Jeanie was careful to be grammatically correct even though it sounded unnatural in context. Her innate knowledge of camera angles made her more self-conscious about being viewed as a college graduate than the fact that she was being recorded as an adulteress. She wanted her sex tape to be hot, but not stupid.

"Go easy, mama." Bad Bob moaned like an Elvis Impersonator. "You're sweet, but it's tender as hell down there."

"Mmmmmmmmmmmmm," Jeanie responded, her mouth full of him. She was able to get him firm but not hard enough to fuck, and she didn't want to be seen trying to stuff his malleable cock back into her pussy on her sex tape. She might have been able to do it by sitting on him face to face, but then the camera would be looking at the unfortunate display of moles on her back. She thought of doing a "reverse cowgirl", which was the preferred porno position, but there was no way she would have gotten his cock inside her from that angle. It just wasn't stiff enough. She reverted instead to a vigorous hand job while watching his face intently. She knew he wasn't going to cum again, but the fact that she had been able to give him enough of a re-erection to make it a possibility was exciting enough.

"Oh, mama. Y'all could raise the dead," Bad Bob said, still doing Elvis. "But mah well's done gone dry."

Jeanie didn't answer him but responded by doubling her stroke and jerking him even more emphatically just to make the point that she was hotter than he was. She was able to face the camera now and pout sweetly as she abused his cock mercilessly. Finally, he stopped her with both his hands and rolled away from her.

"Can't take it, mama. Have mercy," he said.

"You okay, Sweetie?" she said as if they were a long married couple just getting up in the morning.

"Yeah, I'm better'n I've ever been." Bad Bob said trying to calm his cock down.

Jeanie, still playing to the camera, put her yoga pants back on in deliberately slow, incremental stages as if she were doing some sort of reverse striptease. The red light on Camera Two had never wavered nor blinked, and she was momentarily disappointed at the possibility that, perhaps, there *hadn't* been any tape rolling, that nothing had been recorded, and it was just a random camera left "hot" by mistake. She looked the camera full in the lens as if she could tell by doing so if it was being manned in the control room. The notion that the apparent recording might be completely innocent or not happening at all made her even more reckless and blatant. She smiled at the camera and even winked before turning back to Bad Bob. She was indulging herself in the possibility that she was being watched even though, now, in her heart, she had decided that it had all been a voyeuristic fantasy.

She was wrong.

Tape had been rolling and the resulting reel was an instant treasure, more highly regarded than even the Moonie yoga fart tape. It
was years after the show had been canceled, and no one could be
hurt by its existence, that Jeanie ever saw the footage. At that point
she was proud that her body and sexuality had been preserved elec-
tronically in order for her, then, teenage daughter to know, and
witness, her own provenance.

Bad Bob had fallen silent. When Jeanie finished buttoning her
shirt, and his own fly had been zipped, and the cum stains blotted
dry, he slipped an arm around her waist, and they walked silently
off the set.

Three weeks later, Jeanie knew she was pregnant. She made
her doctor try to pick up a heartbeat at six weeks, and he lied when
he said he did. That's when she told Bad Bob she was keeping the
baby.

Eight weeks later she began to show, such was the intensity
of her desire to have the baby. It was around that time that Bad
Bob hastily called a special staff meeting to announce that Jeanie
the Censor was pregnant and was going to have a baby. Everyone
cheered. Jeanie looked suitably demur but proud.

"It's her baby, and it's her business," Bad Bob felt compelled to
add since there was really nothing more to say about the soon-to-be
unwed mother who had miraculously become "with child" without
the apparent benefit of a husband, a boyfriend (Jeanie had never
been seen with as much as a date), or a visit to a sperm bank.

"And if anyone asks you who the father is, you are to leave the
room... *immediately*," Bad Bob said pointing a finger menacingly at
the assembled, "Just walk away and leave the room without another
word."

St Joseph must have made the same speech just before
Bethlehem. In this case, censorship was in the family.

But no one left the room. Everyone knew. The eagle had landed.

CHAPTER TWENTY-EIGHT

Moonie's wedding roll-out was gathering steam, especially with the departure of Roberta who could now only deliver pot shots on "TMZ" about whether the "something blue" on Moonie's wedding day would be her husband's balls or the color of her strangulated stomach.

But the increased plugs and un-credited promotions were becoming a problem for the network. That was the other reason why Bad Bob and Jeanie made their getaways together. It left only Beverly and Mugsy to take the brunt of the problem. But Beverly was not about to let Moonie's unabated schnorring bite her in her journalistic ass even though Beverly had personally approved it all. She retreated to her schizoid pose where she thought no one would ever suspect she was the owner, boss, and *capo di tutti capi.*

When the shit hit the fan over Moonie's wedding plugs, unabated swag, and her hijacking of "The Ladies' Room" to accomplish it, Beverly became a mere "toiler in the vineyard" whose knowledge of the problem wasn't in her skill set and *way* above her pay grade. And when the Feds threatened to get involved—both the IRS and the FCC—she happily agreed to a plenary meeting of the co-hosts as if it were merely a perfunctory orientation session to set guidelines and not a reading of the riot act.

Of course, the elephant in the room was, quite literally, Moonie and the plug fest she had unleashed at the network level. She was the beginning and end of all trouble, and everyone knew it. But no one wanted to be accused of being racist or, especially, anti-Native American. And just to make sure of that, Moonie scheduled herself as the featured celebrity at a special "Moonbeam Brown Day" at the Passamaquoddy Reservation back East in Maine. She was supposed to conduct a seminar for the school girls of the tribe to show them how they, too, could be all they could be *without* joining the army. The tribal kids had prepared for months in anticipation of her arrival, but in the end, Moonie took the plane fare and accommodation allowance for two and spent the weekend on Cape Cod with whatever Kennedy would have her. Then she executed a brief fly-over of the area and honestly thought the waiting school children would be thrilled when, at her direction, the pilot tipped his wings for them. Even so, at 1500 feet, it was the closest she'd come to the reservation since burying her mother there when she was still in medical school.

Consequently, all of the co-hosts were forced to endure the full brunt of all payola warnings and harsh directives which were disseminated equally to the group as a whole but only in the desperate hope that they would be heeded, specifically, by Moonie. The network had suddenly become terrified that the Feds would descend upon them with fines and bad publicity.

Moonie and Beverly sat and took notes during the meeting as if it was all news to them while the other ladies fumed at the inferred payola brush with which they were being painted. Of course, the truth was that all the co-hosts were equally guilty of taking swag, favors, and services far in excess of the accepted limits; but they prided themselves in being more discrete about it and simply not as greedy as Miss Brown. Thus, their high dudgeon at having to attend such a meeting was based on the notion that Moonie was just a *bigger* thief than they were and not because they were blameless.

"All your contracts, in fact every SBS contract, clearly states that no one connected with the show, either on air or off, is permitted to take any gratuity, payment, or promise of such in return for product placement or even an "on air" mention. In other words, no 'quid pro quo'," Sandy Abrumpkin, the glistening network compliance officer, said to open the meeting. Moonie and Beverly dutifully made a display of jotting this down on their pads while Marge and Bambi leaned back and folded their arms defiantly across their chests.

"That includes any promotional items or products that are given to you. All books, CDs, DVDs, and samples must be turned in so they can be given to charity," Sandy went on.

The new draconian enforcement of the rules meant that, somewhere, desperate and destitute homeless people would soon be the recipients of Queen Latifa CDs, tubes of L'Oreal night crème, and enough Pasta Boats to last a lifetime.

"Shouldn't Roberta be here?" Marge wanted to know.

"Ms. Monzon is no longer employed by the network and, as such, is exempt," Sandy replied.

"Well, technically, I really shouldn't be here either," Beverly quickly added, "Because, honestly, darlings, I'm News."

"Even so..." Sandy tried to clarify.

"...Even so, I do it for the good of the show," Beverly continued, "And I suppose I must wear my producer's hat at some point." It was now clear that Beverly was distancing herself mightily from Moonie.

"But Miss 'B', it's okay as long as there's full disclosure. And we've already done that. Isn't that right, Sandy?" Moonie said. Sandy realized he had waded into a free fire zone, and there was no way he was going emerge without at least being wounded; but, hopefully, not mortally.

"Well, yes and no." Sandy said carefully. He knew that Beverly had personally signed off on all the wedding promotions, and he knew that the show was going ahead with most of them. But he didn't know, yet, how invested Beverly was in this, and how many side deals Moonie had made that were not in the proposal. At the same time, he had to protect the reputation of Swann Broadcasting as the family-oriented, clean, and above-board enterprise it had duped the public into believing it was. He began to sweat more than normally. His face became red and shiny at the same time.

"Look," he said. "The point is that no one can get anything for free. You have to pay for everything unless it has specifically been cleared by sales and legal." He took a deep breath knowing he was about to unleash a shit storm. "For instance," he took another deep breath, "Your pool house, Bambi."

There was an audible gasp around the table. No one knew Bambi even *had* a pool, much less enough property to accommodate one. Part of the gasp was because, while the others knew they were thieves and connivers, Bambi's public persona was something that would have made Gwyneth Paltrow feel soiled and fat. Between her cleansings and coffee enemas, Mary Poppins-grade nannies, and immaculate children, she acted like her shit didn't stink. And she could prove it. It really didn't. She had her stools tested and analyzed each day at a holistic laboratory. But Bambi was the least powerful of the quartet, so she became the designated co-host under the bus.

"It's nothing against you, personally, but "sales" has a problem with Target getting exposure while they are trying to sell Home Depot ad space on the show. It has nothing to do with you."

It was too late. Bambi dropped her chin to her chest and began to sob quietly, her trademark lower lip protruding like a chastened child's. Suddenly, Sandy didn't want any part of this job. He had done what he was told to do. He had delivered the message.

"Anyway, that's basically it." he said gathering his papers. "You all know what I mean. We're all grownups. It's just a reminder."

Moonie and Beverly quietly put their pens down. Beverly knew she had dodged a bullet that would have surely gone through her on its way to Moonie, its intended target. Moonie, for her part, leaned back and smiled as if she had just inhaled a roast. God was still on her side. Jesus still loved her, she thought. She was wrong.

Her line of credit had suddenly become too short to schnorr with God. The Devil plugs Prada.

Moonie was on a double path to redemption —make that "triple", if you count the swag. She had risen in her brazenness so that, when her assistant of the week would call for freebies, she was instructed to have the loot delivered directly to her new double penthouse on Wilshire Boulevard in Westwood. Thus, she avoided having to send a U-Haul to the loading dock to remove the samples she had assembled from the various theme shows she insisted on as part of her wedding showers.

Moonie had already had the rooftop of her new Wilshire penthouse fitted out and landscaped for free. (When the "urban landscaper" presented a bill, Moonie sent the man an 8X10 glossy of herself and told him to keep the change.) But the problem was she had installed six propane heaters and a gas-fed barbeque on the roof without a permit or even a thought to the incendiary bomb that she had now placed on top of her apartment building. Leo and Brendan fantasized about calling the fire department for an emergency inspection, but they never did. Of course, the real violation was having Moonie Brown loose on the roof of anything.

As far as Moonie was concerned everything was under control. What she didn't notice was that Beverly had become more and more distant as the time grew shorter before the big event. Most of the wedding roll-out that Moonie had outlined stayed in place, but she, herself, became marginalized in daily increments as the spectacle of materialism proceeded. The network was completely flummoxed by the onslaught of FCC infractions, and they crossed their corporate fingers in hopes that they could get through the wedding without having their license lifted. They did limit her to only one brand name plug each segment, and put their foot down when she wanted to do an entire show on her over-the-top, ridiculously padded, wedding invitations. Those ended up on a special for the Style Channel.

But the real reason any of it was happening was because the public was eating it up. It wasn't that they were so wrapped up in the self-styled fairy tale wedding (although the sexuality of the groom would have qualified it for that); it was that they sensed something else was up. Instinctively, the public knew it was too good a bubble not to burst; and no one wanted to miss the inevitable debris field even if it did mean enduring Moonie's version of the dénouement.

Everybody on the show suddenly had something else on their minds.

Marge was focused totally on her "presidential campaign" which had taken on a verisimilitude unintended by everyone but Marge. She was miffed when she wasn't included in any of the debates but thrilled that she was mentioned and referenced by the actual candidates who were. With the departure of Roberta, the co-host number was cut down from five to four, and this forced Beverly to have her "dessert" daily instead of when she felt like it. But that proved to be a tonic for the ever re-inventing diva because it was visible proof that she had vanquished yet another competitor.

Beverly was still obsessed with her own "TaxiTV" show, and no one could figure out why because it certainly couldn't pay that much. But, ever the populist, Beverly was sure it opened up a "whole new audience for me, darlings, who have never even heard of the evening news. I'm a bigger anchor to those poor people in the back seats of taxis than I ever was on any network. And Swann had nothing to do with it."

Bambi was focused on perfecting Bambi. She was working out twice a day for two hours at a clip and then making infomercials about her own vitamin and cleansing product line. The girl who wouldn't pick up her own wet towel was hawking better ways to take a shit. She actually liked doing her high colonic infomercials because, no matter how distasteful the product was, it was her own show even if her co-host was an enema.

Although Roberta was permanently on the sidelines she was still a presence at "The Ladies' Room". First of all, despite the fact that management hated her and hated themselves for putting her on the show in the first place, most of the innovations she insisted on had endured. The air conditioning was better, and the work week was a day shorter even though the taped show that enabled it was always the lowest rated of the week. The hiatus was longer, and the Christmas break was a full three weeks. On top of that, despite her draconian way of dealing with the tech staff, she had gotten rid of the union deadwood that had been gumming up the works for years. In short, she left the show a smoother running, more easily produced, happier place than she found it,—not in the least, because she had gotten rid of herself as well.

But Roberta was not happy. She knew that the show was enjoying the fruits of her tenure and the elation of her departure. Bad Bob, who had grown a beard and stopped eating while she was there, shaved and regained his former bulk. Even he had ultimately benefited. He had convinced his wife that his firing was imminent and that they should then retire to Florida. Consequently, he bought a huge seaside mansion that once belonged to a disgraced televangelist on Siesta Key near Sarasota and consigned his wife to prepare it for his arrival. He liked the idea that, as a homestead state, creditors could never touch the house which included a studio and control room where he planned to produce web shows, industrials, and funeral legacy tapes for the dying population of the state. But when Roberta abruptly left the show, and everything could then return to normal, he was too far into his venture to let his wife return to California. Besides, wasn't she living in paradise? They had flamingos in the front yard, for crissakes.

Because of the apparent vacuum in network management and the lack of attention span in the other co-hosts, Moonie felt free to carry on her nuptial pageantry. In her own parlance, she felt endorsed. There were "showers" sponsored by Freixenet champagne, trousseau unveilings sponsored by Big and Tall and Chico's. Big and Tall was for the groom's clothes, it was pointed out. There were honeymoon travel suggestions on the show itself with noted travel agents from Liberty Travel all pitching in. The wedding gown was picked out in a taped segment at Neiman Marcus' Beverly Hills bridal shop and then aired in two parts with the "vera wonderful" Vera Wang, herself, commentating. But no reveal. People magazine was given an exclusive on that. And that cost extra.

But there *were* rumblings. The press had picked up trouble within the wedding plans. Or, more correctly, they were given verified reports of trouble by people who knew. In order to simultaneously deflect any sanctions and notoriety for their FCC violations and, at the same time, engineer Moonie's own demise, Bad Bob and Beverly had begun systematically supplying the Hollywood Reporter, The Wrap, Deadline Hollywood, and TMZ with tidbits of her increasingly outlandish behavior. Even Conrad Conroy at The LA Times got his share, but he was used to it since the same favor had been done for him to discredit Roberta.

At the same time, a fake witch hunt was conducted throughout the staff to stop the leaks.

"We will find out who is leaking information to the press, and we will fire him," Beverly pronounced ominously at a surprise mandatory staff meeting in the rehearsal hall. As she said it, she pivoted her body around, Frank Sinatra Jr.-style, in order to finish by saying, "him" while looking directly at Brendan.

Brendan found it amusing that he was the go-to guy for any attribution about the leaks. He wondered if he could be fired twice. He envisioned another meeting with Bad Bob in which Bob would tell him that he was being fired again just for good measure. That's how much Bad Bob and the network didn't want to see him around there anymore. But the truth of the matter was that Brendan was not the source of the leaks, of course, because the executive producers themselves were. And such big, freakin' leaks they weren't. The ridiculousness of the witch hunt was underscored by the fact that, not only were they, themselves, the perpetrators, but Moonie had specifically designed her wedding to *be* a public spectacle.

How could something be "leaked" that was already part of a media deluge?

Bad Bob and Beverly never did find the "leaker" mainly because they never looked in the mirror. So nobody got fired as a result.

Meanwhile, Moonie was actually losing weight. Having every-thing you eat re-routed to a satchel the size of a Balenciaga tote bag will do that. The problem was that the doctors were forced to increase the capacity of the colostomy bag to accommodate her binges, and the sheer weight of the chewed garbage expelled into her new pouch was adding a limp to her gait.

"Here comes Quasimodo." Brendan would say as Moonie came loping down the hall after a "snack" that could feed a family of four at Thanksgiving. "Looks like she finally got a decent buffet under her belt."

Regardless of how she was doing it, the results were tangible. She was losing weight and getting married. In a world where people become stars for merely living in "reality", that qualified Moonie as an expert. But, instinctively, she knew her "window" was small; although "small" in Moonie's world meant there was still plenty of time. She decided to make a video and sell it.

"I'm gonna be the Jane Fonda of self-help. What Jane did for butts, I'm gonna do for empowerment," Moonie declared in the makeup room. "People will buy my video more than the Bible. And it'll do just as much good, too."

The ladies of "The Ladies' Room" automatically rolled their eyes while secretly marveling at her industry and chutzpah. Here was an obese woman, with an upper stomach diversion and double-wide colostomy bag, marrying a homosexual—who was probably more attracted to the surgically constructed anus in her side than any natural orifice—, suddenly deciding to promote the attainment of personal success and marital bliss through her special recipe of honesty, diet, prayer, yoga, and positive thinking.

"You, too, can have it all," she would say in her video. What she didn't point out was that her colostomy bag was where it "all" went once you had it. The idea of Moonie Brown being an expert in love was like Mel Gibson being an expert in tolerance. On top of that, she called the video "The Jig's Up" despite its obvious racist connotation.

"It came to me in a dream," she told her assistant who was horrified at the racist mockery that the title, alone, would create. "It's God's title. It says that you will never go forward until you come to grips with your old ways and self. When you can look in the mirror and say to yourself, 'The jig's up, girl', and mean it, that's when you can start."

She was serious, and no amount of gentle nudging about the loaded nature of the title would dissuade her from her mission. At one point she even admitted that she knew how "The Jig's Up" might be taken, but she still thought it worked for her.

"After all, this "Jig", right here, is definitely up," she told Beverly after Beverly had ever-so-gently pointed out the possible racist implications of her title. Apparently, God was not to be rewritten. On top of that, Moonie was a Native American, so what was the problem?

The video was composed mostly of material that'd already been shot. She had incorporated commercials, interviews, clips from personal appearances, and clips from "The Ladies' Room" to make her point. Of course, she refused to pay for any of it regardless of the union requirements arguing that it was all "news" and fell under PSA and "fair use" exclusions. What she didn't do was inform any of the celebrities included in her clips that they would be seen passively endorsing Moonie Brown's video for a "better you" (And a richer Moonie Brown). Sales of the video went through the roof, and the suppliers to her wedding were incredulous at the return on their paltry product placement costs.

Everyone was happy but Beverly. Beverly kicked herself for single-handedly creating the Moonie monster but, at the same time, she couldn't help marveling at her success. The fact was that, in very short order, Moonie Brown had become bigger than "The Ladies' Room"; and Beverly and the other co-hosts were not making a nickel as a result. But soon, Moonie would learn that it's not nice to piss off the whores you rode in on.

The wedding was at The Cathedral of Our Lady of the Angels. But, even there, Moonie made a deal where she had them to pass the basket (a "first" at a wedding) among her rich and powerful friends "for charity". Of course, there would be a split of the revenue; but Cardinal Quinn was happy with his 20% of the "handle". Moonie had raised it from the original 10% only after the Cardinal agreed to ring the Angelus bells and play "Moon River" on the carillon as the bridal party boarded people movers for the trip to the Jonathan Club. The event was expected to be bigger than the Academy Awards and Midnight Mass combined. Mounted policemen were scheduled for crowd control. But Moonie stopped short of asking them to change the color of the line down the middle of West Temple Street because her color would have had to have been brown, and that would be just asking for trouble from late night television comedians. Besides, Moonie considered hers a "private religious ceremony between herself, Jesus, and Ray Ray". City Hall breathed a sigh of relief.

The ceremony itself was unique in that it was the first Mass in the Cathedral's history that was concelebrated by a cardinal and an even bigger faker, Chief Roy Moore, of the Cherokee Nation in Ventura. The chief hadn't married anyone but drunken cowboys and migrant workers in his current capacity; and so he was, understandably, a little rusty.

Brendan had not been invited to any part of the wedding at first, but he ended up attending the church ceremony only when, at the last minute, Moonie realized that "papering" a cathedral was a lot harder than "papering" a nightclub. Basically, she couldn't "sell out" The Cathedral. So, as a result, last minute "love invitations" were dispatched that arrived as e-mails three days before the event so that "all my working friends and Catholics" could join her at the church but not the reception. God didn't even make *that* cut. The invitations required "white tie" for the unwashed which meant that there was a run on the tuxedo rentals all over the city. Even so, no one wanted to miss the unique display of Rome meets Native America, so the place was, in fact, packed; and the photo op footage would form the basis of a wedding reality show sold to Bravo. It was for that reason that the padded invitations came with a lengthy and iron-clad release form that had to be signed and returned before the invitations became valid and admission to the House of God was granted.

At the reception afterwards, Beverly rose from the head table and insisted on giving the first toast. There were no immediate pictures of her doing so because Moonie had installed Jay-Z and Beyoncé's own security guards (who could put the El Al airport screeners to shame) in order to confiscate all the guest cell phones and cameras. She had sold the photography and video rights to the reception to People magazine, and those rights were exclusive.

Beverly never looked lovelier in all her eighty-three years than she did at the reception. Barry had outdone himself on her hair extensions and spot wigs. She looked younger than Moonie, but she was purposely dressed in red so as to not compete with the bride. Besides, she had a dinner at Bouchon afterwards with the Shah's widow and Bill Gates.

"Moonie Brown is a dear, dear, *dear* girl," Beverly began when the crowd had remained quiet for a full 30 seconds. "She has brought so much joy to our lives, and today she brings that special brand of joy to Ray Ray as his wife. What can I say about someone with whom I have spent more time than with any of my husbands? If Moonie had not come into our lives we would have had to invent her. She was that critical to our happiness and our work. I cannot imagine "The Ladies' Room" without her, and her contributions were so crucial to us, especially in the beginning when we were finding our way. No one will ever be able to think of her without thinking of "The Ladies' Room" and the overwhelming success that it has become. I say all this because now she has fulfilled her own dreams as she had fulfilled ours. And today she has spread her wings to fly to new heights. I wish her Godspeed and hope there is still room in her heart—even on this day when she and Ray Ray are so much in love—that there is still room in her heart to take us all with her to new heights and better tomorrows. We wish her well."

It was vintage Beverly. She never opened her mouth in public that she didn't get a plug in for herself and her next television appearance. But the phrases "spread her wings" and "we wish her well" were chilling for those who knew that, in Beverly's lexicon, it meant, "You're fired". Whether Beverly even knew it, she had chosen Moonie's triumphant wedding to fire her. Moonie, herself, may not have realized it intellectually at that instant, but deep down in her papoose, she could feel the ground shift underneath her—a feeling she had not felt since she had dropped below 400 pounds.

People were teary-eyed at this apparent proclamation of love on Beverly's part, and Ray Ray squeezed Moonie's hand harder than an erection through a glory hole at Rage. At that moment, in the WASP bastion of the Jonathan Club, Moonbeam P. Brown was happier than she had ever been. She had come a long way from Pleasant Point and Eastport, Maine—From Washington County to the Jonathan Club. Moonie had done it; and now Beverly Frost, the queen of California and the diva of all media, had blessed her. Life could only be downhill from there. And it was.

Following the Moonie wedding spectacle, which the network and Beverly survived unscathed, "The Ladies' Room" itself became little more than an afterthought for the co-hosts and producers of the show. The Moonie pageant showed all of them that their various outside enterprises could be much greater than the daily show that was the mother of all them all. The tail was now wagging the dog—the "dog" being what "The Ladies' Room" had become in everyone's mind.

Even Beverly's "TaxiTV" seemed to be taking up more energy than it could possibly be worth.

Marge's "campaign" became her main occupation, and "The Ladies' Room" became nothing more than a nagging obligation in her life like some feeble, infirmed relative who demanded too much attention and whom she really wished were dead. She was like Robert Redford in "The Candidate" who, during the filming of that movie, began to draw such large crowds for real—real and rabid enough—that political consultants thought maybe he *should* run for something; people were that ready to vote for him.

Marge began to pull back when she was "on air" on "The Ladies' Room", afraid that any frivolousness there might undercut what was happening to her outside the show. She was suddenly being asked to comment on issues by legitimate news outlets, even as the "sketch candidate" that she was. Jon Stewart thought it droll to have her answer the Republican and Democratic sound bites of the day. The result was that the line between reality and fiction, between the serious and the inane, became less discernible. As the primaries proceeded and national election became more real, her poll numbers began to rise which only further dampened her desire, or need, to be funny.

Moonie shifted her focus from the wedding to her "Jig's Up" video, figuring that there was still an income stream there that didn't stop when she said "I do". Her weight (when she wasn't carrying the colostomy bag) had shrunk to a point where she was able to have glamorized photos taken and Photoshopped for her "subscription only" website. She had learned that trick from the porn people. She had quietly decided that she could be actually bigger than Oprah because a mere paper magazine about yourself was so "last century". Moonie would trump Oprah with a web presence bigger than "The Huffington Post", and a "Moonie App" for smart phones would supply a tip of the day to keep you going "Up".

Bambi got pregnant which seemed, literally, inconceivable given her cleansing regimen. That any sperm could survive within ten feet of her bleached anus was a Darwinian triumph. In fact, she actually *was* un-conceivable and had engaged a surrogate to carry the baby this time. Normally, a co-host pregnancy was good news and would usually be timed to have the announcement during November "sweeps" and the birth during the May ones. But the surrogate decision put her well beyond the purview of "The Ladies' Room's" demographic and into a separate "celebrity-weird" realm so that the net effect was detrimental to the show. She would arrive at the show each day glistening with a spectacularly clean body and a perfect shape that defied gestation so that any talk of her "pregnancy" or her so-called sympathetic "baby bump" created a cognitive dissonance that made viewers turn away. On top of that, TMZ had obtained a tape of Bambi interviewing the surrogate mother in a Kentucky trailer park in which she sounded like a horse trader dickering over a nag. She literally looked into the poor girl's mouth to check her teeth. Most celebs going this route treated the surrogate mother as a sister or a godmother. Bambi treated hers as an embryo mule. She would have killed her after the birth if she could have.

All of this meant that the show was headed in a direction of decidedly less comedy and certainly no fun. The women were effectively firing Brendan faster than Bad Bob could. In effect, while Bad Bob had to wait until the end of the contract (only because the thought of paying Brendan for not working was more abhorrent than enduring his lame duck employment), the women of "The Ladies' Room" could sever their ties with Brendan immediately. And they did.

"I really have nothing to say," Marge would announce day after day to him as she sat in her make-up chair endlessly staring at her hair. "Write whatever you want."

She found more inspiration on her iPad than from her writer now that she had become a "cultural icon" alongside the Energizer Bunny and Flo, the Progressive Insurance girl. Her catch phrase, "Pul-leeze!" had gone viral even though she had never actually said it. When she was accurately lampooned on "Saturday Night Live", they had used "Pul-leeze!" to stand for her habit of verbal short-cuts and dodges in response to any complex question. The caricature phrase became so popular that even Marge began to use it, as opposed to anything she'd actually said, as her trademark catch phrase on the show and in her phony political campaign. The phrase ended up sticking more than her attempts at seriousness about the issues. Thus, in short order, her new-found fame and political verisimilitude became based directly on a lampoon rather than on anything real that she had ever said or done. No wonder America loved her. Pul-leeze!

CHAPTER TWENTY-NINE

"I thought Kolodny was going to fix you up." Dr. Benjamin said.
"He's a little sleazy, Kenny," Brendan replied. "The Wife didn't like him."

"I don't remember feeling *her* prostate. Yours is the one with cancer, remember?"

"Right."

"You want to ruin not only my weekend but Purim as well?" Benjamin said, "Your PSA is up. You have to have another MRI so we can compare it to the first one. What the fuck've you been doing?"

"I've got problems at work. Trying to keep my job. Things came up. Besides, Sykes said it was slow growing, and I still don't have any symptoms to speak of."

"Neither do dead people. We've got to get ahold of this. Right now."

For the first time Benjamin was deadly serious. His tone frightened Brendan because Brendan had always been used to all bodily disorders being temporary and fixable. It wasn't a question of being cocky, just confident in his own manifest destiny. Brendan always thought of himself as someone who would always prevail;

except, that is, in long term relationships and employment. He went for another MRI.

The MRI showed that Brendan's particular strain of prostate cancer had proven to be uncharacteristically aggressive. The radiologist told Dr. Benjamin this news as if it wasn't *his* fault he'd missed it the first time around. He'd been hoodwinked. It was close to breaking through the prostate shell and was poised to metastasize to other organs and the bone. The tumor was still officially a T2C, but it was a "T2C with a bullet", almost a T3A now. But the most pressing problem, both figuratively and literally, was that Brendan's prostate had enlarged. That fact was benign compared to the cancer, but it presented an immediate problem with urination.

Brendan was in trouble, and he knew it. The weight loss he thought was of his own choosing—getting "in shape" for the operation—was now suspect. But in his crazy mind, Brendan's first thought upon hearing the dire report was that it would buy him time at "Ladies'." They would never fire someone with incipient bone cancer especially if he was still funny, although when Steve Corrigan, the technical director, had fallen ill with Parkinson's, they had hired a younger AD to shadow him like a circling condor just to remind him daily that he was overstaying his usefulness. Corrigan had committed suicide rather than endure the kid, almost literally, checking his watch every time they passed in the stairwell.

"You've got to be aggressive about this and take it seriously," Benjamin told Brendan. Suddenly, the doctor with no time for an appointment wanted to see him every week.

"Should I 'get my affairs in order'?" Brendan asked half facetiously.

"If that'll clear your head so you can deal with this, yes."

"Hey, but the good news is I don't have to make any more dentist appointments," Brendan said. "No more flossing. And no more sit-ups anymore, either. There *is* an upside, you know."

"Don't be an asshole." Benjamin said as he got very busy with Brendan's medical file. Brendan noticed that it was uncommonly thick. Either he had been sick all his life, or Benjamin was obsessive about his notes. Maybe that very file was the novel Brendan had never written. It had the heft of a proper manuscript, and it certainly told the tale. But the ending definitely needed work.

"I think I'll get a dog," Brendan said. "They say you live longer with a pet. We had a guy on the show."

"Great. Do that." Benjamin said writing something down on his prescription pad. In the meantime, here's an oncologist. He's at UCLA. I usually don't refer over there, but you're not only a patient, you're a friend. He's the best."

"What about "watchful waiting"?

"You watched enough. You gotta do something now." He handed Brendan the piece of paper. "And I want to see you back here in a week. Don't fuck around this time."

Brendan couldn't wait to tell Bad Bob and the others at "The Ladies' Room" about his apparent turn for the worse. The funny thing was they all expected it. He could see them composing the announcement in their heads for the "Wall of Woe" as he was telling them the cancer had gotten worse. It didn't inoculate his firing as much as it confirmed it. Secretly, Bad Bob instantly considered himself a managerial genius for anticipating it. What Brendan learned in short order was that it was all the same. Everyone had already considered him finished anyway. Anything additional was old news. Brendan could see it in their eyes as if they were saying, "What did you expect?"

Brendan told Marge about his developing cancer as he was standing next to her after the "CrossTalk" meeting while she was, once more, getting her hair washed.

"So now what?" she said leaning back with the top of her head in the sink.

"They give me female hormones."

"Estrogen?" she said. "Be careful. I'm off that."

"No, something else. Lupron or something. I forget the name. But apparently it works like a charm...except for the extra tits."

"If that ever happens to me, my doctor says he'll put me on a morphine drip, and I won't know a thing. Pul-eeeze! And that's the way I want it." Marge said missing the point.

"That's great," Brendan said. "How's your campaign?" He wanted to see how long he could jerk her off into talking about herself as a response to his announcement about his cancer.

"Whatever. I'll still get more votes than any third party candidate. I'm the biggest thing after Republicans and Democrats. That's what the latest polls say. This thing is huge. It's got a life of its own."

"That's great. I'm happy for you," Brendan said, strangely amused that she had taken the bait and carried on in true form.

"That's why I don't need this show any more." Marge added.

"Yeah, but what about me?" Brendan said with a smile.

"You'll be fine." Marge said. "You've got bigger fish to fry."

"You mean, the cancer," Brendan said in mock seriousness. Now they were in a black comedy zone. Marge lifted her head up out of the curved notch in the shampoo sink. She turned and looked straight at him.

"You love it," she said. "I know you. You'll work this for all it's worth. You're not going to die. I checked it out. You'll be fine."

Marge laid her head back down in the notch so the stylist could rinse her. Her statement was typical of all celebrities: a) They consider themselves magically blessed and capable of changing reality by proclamation; b) They really don't want to deal with anything uncomfortable; and c) They think their own information is so inside and proprietary that a "civilian" should never question it.

Marge really thought she was putting his, and her, mind at ease by proclaiming him healed. But, unfortunately, Brendan knew she was only talking "Celebritese". And the smug and satisfied look on

Marge's face as she closed her eyes and allowed Celeste to bathe the back of her head in soothing warm water only made him feel worse.

Shortly thereafter it became necessary for Brendan to be catheterized. The prostate gland had grown in size to such an extent that it was impinging on his ability to urinate. The thinking was that he would piss through a catheter until he could either be operated on or get some form of radiation. They also wanted to allow the Lupron to work. The procedure had been performed at Cedars on an outpatient basis. Brendan had made the macho mistake of saying he didn't need to be unconscious for it. Suddenly, his pecker became a two-way street as if that's what it was built for. First, a cystoscope was inserted. Then it was withdrawn. And then the catheter was put in place. His request for a "happy ending" was met with stares all around. Apparently, he was in a place where penises had nothing to do with pleasure.

The catheter was of the "Texas" variety and was connected to a bag that could be strapped to his leg. He was required to wear it for at least ten days and probably more. The strange thing was that, rather than free him from trips to the bathroom; it made the visits more frequent as he became somewhat obsessed about emptying the thing. And it did bring him closer to Moonie.

It had nothing to do with the fact that now they both had bags because Moonie never admitted she was "carrying". But Brendan knew he was in bad shape when, several days after she returned from a promotional tour for "The Jig's Up!", Moonie appeared at his office door to pray over him.

"I know we've had our differences in the past, Brendan, but Jesus ministered to lepers, thieves, and prostitutes so I guess He would want me to minister to you."

"Thank you, Moonie, but it really isn't..."

Brendan tried to demur, but she was already in the door and had set her oversized purse down on his desk. The purse was "oversized" because she thought it made the rest of her look smaller.

"You don't know the power of the Lord," she continued as she came around the desk and took his two hands in hers.

"Did you have a nice honeymoon?" Brendan asked looking straight up at her face. She really was decidedly smaller since the second stomach bypass procedure. He could see where her cheek bones were supposed to be. She had beautiful teeth, and they were her favorite part of her body. She spent thousands of dollars each year on their maintenance, but it was all for naught. She was like a hippo with a Maserati. Teeth were not the issue.

"My honeymoon was a dream come true. I called out Jesus' name more times in that hotel room than I ever did in church."

"And probably spent more time on your knees, too."

"Now don't you go gettin' nasty on me, Brendan," Moonie shot back. "Our union was sanctioned by God, Himself, in your own bad-ass cathedral church. And that means anything we do now is all right with God."

"Well, I'm sure you make a lovely couple," Brendan replied in his best Groucho.

"Now, I'm gonna pray over you, Brendan White, and despite our differences in the past, I am your last hope of becoming whole again. Where exactly are you sick?"

"My prostate. You going to pray over that, Moonie?"

"God works in wondrous ways. If the evilness is in your prostate, Jesus will find a way."

"That's all I need. Jesus up my......"

".....Hush!" she cut him off. "Let us pray."

Moonie closed her eyes while holding onto the fingers of both of Brendan's hands. She began to sway slightly as if in a reverie. Then she began to hum quietly to herself. Brendan took the opportunity to look out into the hall to make sure no one was walking by. Then he checked the time and looked at the front page of Variety on top of his desk that was announcing, "Reality Bites!" because someone on "Survivor" had resorted to cannibalism in order to win.

"Oh, Jesus," Moonie began in a low growly voice that Brendan had never heard before. "Oh great Spirit that dwells within us and in every living thing you have created from the sardines that swim free before being canned to the pollock and cod that will always remain plentiful, thank you, Jesus."

She was going all the way for this one, thought Brendan, and plugging into her semi-Native American roots.

"Heal this boy in front of you. Take his prostate in your hand and make it free of the cancer that is not of your bidding but of Satan's. Forgive him for the sins he has committed against you and against certain individuals on this show. He is your fool, and only you know the truth of his tomfoolery. Oh, Great Spirit, he didn't mean it. It was a joke, that's all. Like the juggler who can only serve you by tossing his balls in the air, this sorry wretch in front of you juggles mockery and put-downs to try and get your attention and Writers Guild minimum. God, I beg of you to make his rotten prostate *your* joke and not the death sentence it will surely be if he does not embrace you as I have. Let him know that Jesus is the Flomax of your love. In God's name we pray. May the Great Spirit, in whose bosom our ancestors lie, smile upon us this day and be moved by our song and our dance to remove that nasty cancerous gland and return this boy to normal urinary life."

Moonie paused momentarily. Brendan thought she was finished. But her eyes remained closed, and her trance-like state made her head weave back and forth in a deep, dark swoon. Then she began to chant something that sounded at first like she was clearing her throat but then became vaguely melodic although still guttural and not in English. At the same time, she began to stomp her feet, lightly (for her) at first, but then she began to punctuate her chant rhythmically by emphasizing every fourth step. Brendan realized Moonie was conjuring the full Passamaquoddy on his behalf. What had originally been designed to ensure a plentiful catch of pollock and cod in the Bay of Fundy, was now being asked to do the work of a radical post pubic prostatectomy on an aging comedy writer. The chanting and stomping went beyond the merely perfunctory, and Brendan feared the worst: Moonie Brown was performing the *long* version.

The Moonie Prostate Dance went on for several long minutes. She was obviously misguided but deeply sincere, and he had to respect all that for as long as it took. Finally, she stopped and opened her eyes. Brendan exhaled audibly as he would have at the end of a long, wincing, dental procedure.

"Here. Take this." She said handing him a DVD of "The Jig's Up". "This will help when I can't be with you in person."

She dropped the DVD in his lap. He looked down and noticed a hole punched in the corner indicating it had been remaindered.

"Thank you," Brendan said. "For everything."

"And that's the limited collector's edition," she said. "It has bonus material. You should watch and listen to it every day. It's my prayer for you, Brendan."

"I will, " he said because he could see that she was deadly serious. Moonie really thought she was better than chemo.

Brendan's option for surgery became problematical when the results of a new CAT scan and PSA came back. His PSA was suddenly in double digits. His treatment went from "cure" to "holding"; from "watchful waiting" to "delaying the inevitable". The only upside was that grave illness does tend to get people's attention. It's only a shame that it all has to come to an end in order to do so.

When The Wife figured it out, she was completely undone. She even told the Governor. The Governor immediately suspended all sexual relations between them out of respect for the infirmed, and because he really thought it really might be catching. The Wife became obsessed with caring for Brendan mainly because she was afraid that being a widow would make her read "old", and it would ruin her relationship.

She had to admonish Zeke to stop randomly punching his father's midsection for fear that it would dislodge the catheter and spill urine on her oriental rug. "Don't step on your father's bag" replaced "No balls in the house" as her standard admonishment. Zeke, for his part, replaced the punching with mock CPR. He even got the correct compression rhythm after Brendan taught him to sing, "Stayin' Alive" as a metronome. Brendan and The Wife would smile sweetly each time Zeke would shout. "Clear!" before placing imaginary paddles on Brendan's chest while they all watched television. Brendan was afraid Zeke thought it was all a game.

Actually, Zeke was fairly cool about his father's sickness. Having a father with cancer played well at school, and he enjoyed the perks. At home, the catheter and urine bag quickly became normal and as instantly acceptable as a new pair of shoes. Of course, Brendan flaunted it. He would ask The Wife if her boyfriend knew she was sleeping with a man *and* his urine. The Wife was not amused. The catheter obviated any sex between them, and that was a relief. She didn't really think the disease was catching, but she couldn't take the chance of infecting the Governor of the most populous state in the union. She was afraid he might classify her as a "terrorist" or put her on a "watch list" for even a blow job.

Then one Sunday morning Brendan was watching Zeke play a new video game he had just bought for him. In the game, like most tales for children in America, the father of the young hero was benign but remote. They lived together in a post-apocalyptic underground bunker. Then, just as the main action of the game is about to begin, and not unlike the "Lion King", the father dies, and the boy is left to pursue his life-quest outside the bunker alone. The plot element was so arbitrary that Brendan had never anticipated it nor even paid much attention to the story as it had unfolded.

But suddenly Zeke's thumbs stopped on the controller, and he stared at the screen where his avatar, an idealized young boy, swayed drunkenly in "pause mode" at the threshold of the bunker, waiting for Zeke's command to leave the enclave and go forth into a hostile world. There was a long stage wait while Zeke said nothing, his thumbs frozen on the controller. Brendan was confused. Tears welled up in the boy's eyes. Brendan still didn't understand.

"I don't want to play this anymore." Zeke said setting the controller aside. He stood up.

"What's the matter?" Brendan asked. "I thought you liked it."

"I don't want to play it anymore," Zeke said. "That's all." His voice thicker than normal.

"You mean, ever?" Brendan was still dismayed and frustrated by his failure to, now, even provide an acceptable video game for his son.

"I dunno." Zeke said, "Maybe later." Then he left the room without another word or even a glance at his father.

Brendan sat there for a beat, not following him out. He studied the monitor screen for some clue as to what had happened. All he saw was the cartoon character of the young man (who had been carefully customized by Zeke to resemble a game version of himself) standing at the door to the fortress weaving in an endless loop of unfulfilled anticipation. Then he got it: the connection between the video game story and what, now, Zeke had realized it was his *own* narrative: The death of the father and the necessity to go forth, alone, into the world. The swaying character on the screen was a glimpse into the future for both of them. In a strange way, even though he had left the room without talking about it, Brendan felt closer to his son in that moment than at any time before. But neither of them would ever bring it up again.

At work Brendan was determined to stay on until they escorted him out the door at the end of his contract. The removal of Moonie Brown, however, was more problematical. Reverting to her mob roots, Beverly took a page out of "The Godfather" and began to work on Moonie the way Michael Corleone had worked on Frankie Pentangelo. Moonie was just as untouchable, in a sense, although not in federal custody—yet. The first step was to convince Moonie that she had not prevailed unscathed after Roberta had self-immolated. She was still under review.

"You can't promote "The Jig's Up" any more on 'The Ladies' Room'," Sandy Abrumpkin told her one day after the show. "We have to adhere strictly to the FCC guidelines."

"Maybe I should've invited the FCC to my wedding," Moonie said with an uncharacteristic glower.

"You did. They were all over it."

"Then why didn't they say anything?"

"Because of Beverly. They didn't want to embarrass her."

"The FCC?" Moonie said incredulously. "Miss Beverly Frost makes the FCC look the other way, but a Native American, who has done more for Indian folk than Sacajawea, *she* can't promote her inspirational video on the white man's magic lantern where she's tryin' to help tribal kids, all jammed up on their reservations, into being something in this country other than a logo, car model, or sports mascot? You wanna talk to me about the "Redskins?""

"That's right," Sandy said quietly. "They're watching you."

"Well, then you tell them they better watch out for Ms. Moonbeam P. Brown," she said and stormed off. But it was all part of a plan to increase the heat and thus, eventually, get Moonie to do the right thing in a Frankie "Five Angels" kind of way.

Next was the Escalade. Moonie had wrangled a deal with a local dealer for her own super-sized, smoked window, Cadillac Escalade to replace the ordinary Lincoln town car that the show provided. She still availed herself of the driver, of course, so it didn't save the show anything. But it was a master stroke of schnorring in that she was able to turn a legitimate perk that even the IRS could love into a scam that would've made Bernie Madoff squirm.

But since everything is relative, especially among freeloaders, the vision of Moonie getting into a bigger and better car each day after the show ate away at Beverly's heart like a trapped rodent gnawing its way to freedom.

"Darling, what do you think Moonie had to do to get that car?" Beverly said to Marge as they waited together on the loading ramp for their cars to arrive. It irked them that in addition to the size and macho grandeur of the Escalade, the driver always managed to get there ahead of the others as if part of Moonie's score was having the other co-hosts watch it in action.

"Beats the shit out of me," Marge replied. "Must be something from 'The Community'".

"You mean 'The Tribe'," Beverly pointed out.

"No, Bev. You're 'The Tribe'. Moonie's with the rappers."

"Really?" Beverly said. It was an angle she hadn't considered.

"When do we get ours?" Marge said with a smile. She didn't really care, but she knew it bothered Beverly.

"Just wait." Beverly said ominously, but Marge knew her answer didn't mean that they would all be getting Escalades compliments of the show. Beverly had dropped into her "mob mode", and it was not healthy to be on the receiving end when Beverly did that.

"Just...wait," she repeated.

It turned out that the car dealer was an Indian from India who called himself "Jambalaya Motors" which accounted for Moonie's sudden interest in Cajun cuisine on the show and her repeated mentions of how much she "loved mah Jambalaya". It was so pervasive that viewers sent in recipes, and there were cooking segments with Paul Prudhomme. Then, the Mayor of New Orleans offered her a place in the Mardi Gras parade which Moonie promptly parlayed into a sky box at the Superdome which she then leased out to some Native American Indians running Riverboat Casinos on the Mississippi in return for being comped at their tables plus part ownership in two cell phone towers in Desoto County, Mississippi, south of Memphis. Thus, she was able to turn a "Jambalaya Motors" bumper sticker and license plate holder on her free Escalade, which she insisted on bringing to every event in Los Angeles, into a money making situation in Bad Bob's backyard in Tennessee. It boggled Beverly's mind and challenged Bad Bob's balls. She had to go.

The chink in Moonie's armor turned out to be a Haitian. It was the driver, Maurice, who, although devoted to Moonie, was also devoted to staying in the U.S. Instead of the single destination (studio to home) that the show had contracted with the limo company to provide, Moonie was logging in up to 27 stops a night, every night; and Maurice was dutifully turning in a chit for every single one of them. Moonie was making more stops around the city than a coke dealer, and the show was not above intimating the possibility of that as well in order to trigger the "morals" clause in her contract, an FCC probe, and an alert to local law enforcement.

"You will be required to compensate Swann for your excessive use of the driver," Madame Defarge informed Moonie in an e-mail. "The show provides a car and driver for the convenience of the co-hosts traveling to and from the show and not for their personal use or commercial purposes."

It was the "commercial purposes" reference that threw down the gauntlet. It meant that the show, and more specifically, Bad Bob and Beverly, were on the warpath and were specifically targeting Moonie. The minute she read the e-mail, Moonie stormed out of her shoe-filled dressing room and headed straight for the elevators to make a rare appearance in the windowless basement production office of the show that housed a conference room, grid "whiteboards", editing rooms, graphics facilities, Mugsy's exercise rooms, and a locked office containing high-end swag.

"What the hell does *this* mean?" she said standing in the doorway of Gloria's office, waving a print-out of the e-mail in her hand.

Gloria remained seated at her computer. Moonie did not have to announce herself. Her presence in any doorway was usually like a total eclipse of the sun and would form an airtight seal that threatened any living thing trapped inside.

Gloria continued to stare impassively at the blank screen. The computer wasn't even on. Then, after a beat, she languidly turned her head, like an imperious cat that had been mildly disturbed but in no way felt threatened.

"Is anything wrong?" she said fluttering her eyes back into her head and with a slight patronizing smile like an uber shop girl.

"You tellin' me I cannot use *my* car that I provide at my own expense just because I happen to make a stop on the way home for health reasons and to promote the show?" Moonie said while suddenly realizing that, now, she actually *could* fit though the door without turning sideways. Thank you, Jesus.

"You're free to use your own car however you wish, Moonie." Gloria said quietly. "You just can't use the driver we provide unless you compensate Swann every time you do."

"What?" Moonie was truly incredulous. For an instant she wished she were back to her old weight. She could have used the extra pounds for intimidation. She hitched up her double wide colostomy bag instead, just for emphasis. "Is this the same bullshit as the mail?" she said pronouncing it "boolshid" as only a Native/African American could.

"If you mean, will the show pay for your personal mail and transportation, then the answer is 'no'. I mean 'yes', it is the same policy. Inappropriate use of business mailing privileges is the same as running around all over Los Angeles on the show's nickel," she said evenly. Gloria was a company gal. Swann was all she had, and she was sticking to it.

Moonie was getting steamed. The contents of her colostomy bag were almost boiling. She placed both hands on Gloria's desk and leaned in close enough to the impassive network executive to take a bite out of her.

"Now I want you to tell me exactly how y'all know exactly who, what, where, why, and—as we like to say on the reservation—'how' I am abusing my privileges, mail or driver-wise?"

"It's pretty obvious, isn't it?" Gloria said calmly, with her eyes almost fluttered shut.

"Oh yeah? You mean, when I put a letter in the 'out' box; and it gets taken up to the mail room, and the girl up there, Blind Bertha, puts it to her head like Carnac and decides whether it is business or personal?"

Moonie was referring to Swann's proud employment of a legally blind woman in the SBS mail room which, while it satisfied their hiring requirements for persons with disabilities, made little practical sense in terms of mail sorting and delivery. On top of that "Blind Bertha" spoke mainly Farsi, so she wasn't even blind in English. Standard English Braille was Greek to her. But somehow, if Bertha felt that a piece of mail was personal rather than business related, she would kick it back to Gloria who would then return it to the sender, usually Moonie and sometimes Brendan.

It was as offensive to Brendan as it was to Moonie, but Brendan got around it by sending everything in official SBS corporate envelopes and listing Gloria, herself, on the return address regardless of the addressee.

"Then send me a bill." Moonie said angrily.

"I think we already have."

"You don't know how much I do for this show and in ways that neither you nor anyone else knows or could ever figure out. My stops are as important as my letters to Miss Diane Sawyer and Mister Les Moonves—my name brother—, or to anyone else. It's called show business, Gloria. And Moonbeam P. Brown is takin' care of business big time. If you want to challenge that, girl, then you're gonna have a fight on your hands that you will lose."

"I'm sorry."

"No, you're not. But you send another piece of mail back to me, and you better have a signed court order that lets you do it. And don't think I won't hold your feet, the show's feet, the network's feet, and Swann's feet to that federal fire. I know my rights as an American and a member of the Passamaquoddy Nation."

Gloria quietly turned away and stared at her blank computer screen again. She had begun to be physically afraid of Moonie and physically ill from the smell. Moonie held her stance over Gloria for a few more silent beats. Then she abruptly turned and left, knowing she had raised enough hell to keep her in free limo-stops and postage for as long as she was on the show.

"Please remember, everyone: 'The Ladies' Room' —*our* 'Ladies' Room'—may be occupied, but it's always open. So please join us here every day. You'll feel better when you do." Beverly would repeat that, word for word, at the close of every show. Brendan had written it for her before the show had gone on the air because the "newsies", who were running things, felt Beverly needed a signature "sign-off" like Cronkite, Murrow, and other beloved newscasters.

Moonie had now taken that invitation to the extreme. She knew instinctively that the last thing Beverly wanted in the twilight of her journalistic career was a nasty public fight over questionable practices. And Moonie was right...up to a point. What Moonie hadn't figured on was that Beverly had no intention of retiring, and she was fighting just as hard for her own survival as for her legacy. Indians may have beaten the white man at Little Big Horn and at tax-free casinos, but they were no match for the Mob. When Beverly heard about Moonie's little *tête-à-tête* with Gloria, she redoubled her plans for a Moonie "by-pass" of her own.

Brendan was becoming more fatigued, but he insisted on showing up for work every day. The Lupron and radiation to shrink the prostate made him drifty and disoriented. He could no longer bound up the stairs to the studio with new joke cards during commercials, and often he would fall asleep at the computer—although never before the live show in the morning. He was pale and thin, and the Texas catheter made him walk with a limp like some television character or Moony with her bag.

When he was single, Brendan used to spray deodorant under his arms first and then spray an equal amount on his genitals just in case the opportunity for a blow job presented itself during the day. Now, he found himself spraying deodorant on his crotch once again, but this time it was to cover up the smell of urine from the catheter and bag. Things change in a man's life.

"Why don't you just go home?" Mugsy said to him once after she had just come out of her shower before the show. "Get some rest."

"What? And give up show business?" Brendan had said and then hobbled back toward his office to do more monologue.

He didn't want to give them any ammunition. But he did have to come to grips with the fact that time was running out, and he was not building up a record that would help him in any material way.

CHAPTER THIRTY

They got to Ray Ray. Ray Ray fancied himself a financial genius mainly because he'd taught himself to say "derivatives" and "the Fed" like a true Wall Street asshole, but don't ask him what a hedge fund is other than money put aside to trim your shrubs. Ray Ray's plan was to use Moonie's money and connections to create a hip-hop and pro athlete business management empire. A black IMG. He wanted to be like Jay-Z but with smaller lips.

"You can talk to those people better than anyone else." Bad Bob told him over drinks while they were waiting for Moonie to arrive at the "Hair Hall Of Fame Awards" where she was receiving a "Weavie". Bad Bob was there to represent "The Ladies' Room" and also because he was getting a "Lifetime Achievement Weavie", of all things, for overseeing the hair styles of five women every day for fifteen years.

The Palladium ballroom smelled like burnt rubber. Actually, the "Weavie" people had originally wanted to give the award to Beverly, but she considered the honor—and a "Lifetime Achievement" one at that, for *hair*—far beneath her station as a serious journalist and friend of the Royal Family. But she thought the award would be perfect for Bad Bob.

"You're huge, man," Bad Bob went on, being overly expansive for Ray Ray's benefit. "It's virgin territory." He figured the "virgin" part would really hook him.

"Yeah, I been thinking a lot about ventures. You know, leveraging the equity I got in this thing. Like we did when we did that YouTube deal."

Ray Ray claimed to have been part of the M&A team that masterminded the takeover of YouTube by Google. The truth was he probably was *on* Google, learning e-mail, when that buyout took place.

"Well, then, you know. I don't have to tell *you*," which is what Bad Bob usually said when the person he was talking to was completely full of shit.

"Yeah," Ray Ray mused. "I think I see where you're getting' at. Me and Moonie see these dudes all the time. And most of them don't know what to do with their money. You know how much money Jay-Z made last year? 148 million dollars. And all he wanted to do was buy Mike Tyson's old crib in Connecticut to prove he was badder than Iron Mike. And that place don't even got a helipad."

Bad Bob knew he was getting to Ray Ray because Ray Ray was becoming more ghetto now and dropping the "Wall Street" lockjaw he'd learned from the movie.

"Then you da man," Bad Bob said, matching his jive. "You should be spending half the year back in New York—where it's all happening."

"Yeah," Ray Ray said, relishing the thought of Chelsea on a Saturday night.

"Yeah," Bad Bob repeated. "Think about it." At that point Moonie hove into view like a freighter on the horizon. And she headed straight for them.

"Whatchu boys talkin' 'bout?" she said kissing Bad Bob and squeezing Ray Ray's hand.

"Your future, baby," Ray Ray said as Bad Bob nodded dutifully like his posse.

Their marriage seemed to be going well at the moment. But Bad Bob knew he had to get to Ray Ray and Moonie while they still thought they were "Oprah and Steadman" and, therefore, far above the tedium of a daily talk show with three other mere "mortals". He even thought of taking the show to New York for a week to make them taste the bright lights together.

But what Bad Bob really wanted at that moment was to get away from both of them and soak up his brief moment in the spotlight as the recipient of the coveted Weavie "Lifetime Achievement Award". He'd even hired a public relations firm to make the most of it and to combat the inevitable guffaws from colleagues and even strangers.

Bad Bob turned away from Moonie and Ray Ray and left them to wallow in their own artifice. Then he took out his iPhone so he could interview himself while heading for the entrance to the event in order to make an unprecedented *second* appearance on the Hair Hall of Fame red carpet as if he had arrived twice.

Moonie became obsessed with "expanding her brand" after the wedding. She put out a series of soft cover self-help books that showed her and Ray Ray in various stages of wedded bliss. People asked her if she were trying to become the next Oprah.

"I'm trying to become the next Pocahontas," she would tell them.

But Ray Ray was Captain "John Smith" only when he needed an alias at the Inglewood Holiday Inn, or wherever he would find himself at the end of an evening with the boys. Interestingly enough, his marriage to Moonie actually increased his currency in the clubs because it gave him the patina of being straight while his sex drive remained intact and overwhelmingly gay.

Moonie was riding high with her new figure and glam make-up to match. When the show refused to shoot a new group "cast" shot for the show, Moonie insisted that they take a single portrait of her in her new body and "Photoshop" it in where her old self used to be. The only problem was there was so much white space on either side of the "New Moonie" that it looked like the other co-hosts were avoiding her—which they were. The cheese stood alone in the group shot, as well it should have.

She also believed that her new body was suddenly overwhelmingly attractive to straight men. It wasn't, of course. Because, like a bad tit job, while Moonie looked presentable in her wrap dresses which she now preferred; there was still something about her that "just wasn't right". And it wasn't the colostomy bag which she put on a strict diet of being emptied after even a snack. It was a "ghost obesity" that had stayed with her. You couldn't see it with the naked eye, but you could sense it. And so could she whether she admitted it or not. It's called "Fat Head" disease: the disorder that causes formerly fat women to look at their new bodies but still see themselves as just as huge as they used to be.

Even so, Moonie was on the make if, for nothing else, than because she needed the validation that she was now thinner—not thin, just thin-ner.

"Keep it in your pants, Goldblum!" She shouted to Jeff Goldblum a week after she was back from her honeymoon and feeling good about herself. And she said it loud enough to make everyone on the floor think that an actual pass had been made when all Jeff did was merely stick his head out of his dressing room door at the precise moment Moonie was sashaying past it before the show. Goldblum never fully understood what she was talking about and certainly couldn't imagine any sexual innuendo. After all, this was a man whom Streisand had fired off "The Main Event" because he wasn't attractive enough to play even her *ex*-husband. But Moonie's admonition to Jeff was so absurd and needy that "Keep it in your pants, Goldblum" became the instant catchphrase around the office and would always draw a laugh even from people who hadn't been there to witness it.

With Bad Bob's tacit approval and deft manipulation, Moonie began to miss shows because of her "other obligations". The network seized on the absences as an incipient breach of contract and sent inter-office memos warning all the co-hosts of conflicts of interest. The network was too afraid, or too Machiavellian, to ever confront Moonie directly. They knew of the new "Indian Wars" that would ensue if they did. Moonie took the admonitions at face value and never applied them solely to herself; but the rest of the ladies did immediately, and they were not happy about the meetings that were prompted by her behavior alone. All of the co-hosts were curtailed and reprimanded because of her excesses. And their own private scams were suddenly scrutinized and put in jeopardy because Moonie thought she was bulletproof and invisible. Pressure was mounting on Moonie from all sides.

"Now I know how Custer felt," Marge said. "That fat fuck is too blatant. She's going to bring us all down."

"Just wait," Beverly always replied ominously. "Just wait. It will all work out."

Beverly was in her favorite position as both the perpetrator and the benefactor of mob justice. Sometimes she played the innocent school girl and sometimes the ruthless Don. She could courtesy one moment and "Coreleone" the next. But her favorite pose was the "beset upon damsel in distress".

"If Beverly puts the back of her hand to her forehead and does that fake swoon one more time on air I'm going to throw up," Brendan said to the little group of malcontents who sat and watched the live "feed" of the show each day in the wardrobe room. They would meet there as soon as the show went on the air because it was secure, smelled better than their own offices, and there were fewer mice. The wardrobe people had fashioned their own little boudoir around a monitor located behind the racks of dresses and accessory tables.

"Something's up with Moonie," Janet, the wardrobe coordinator, said. "She's just sitting there. And scowling every time one of them speaks."

"Her double order of bacon was late this morning," Brendan said.

"No. She's pissed." Presently, everyone in the little group turned their full attention to the television screen.

"She hates Beverly. They must have had a fight."

"Actually she was uncommonly silent during the "CrossTalk" meeting. I chalked it up to indigestion. Or something bad in the bag." Brendan said without really paying attention.

On any given day, the ladies unwittingly carried their problems or feuds onto the live show. A discerning viewer, who had a sufficiently empty life to actually care, could easily parse which cohost had had a bad time the night before, or which lady had insulted the other, or whose contract was short, or who was being left twisting in the wind by the co-host/owner of the show. As a cover, Beverly would constantly verbalize the phony subtext of "The Ladies' Room" as if it weren't abundantly clear and even more abundantly bogus.

"Ladies' and gentlemen, you must know, we all really love each other on this show," she would say in the middle of a hot discussion, thereby killing any sense of spontaneity. Then, with her fingers splayed like a daytime Norma Desmond, she'd continue, "But I can't *believe* some of the language that comes out of the mouths of my dear, dear, sweet colleagues," she would opine apropos of really nothing extraordinary in the conversation. But the back of the hand would go up to the forehead, and she would throw her head back as if swooning from the vapors of the scandalous talk. "And to think that this all is happening on our little show on daytime television," she would remind the audience in case they weren't sufficiently appreciative of the fact that she, Beverly Frost, was actually gracing their insignificant, pitiful, homebound, daytime lives before 6:00 PM.

On this particular day she was doing her signature star-turn of lying through her teeth while apparently speaking the "truth" from the bottom of her journalistic "heart". They were discussing a subject as innocuous, but pervasive, as whether "stay at home moms" worked harder than professional women. But when Beverly had something on her mind, nothing—neither teleprompter, cards, script, nor commercial breaks —could keep her from getting it in and on the air, no matter how tangential or irrelevant it was to the conversation.

"Ms. Moonbeam Brown is so incredibly talented and diverse," Beverly began, gently tapping her blue cards with the tips of her fingernails to indicate she was "serious" now. "She can do virtually anything."

Then she turned to the audience for mock affirmation. "I mean, the books, the lectures, the DVD's, her own line of clothing, the nail salons, the wigs, the paper dolls. Yesterday I saw a protein bar with her name on it." Beverly became, apparently, speechless and out of breath at just the thought of it all. "It's all just,..whew!"

Now Beverly dropped her arms to her side and slumped in her chair glassy-eyed as if pretending to be completely overwhelmed. But she wasn't finished. She straightened herself up immediately.

"Not to mention a little something called "The Ladies' Room" which is, for most of us, our only job." Then she turned to Moonie and put her hand on hers. "We love you, darling. And we couldn't do the show without you." Then she turned, like the pro she was, full-on to "Camera One" that she knew was always "iso'd" on her. "There have been a lot of rumors recently and items in the press that you might want to spread your wings and fly away to any number of opportunities that may be out there waiting for you, but we had you first; and we intend to keep you here by our side and at this table for as long as you want to be here. You are, and always will be, one of us, right here at "The Ladies' Room". This is your seat and your show."

In other words, you're fired, and we're not renewing your contract.

Moonie knew it, and Beverly knew it. But the audience took Beverly's unprompted endorsement as a major applause "suck" and burst into a thunderous applause of acclamation and affirmation that evolved into a standing ovation for Moonie. The love went on for close to three minutes before the audience sat back down to see the fruits of their outpouring.

Moonie had tears in her eyes. Beverly stood and stepped over to her chair and hugged Moonie where she sat. But Moonie's tears were there because she knew that Beverly had just given her the *bocce morte* as surely as Michael Corleone had planted one on Fredo in "The Godfather".

"Thank you, Beverly" Moonie said in her best church girl persona, "This is my home. And, as my tribal elders always taught me, as high as the eagle soars, he always has to land. And wherever he touches the earth, that is his home." Then she turned to Beverly as if they were exchanging vows at a gay wedding instead of doing a talk show. "And Beverly, my talons are right here with you."

There was another round of perfunctory applause. The audience was exhausted by this shadow dance of love and had become slightly suspicious of it. The operative word, of course, was "talons" which had bubbled up in Moonie's subconscious from her sense of what was really going on. And everyone else knew it as well, if only instinctively.

"Bye-Bye," Brendan said to the television screen and the assembled kibitzers in the wardrobe room.

"She's toast." Janet, added.

"That's incredible," Leo said. He always joined their little group, but he rarely joined the conversation. "Whaddya think'll happen now?"

"New co-host," Janet said standing and then sauntering out of the room. "Let the search begin."

The next day, Moonie was agitated during "CrossTalk" and not paying attention or saying much. Beverly had turned a conversation about custom monogrammed condoms as wedding gifts into a discussion about her friendship with Imelda Marcos and how they would go shopping together because, it turns out, they both wore the same size shoe. But Beverly had no idea Imelda had so many shoes until she opened Imelda's closet when she interviewed her in the Philippines after Marcos was deposed. And that was when Imelda personally gave Beverly the actual pair of shoes that she had worn when Marcos was inaugurated and which Beverly has treasured to this day and has never shown *anyone*, much less a network daytime audience, until right now.

"Hal, put the camera on me," Moonie blurted out apropos of nothing.

She then proceeded to quit right there on the air saying she had decided not to renew her contract in order to pursue the path the Great Spirit had laid out for her. A fleeting smile flashed across Beverly's face before "Camera One" picked up her shock and pain at being "blindsided" by the announcement. It was as dramatic as when one of those local news anchors blow their brains out, live, on the Six O'clock News. Moonie had dutifully opened a vein and bled out, like a good soldier, prostrate before her *capo di tutti capi*, in abject supplication.

The next day she was gone, vanished. This time, Custer won. As a replacement, the daughter of a socialite friend of Beverly's who was certifiably insane, but fancied herself an iconoclast, was in her seat. And Moonie Brown was forgotten immediately as if she'd never been there at all. Such is the disposability of daytime television.

Moonie's concrete chair had outlasted her.

CHAPTER THIRTY-ONE

B rendan's situation had deteriorated medically so that even the cancer doctors were flummoxed. He had quickly moved beyond surgery, so the question then was how best to circle the drain: chemo, radiation or both. They had initially chosen Lupron, a hormone inhibitor, to reduce the prostate and mitigate the raging PSA that was being urged on by his own testosterone. After that, he had become no better off than a frog being dissected in Biology 101. His end was clear. The path and pain were not. The cancer had grown. They were waiting for the radiation to kick in and shrink the prostate, but Brendan knew he was slipping.

"Whaddya mean, we can't fix it?" he said sitting in Dr. Benjamin's office.

"Because now we can only arrest it.....if we're lucky. You're talking about a mortality of anywhere from one to ten years," Benjamin told him.

"I'll take 'Cancer' for ten," he said like a Jeopardy contestant.

"It's not that funny although I suppose it's your way of dealing, so I guess it's okay."

"Am I dying?"

"We're all dying."

"Is that what they taught you to say?"

"No, that's what I teach my students to say. Look, my friend, I'm in the postponement business. You could be as healthy as a horse, but I'd still be only delaying the inevitable." He leaned forward very un-doctor-like. "You know why I'm fucking depressed and anxiety ridden every fucking day of my life? Because I'll tell you a little secret. I'm a fraud. I can't cure anything. I can only, maybe, help you dodge a few bullets; I can't stop them. Sometimes I have a good day dodging, and sometimes a lousy one. If I'm a good doctor, I'm about 5% more effective than if you never met me. If I'm a lousy doctor, you lose. But, then, on the other hand, it cuts down your waiting time. As your doctor, I'm no better than a barker in front of a carnival dunking stool. You're on the stool. I make money, we're in cahoots, but you're still gonna lose. The longer you stay up, the happier we both are. But when the right ball hits the bull's-eye, down you go. That's the object of the game. Right now I've got to keep you dry for as long as possible. That's why I'm putting you on Coumadin," he said writing a prescription.

"I feel better already," Brendan said, still cocky and high from the fact that he'd actually gotten Benjamin's attention. "Why Coumadin? Isn't that rat poison? I thought the guys at UCLA already had me on the good stuff."

"That's for your cancer. I don't want your A-fib or metastases to throw a clot while they're fucking with you over there. Then I look like an asshole."

Marge's "campaign" was heating up to the point that she was becoming a bigger star as a "candidate" than she was as a co-host on "The Ladies' Room". The line between real and mock had become so indistinguishable in her own mind, as well as the public's, that she now thought she *should* be president, sort of —like Sarah Palin but without the sanctimony.

"These jokes are inappropriate," she would say to Brendan, scowling as if she were looking at a bowl of shit instead of at seven newly minted blue cards with up to the minute comedy material on them. "I can't say this about a member of Congress."

She, of course, was talking more as a canny politician than a comedian. There had been a time when she would have said anything about anybody, like any other comedian. But now she was ostensibly running for president, and people actually asked her for her opinion and then leaned in with their pencils poised for her answer. It was the death of comedy—being actually responsible for what one said and, worse, actually caring what they thought about you afterwards. Suddenly, potshots became policy. In the back of her mind she figured the upshot of her "Run for the Presidency" on Comedy Central would be that she would emerge as a viable political commentator, a pundit, an irreplaceable addition to the cable mix of endless bloviating experts, a split-screen talking head in her own "Bloomberg Box". She would get "the respect" due her as the first college graduate of her family.

Brendan's mission was to keep his job while he was still alive. He never argued with Marge when she squandered perfectly good monologue material that scooped the late night funnymen. At first he thought she must be banking it for her political show and the campaign she'd summarily shut him out of. But ultimately, he realized, she had completely forfeited her comedy chops for celebrity legitimacy. She was *responsible*, now; head of her own reality show if not "Head of State". Nothing was funny, and everything was important. But it wasn't that she was exploiting, or even ignoring Brendan, since both of those attitudes would presume a certain recognition of the value of what he presented to her each day. She had simply let herself slip into adulthood. She had become responsible for what she said, accountable for her behavior and her words. She had ceased to be funny because she was important now; the fodder for other comedians while tirelessly plowing the furrows of self-aggrandizement. She was running for President of the United States, for crissakes, while everyone else was making jokes. She had a job to do and a franchise to protect and had no time--nor inter-est—in rocking the boat she was standing up in.

Brendan was able to show up for work and actually, like some disembodied head, churn out a show's worth of jokes for Marge de-spite his discomfort and inability to bound up the stairs to the studio two steps at a time like he used to during commercial breaks in time to hand Marge new material. But in a strange way the writing was better because of it. Knowing that he didn't have another shot at a subject during the commercials made him bear down harder on the page at hand. It was as it always had been. Adrenalin and an-ger equaled comedy. When he had been well and Marge had been funny, Marge would often purposely turn down adequate takes on a subject just to see what a second turn, done in anger and frustration, and fueled by the descending minutes before a show, would produce. She was always rewarded with something better despite Brendan's glower and a "Take that, bitch" attitude when he would hand her the new material. Brendan knew the forced material was better, but he would never admit it. Just like Secretariat, even Brendan sometimes responded well to the whip.

"I think the bathroom lights take longer to go on when I enter now," Brendan told Leo one afternoon. "It's as if I'm losing mass, and it doesn't sense me until I'm almost at the urinal."

"You're crazy," Leo told him. Brendan always thought Leo was the happiest man on the planet. He loved his wife, he loved his family, and he loved the job of making Beverly sound smart, con-cise, and coherent. Brendan always respected Leo as a comedy writer who was as funny, or funnier, than he was; but Leo was rarely given an opportunity for any of that on the show. That didn't seem to bother him as much as it bothered Brendan. Brendan squirmed under the torture. Leo simply never acknowledged it. Hence, his sunny, upbeat disposition.

Despite Brendan's brief Vegas dalliance with Beverly, Leo had a much longer history with her because she had discovered him when he was a runner at PermaFrost who would happily do errands in the rain for her and her specials. Beverly felt she had raised him as a writer who could fix anything in preparing her interviews. She considered him another one of her lifetime achievements as if she had personally fed him with an eye dropper of milk after she found him, graduating to baby bottles administered as if to a motherless lamb in her arms, and then to solid food when he could finally stand, wobbly, on his own two feet and fetch for her. The fact that she called him "Lenny" instead of "Leo" didn't diminish the affection she thought she felt for him. Leo was the son she never wanted.

"I'll prove it to you," Leo said to Brendan. He really didn't want to move. He liked staring wide-eyed into the computer monitor. Leo only had two positions in his office: staring intently at the seemingly endless template of the show script on his screen or on the phone with his extended family. Of the two, Leo preferred staring into the screen

"You don't have to prove it to me. I know it." Brendan said. "Raoul even fixed it. The fucking lights used to go on as soon as I opened the door. I couldn't get two feet inside before the room lit up. Now, I have my dick out and get all the way to in front of the sinks before the lights go on. The next thing you know I'll be pissing in the dark. This cancer is powerful shit, man."

"I thought you still had the bag. What difference does it make?" Leo said trying not to have to move from his chair.

"I was speaking metaphorically."

"C'mon," he finally told Brendan, pushing his chair back and standing but still looking intently at the computer screen. The page of the script on the monitor was like a meditation mantra he always thought would ultimately reveal something to him about what he was doing with his life. "Let's check it out."

They walked together to the men's room door across the hall.

"You go first and tell me when the lights go on for you." Brendan said.

"Right. You stay here. Like one of Kanye's security guards," Leo said.

It was a standing joke among the staff as to which celebrities felt they needed personal security guards when they appeared on the show. The practice had escalated until now the new distinction, initiated by the rap artists, was to have a guard at the bathroom door to prevent any civilians from sharing the facility with the rapper. The next level would probably be a man carrying a toilet seat like the one the Queen of England gets to use exclusively. That was right up there with the "no looking" memo for Mariah Carey in the elevator.

"Okay," Brendan said. "I really appreciate this. You know, with 'my condition' and all," he added sarcastically.

"Anything to help. Here I go."

"Act normal." Brendan said quickly.

Leo hesitated for a beat.

"Too late," he said. Then he opened the door and went into the bathroom.

There was nothing wrong with the lights. So he immediately came out again.

"You're full of shit. The lights come on like they always do."

"Sure, for *you*." Brendan said. "Look at you. The picture of health. But me? Nuttin' ."

"Well, I gotta break something to you, pal. We can't try this with you because, now, it'll take five minutes for the lights to go off again." Leo said. "And I ain't standing here with you outside the men's room. It may even be a Human Resources issue."

"But it's true. I'm losing it. I'm disappearing. The lights don't lie. I'm going to have to go over your head to Raoul. He'll tell me."

"You do that, and get back to me." Leo turned and left Brendan standing at the bathroom door.

"But, in truth, it's actually impossible to test because if we walk in together to demonstrate it to you, it fucks up my critical mass theory." Brendan continued raising his voice because Leo had walked back to his office. "And if you stay in there to watch, the lights will never go out. I'm the only one who knows. I'm the only one who'll ever know. Unless I could get Raoul to hide in one of the stalls, perfectly still, until the lights went out. But I think I'd have to pay him. How much do you think I should give him to do that? But even then it wouldn't work. It's a Heisenberg problem. The mere observation alters the validity of the result. I'm a fucking Heisenberg conundrum. That's *worse* than cancer."

By now Brendan was doing a bit. But he was kidding on the square. He really did think that, somehow, the bathroom light sensor was picking up on his diminishing health or, worse, anticipating it.

"You've got a Marge intro," Leo yelled from his office. Brendan turned and went back to work.

The last thing Leo wanted to do was to buy into Brendan's self-destructiveness about his health. He continued to treat him as if he had a cold or something. Not only did Leo not want to face it, but he knew neither did Brendan. Brendan did confide in him his wonderment about death. That he hoped he "did it well" when the time came just like Cary Grant had worried about doing *his* death well. Brendan was afraid of the pain, but Leo told him the good thing about death was that, as bad as the dying got, you wouldn't remember it as soon as it was over. At least, that was what he was counting on. But with Brendan, Leo had the feeling, the pain might just last longer. Much longer.

The Wife was conflicted by Brendan's condition. On one hand, she wanted to fulfill the role of the stalwart life partner devoted to the care and comfort of her infirmed husband. On the other hand, she didn't want it to fuck up her relationship with the Governor. What started out as a family effort quickly turned into just another one of Brendan's annoying gambits like internet porn or doing bits in elevators,

"If you die, I may not tell Zeke." She told Brendan when they were alone. "I'll just say you took a trip. That you're on the road."

"And when I don't come back?"

"He'll just think you didn't come back. I think it will be easier for him."

"Not even a letter? A phone call?" Brendan wondered. The wife shook her head. She'd obviously thought this all out.

"No. it'll be easier. I mean, he'll find out eventually—in, maybe, twenty or thirty years. But by then he'll be able to handle it. I think it's best. I'm not going to tell him.

"That's the craziest thing I ever heard," Brendan said to her.

"Thank you," she said. "I came up with it all by myself."

"Really?" Brendan said sarcastically.

"You'll beat it," people at work started saying to Brendan when they heard he was doing a course of chemo and radiation. "Hang in there," became the preferred way of closing even the most casual conversation. Of course, Brendan couldn't recognize it in himself, but he had unquestionably developed "the look". His co-workers couldn't avoid the skull quality that had taken over his face and the slight tightening of the lips across his teeth as if the skin on his head was shrinking and no longer fit.

"If one more motherfucker says to me, 'You'll beat it,' I'm going to fuckin' explode," Brendan told Leo one morning after the "CrossTalk" meeting. "Or 'Hang in there'. *'Hang in there?'* 'Go fuck yourself,' I'd like to tell them. 'Fuck you with your fucking 'hang in there'. Je-sus Christ! Beat *this*," he added grabbing his balls more aggressively than was comically called for.

Brendan's lack of piety about his own condition was actually a relief to his close friends. It broke the tension. The comic rage, or whatever stage of dying Brendan was supposed to be in, kept the beast at bay, or, at least, moved it over to the to the corner where it was no longer in the way.

Brendan found himself reading the announcements posted on the "Wall of Woe" with increased morbid interest and a hint of competitiveness. The endless series of bad news bulletins continued unabated. One posting asked for platelets for a transfusion-needy daughter of someone in wardrobe on the soap who was going through a bone marrow transplant. Another announced the death of an audio technician's father. Another telling of a tape editor's wife's double mastectomy. Even the birth announcements were tinged with tragedy. Preemies with holes in their hearts, or cleft palates, or unplanned triplets—all requiring copious outpourings of sorrow and prayer..

Brendan concluded that the soap people lived their lives as they plied their art: on their sleeves and on the "Wall of Woe". The litany of hardship and tragedy that played out in standard letter-size 8 ½ x 11 inch postings on the wall was no different than the endless fictional troubles that were acted out by them in the studio within.

The other thing that Brendan noticed was that none of the stars of the soap opera were ever beset with any "real-life" hardship. It was only the crew and production staff that seemed to be falling apart every week. The perception was that the actors and creators of the soap operas somehow were able to expunge all their troubles on stage whereas the "dear crew", behind the scenes, had to go through *their* disasters in real life and in real time. The stars owned the scape-goat. Their "vale of tears" was only on camera. "Disaster" for them was when their limo was late. Everyone else was fucked—big time. In other words, once again, the "Wall of Woe" proved that it's better to be a star. Much better.

One of the soap actresses actually had the balls to volunteer at actual breast cancer rallies in order to testify to the crowd, in great detail, how her *character* had famously endured Stage Four breast cancer for 13 weeks on her show, but then she had miraculously been cured! (Applause). What she didn't tell them was that the "miracle cure" was the signing her new contract.

"So like all of you, I'm still here!" the very healthy actress would proclaim. Then the real cancer victims would wildly cheer the fake one as if getting into stage four cancer make-up every day was just as heroic as a double mastectomy with chemo and radiation.

Brendan's time at "The Ladies' Room", per his contract, was winding down. Despite all his activity to the contrary, he had been working under the edict of being dismissed as soon as the 26 week guarantee in his contract played out. While he had avoided being escorted from the building as other fired individuals had been, neither had he been informed that Bad Bob's decision to fire him had, in any way, been commuted or was under review. The threat of adverse publicity, and the innate cheapness of the Swann Company, had probably combined to keep Brendan on the job; but now it was witching time, and Brendan had to prepare.

"You can have my chair," he said to Leo as he rolled his special "Backopedic" office chair into Leo's office. Brendan had had to produce three bogus back X-rays that actually belonged to his dead brother in order to convince the Swann Company, and, specifically, Gloria, to spring for the chair. It was his most prized piece of office equipment, even more than the assortment of incandescent lamps he'd glommed from the soap sets to replace the deadly overhead fluorescent lighting. The arrival of Brendan's chair, actually made Leo turn his head away from his computer screen and look at Brendan with a certain amount of dread. It was not clear to Leo, nor was it to Brendan, which termination he was preparing for.

"Whaddya doing that for?" Leo asked. "Bad test results?"

"My contract's up tomorrow. Remember? Dead man walking. Six months and 4 weeks."

"Bullshit. They're not going to actually fire you."

"Bought and paid for, baby," Brendan said. "I got some lamps, too. Come into my office and take what you want."

"Bullshit," Leo said again.

Brendan could see that his firing and his cancer had met in a nexus of overlapping metaphors. It was no longer possible to discern which demise was more imminent or which one they were talking about.

"Go on. Take it. That piece of shit you sit in will kill you. Don't make me leave this thing for them. I worked too hard for it. I want you to have it. C'mon, it's like Joey's jacket in "On the Waterfront". I'm passing it on to you.

"Okay, I'll take it," Leo said getting up and rolling his own chair back. "Thanks. But I feel funny."

"Good. Then you can write for Marge."

Leo slowly placed his hands on the chair and tentatively rolled it into place as if it were a gurney with a comatose patient on it. Then both men looked at it for a beat when it was in front of Leo's desk.

"Perfect," Brendan said. This makes me very happy. And I'll take yours until I leave." He then rolled Leo's chair out of the office.

"Right." Leo said looking intently at his new chair as an excuse not to have to look at his doomed friend.

Back in his office, Brendan felt a certain rush at the impending change. Something *different* was going to happen. He downloaded all of his documents onto a CD and then deleted anything else he had put on the computer that he didn't want. He would have re-formatted the hard drive if he'd known how. He wanted to be absolutely ready for when they came to get him. If he was going to be naked and carried out, he had to be eminently portable.

Next he rummaged through the debris on the counter along the back wall of the office to see if he'd left anything of value there. Before serving as the office of an esteemed veteran comedy writer, the windowless cell had been a dressing room for soap extras. There was a working sink underneath the pile of junk that was totally useless. Even the water that came out of the spigot was the color of shit. But like a back eddy of a fetid pond, the detritus collected on the counter was a virtual archeological dig of Brendan's fifteen years working at "The Ladies' Room".

Decade old bags of potato chips and cookies, unused reams of paper, bad self-help books sent to the show in hopes of an appearance, beauty product giveaways, cheaply made bad toys, logo shopping bags from stores long closed, T-shirts heralding strange enterprises and forgotten campaigns, pencils, cellophane wrapped packs of blue cards, open reams of mysteriously stained three-hole

punch paper, a rope, a bottle of promotional vodka from an unknown country, a cardboard doll cut-out of an idealized, semi-fat
Moonie Brown in her underwear that had been part of a failed
paper doll fashion collection, a poster of nuns with rifles, the skull
of baby alligator, a talking Stewie doll from "Family Guy", copies of
an old ABC fall line-up campaign consisting of black letters on a
solid yellow background saying things like "Not tonight, Willow, I'm
watching 'Who Wants To Be a Millionaire?'", socks, a mouse trap
(empty), a mouse trap with a petrified mouse in it, an entire box of
plastic coffee stirs, a baseball bat, 10 Pollo Loco take-out menus, a
holiday gift assortment of Altoids breath mints with one tin missing, a mini blanket with "The Ladies' Room" embroidered on it,
a "Roberta's Round Up" cowboy hat. An assortment of seasonal
"The Ladies' Room" coffee mugs, Play-Doh, a "Swann Employee
Essential Response kit —West Coast Version" given out eight years
after "9/11" containing two 4 ounce water pouches, 1 Millennium
Bar, 1 Emergency blanket (tin foil), 2 dust masks, 1 plastic whistle
w/ lanyard, 1 Twelve-hour green lightstick —all contained in a wa-
terproof pouch (medium), w/custom lanyard 42", a copy of Medical
Myths, a box of Dr. Siegal's inedible chocolate meal replacement
diet cookies, a "Pasta boat" as seen on TV, an unattached computer
keyboard, a box of individual "Kid's Flossers", an empty toner car-
tridge, a "live" Christmas tree in a box (long dead), three old fashioned seltzer bottles.

Brendan went out into the hall to where a large industrial waste
barrel with tiny wheels was stationed and rolled it into the office.
Then, in great unceremonious armfuls, he indiscriminately, and
without a hint of nostalgia or affection, transferred the heap of garbage and memorabilia from the countertop to the garbage can.

"Brendan White, please come to Bob Vapors' office. Brendan
White, please come to Bob Vapors' office," the PA speaker outside
his office announced.

Anita, the angry receptionist, was paging him. It always made
Brendan slightly crazy to be paged publicly when he was, in fact,

sitting at his desk in front of his phone. But angry Anita often did that just to exert her self-appointed prerogative. As always, the page came in twos, the second one sounding slightly scolding like the redundant, public address, "No Parking" announcement at LAX that looped endlessly at curbside: "(I said), *'No Parking'.*"

Brendan looked at the phone waiting for it to ring, but it did not. But, instead of calling Anita and complaining to her, he decided to dutifully present himself, instead, at the executive producer's office downstairs.

The main production office of "The Ladies' Room" was filled with people essentially doing nothing. There was a lot of sitting and staring. Bad Bob had an open door policy to his office, but anyone looking in would see him deep into the subdued browns of the room staring blankly at his computer screen, never typing, occasionally talking quietly on the phone, but never especially engaged in, nor reacting to, anything he saw or said there.

Angry Anita ruled the office space from her reception fort just inside the door to the complex. The fact that she answered the show's phone but somehow managed to never actually be *on* the phone enabled her to monitor the comings and goings of practically everyone in the building even though she was stationed in the basement.

The rear portion of the office complex housed the conference area whose main function was as a lunch room and swag distribution center for the segment producers whose offices branched off the two corridors leading back to it. The research department, located in an office off the conference room, was another oxymoron. The two researchers never moved from their desks, and they were never seen reading any of the mountains of papers and magazines piled up around them, yet they knew the most minute details of any ongoing tabloid scandal.

The main feature of the conference room was the display of large white "grid" boards that covered three walls and announced six weeks of upcoming shows. During "grid" meetings, producers would stand and stare at them like Allied commanders studying maps of Europe during WWII trying to decipher troop deployments and lines of battle. For all their strategic musings and chess-like feints at programming master strokes, nothing on those boards ever radically changed from the time that Serena Faust, the PA with the best hand writing, wrote the booked guest's name in black magic marker in the designated segment box on the board to the time when she wiped it off and entered a new name or subject five weeks hence. Time, in the back conference room, marched along in week by week blocks as inexorably as life itself, continually changing but never different. Week after week after week; guest after guest after guest; seasons sliding into new seasons; shows bursting into existence like a struck match and then disappearing from memory completely as if they'd never existed. It wasn't the circle of life because there was no return. It was the banality of life: an endless, straight-line march to oblivion.

"What's up, Chief?" Brendan said after taking one step into Bad Bob's office. Bad Bob maintained his silent Copernicus-like contemplation of his computer for an extra beat and then languidly turned his head as if he had forgotten why he'd summoned Brendan. Then it dawned on him, and a flicker of animation momentarily illuminated his massive hang-dog face like a fleeting patch of sun across a corpse.

"Oh. Right," he said without moving out of his chair. "We've decided to pick up your option. You've demonstrated you can contribute to the show in multiple areas."

"Great." Brendan said. He was strangely unmoved by this redemption. Maybe it was because the motherfucker had waited until Brendan's last day to bestow it.

They looked at each other for a beat. They both knew that this was neither Bad Bob's decision nor his wish, and he did not hide the fact that he had backed into it, or had *been* backed into it. It didn't make any difference. Bad Bob no longer wished to deal with either Brendan or whatever the issue was that had precipitated the firing. There was nothing that pissed him off more than having his so-called authority usurped or challenged, even subtly. He really meant it when he would talk about "*my* show", and no one was allowed to make any more money than what had been allotted to them on "his" show.

In the early days, Brendan had forced the show to pay full WGA minimums to the writers instead of the niggardly "spot supplier" rate the network tried to get away with. Bad Bob had acted as if the increase was coming out of his own pocket and had admonished the writers to "never come into my office again asking for money" when he had to tell them they'd achieved what they had fought for. Later on, he cancelled the overnight repeats of the show because the writers got residuals for the airings while he got nothing. Asking him for a raise was like asking for blood. He really did believe that everyone should be happy they were working at all, regardless of their compensation. Back in Memphis, he had viewed the African-American garbage strike there that merely sought a living wage for minority workers as tantamount to a treasonous uprising.

"Keep up the good work, man," Bad Bob said and turned back to the unseen screen on his desk. He could have been looking at porn for all anyone could tell. No one ever saw what the fuck it was he stared at all day. It had to be porn.

"Thanks," Brendan said like a schoolboy and turned and walked out of the office. He had almost felt like clicking his heels and snapping into a beaming salute, saying, "Yes, *sir!*"

Brendan's first thought was not one of elation that he had saved his job but, rather, immediate remorse that he had given away his chair. He walked back to the elevators slowly trying to parse the situation.

Obviously, what had happened was that Beverly, who was up the ass of every prominent doctor and medical institution in California in her quest for eternal life, had gotten to his doctors, HIPAA or no HIPAA. The fact that he had just *not* been fired was more devastating than if they had cleaned out his office while he was seeing Bad

Bob and carried him out of the building. It meant that he really *was* dying. Thanks to Beverly, it finally hit home. The doctors had all been hedging their prognosis and telling him that the cancer was treatable. But, now, coming from Beverly Frost, there was no hope.

Beverly had always treated Brendan as if he were invisible except for the occasional glimpses of acknowledgement whenever she actually needed something from him, like getting fucked up the ass in Las Vegas.

Several weeks before, after a long holiday weekend, Brendan had decided to approach her, as part of his comeback campaign, while she sat alone in the lead director's chair before the "CrossTalk" meeting had started. He was eager to engage her because he actually had something complimentary and pertaining to the greater glory of Beverly Frost to share with her. (Celebrities will listen to civilians only if they have something laudatory to say about them.) There had been a moment of panic when he realized that, by standing next to her when she was sitting in her director's high chair, he was much closer to her face than she would have ever allowed had she been standing. In the instant before he spoke he noticed the lines of make-up etched along her thinly carved upper lip that was the only remaining moveable part of her face, the rest having been frozen into an imperious and dismissive scowl by hidden engineering that defied physics and gravity.

When she had determined that Brendan was not going to move away by the sheer fact of being ignored—that Brendan had come to actually *speak* to her—Beverly grandly rotated her head to face him without erasing her disgust at having to do so. She made up for his intrusion by not verbally acknowledging him in even the most perfunctory way. No "Hi" or "Good morning" or "What's up?" Newspaper vendors and cops were more engaging with strangers than Beverly Frost was with a co-worker of 15 years. Brendan remembered, on his first day of work, being horrified at his first sight of a no make-up and un-coifed Beverly. At that first staff meeting she had apologized, in advance, that she would have trouble remembering names but that staff members should not be offended by it. Fifteen years later, she could have made the same speech. What she hadn't said on that first morning was that she really couldn't *care* to know anyone's name less important than herself.

As Brendan stood there, Beverly looked blankly at him with her turtle face, waiting for him to come up with something that would justify this presumptive intrusion. And after a beat, Brendan realized he would have to go first.

"Beverly, your name was in the Times crosswords puzzle this Sunday. The clue was 'TV Talker'," Brendan had begun. Beverly's blank stare indicated that, already, the encounter was not going well. Brendan then circled back trying to show he had come in peace. "Anyway, it was interesting because yours was the only celebrity's name in the entire puzzle. It was all about national treasures like Mount Rushmore and not about television."

There was a beat of dead air. Brendan couldn't think of any other elaboration on the seemingly innocent subject that might ameliorate the fact that he had chosen to speak to her.

"I do not find that funny," she said flatly and with a royal finality like the Queen she so desperately admired. She probably really meant to say, "*We* do not find that funny." Then she rotated her head back away from him. The conversation was over. Brendan then backed away, as if from an open casket, and returned to his seat at the back of the room.

In retrospect, the mistake had been that he had made her turn her head at all as if what he had to say was of vital importance to her. The staff had learned that the co-hosts, and especially Beverly, preferred to be addressed indirectly into the make-up mirrors in front of them so that they didn't have to turn their heads to address anyone face to face. Talking exclusively into a mirror to someone right at their side provided a comfort layer of separation, distance, and deference—not unlike having an intermediary to buffer any physical intimacy. It also enabled them to multi-task—to talk and admire their glorified selves simultaneously. The custom was so pervasive—whether in the make-up room or their dressing rooms—that often a producer or PA, out of habit, would talk to one of the co-hosts in the hallway staring straight ahead as if they were in front of a mirror when obviously they weren't. It was a crazy mistake, but it did avoid eye contact; and for Beverly, that was paramount—like Mariah Carey in elevators.

When Brendan got back upstairs after speaking to Bad Bob he didn't stop in Leo's office to ask for his chair back because he knew that he had done the right thing for the wrong reason. It was only a matter of time. He sat in his, now, unfamiliar chair and pondered his end. Talk about ending with a "whimper", this was it.

The next morning, standing before Marge Foley, he told her.

"I got re-hired," he said flatly.

"I figured as much," Marge said. "Beverly never mentioned it to me again, so I figured something was up. The cancer saved you. Now all you have to do is stay in your office, keep your head down, and try to keep your job.

Brendan didn't have the energy or inclination to point out that even in her own self-serving version, the most she had done was passively accede to Beverly's *fait accompli*. Marge had not gone to bat for Brendan at all. She had merely accepted Beverly's gesture of accommodation for reasons that were entirely self-serving for Beverly. Once again, Beverly had "Godfathered" the situation by making Marge believe she had extracted something that was already a done deal.

Of course, the truth of the matter was that Brendan's call to the Writers Guild informing them of his imminent demise had triggered a call from the Executive Director of the Guild to Labor Relations threatening an EEOC age discrimination filing. In the end, it was SBS Labor Relations throwing a meaningless bone to his union that did the trick. Marge had merely been a bystander to a bigger issue. The last thing Swann wanted was bad press or even a hint of discrimination. HR may have even concurred. That and, of course, the fact that Brendan was apparently dying made the whole termination issue academic and unnecessary. As in most things, God was on Swann's side.

"Thanks, Marge," Brendan said. He didn't want her to think he was ungrateful for something she didn't actually do.

Marge sat back in her chair with a satisfied smile. She was so busy with her mock campaign that she couldn't think about anything else. The Sunday Morning political shows had suddenly become interested in her because they detected a cultural phenomenon in a dull presidential campaign that might boost their ratings. But Marge took it as validation of her intelligence. The verisimilitude was running thicker than the real, and the last thing Marge wanted to be was a jokester on a daytime gabfest. The daily discourse bored her now, and she couldn't be bothered to sit there for even the hour required by her contract. Besides, she now had a press secretary, supplied by Comedy Central, dressed in black like a bodyguard or hit man, who would quietly sit in on the "CrossTalk" meetings and nod or wince to Marge as the topics were floated depending on their usefulness to her campaign and her new career. It was the PR guy, now, who actually ran the meeting, and everyone knew it.

Beverly, for her part, was only interested in using the show as a Beverly Frost legacy machine. She knew exactly what Marge was doing and was publicly supportive of the successful life she had created outside, and competitive to, "The Ladies' Room". But privately she was hard pressed to figure out to how to turn Marge's growing popularity into a windfall for herself. In the meantime, she redoubled her insistence on topics relating only to herself; or, if world events actually overshadowed her lunch date the day before, she would insist on a clip from one of her ancient interviews regardless of its tangential relevance to the subject.

Beverly was a master of the venerable television dictum: "Tell them you're going to tell them, tell them, and then tell them you told them." She had no problem plugging one of her "Conversations" or "Teaching Moments" relentlessly on "The Ladies' Room", but then she would also plug her upcoming appearances on other shows where she was booked to make *more* plugs. Then, the next day on "The Ladies' Room", she would show a clip one of those self-serving appearances in case anyone missed it. She would then even continue to plug her specials after they had aired as if the actual broadcast itself was breaking news, and plugging it could somehow paste an audience onto the rating after the fact. Her life had become the eternal present. There was no future; the past was merely the hand maiden of the "now"; and the "now" would live, incorruptible, forever. "Live to Tape" will do that.

Watching the spectacle of Marge and Beverly revolving on their separate spits of solipsism made Brendan sicker than he was. As invisible as Beverly made him feel in life, he knew he would be eminently forgettable in death. He wondered if Zeke would find the folders upon folders of jokes he'd saved in storage boxes from his fifteen years at "The Ladies' Room" and say, "So *this* is what the 'old man' did," and be just a little proud of him, instead of embarrassed.

Marge could not be bothered by the sudden sea change in Brendan's prospects. Her hair was being washed, and her eyes were closed in the celebrity ecstasy of having, yet, one more personal chore silently attended to by someone else.

"So what do you want to do about these topics?" Brendan said once more, knowing full-well that she could only half hear him and what her answer would be if she could. The hair dresser squeezed her heavily dyed hair that looked like it was rotting at its grey, unretouched, roots, and lifted her head out of the sink. Marge rose up, zombie-like, as out of a grave and regained a semblance of consciousness.

"I can't be bothered today. I'm just going to listen and react. Do what you want. You know what to write."

Writing monologue material for Marge had become worse than offering "pearls before swine". Actually, that would be an insult to pigs. It had become, instead, "feeding caviar to a corpse".

Marge was conserving her energy for an interview on Fox News later. MSNBC was also using her as the go-to commentator on the legitimate campaign. She was getting more air-time than the legitimate minor party candidates, and there was a Facebook campaign to include her in the nationally televised debates. Suddenly, being sponsored by an enterprise called "Comedy Central" was cutting into her legitimacy, and she wanted to separate herself from all things "comedy" as much as possible. Consequently, the last thing she wanted was to be funny with women in the morning. Brendan may still have had a job, but there was less and less for him to do. He found himself humming "September Song" and meaning it. His own "precious few" days would be spent servicing a "horse" deader than he would soon be. It wasn't even "the sound and fury signifying nothing". It was his etherized body of comedy material falling like a tree in the forest with no one to hear. On the other hand, he could think of no better way to prepare for the abyss. The transition from one world to the other would not be shattering. He would slip from meaninglessness to nothingness so effortlessly that no one, especially himself, would be able to spot the seam joining one to the other.

"Why don't you take a few days off from work," The Wife said that night after Brendan had told her of his redemption.

"I just got my job back. You want me to take a vacation?"

"Well, you're guaranteed for thirteen weeks. So why not? You deserve it after what they put you through."

Brendan looked at her. What was she saying? How did everyone seem to think that God worked, not in strange ways, but in 13 week segments like a WGA contract?

"I don't think I should take any time off. I want to show them I can do it." Brendan said.

"Do what? Write your stupid jokes?"

"Yeah, especially the stupid ones."

It wasn't that The Wife was demeaning his ability, but she knew the futility of the process he was locked into with Marge, and she was just being loyal—in her way.

"Well, Zeke needs you. You should spend more time with him."

"I plan to," Brendan said. "You better warn him."

"I didn't sign him up for fencing lessons this time, so he could be with you."

"When?"

"Tuesdays."

Brendan looked at her. He knew she thought she was making the supreme sacrifice with the fencing class cancellation.

"That'll be a tough one for ol' Zekie. Fencing or face time with his dying father."

"You will not tell him you are dying. That's selfish and hurtful."

"What should I tell him then? I'm picking him up at school out of the blue on Tuesdays because I'm feeling great?"

"He doesn't have to know. He already knows too much. You want him to remember you, don't you?"

"Yeah, all fucked up and with a bag attached to my dick."

"He thinks that's funny."

She had a point. As shitty as he felt and as clumsy as the catheter and bag were, if it read funny to the kid, then maybe it wasn't so bad. Zeke would remember him as funny, and that was the whole point of everything, wasn't it? Brendan really wanted to go out in a way that that was at least somewhat pleasant for all assembled. It was his sense of audience, the same that had made him a good television writer. The ten Oxycontin a day helped. It made him goofy and drifty like a 60's hippie, and people took that as evidence that he was getting better. At times it even seemed like he really *was* "beating it", or, at least, "hanging in there"; and that made people relax and feel good when they were around him.

"I want a dog," Brendan said to The Wife the next morning.

"Why?" she said.

"I had one when I was growing up. I think Zeke should have one, too."

"We're not getting a dog. We've got too much on our plate as it is. How're we going to cope with an animal?"

"I'll take care of it."

"No, I'll be the one who'll end up taking care of it, like everything else." This last, inadvertently true, statement made them both pause and contemplate each other. Brendan thought of making a joke, but for once in his life he thought better of it.

"We are not getting a dog. We live in the Hollywood Hills. It's completely impractical," she finally continued.

"But that's the point. Impractical but lovable. Like me." She looked at him silently for a long beat. He could see her running the numbers on his situation in her head.

"I'll think about it," she said.

"I'm taking that as a "yes'. Zeke will be thrilled."

"Do not tell Zeke until I've made up my mind. What kind of dog?"

"A golden retriever." Brendan said knowing it would push her over the edge. He was right. Her shoulders slumped in resignation.

"Come on, Brendan," she said pleadingly. "Don't do this to me. Who's going to walk a golden retriever? They need exercise. They need to run free. This is Laurel Canyon. Are you going to come home from work in the middle of the day to walk him? You know that's not going to happen, and then we end up paying for someone to do it. Think, Brendan, think," she said tapping the side of her head.

"If it was your second child you would do it."

"Do what?"

"Come home in the middle of the day to walk it."

"Well, that could happen."

"We're getting a baby instead of a dog?" He felt like an absent-minded husband all of a sudden.

"That nice doctor who wouldn't shake hands with you is waiting until I have enough eggs."

"Oh," Brendan said. "We're going to have a baby?"

"Maybe," The Wife said. "You never know about these things."

"Yeah, I'll say. Especially me."

The Wife actually looked at him with deep affection and some guilt at not involving him more. Her eggs and his thawed sperm were having more sex than they were. She put her arms around his waist and kissed him lightly on the lips.

"When you get rid of the catheter and the bag, you can have your dog. But I want nothing to do with it."

This last statement brought Brendan up short. It was a Beverly Frost moment. Like getting re-hired at "The Ladies' Room". Whatever joy there was in getting what he wanted was immediately mitigated by the profound implication of the grant. The Wife allowing him to have a dog was another death sentence. He was not only a "dead man walking". Now he was a "dead man walking a dog."

That night he did something he had never done before and had always sneered at when he heard of women doing it with no apparent emotion. He went through the bundles of family snapshots from Shutterfly on The Wife's desk and threw away all the bad ones of himself. It didn't take long. As the only one in the family who ever bothered to pick up a camera, 99% of the photographs were of a smiling wife and child in countless stages of merriment. As the picture taker, he was nowhere to be seen, his presence in their lives only implied at best. The metaphor was not lost on Brendan. It was as if this moment had always been planned, had always been writ. He was reminded of the problem divorced wives were faced with when the divorce is final: The problem of having to either destroy all evidence of their former life or skillfully excise the offending husband from every photograph with a pair of scissors. The Wife's family album, on the other hand, came ready-made. The Governor would be pleased.

The question then became why go to work? He had saved his job. He could still write a joke, and it didn't matter whether Marge used the material or not, at least not for thirteen weeks. Marge seemed to be spending more time reclined with her head submerged in the shampoo sink than worrying about the show or the relative merits of Brendan's joke output. She rarely used the material, but she liked getting it nonetheless. Brendan decided that she was using the jokes as crib notes for the topics themselves. By reading the jokes she got a sense of what the discussion would be without having to actually delve into the source material and articles provided by research. In her quest for legitimacy, even the faux legitimacy of a mock presidential campaign, she had come full circle as a comedian. Whereas, before, she would use the news and current events to trigger humor and silliness, she was now retro fitting those jokes back to their source in an attempt to seem intelligent and informed. It was a long way to go and circuitous, and the result was that she came off as merely cranky and superficial. The audience could spot her intellectual laziness a mile away and did not buy her glib pronouncements for a second. When she had once been funny, the shorthand was delightful and facilitated the laugh. Now that she was trying to appear "informed", instead, her presumption was laughable. Thus, finally, Brendan was able to achieve his secret passion: even dying, he was, at last, funnier than the comedian he was writing for.

But Brendan *did* go to work, more as an act of aggression than out of any sense of duty. He wanted to be all up in their face. Like the Mayor of Cork starving himself to death on the doorstep of his oppressor. He knew he was in trouble and probably actively dying, although, except for the fatigue, he really didn't feel *that* bad. What he did learn was that since the very organism that was shutting down was the same one that was feeling it, there was a certain peacefulness to it all rather than the terror that a healthy person, inexplicably remaining healthy while dying, would experience. His consciousness was in "Stage Four" as well as his cancer.

At work, he was treated with the deference usually reserved for Clarence, the brain-damaged mail clerk. Nothing but smiles were ever directed at him; he was over-praised for the minimal performance of normal duties; people laughed loudly at his jokes and marveled at his "wit"; and secretaries freely shared their chips and candies. It was not unlike being a precocious child, an agreeable dog, or a Catholic priest. To compensate, Brendan tried to do more than just monologue material for Marge. He even gave Beverly some lines that she actually used and got big laughs with for the first time in her life. Suddenly, she knew what it was like to be a wise-cracking Vegas dolly —the kind of girl her father would have loved.

Marge felt the shift in devotion immediately, and she didn't like it.

"I wish you'd tell me when you're not going to do cards for me," she said one day after he had been helping Leo with some last minute intro rewrites and teleprompter copy.

"I forgot." Brendan told her. The truth was he hadn't even thought she would notice since she did precious little material as it was. And the few lines she did do, she usually botched. Politicians, even sketch ones, are not known for their comic ability.

"I have other sources," she proclaimed ominously just to remind him, once again, that she didn't need him.

Marge now had young, smug Harvard types working on her gag political campaign as well as the legendary Mark Solomon So, in the end, with Marge, it wasn't about the material at all, only the attention. She needed to make up for all the neglect she'd endured growing up in her Irish menagerie of a family back in Chicago.

But in true stand-up fashion (even though she eschewed all stand-up now), Marge was protecting her sources in the way a cat always knows where its next bowl of cat chow is coming from. As soon as she knew, for sure, that Brendan was dying, she had secretly begun importing material to "The Ladies' Room" from her cadre of writers on the campaign reality show. It didn't matter that it was professionally offensive and insulting to Brendan and exploitive of the non-union writers working on her other show and also completely against the WGA union rules that she so steadfastly supported as a faux Communist. But, like a true junkie, the only thing that mattered was her fix. She thought she was putting one over on Brendan when she ordered the research department to send her, by e-mail, the topics and rundown for "CrossTalk" which she would then forward to her "other" writers. Then, as if she were doing her own research for the show, she would transcribe their offerings onto the backs of the unread cards that Brendan gave her.

She refused to do Brendan's material because Brendan was a dead man; and, besides, his very presence gave her the creeps now. In addition, she figured that hearing their material on a network show each morning would function as some sort of compensation for the writers who were doing their daily scabbing for Marge on her cable show at sub-standard rates.

For Brendan, it was a dagger in his heart each morning to see her bend over backwards to fit marginal material from her reality writers into the conversation while leaving his jokes unceremoniously dumped in her dressing room wastepaper basket before she even went on air. At first it made him bear down harder and try to beat them with better material, but then he soon realized that, in Marge's world, he simply no longer existed. Even his material was nonexistent. She had killed him before he was dead. It was very mob-like.

Brendan had become obsessed with "getting it all in" as his friend, Sam Amos, loved to say. He had always assumed that Sam was talking about his carefully plotted daily rounds of errands, stops, bits, and visits rather than anything more sinister like where he was going to put his cock. Brendan's version of "getting it all in" consisted of phone calls and the disposition of extraneous items and loose ends that had to be attended to. His brother had called it the "non rev" elements of daily life.

A week after he'd gotten his job back, Marge was getting her hair done once again after the "CrossTalk" meeting, and Brendan was standing over her, as usual, trying to elicit some direction for the topics or, at least, a modicum of interest in what she was going to do on the show.

Suddenly Raoul appeared in the Make-Up room as if he had materialized there rather than availed himself of a door. His presence was unremarkable but unique at the same time. Such was the invisibility of the Yale Maintenance crew. Their presence anywhere went largely unnoticed. They could, and did, go everywhere; and their uniform made them, at once, ubiquitous but inconsequential. It wasn't that they were expendable; they simply never rose to the threshold of being acknowledged to the point of being ignored.

Brendan saw Raoul immediately and counted yet another instance of them both being in the same place at the same time. It gave him a chill.

It was strange having Raoul in the make-up room but, like the NBC pages of old, as long as they were in uniform, "Yalies" could go anywhere. And if you actually noticed any of them somewhere out of context, it was like seeing a Con Edison truck in New York City—you could assume there was some kind of an emergency, but it didn't affect you.

Thus, when Raoul showed up in the Make-Up room just as the meeting was breaking up and Marge had moved from her make–up chair to the shampoo chair, it was incongruous but not remarkable. Brendan proceeded as if Raoul weren't there since the assumption was that the he had more important things to do in the room than watch Marge get her hair washed.

"So what do you want to do today?" Brendan asked *pro forma*, knowing what the answer would be. Marge did not answer as her eyes closed, and Celeste ran the pre-warmed water over the top of her forehead and hair. Brendan could see Marge's face relax into a solipsistic ecstasy as the water, warmed to her specified temperature, washed away all cares about her career, the country, and especially the show she was about to appear on.

Then it happened.

Like a cat pouncing on a mouse, Raoul suddenly leapt between Brendan and the sink. At the same time, with his forearm, he swept Celeste out of the way. She dropped the water nozzle automatically. It landed on Marge's head spewing warm water on her forehead and face instead of back through her scalp. But Raoul didn't bother picking it up or moving it. It continued to stream water down Marge's face as if she were being waterboarded instead of shampooed.

Raoul's hands were immediately around Marge's neck with his two thumbs pressing down on her throat just beneath her Adam's apple. He was choking her to death.

Brendan was strangely immobile as was everyone else in the room although most of the people had no way of knowing what was transpiring. For a moment, it could have easily been Raoul responding to some sort of minor emergency—not causing a major one. At first, Brendan strangely and very calmly leaned over and observed Raoul's thumbs disappearing into the soft Irish flesh of Marge's neck completely obliterating her Adam's apple. It looked as if he might push through her entire neck or even puncture the skin with his thumbs.

Marge's eyes flashed open in response, but she couldn't make a sound which meant that only Celeste and Brendan knew what was really happening.

If truth be known, there then occurred a full beat off inaction. But let the record also show that it was only a beat. Marge's face looked like one of those rubberized squeeze dolls whose eyes bulge out when its torso is squeezed. In this case, Marge's expression was one of pure amazement that this was actually happening to her. On top of that, she didn't fully recognize who was choking her. Raoul, without his broom and long handled dustpan, was completely out of context for her. While she couldn't make a sound or lift her head out of the sink, her hands and legs flailed slightly making everyone think she had slipped or fallen while leaning back into the sink.

"Raoul! Stop!" Celeste screamed. Then, turning to the room she shouted, "He's choking her!"

Brendan was the first to react after the long beat of comprehension had run its course. Standing, now, at Raoul's back, he grabbed Raoul's elbows and tried to pull his arms away from Marge thereby forcing him to release his death-grip on her throat. Marge, even *in extremis*, instinctively and carefully reached up with one hand and gently checked to see what stage of shampooing her hair was in even as she was being choked to death.

Brendan quickly realized he could not effectively pull Raoul's crazed hands away from Marge's neck, so he wrapped his arms around Raoul's chest and tried to lift him bodily away from her instead.

Raoul was not a big man. He was smaller than Brendan but wiry and strong. By arching back while tightening his grip on him, Brendan was able to lift the self-proclaimed Spanish Hungarian off the floor and swing him back, away from the sink. But in so doing, Raoul, with his hands still around Marge's neck, lifted her head out of the sink and turned her body sideways on the reclined shampoo chair.

Brendan then had no choice but to take Raoul down to the floor with him in order to make him release his grip which Raoul finally did but not before knocking Marge's head on the side of the sink. Celeste reacted immediately and rushed to attend to the, now, freed but dazed co-host while Brendan and Raoul rolled away from the shampoo area toward the center of the room.

The first casualty in the fight was Brendan's catheter and collection bag. The catheter was summarily pulled out of his penis, and the bag came loose from his leg, spilling its contents out all over the floor. Brendan and Raoul were then rolling in a pool of a comedy writer piss.

Had he been healthier, Brendan could have easily subdued the feisty maintenance man; but in his present condition, it was a fair fight, neither one getting the upper hand. For Brendan it was like trying to wrestle a hitherto lethargic pet that had suddenly become uncommonly sinewy and strong through some atavistic triggering of its feral survival instinct.

But then Raoul freed one hand sufficiently to reach into his pocket and produce a switchblade knife which he opened expertly with a deafening "click" that spelled trouble for all who saw it flash, almost cartoon-like, in the lights. It was obvious that this was not the first time Raoul had ever pulled his knife during a fight nor opened one for a deadly purpose. It made the room audibly gasp.

A switchblade? Brendan thought even as he was fighting for his life. What is this, "West Side Story"?

That was the last thought Brendan had. As they rolled on the floor, Raoul held the open knife high above their two bodies waiting for an opportunity.

"You no suffer!" Roaul shouted.

Then he plunged the knife deep into Brendan's chest.

The blade ran easily between Brendan's third and fourth rib and stopped only at the hilt. The point of the blade pierced Brendan's heart and severed the ascending aorta in the process. It killed him instantly. It wasn't like in the movies. Death came all at once. There was no "death scene" or a look of surprise, confusion, or wonderment on Brendan's face. Just death.   He lay there with the foolish switchblade sticking out of his chest.

Then Bad Bob got out of his chair.

The room erupted. This was not a phony fight like the arguments the ladies had on the air, or the so-called battles and feuds they carried out in the press. This was the real thing. A real fight and a real death. A real person lay murdered on the floor of Hair and Make at "The Ladies' Room".

Beverly immediately felt validated. This time, really and truly, she actually *was* at the center of a big story. She instinctively started composing the lede for her "stand-up" while moving down off her high director's chair with carefully placed steps to avoid getting blood on her new Manolo Blahniks.

Brendan died with his eyes opened. He could see everything that was happening in the room around him even though his brain could no longer process it. No more jokes. But no more rejection either.

Marge was alive. She recovered in Celeste's arms, coughing; but she still could not speak. Of course, Marge considered herself in much worse shape than the dead writer on the floor. Leo took Brendan's place in holding Raoul down, but Raoul needed no restraint now. His mission had been accomplished.

It had all worked out better than anyone—Marge, Beverly, Bad Bob or even Raoul could have ever hoped for. Even Brendan benefitted from his summary execution rather than the uncertain future he faced.

And best of all, the Daytime murder was a ratings monster for "The Ladies' Room".

CHAPTER THIRTY-TWO

When The Wife heard, she was with Zeke at the Governor's hideaway in Montecito. The Governor provided a car and driver to get her back to L.A and, more importantly, off the property, as fast as possible. But when he heard the funeral might be at The Cathedral with all the ladies of "The Ladies' Room" and, especially, Beverly Frost in attendance, he insisted on being part of it.

Zeke didn't believe his father was dead. He thought it was just another one of Daddy's bits or that "Daddy was being crazy" again. But when The Wife explained that Daddy now was just like "Jingles", the Governor's Siamese cat, who had choked on a hairball and croaked right in front of them one weekend, it brought up all the memories of the beloved cat and the spectacle of the animal "coughing it up", literally, in Zeke's lap. Having been reminded of Jingles' demise, Zeke then cried in the back seat of the limo all the way from Montecito to LA and would not stop his keening until The Wife promised, as they turned off the Ventura Freeway, that the Governor was going to get a new cat, and it would be Zeke's, alone, right after his father's funeral.

Zeke, for his part, preferred the notion that it *was* just a bit. And it made him smile privately at the paroxysm of news coverage, preparations, and rigmarole that his dad's comic turn with the

switchblade had produced. He was his father's son, so he understood and appreciated this one last laugh. "Thanks, Dad," he said
to himself. And this time he didn't mean it sarcastically. He was
proud of his father, not because he had died trying to help another
human being, but because he had died with his clown shoes on,
writing comedy.

The funeral wasn't downtown after all but at the Church Of The
Good Sheppard in Beverly Hills because of its proximity to celebrities, the Wilshire Hotel, and better catering. Besides, with the cast
and crew of "The Ladies' Room" attending as well as the press, crowd
control was easier there than at The Cathedral with its wondering
tourists in the aisles. In addition, the Cardinal had already been
burned by Moonbeam P. Brown, and he was still pissed.

Because it was a showbiz *murder* funeral, the paparazzi and network news crews were swarming all over the place as if they expected a repeat stabbing to occur as a denouement of the original one.
Thus, in death, Brendan achieved a modicum of celebrity and was
even anointed, by the press and even Marge herself, as a "comedy
genius" which was far greater than what he had ever dared aspire to
in life. Even Zeke was impressed.

The Beverly Hills Police were called in to keep some semblance
of order even though the whole affair was considered by them as
just another example of craziness that always seemed to happen in
"The Valley".

But it was then and there that The Wife stood up and stood her
ground for Brendan proving, once and for all—if not a little late—
that she really *did* love him, and she respected what he had tried to
do in life.

Loyalty trumped ambition, and The Wife was standing defiantly
at the top of the steps outside the church when Marge's "presidential limo", with little Comedy Central flags on the bumpers and two
motorcycle escorts in front, pulled up behind the hearse. The Wife
had been married to Brendan long enough to know to wait until
Marge's reality show camera crew had set their "white balance" and

had "synched sound" at the curb. But the news cameras and paparazzi were ready immediately, and they pressed in for the "money shot" of Marge arriving to honor the writer who had died saving her life.

Marge emerged from the limo wearing a large white neck brace which she didn't really need, but it sent a message to everyone that she was also a victim. It also covered up the large, purple thumb marks that Raoul had left on her throat. But then, just as Marge and Lars were making their way up the steps of the church, The Wife stepped forward to meet them, flanked by her own crew of pallbearers.

"Stop!" she said holding her hand up like a Supreme when the cameras and shotgun mics were in range, "No politics."

She paused slightly. Then she continued, "No politics," she repeated. "No 'reality'. And no...," she paused again, deliberating her next word. She wanted to say something with a "C". Was it "Controversy?", "Cameras?", "Candidates?", "Commentators?" One thing for sure, it wasn't, "Comedians," because she knew that no longer applied.

"And no...YOU!" she finally said. She had avoided saying, "Cunts!" because she felt it was too obvious and redundant.

"Just *go*," The Wife said. "We don't *need* you, Marge," she added pointedly for the cameras and directly at Marge. "We don't *need* you."

Marge stopped in her tracks, knowing full well that her cameras, and all the other cameras, were catching the moment, and a "reality" one at that, which had not been scripted by Mark Solomon or "The Harvards".

"Pul-lease!" Marge uttered half to herself and half for the cameras' benefit.

Then Marge looked back toward Mark Solomon for help, but all he could come up with was an effete shrug. He had no comeback for her or an "alternate ending." The pallbearer goons then stepped forward, happy to do anything but heft the casket again; and the cameras continued to roll silently for a beat. The Wife watched as the pallbearer's heads swiveled from her to Marge and then back again. She knew at that moment that the video of Marge Foley being turned away at her writer's funeral, and the man who had saved her life with his own, would go viral faster than Jeanie Murphy's sex tape.

Marge could do nothing but turn and pick her way back down the steps in her high heels, happy, at least, that she'd done full hair and make-up for the event even though she'd just been barred from it. The limo driver hurriedly got out of his vehicle and ran around to try to meet the retreating former comedian, but he did not get there soon enough to rescue Marge who had to stand helpless at the door of the limo waiting for someone to open it for the "candidate".

Suddenly, the stretch limo, presidential-type flags, and motorcycle escort seemed doubly silly and stupid. In fact, one of the motorcycles couldn't get re-started, and its rider had to push the dead bike ahead of the limo, trying to keep up with the other functioning one, as the pathetic procession slowly turned the corner at Roxbury and disappeared.

Only then did The Wife turn and go back into the church to bury her husband, feeling more in love with him at that moment than when Addison G. Rage had "married" them; and confident now, that somehow, in some way, she'd consummated their union by, somewhere, making Brendan laugh.

She had told the Governor not to come to the funeral for the same reasons that she had given Marge. Marge ultimately took the "no politics" rebuff as a compliment. After all, she was rejected as a politician; and no one questioned it. But the Governor took it as an indication that he wasn't going to get laid that night.

The funeral itself proceeded in the usual self-serving, show business "he would have wanted us to be happy" way. The only hitch for Beverly was the fact that, in order for her to walk from her pew to the pulpit, she would have had to do the "Frosty Shuffle" in full view of the assembled mourners and public. She had developed an old lady's gait as a means of locomotion to insure that she wouldn't fall and break a hip. It was the only obvious part of her demeanor that showed her age. If they would only develop some sort of cosmetic surgery for motor functions, she'd never grow old. But, alas, despite the wonders of surgery, lighting, collagen, mainlining Botox, and around the clock attention by "Syd Vicious" and her medical crew, Beverly's halting locomotion betrayed her.

Bad Bob put in a request that she be "pre-set" on the altar, but the Monsignor saying the mass would have none of it. He didn't need another queen upstaging him. It was then decided that after being seated in the front pew, she would then excuse herself at the start of the service and be heavily escorted to an area in the sacristy behind the altar. Then, at the appropriate time, she would make her entrance from the wings and proceed directly to the pulpit like a priest. This would enable her to not have to sit through a Catholic Mass and also put her in total control of her cameo appearance. Beverly agreed that, as long as she could keep her iPhone with her, she'd be fine.

Everyone knew that Brendan had been sick, and that reality mitigated somewhat the horror of the murder. A special "repeat performance" of 'The Ladies' Room" had been inserted into the SBS Daytime schedule to accommodate the other "live" event that day starring the ladies. But the real drama of the morning was the appearance of Beverly Frost at another funeral and her long-awaited eulogy.

Beverly ascended the pulpit like the pro she was and was totally comfortable being exactly where she always wanted to be. As she had declared before to Sandy Abumpkin right after the departure of Roberta, she was "back in the game."

"Brendan White was a dear, dear, *dear* man," Beverly began after standing silent in the pulpit for a full 30 seconds. She learned that in drama class at Wellesley. It allowed the room to "gather" and draw the focus inexorably to her.

"He brought so much joy to our lives, and even today he brings that special brand of joy to this very sad occasion. What can I say about someone with whom I have spent more time than with any of my husbands? If Brendan had not come into our lives we would have had to invent him. He was that critical to our happiness and our show. I cannot imagine "The Ladies' Room" without him, and his contributions were so crucial to us, especially in the beginning when we were finding our way. No one will ever be able to think of him without thinking of "The Ladies' Room" and the overwhelming success that it has become. I say this all because now he has fulfilled his own dreams as he has fulfilled ours. And today he spreads his wings to fly to new heights. I wish him Godspeed and hope there is still room in his heart—even on this sad day when we feel nothing but his love—that there is still room in his heart to take us all with him to new heights and better tomorrows. We wish him well."

Beverly was the best anyone had ever seen her that morning. She held the congregation in the palm of her emaciated hand. Her eulogy was breathtakingly dear and personal. But for those who knew, and for those who remembered, her heartfelt words were recognized as *exactly* the same as the toast she'd given Moonie at her wedding. Word for word. Even down to the chilling "spread his wings" and "we wish him well" which meant, of course, that she *did* fire Brendan, after all.

When she was finished there wasn't a dry eye in the church. Beverly paused demurely for the long round of muffled sobs from the congregation that replaced what would have been her applause. Then she turned and made her way down from the pulpit in slow, deliberate, and precisely placed egret steps as if she were coming down off a ladder. Then she exited stage right. In doing so, she missed the sidelong glances from Leo and the rest of the knowing staff and wardrobe room kibitzers. She also missed the stunned look on Moonie's face who, to her chagrin, had always thought Beverly meant what she had said at her wedding.

And Brendan? Brendan was happy at last. Dead in his coffin, his body shifted slightly onto its side when they removed it from the church; a faint smile etched on his frozen face as he slept the Big Sleep. It was roughly the same position he had assumed when Bad Bob fired him.

Warm fur cozied up to his cheek as they lowered the coffin into the grave, and he embraced whatever had been put in there with him. A dead golden retriever had been lovingly laid alongside Brendan's body by The Wife in order to keep her end of the bargain and to keep him warm for eternity while his sperm, deep within her, swam ever northward in search of a soft place to lay its head.

www.ingramcontent.com/pod-product-compliance
Lightning Source LLC
Chambersburg PA
CBHW072108250626
47159CB00007B/2353